Lost Prince

Lost Prince

Chelsea Quinn Yarbro

BORDERLANDS PRESS
Baltimore, MD ❏ 2008

Lost Prince Copyright © 2008 by Chelsea Quinn Yarbro

ISBN# 978-1-880325-98-8

Typesetting and page design by E. Estela Monteleone
cover by Mario Martin, Jr.

Printed in the United States of America

Borderlands Press
POB 660
Fallston, MD 21047

800-528-3310

www.borderlandspress.com

It's high time I dedicated a book to
David Nee
so this is it, Dave,
and it comes with my thanks and friendship

There was never a Spanish Hapsburg King of Spain named Alonzo, either the First or the Second. There was never an heir to the throne named Rolon. There was never a Grand Inquisitor named Juan Murador. All the other characters are equally fictitious. Nevertheless, there are very deliberate resonances to the historical King of Spain Felipe II, and although this work is fantasy, it is not entirely divorced from reality.

Prologue

THE HERETIC

November 1564 through March 1565

Oh the flames were glorious, competing with the splendor of the sunset as it faded over Valladolid. The church bells, muffled for Holy Lent, throbbed with the pulse of the burning pyres for the triumph of faith The Plaza del Rey was filled with the faithful who had come to see their devotion vindicated by the deaths of pernicious heretics. There were still seven pyres to light, the ones farthest away from the royal viewing stands, for these were the least important of the offenders, persons of no account who had turned from God and were now to pay the price.

From the Catedrál came the last of the procession: two men, one a priest, one a layman of acknowledged piety, flanked each of the heretics, still exhorting them, even as they approached the stake, to repent and be received again into the Grace of the Church before the fires could consume their flesh. Soot hung around them, obscuring the figures, and the sound of the flames and bells and screaming of the dying almost obliterated the arguments of those accompanying the heretics. Occasionally those in the crowd gathered to witness this auto-da-fé would spit or throw rotten food or offal at the heretics, but such missiles landed imperfectly, and often it was the good Christians who were struck and not the unhal-lowed men and women they guided.

Frey Juan Murador had the pulp of a melon spattered over his vestments, ruining the fine embroidery of the chasuble he wore instead of the usual dark brown habit that traditionally covered the white alb of his order. This was a holy occasion and he was dressed as befitted his special functions. It galled him to think that the magnificent garment was soiled. He tried to concentrate on the castigations he was supposed to deliver the heretic, but he could not take his mind away from the fascination he had for the fires. How tremendous they were! How they shone in splendor! He was sure that the Throne of God had just such a radiance about it, and it awed him.

Ahead, the procession faltered as one of the heretics—the second in line—turned away from her guides and broke free of their grasp. As she shambled toward the royal platform, there were shouts of alarm and several guards rushed for-ward, their pikes uplifted.

"Stay!" came the command from the slight, dyspeptic man who was Rey d'España.

"But, Majestad . . . " one of the armed men protested, preparing to run the woman through with his lance.

"No. I will not tolerate any action that cheats God of His Revenge," Alonzo II declared, shouting to be heard. "She is condemned for a far greater sin than assaulting us." He rested his arms on the arms of his chair, the stiff padding of his brocaded sleeves making it impossible for him to bend his elbows. "Take her. You see that the wretch cannot move."

Two of the soldiers reached for her, but before they could touch her, the woman threw back her head and shrieked.

"You! You call me sinful!" She tried to get to her feet, but could not. The strappado had dislocated her hips and now her legs could not bear her weight for more than a few steps.

"You!" Her hands reached up toward him, hands that were still caked with blood where her nails had been pulled off her fingers.

"Take her," Alonzo said, no longer concerned with the woman. "The pyres are waiting."

But the woman writhed on the ground and bit the first man to lay a hand on her. With a last effort, she reached for the wide tapestry that hung down in front of the royal box and tried to drag herself to her feet. "You have condemned me, though I am innocent of all wrong. I am a faithful Christian! I die innocent!"

"Then God will welcome you as a martyr," said the monk who had walked beside her as he at last reached her. He was a portly man, not given to worldly exercise, and he puffed as he knelt beside her. His remonstrances came in breathy spurts, not loud enough to be heard by anyone.

"If God demands I be His martyr, then God will be revenged for my death." The woman was speaking clearly now, and it was not good to hear her.

"Take her away," Alonzo repeated,' and deliberately turned his head toward the nearest pyres, ignoring the woman entirely. Beside him, his Reina trembled and pulled out her lace handkerchief to hold before her eyes; she was a pretty woman who had often been called an angel though the sweetness of her features did not come from virtue but vapidity.

The woman refused to be ignored. "As I am innocent and suffer, so your innocents will suffer. Mark that, proud man: where you garner up your hopes, there you will find a ravening beast; where you sin the least will be the greatest sacrilege and nothing you do will deny it or detain it."

For a moment there was a horrified silence, and then the boldest of the soldiers brought the pommel of his sword down on the woman's back, pounding her three times with all his strength. He was strictly forbidden to unsheathe his blade for this religious occasion and he had been given orders not to make killing blows, so, much as it galled him, he struck the woman on her back, breaking her ribs.

The woman screamed, and then the sound faded to a sigh as she went limp, her back broken and her lungs punctured. Blood ran from her mouth and nose as she slumped forward under the tapestry.

"That was ill done," muttered the corpulent monk as he made the sign of the Cross over the body. "It is fitting that she burn, but not that she be slaughtered."

Alonzo stared down at the dead woman. "Burn her anyway. She was condemned to the flames, and to the flames she will go." He glanced at the old bishop who stood at his side "Mi Padre, is this not the best way?"

"It is, my son," the bishop murmured and signaled the monk to continue with the procession.

As he watched the fat monk and the old grandee lug the woman's body away to its pyre, Juan Murador felt a surge of excitement, and he tugged at the arm of the heretic at his side. "See!" He pointed to the body being dragged toward the faggots. "There is no escape in this world and there will not be in the next. God does not permit His power to be mocked. He will judge you for your sins and you will be cast into everlasting fire; by comparison to these pyres, the death you shall suffer is as nothing. You must see how gross is your error and how grievous your trespasses."

The man looked at him with sickened eyes. He had two great supurating wounds in his shoulders and his face was bright with fever. "I know nothing," he whispered. It was the only thing he had said since he was taken by the Inquisition. "Nothing, nothing."

"So you insist," Juan said with disgust. He had been warned that this heretic was obstinate, and he had spent the afternoon trying to coax a confession out of the man without luck.

They had reached the pyre now, and Juan pronounced the Anathema on the unrepentant man beside him. There were men-at-arms of the Holy Office approaching to take the man the last few steps up the ladder to his doom. Juan thought of the woman he had seen die so little time before and pointed to the pyre. "You believe that death will release you, but Our Lord promised that this was not so. You are guilty of heinous sins and for that you must pay the ultimate price. Do not die with worse to come. Offer your suffering to God and He will perhaps have mercy on you in your plight."

"I know nothing," the heretic said again. He looked at his other guide and shook his head.

With a gesture of frustration, Juan released his heretic to the officers of the Secular Arm of the Holy Office. "He will not repent," he informed them needlessly, and affixed the imp-covered San Benito. "You must do your task." He stepped back and blessed the officers, then turned toward the viewing area set aside for clergy. As he took his seat, he glimpsed some motion in the royal box, and allowed himself to be distracted by it.

"Frey!" the monk at his side whispered sharply, tugging at Juan's sleeve.

"Forgive me," Juan said automatically, and once more directed his gaze toward the pyres as the last one was ignited.

"What happened with that woman?" the monk asked in an undervoice.

Juan was staring at the enormous fires, entranced by the sight of them, and so had to be questioned a second time before he answered. "Oh. She cursed el Rey. You know what creatures these heretics are."

"Cursed on the last night of Lent," the monk said, clicking his tongue in disapproval. "A bad business."

"To be cursed by a heretic?" Juan responded, paying more attention now.

"Any curse is evil, and those of heretics especially so, as they come from Satan himself. El Rey must take care. We will offer a Mass for him tonight and another tomorrow night. Otherwise, who knows what might befall?" He crossed himself as he stole one look at the royal box. "La Reina looks faint," he observed.

"A pale little thing like that, it isn't surprising," Juan answered uncaringly, his eyes bright with the reflections of burning.

"Still and all. The curse must have upset her. A pious woman like her, she can't be expected to—". He rose in his seat and pointed to one of the largest pyres where a blacked figure had crashed forward, toppling off the tower of burning faggots to land much too close to the royal box. "God keep and preserve us!"

"Amen," Juan said at once, trying not to picture in his mind the destruction that might have happened. Soldiers were already using their pikes to push the charred thing back toward the fire. Monks converged around them, crosses upheld in their hands, a few kneeling to recite the Rosary.

Juan Murador longed to be with them, to join them in their prayers for the heretics, near the burning proof of his faith. He looked again toward the royal box and saw that la Reina was reclining in her chair, her hand to her pale brow. Two of her women hovered over her, one holding a pomander under her nose, the other fanning her with a stiff bit of brocade. As la Reina leaned toward el Rey, Juan heard the pyre of the woman who had cursed them burst into full flame.

From somewhere behind the royal box there came a long, despairing wail from a dog. It was an eerie sound that cut through the muttering roar of the crowd gathered in the plaza, through the muffled toll of the bells, through the rush and crackle of the fires and the screams of the heretics. For an instant, there was no other sound in the Plaza del Rey. And then the bishop began to intone his prayers.

In the middle of the Mass, la Reina was led away as unobtrusively as possible, and el Rey, his severe expression showing as little as it usually did, was thought to be displeased. Once or twice he wiped his fingers on a lace handkerchief.

Only when the last fires were nothing more than smoking heaps of embers and ashes did the people depart. By then it was almost midnight and the first of the Paschal Masses were beginning in the Catedrál. Most of the nobility attended the first three Masses of Easter, and then went home for an afternoon of prayer and contemplation before the elaborate feasts of the late evening.

Juan Murador remained near the smoldering rubble. He stepped warily to avoid the dark, burnt streaks on the paving stones, which were all that was left of the rivulets of human fat that had run, burning, from the flames. Before sunrise, he and two other monks would rake the ashes for bones and other tokens to present to the Holy Office for their benefit. It was a task that was thought to breed humility by its nature, so Juan never told anyone that he enjoyed it. For him, it was exhilarating to sift the ashes for the bones and trinkets of the burned heretics, almost like a treasure hunt. This was the third time he had drawn such duty since he became a novice monk and he had ceased to wonder why the grisly work thrilled him so. He recited the eighty-eighth Psalm when he was through, mildly regretting that it would be another year before he would be able to do this again.

It was late the following October when Reina Concepción daughter of King Pao of Portugal, wife of Alonzo II of España, died while bringing the Infante Real into the world. Death in child-birth was woman's heritage from Eve, and the Archbishop who heard her last, whispered, incoherent confession before administering Extreme Unction, reminded those who stood around her enormous canopied bed that La Madre Maria would welcome Concepción to Heaven for attending to her uxorial duty so well. The ladies-in-waiting attending her bowed their heads, most of them secretly hoping that they would come face to face with God some other way. The little Reina's suffering had been dreadful.

Once again the bells of Valladolid were muffled as they had been at Lent, and Masses were ordered throughout España and Portugal for the repose of the soul of Reina Concepción.

Juan Murador was in the refectory when he heard the first, mournful tolling that announced her death. He stopped his reading of the lesson and crossed himself, not noticing whether or not his fellow monks did the same. He could not forget the words of the heretic woman as he listened to the sound of the bells. He prayed automatically, hardly aware of what he said or the murmur of other prayers that rose around him. Now that Reina Concepción was dead, he thought. It would surely be the end of the curse of the heretic woman. She had pronounced destruction on those innocent, and no one in the royal family was so innocent as the young, vapid Reina.

"We are to pray for la Reina, who has been taken from this life to the Glory of God," the Prior announced to the assembled Dominican monks when the first orisons were over. "We are also asked to address Heaven on behalf of the Infante Real, Rolon Andres Esteban Angel Castelar de Astuarias, Aragon, Leon y Castilla."

Obediently the monks commenced their thanksgiving for the safe delivery of the heir to the throne, a thanksgiving that was to spread from Burgos to Barcelona to Sevilla as news of his birth and his mother's death were carried through the kingdom of Alonzo II.

Part I

November 1564 through March 1565

I

Below them, the walls and towers of Zaragoza thrust into the sharp angles of the sunset, bastions against the night, reaching for the last benediction of the day. Around them the air was clear and cold, biting through the short, fur-lined cloaks and jeweled leather gauntlets fashion more than good sense demanded. Only the dwarf on the fractious mule had wrapped himself in an engulfing cape and pulled a fur hat down over his brow and ears; since he was a jester, no one was offended.

"There will be food waiting at El Morro," one of the courtiers panted as he came abreast of the men in the van of the little party.

"And a fire, I hope," Capitan Iturbes said to the young Conde.

"At least the moon is nearly full," he remarked before dropping back to his place in the group.

"The moon is getting full," said the Infante Real with an apprehensive glance over his shoulder toward the east. He was the most elegantly dressed of the group, as was fitting to his rank and station, with velvet tops to his boots and pearl buttons on the collar of his cape below the ruff.

"We'll be at El Morro before it rises," Capitan Iturbes assured the Infante Real with enough bluster to cover his doubts.

"Por Dios, I hope so," the youth answered, pulling his cape more tightly around him.

Capitan Iturbes was not the sort to presume upon the goodwill of royalty, and so he said nothing. Don Rolon, the Infante Real, was known to be a moody lad, given to study and silence. At least, thought Iturbes as he rode beside the heir to the throne, the prince was not like his father, whose forbidding austerity made him an object of awe and rancor to his military officers.

In the rear, Lugantes kicked savagely at his mule and cursed his fortune once again. The little man with the misshapen body hated these treks into the country. It was bad enough to have the mockery of the court around him, but to be scorned because he could not ride as the courtiers did and suffered when he tried was almost more than he could endure. But, he reminded himself, there was Don Rolon, his prince. Something in that unhappy young man struck a responsive chord in the jester, and he could not begrudge the Infante Real his company, even on these dismal hunting parties. So he took out his ire on the mule, delivering a more vehement kick than usual, and prayed that he would not be asked to sing and dance while the others had their evening meal. By the time they arrived at El Morro, the only thing he would be good for was a bowl of soup and long hours of sleep.

"The Infante looks worried," el Conde del Aranjuez said to the man beside him.

"He always looks that way," came the bored rejoinder. "Don Rolon looked sour the day he was born." Don Enrique Hurreres was only a Cabellero, but he was related to some of the oldest and most revered families in España, and was to be found in company not often accessible to mere knights.

"How much longer, do you think?" el Conde asked, willing to risk Don Enrique's jeers if only he would provide an answer.

"Chilblains or saddle sores?" Don Enrique inquired sweetly. "I'm tired," the other admitted.

"I give it an hour. No more, unless that fool Iturbes has forgotten the way." He looked up the rocky trail with resigned disgust. "El Rey never leaves any doubt when one is in disgrace."

"A hunting party is not disgrace," el Conde objected hotly. If he had not been so tired, he might have made more of his argument.

"A hunting party at El Morro is a disgrace, believe me." Don Enrique shrugged. "There are five of us, that's something—and Lugantes, of course. We'll have something to laugh at besides the sheep." He slapped at his gelding's withers with the ends of his reins, his face made ugly with dissatisfaction. "Impossible beast!"

"He's as tired as the rest of us," el Conde said, wishing he had worn a warmer cloak and ignored the dictates of fashion.

"What's that to me?" Don Enrique demanded and gave an inward smirk when his companion did not answer him. He flipped the last of his riding crop so that it bounced against his boots; he felt his horse shiver at the sound.

Lugantes watched the two young noblemen ahead of him and smiled briefly at their impatience. That unrest would haunt them if he were given the chance to talk in the next day or so. He had a knack for mockery, having endured so much of it in his life, and nothing pleased him quite so much as planting the thorns of his wit deep in a well-born hide. He clung to the saddle, cursing quietly, anticipating that brief satisfaction that would be his in a short time.

As they crested the steepest rise of the trail, Capitan Iturbes drew rein and pointed to a squat, massive fortress on an outcropping of rock. "El Morro, Alteza," he announced.

Don Rolon stared at it. "Very good, Iturbes: how long do you think it will take to get there?"

"An hour," Capitan Iturbes answered promptly and with real confidence.

"Night will have fallen by then," the Infante Real said uneasily. "Couldn't it be sooner?"

"The moon is nearly full, Alteza," he pointed out. "It will not be hazardous."

"But the moon . . . " Don Rolon let his objection fade away. "If we hurry, it would be less time."

"On this ground?" Capitan Iturbes protested. "If it is what Su Alteza orders, then we must do it, but I will not be answerable for our safety over these rocks."

"Of course," the young man said, and pretended to stifle a yawn. "Set the pace, Capitan, and we will oblige you."

"Gracias, Alteza," the officer said with feeling. "There is a little way we can trot, but our horses are tired."

"I have told you to set the pace. Use your best judgment." He sounded exhausted, as if he had just lost a battle instead of a mild dispute.

"Muy bien," Iturbes said with a brisk salute as he took the lead and held his horse to a brisk walk.

Sangre de Cristo, thought Don Rolon, but El Morro was desolate. What was there to hunt here but the sheep of peasants and fleet-footed wild goats? Here the whole world was made of stone, hard and forbidding. He listened to the hollow sound of his horse's hooves on the track. The place reminded him of his father. He bit his lip, knowing he would have to confess so treasonable a notion. He wished he had brought his own confessor with him rather than that creature of the Inquisitor General, but there had been no opportunity to request that Padre Lucien accompany him, his father had seen to that. He shook his head. Another sin to confess, and his soul so heavy within him already.

"There are torches at the gate," Capitan Iturbes pointed out, thinking to cheer the small band of men, but no one paid much heed to his remark, either because they were not listening or because they had ceased to care.

Don Enrique let out a cry and pointed off to the side of the trail where a large owl had fallen on a half-grown badger. The two were locked in deadly combat, each holding the other in a passion of rage. "And the sun is not quite down!"

El Conde crossed himself, and an instant later, so did Don Enrique. Immediately behind them, Padre Barnabas copied the gesture and noted that none of the others had guarded themselves against so ill an omen. He heard the jester chuckle and determined to watch the little man closely for overt signs of heresy.

"I don't like it," Don Colon muttered, turning away from the struggling creatures.

"Alteza," Capitan Iturbes called out over his shoulder. "The way is very narrow here. We must go cautiously. Be careful of the overhang." He pointed ahead to a rocky defile like the darkened maw of a ravening beast. "It isn't long."

"What is this place?" Don Rolon asked aloud, his hands cold fists on the reins now. His horse was laboring, for the path was steep here, yet he gave no more than passing thought to the gold-and-silver Andalusian stallion. Ordinarily he was more considerate of the magnificent horse, since it was one of the few concessions to his position his father had permitted him, for only royalty could ride these horses with the light gray coats and golden manes and tails.

"The peasants here say that this place is haunted, Alteza."
"Haunted?" Don Colon looked about uneasily as the frowning rise of stone loomed over them.

"Peasants!" Don Enrique sneered. "Who pays attention to peasants?"

"This is their country, mi señor grande," Lugantes quietly reminded the sarcastic young hidalgo, his large, misshapen features showing how much he wanted Don Enrique to understand. He did not hate these arrogant courtiers, he loathed them. Don Rolon was not cut from the same cloth, and for that reason Lugantes served him with passionate devotion.

"I want no part of those who dig in the earth," Don Enrique laughed harshly.

"They are my people, Don Enrique," Don Rolon corrected him sharply. "Do not speak of them in such a way, I pray you."

"Si to quieres, Alteza," Don Enrique said at once, doing as much of a bow as he could from his perch in the saddle. Then he added to el Conde in an undervoice, "He may be out of favor now, and we with him, but he will be el Rey one day, and those who gain his favor now will not be forgotten."

"And so you pander to him," el Conde muttered, disgusted. "You're as bad as the French, with their licence and debauchery because the Roi orders it to amuse him. And for his excesses he will burn in Hell."

"While you sing hosannas at the Right Hand of God," Don Enrique shot back.

Padre Barnabas, riding ahead of Lugantes, overheard the two young noblemen with a degree of satisfaction that worried him. He knew that he would report this irreligious banter to his superiors on his return, and they would mull it over. In time, he might rise in their esteem through the fall of Don Enrique. His conscience was clear, he told himself, and vehemently began to recite his evening prayers in a low, penetrating voice. A man of his station must uphold his office, he insisted as the familiar words of the *Ave Maria* droned on. It was his responsibility, his obligation to see that men of high rank be of the finest stamp, untouched by corruption and heresy. His prayers grew louder.

By the time all the men were on the dangerous trail, not one was free of the apprehension of the place. The rocks, made more massive in the advancing darkness, changed the sound of the horses' hooves to an echoing, hollow clatter, like the beginnings of an avalanche. Their progress through the dark was silent but for that ominous sound, and even Padre Barnabas was quiet, his prayers continuing by the movement of his lips.

"We are almost out of it, Alteza," said Capitan Iturbes, his comforting words distorted and mocked by echoes. "Excellent," the Infante Real responded with genuine relief. "When we leave, we must pass this way in daylight."

"Indeed, Alteza," he agreed with fervor. His years of soldiering had steeled him against the dread and anger of battle, but not against the fear that possessed him when he could not identify his foe.

"How much farther to El Morro?" Don Enrique yelled, and his question came back to him, broken and sharpened by the stone.

"You will dine within the hour," Capitan Iturbes promised him, and was comforted by that reassurance himself.

"With the aid of God," Padre Barnabas interjected in a warning tone that the others caught and made note of with an emotion not unlike their apprehension in this defile. El Conde crossed himself and Don Enrique laughed.

Suddenly Lugantes made a hissing noise and turned it into an unearthly howl. His mule halted, long ears back flat, and the other mounts whickered uneasily, sidling on the rocky trail. Lugantes chuckled. "You thought it was the haunt, didn't you?" His laughter increased and the rocks took it up so that the air rang with malignant chuckles. "Anyone whistling in this place would be thought a haunt. What do you say, Capitan?"

Now that the first shock of terror had passed, Capitan Iturbes had a fighting man's rough humor to guide him. He chuckled richly. "Señor Jester, you are a most irreverent man. Surely you're right about the haunts."

"Never do such a thing again!" Don Enrique shouted, turning in his saddle, his face contorted with rage. "Fool! Dolt! Monster!"

"Do not speak to him so, Don Enrique," Don Colon said sharply. "I deplore his jests sometimes, as I deplored this one, but you are not permitted to treat him badly. His task is not an easy one, and he is as tired as the rest of us." He looked through the darkness toward the place he knew Lugantes had to be. "I'm sorry I could not find it funny, mi amigo. Perhaps next time."

The little party resumed their progress in silence, and when a few minutes later they passed out of the defile, each of them was silently glad to be free of the narrow stone walls and their disquieting echoes.

"Ah, see there, Alteza," Capitan Iturbes called, pointing to the east where a white shimmer was gathering on the peaks of the mountains. "The moon is rising!"

The left side of Don Rolon's face was still touched with the fading luster of sunset, and the right, toward the pale brightness, was in darkness. "They say that madmen roam at the full of the moon."

"It is the spell of Lilith and the depraved ones who worship the Devil," Padre Barnabas announced with authority. "If we are true in our service of God, there is nothing we need fear but His wrath on the Day of Judgment."

"De seguro," Capitan Iturbes said automatically, having learned long ago not to argue with prelates.

"You're being unwise, then," Don Enrique declared, determined to show how removed he was from all that. "We are taught to fear the Devil and his works and to fear the Coming of God. We take refuge in faith, hoping that it will aid us on that day. Others suspect that they will not be worthy, and turn to a less demanding master." He was able to smile, but no one saw it. "Padre Barnabas will tell you that his brethren are stern taskmasters, but they are as nothing compared to God. Is that not so, Padre?"

The priest gave a sour answer. "We pray that there be no sin in the world, that God may come more quickly."

"And you do what you can to eradicate it, don't you?" He did not wait for Padre Barnabas to speak, but said to the others, "That is why we must have autos-da-fé, to purge and cleanse us, those who are pious, of the least taint of sin."

"The auto-da-fé is the triumph of faith," Padre Barnabas reminded them all in careful accents. "You would do well to remember this."

"But so high a price to pay," Don Colon said quietly. "God gave us His Son, I know, and we did not honor him. But still ..." He stopped.

"Your own mother was destroyed by the curse of one such heretic, and you do not wish to be revenged?" Padre Barnabas inquired.

Don Rolon had heard that tale since he was old enough to speak, and it had horrified him once, but now it filled him with a coldness that was not quite sickness. If the heretic woman had not been accused, tortured and burned, she would have had no reason to curse Concepción, and both women might be alive this day, content to live out their lives as virtuous matrons. He had not always felt that way, but in the last five years he had come to despise the autos-da-fé his father so adamantly approved; the hatred he felt once for that unknown woman had faded years ago.

"There is El Morro, Alteza," said Capitan Iturbes as they came around a bend in the trail. "We will arrive shortly."

"El Morro," Don Rolon repeated. If his horse had been fresh, he would have made a quick gallop to the gates, but as it was, he resigned himself to another several minutes in the saddle. His legs ached from the cold and his face felt stiff.

"How elegant," Don Enrique observed sarcastically. "Your father does well by you, Alteza, doesn't he?"

"My father is el Rey, Don Enrique. If it pleases him to send me to the wastes of the New World, it is his right to do so, and my duty to go." He paid no heed to the quick intake of breath that was Don Enrique's protest, but kept his eyes fixed on the massive gates of El Morro.

"The torches are lit, Alteza," el Conde pointed out, glad to see them.

"There are servants waiting, and guardsmen, Alteza," Capitan Iturbes informed Don Rolon, hoping that the Infante Real would not be too disappointed in the stark fortress.

"Not quite a French hunting lodge," Don Enrique observed to the air.

"Has it a chapel?" asked Padre Barnabas.

"A small one, mi Padre," the Capitan assured him. "And an old priest, or so I'm told."

"Good." He turned back toward Lugantes. "You may not have much to do, jester."

"Then I will amuse myself," Lugantes said at once. "I have learned to enjoy my own company, since few others have cared for it."

There was the sound of a ramshorn blowing, a blatant, unmusical sound that reverberated through the stony peaks as the massive gates of El Morro swung open, and the little party passed through.

2

Since the three young noblemen had not been allowed to bring their valets, el Conde and Don Enrique had to fend for themselves while Lugantes handled such duties for Don Rolon. He presented himself in the Infante Real's chamber on the second morning they were there to find the room in complete disorder and the Infante Real tossing in exhausted sleep on the fur-covered bed. Lugantes clicked his tongue, supposing that Don Rolon had drunk too deeply the night before; he set about putting all in order, and was quite pleased that he accomplished this task before the young man came sluggishly awake.

"Good morning, Alteza," Lugantes said as he finished setting out the hunting mantle beside the padded pourpoint with a modified lace ruff.

"To you, Lugantes." He put his slender hand to his eyes. "Madre de Dios, what a nightmare!" He started to get up, then lay back with a groan. "My body aches."

"Wine fumes," Lugantes said sympathetically. "They have only raw vintages here."

"Perhaps," Don Rolon said as he rubbed his brow. "I did not think I drank so much."

"Well, Alteza, you have a glass, and then another, and then it is easy to forget the first, and so have another. . .In time, you have a great many but it seems no more than two or three." He did not remember seeing Don Rolon take much wine, but the other two young men were so besotted that he assumed Don Rolon had followed their example.

"Perhaps," he repeated, then made another attempt to get up. He sat for a little time with his legs dangling over the side of the bed, his shoulders hunched as if to keep him from being struck. "There were such terrible things in my dreams," he said to Lugantes as the jester brought his leather hunting leggings to him. "It must be this place."

"A bad place to dream, certainly," Lugantes said, not paying too much attention to Don Rolon's words. "That, and the hunting."

"Goats!" Don Rolon scoffed. "My father knew how I would feel, hunting goats."

"Still, it is better than sitting in a courtyard in Madrid, isn't it?" Previously when Rey Alonzo wanted to punish his son, he had sent him to one of the private estates he owned in Madrid, with instructions that the Infante Real was not to leave the premises. "And you have too many friends in Madrid."

"I wonder if I do," Don Rolon said, beginning to draw on the leggings without protest. "My father would prefer I have none, and there are others . . . "

"Gil?" Lugantes suggested. He disliked el Rey's bastard son almost as much as he disliked Alonzo himself.

"In some ways," the youth said cautiously. "It would be easier, I think, if our roles were reversed. Then my father could have the heir he wants and he would leave me alone." He stood up. "My feet are sore. What have I done?"

Lugantes recalled the state the room was in, and said nothing. He picked up a pair of boots and held them out. "Will these do?"

"As well as any. I feel as if I spent the whole night running." He donned the boots gingerly and then pulled off his night camise. "I suppose I am not used to the bed."

"Strange beds breed strange dreams," Lugantes said, hoping to reassure him.

"Then this one is very strange. I thought I heard screams and saw men running. I thought there was blood everywhere and men crossed themselves as if to find protection from the Devil himself." He blessed himself without thinking. "What would Padre Barnabas make of this?"

"There's no reason to trouble Padre Barnabas with dreams. He has enough to think of with the sins he searches for." Lugantes made a face. "That one is dangerous, Alteza. He is ambitious and does not know it."

Don Rolon shrugged. "Very well. I will be careful of him, but to dream so and have no comfort . . . " He fastened his belt and held out his arms for the knitted woolen camisado, tugging it over his tousled head impatiently. "Hunting for goats. My father will be delighted. He has always liked to have me busy with something." He coughed once, to cover his shock at his denouncement of his father. "I do not mean anything disloyal to the Crown, Lugantes."

"Never, Alteza," Lugantes agreed promptly. "You are not here for disloyalty, but because El Majestad suffers from fits of pique. And that is not disloyal to the crown, either. No one who has been at Court believes that your actions are disloyal. Unwise, yes, on occasion, but never disloyal."

Don Rolon drew on his pourpoint and fussed with the ruff so that the lace would not press against his neck, then reached for the sleeves. "Use the iron pins, Lugantes. There is no reason to wear jewels here." He could not admit that he enjoyed being less conspicuous than the court life permitted him to be. "I will use the simple leather gauntlets. No reason for anything fancier."

"Very sensible, Alteza." He went to the larger of the two cases Don Rolon had brought with him and searched it quickly for the desired gloves, holding them out as the Infante Real finished pinning his sleeves to his pourpoint. "Is there anything else?"

"I must wear my ring. With that, I am ready." As he took the ring, he had a dizzy moment, as if he were setting it aside as he had done at some late hour the night before. He once again had to control the cold, sickened sensation that coursed through him, and when it had passed, he could not recall it enough to learn why he had had it in the first place. His laugh was shaky. "You may be right about the wine."

"It's not impossible," Lugantes said quietly but with a twinkle in his glittery eyes.

"I must be more cautious tomorrow, or . . . " He stared down at his hand and saw that the nails were broken and torn, that there was dirt on the fingers. "What? . . . Lugantes . . . " He was about to show the jester his hand when he was overcome with a nameless fright. "Bring me my basin. I should wash my hands before putting on gauntlets." To his own ears he sounded jittery and unhappy, but apparently Lugantes did not notice this.

"In a moment, Alteza. The water is cold, I fear." He stepped into the dressing room beside the bedchamber and took the ewer and basin from the top of an old chest. He was out of charity with himself for forgetting so basic a service. He knew he was fortunate that the young man had not chided him for the oversight, and took it as further proof of Don Rolon's innate humanity and royal courtesy. As he brought the articles back into the bedchamber, he said, "I will ask that the water be heated in future if you wish it, Alteza."

"It won't be necessary," was Don Rolon's distracted reply. He could not imagine how he had come to have his hands so smirched. Where had he been, that he had broken his nails or dug in the earth? He searched his memory and could find nothing. He vaguely recalled a similar problem about a month ago, when he had been visiting the gypsies outside of Valladolid. His hands had been filthy and his clothes torn. At the time, he thought he had had more of an adventure there than he could remember, but now . . .

"Are you troubled, Alteza?" Lugantes asked, seeing the distress in the young man's dark eyes.

"Urn?" He looked up sharply. "No, not troubled. I'm . . . wondering." He dipped his hands into the water and rubbed them quickly together, not watching too closely to see what was washed off.

"Do you require anything else?" Lugantes asked. "Aside from Ciro?"

Ciro Eje was Don Rolon's valet, a soft-spoken efficient man in his mid-twenties, one of a distinguished family of conversos who had not entirely forgotten their Jewish heritage. Ciro continued to honor his grandparents and great-grandparents, though they were considered enemies of the Church, and had occasionally boasted that his oldest uncle was one of the conversos who made up the crew for the Genovese Colombo when he had first sailed to the New World. Ciro Eje was one of the few servants in the royal palace who took the time to speak sensibly with Lugantes. "Ciro would be a help, but you are doing very well, Lugantes," Don Rolon said wistfully.

"You will be back in Valladolid soon, Alteza, and there you will require more adept services than mine. Ciro will be horrified to see what I have done to your clothes, but he is an understanding man. He won't be too angry with me." He shrugged. "For a jester to be a valet, well, the French would make a comedy out of it, wouldn't they? one of those farces with music and dancing. And the courtiers would try it out for a while, until they became bored with it."

"This is not France," Don Rolon said in a flat tone. "And to do a play, about a valet or anything else, would bring too many questions from the Inquisition, I fear. My. . .mother told me so, in any case, when they refused to let her have such a performance." He dried his hands carefully, quietly thankful that Ciro had not seen this, for he was acute enough to make inquiries Don Rolon did not want.

"Your father is most fortunate to have so lovely a Reina, and it is sad that he has so little affection for her," Lugantes said, and saw Don Rolon wince. "The French are still pleased with the match, are they not?"

"They have been," Don Rolon said as he started toward the door. "We are going to hunt until midafternoon, or so I am told. Do what you can to make this place as livable as possible. I don't expect miracles, but there must be something you can do that will make it . . . less like a dungeon."

"Si, mi Infante. But it will not be easy."

"I know that, Lugantes. Do what you can." He lifted his hand to wave, closed the door and was gone.

Only when Lugantes was certain that the young prince was gone did he pick up the basin and stare thoughtfully at the muddy water.

Just Don Enrique was waiting for the Infante Real in the little stone courtyard. He was much more elegantly dressed than Don Rolon, and permitted himself the luxury of pointing this out, relishing the contrast his appearance made to that of the heir to the throne. "You're worse than the local landowners, Alteza," he said after summing up his opinion of the Infante Real's clothing. He added with more than a little scorn, "You are Infante Real; they at least have the excuse of bad example and little money."

"Ah, but I have one, too," Don Rolon reminded him unhappily. "I am here as a sign of disfavor. It is better than many another prison would be, but it is not fitting that I dress as if at a festival. This is penance, and we all know it, Don Enrique." He signaled for his horse before asking, "Where is el Conde? Is he joining us, or has he changed his mind?"

"He has not come down. That swill we drank last night, you know." He too looked less than himself. His temples still throbbed and the sunlight hurt his eyes.

"Is he coming?" Don Rolon inquired, not caring particularly whether the young man did or not.

"I haven't seen him, Alteza," Don Enrique admitted. "He told me last night, when we went up to bed, that he was going to take a walk to clear his head. The majordomo here said that he did not respond to his knock this morning. The man's incompetent, of course. You could not hope for anything else in such a place." He looked up as the horses were brought from the stables. "I'd best try the girths before we mount, Alteza. There is no telling how the saddles have been put on."

"I will see to my own," Don Rolon said, holding out his hands for the reins of his horse. He had learned how to care for the animal when he was first given the stallion and now felt cheated when he could not tend to him. He blew in the horse's nostrils and smiled at the nudge the stallion gave his arm.

"That majordomo," Don Enrique said when he was sure that his girths were properly fastened. "He told me this morning that the peasants hereabouts are sure that there is another haunt in the neighborhood. They told their priest, who's probably a half-mad ancient, that they heard the Devil in the hills late last night." He got into the saddle without his usual flair, and blinked at the pain that lanced down his back.

"The Devil?" Don Rolon asked. "What makes them believe it was the Devil?"

"Anything they cannot explain at night is the Devil," Don Enrique said with a sarcastic flourish of his hand. "Even Padre Barnabas would agree with that, and that should convince you."

Don Rolon mounted and steadied his horse. "What does Muñoz have to say to that?"

"Who?" Don Enrique demanded without ceremony.

"The majordomo, Salvador Muñoz. What has he said about it?" Don Rolon reached down to adjust the stirrup, and when he looked up, Capitan Iturbes was coming toward them, and he put the gossip of peasants out of his mind.

"A fine day, Alteza," the Capitan declared with such jauntiness that both Don Rolon and Don Enrique were ready to strangle him. "They say that there are wild goats farther up the crest, and we should get in a chase or two."

"Fine," Don Rolon said, weary already. "Will we have dogs?"

"Two. Muñoz needs an extra one to stand guard, he says, and I have not made an issue of it." He gave an easy sign to the stablemen and stood confidently waiting. "El Conde is not with us?"

"Apparently he is still asleep," Don Rolon answered. "The wine last night . . . "

"Wonderful!" Capitan Iturbes enthused. "Better than what we have in the army, I can tell you. I wish I'd had more of it."

"I will be sick in a moment," Don Enrique vowed quietly.

"Still, that's the advantage of these fortresses," Iturbes went on blithely, "where you can get a store of foods and goods, season after season. Barley and rice, and mutton whenever you want it. There's cheese and oranges and enough honey to sweeten a wagonload of bread. These people here, they have the good life." He took the reins of his gelding from the stablehand who led him out and vaulted into the saddle without pausing to look at the girths. "The good Padre has said he wishes to fast and pray this morning, and so we three are all the hunters." He brought up his riding whip. "Bring the dogs!"

One of the stablehands went running across the courtyard to the kennels, shouting to the keeper to bring out his treasures. Shortly afterward, he came back, almost dragged by two large, lean-bodied hounds that barked and growled as they neared the three men on horseback.

"Pardon, Señores, but they do not know you, and they are fierce," said the stablehand, trying to excuse the way the dogs behaved.

"Guard dogs should not be sweet-tempered," Don Rolon said at once, and nodded to Capitan Iturbes. "Whenever you are ready, we will leave."

"Bueno, Alteza," said Capitan Iturbes with a wave to the stablehand. "Celease the dogs!"

The two hounds leaped forward as the gates opened, racing out into the bright morning light along the narrow trail that led to the upper peaks. Capitan Iturbes grinned in anticipation of great sport, then dug his spurs into his gelding's sides and bounded after them.

Don Enrique was less eager, but he followed with grim determination, not looking to see if Don Rolon was with him or lagging behind. Properly he should not take the lead from the Infante Real, but he could not resist that first exciting rush from the fortress. He flicked his lash over his horse's rump and grinned at the nervous response. Headache or no, Don Enrique was determined to have his pleasure hunting.

It did not trouble Don Rolon to have Don Enrique take the lead. He was still in the grip of the malaise he had awakened to, and now wished he had followed el Conde's example and remained in bed for the morning. But word of such petulance would reach his father, and then there would be the letters of admonition and arguments, which was more than he could bear. He clapped his heels to his Andalusian's sides and resigned himself to a day of chasing hounds through the mountains. He touched the crossbow hanging from his saddle and felt the packet of quarrels, disappointed to find so many.

Had there been fewer, they might not have had to spend long on the hunt. As the doors closed behind the Infante Real, he had a moment of stark fear, as if he were being banished to the fastness of the mountains with no redemption or succor left to him. This impression faded quickly, but left behind it a wretchedness of spirit that did not lessen its hold on him for several hours.

By the time the hunting party started back toward El Mono, there were three dead wild goats strapped to the cantels of their saddles, and the dogs trailed them with pink tongues lolling. This time they had to wait while the gates were opened, and when they came into the courtyard, two cooks bustled forward to meet them, reaching for their prizes before the stablehands came to take the horses to be fed and watered. The hounds slouched away to their kennels, heads low.

"Not much to brag about," said Don Enrique as he dismounted. His headache had disappeared some time before, replaced now with insistent hunger. He resolved to be more careful with the wine this time, and to take more of the simple meats the majordomo offered.

"There is nothing more to hunt," Capitan Iturbes said laconically. "In the army we've had to run down geese, sometimes. Once, in Flanders, three of us went out with pikes and pronged half a dozen ducks. We were out of other food and the farmers would not sell us any, since most of them were Protestants, and not anxious to—" He broke off as he saw Padre Barnabas coming toward them, his face grave and his manner reeking of bad news.

"Señores," intoned the priest, "your prayers are required."

The others in the courtyard paused to cross themselves and a few made the sign against the Evil Eye, averting their faces so that they would not offend the Infante Real.

"What is it, good Padre?" Don Rolon asked as he unbuckled the girths of his saddle. It was good to be on the ground again, he thought, for as much as he loved to ride his Andalusian, he often longed for the simple satisfaction of walking, and a long day on horseback inevitably made him happy to be out of the saddle.

"It is el Conde," Padre Barnabas announced solemnly.

"Is he ill?" asked Don Rolon, secretly wishing that Padre Barnabas would come to the point.

"No, would it were so, mi Infante. El Conde was. . .found dead by shepherds, at the very edge of that defile we came through the day before yesterday. They told me it was the work of the minions of the Devil." This pronouncement brought about quiet, terrified whispers among those who stood in the courtyard to listen, and Padre Barnabas nodded portentously. "Yes, the Devil is working here, with willing servants, if the condition of the unfortunate young hidalgo is any indication of their malice."

"What . . . how did he die?" Don Rolon asked, his throat suddenly so dry that his voice cracked.

"The Devil: you heard him," Don Enrique said roughly. "Spit it out, man, how did el Conde . . .die?"

Padre Barnabas did not like to have his hand forced, so he folded his arms and said as bluntly as he could, "His throat and entrails were torn out."

Though rumors of this had spread through the servants of El Morro, hearing it announced so badly and cruelly silenced them, and one or two of them whispered prayers, though not all were to the Virgin or Saints.

"Mercy of Jesus," Don Rolon murmured; his chest tightened with shock.

"Shepherds found him and brought him here," Padre Barnabas went on, satisfied now that he had the attention he wanted. "He has been laid out as best he can be in the chapel and I have offered prayers for the repose of his soul. But the way he died, it is possible that he has fled to Hell where pious petitions may not touch him and bring him the salvation Our Lord promised."

"What?" Don Enrique demanded.

"Those who die as sacrifice to the Devil are given to him as tribute and we of the Church Militant can do nothing to save them. That is why it is so necessary to eschew all the works of the Devil, for there is nothing more terrible to a good Christian than the loss of his soul to the powers of the Great Enemy of mankind and God." He was warming up now, and took advantage of the moment to deliver an impromptu warning. "Those who preach tolerance and understanding for heretics and Devil-worshippers are themselves serving the interests of the Evil One. They are as much the enemy of every sincere Christian as those who actively seek to subvert our faith. When one man declares that there may be no harm in opposing thought, he is setting himself with those who oppose God Himself. Who can tolerate that, and be worthy of the gifts God has given us? Yet so many look for excuses that will free those they defend from the penalties God has decreed must be theirs. In that, they set themselves against God and His Holy Word. Think of this before you condone the acts of those who are not practicing our faith, and who give comfort to those who serve that Other Master. It is your own soul and salvation you trifle with; in that time of judgment, God will see your errors and cast you from Him for the betrayal that is as great as the betrayal of Judas."

Capitan Iturbes cleared his throat in the silence that followed Padre Barnabas' impassioned words. "When was el Conde discovered?" This inconsequent question was so startling that it caused a minor shock of its own.

"Is it important?" Don Enrique said, glaring at Padre Barnabas.

"Yes. If it has not been long, there may still be signs I can read that will tell us who else was there with him. It may be that if he was . . . mauled as you say, Padre, that it was the work of animals and not men. If it is a dog or a wolf, we may be able to hunt it so that men need not fear him." He snapped his fingers for a stableman and told him to lead off his horse.

"A dog or a wolf would do this, and leave him in such a place?" asked one of the more credulous servants.

"Of course," Capitan Iturbes said. "You admit that no one goes there at night. What better place for a beast to bring its prey, for it will not be disturbed." He looked up at the sky. "There are four more hours of light left to us. If you will saddle a fresh horse, I will ride out to investigate."

"It is a waste of time, Capitan, and possibly dangerous," warned Padre Barnabas.

"Perhaps so, mi Padre. If I delay any longer, it certainly will be." He turned toward Don Rolon. "Have I your permission, Alteza?"

"As you wish, Capitan," Don Rolon said, wishing that he had the courage to offer to go with him. "Will you need . . . help?"

Capitan Iturbes smiled. "No, Alteza. Best I go alone. It's daylight still and I will not be gone past sunset. If there is anything to find, I will come upon it quickly." He started toward the stables, walking quickly.

"And what if . . . he doesn't come back?" Don Enrique demanded loudly. "What if he is attacked—or merely deserts. Soldiers desert all the time, don't they? Why should not Capitan Iturbes do so, since there is no one here who can follow him." He stalked across the courtyard toward the central keep. "It's all very well to let him go, but I tell you that we ought not to expect to see him again."

Although Padre Barnabas agreed with Don Enrique's prediction, he felt compelled to defend the Capitan for form's sake. "Instead of castigating the man, offer your prayers for him. Once you have seen el Conde in the chapel, you will know what true bravery our Capitan is showing." He blessed the servants in the courtyard, then gave his attention to Don Rolon. "If you will attend me, Alteza, we will begin the service for the dead. There is a priest here, but I fear he is not of the best, more of a peasant than a priest and unaware of the significance of most ritual." He turned and swept through the squat arch of the keep door, enjoying the luxury of having the Infante Real in his wake.

Don Rolon tried to quiet the turmoil in his mind as he followed the priest, but the nightmare that had plagued his sleep filled his soul with apprehension and dread. Had he heard something, seen something, known something that warned of el Conde's death? While they drank together—just the night before!—was there a remark of some sort he should have paid more attention to, a gesture of curiosity that might have shown the fatality that hovered over him? With these questions roiling within him, he went to see the body of his courtier.

Capitan Iturbes did not return for several hours, and when he did, he called for hot wine and food before speaking on what he had discovered. He pulled off his muddy boots and sat with his feet toward the fire in the great hall, then addressed Don Rolon.

"Did you find anything?" Padre Barnabas demanded just as Iturbes was about to speak.

"Not conclusive, no," the Capitan said with a scowl at the priest. "Alteza, I found tracks that led near the place, but I could not see where they came from. None of the peasants in the village know anything about it; or they say they don't. Padre Hernan tells me that everyone is afraid of the place, but we knew that."

"What were the tracks like?" Don Rolon asked quietly. He was curious and repulsed at once.

"It could be a wolf, and if it is, it's a large one. There are wolves in these mountains, Alteza, and that means we should be on our guard against them. I'll speak to Muñoz in the morning, and he may wish to set traps for them." He looked into the fire as if finding secrets in the flames. "I've never hunted a wolf. It would be a great challenge. If it strikes again, let us go after it."

"Don't you expect it to attack once more?" Padre Barnabas inquired, crossing himself for protection against the beast.

"It could be a rogue, and they never stay long in any place, or that's what the shepherds tell me. That is what they pray it is, because they hope to keep their flocks safe. But they may be right. A wolf that size would be noticed if it hunted around here most of the time." With a sigh, he leaned back, smiling up at the ceiling beams. "This is the life, having a place like El Morro. Nothing to bother you, no one to fight you, and if they try, all you need do is lock the gates and wait them out. Not like riding into the field with cannon and lances, where you know that half of you will not leave the field intact. The last charge I rode to, eighty men were dead in a quarter of an hour. But here, there's good food and a sturdy fortification. These people don't know how fortunate they are."

"They are also isolated," Don Enrique muttered as he looked up from his cup. It was the first notice he had paid of the conversation.

"That's not a bad thing, Señor. It can have many advantages. A man in my profession comes to love solitude." Iturbes finished his hot wine and called for more. "You know, Alteza, you should remember this place. When you are el Rey, you may need such a retreat when Court life weighs too heavily upon you."

"I pray God that day is far off," Don Rolon said automatically, certain that every remark he made about his father would be reported to him.

"As do we all," agreed Padre Barnabas at once.

"But one should keep these things in mind, Alteza," said Iturbes as he held his cup out to the servant. "Gustav has his retreats, that one in Austria and that other one near the Danish border. Your uncle is a clever man. Well, he'd have to be to keep his crown, wouldn't he?" Almost half the wine was gone in a gulp. "Better. A little more of this, and I'll sleep as if in my old nurse's arms."

Don Enrique sneered. "You like it up here, you can stay when we leave."

"That's not how I was ordered, Señor, if you will permit me to remind you," Capitan Iturbes said with a touch of disgust in his tone. "Oh, yes. I've talked to the villagers, as I said. They're going to keep the way clear from here to Zaragoza, or so they've promised. It won't be an easy journey, but if we break it along the way, we should be able to go safely and not risk being out at night." He looked around for Muñoz. "I want meat, man. I'm famished."

"It is coming," Don Rolon said. "Will the ride be dangerous?"

"No more than it was coming here," Iturbes answered. "Don't be troubled, Alteza. Time will pass quickly and you'll be back in Valladolid before half the city knows you're gone."

"If it pleases my father," Don Rolon murmured.

There was no response to this, and a few moments later a servant arrived with a trencher for Capitan Iturbes. Padre Barnabas repeated the blessing and had a token of meat with the Capitan, and Don Rolon called for Lugantes to entertain them. For the rest of the evening, it was much like any other night in a mountain fortress.

3

A week after the body of el Conde del Aranjuez was consigned to sacred earth, there was a dusting of snow on the highest peaks around the fortress. Wind slid down the mountains, insinuating its icy presence everywhere. El Morro escaped the snow at first, but there was frost every morning and the water in the cisterns froze at night. The little party was no longer inclined to hunt, for the weather made tracking the goats in their high, foggy crags almost impossible. So the courtiers stayed in the great hall of the keep, near the heart and its fire while the servants crept about, anxious not to disturb their important guests, and too chilled to be active themselves.

Don Enrique became surly after two days and struck his manservant with a wooden serving ladle. The man did not complain, being too much in awe of the hidalgo, but word of it spread, and eventually Don Rolon took Don Enrique aside and chided him for this churlishness; it was agreed that the incident was forgotten.

Padre Barnabas kept long vigils in the chapel, emerging only twice a day for meals and to exhort the three men on the evils of sin and improper behavior, reminding all that sloth was numbered among the capital offenses against the Holy Spirit. He called upon the Saints to witness his efforts, then sought the chapel again.

For one afternoon, Don Rolon busied himself in the stable tending to his horse and tack. The stallion was restive with confinement and nipped at his master's arm. Don Rolon quieted the horse, but his interest flagged, and he asked the stablehands to attend to his Andalusian, suggesting that they let him run about the courtyard once a day so that he would not start kicking down his stall. Later, he asked Padre Barnabas for a Bible or Prayer Book to read, there being nothing else in the fortress.

By the end of the second week, the snow had reached El Morro and it was cold enough to make all the servants dress in wool and furs. The terrors of el Conde's death faded from their thoughts except when Padre Barnabas chose to remind them of it during his interminable evening prayers. As a result, there were two days of hunting sallies, and each time Don Rolon and Don Enrique returned with wild goats, but it was no longer sport but hunger that drove them into the snowy mountains.

Of the wolf, there was no sign.

There was ice on the courtyard cobbles and a seer wind out of the north when el Rey's Messenger came up to El Morro. He carried the herald's banner on a crook instead of a lance, symbolizing the peaceful intent of his mission. His horse was lathered and panting in spite of the cold when the gates were opened to him and Don Rolon, hastily wrapped in a long fur mantle, came out of the keep to kiss the ring he bore.

"How is it with El Rey?" he asked, his breath clouding the air.

"He sends you his blessings and this letter." The messenger held up the folded parchment so that all could see the royal seal impressed into the wax.

Dutifully Don Rolon took the parchment and kissed the Arms of España. "It is my pleasure to serve el Rey in all things." He had said that so many times in his life that the words had ceased to make sense. They were more unreal than prayers and hymns, he thought, and could not find it in himself to be shocked at the notion.

This formality over, the messenger dismounted and handed his horse over to the stablehand who arrived at a slow run, looking put upon. The messenger offered the other man the reins and turned to Don Rolon at once. "It is the best news, Alteza. Word is already spreading, and all the country rejoices with you."

Don Rolon frowned, puzzled. "You please me, naturally, but I fear I do not understand the reason for your good wishes."

"Why, the Doge has agreed to your father's offer," the messenger beamed, as if this made all clear.

"It is fortunate for my father," Don Rolon said politely. "But how does it touch me?" He had asked Rey Alonzo many times to send him away from España, but this request had always been denied, and so he knew that it could not be the reason for the Herald's delight. As Infante Real, he was not permitted to be part of a diplomatic mission to any country not allied with España and the Holy

Coman Empire, which restricted his movements as much as Rey Alonzo's dictates. How, then, did the Doge—of Venezia or Genova? —enter his affairs? It was improper for Don Rolon to read the letter here in the courtyard with others looking on; he would have to wait until Don Enrique or Padre Barnabas could act as his witness. The parchment felt hot in his hand, as if the words written on it were burning their way through to him.

"You will be expected to return to Court in a month, Alteza," the messenger was saying, "so that preparations may begin for the festivities. There are state visits and other functions that you must attend."

"I?" asked Don Rolon, who had not been listening closely to what the man was saying. "I am eager to do as El Majestad desires, but it is not . . . often that such honors are visited upon me."

"Indeed, no," the Herald declared with a chuckle. "And with the aid of Heaven, you will have these festivities only once."

Don Rolon looked closely at the messenger. "Señor, tell me. Does this concern my marriage?" He knew that his father had been considering such a move ever since the Infante Real reached the age of seventeen, but the personal enmity he felt for his legitimate son kept him from pursuing the matter. Now, perhaps, Rey Alonzo's brother, the Emperor Gustav Humphrey, was pressing the issue: his own son, Otto, was to be married at Easter.

"I cannot answer what the letter contains, Alteza. I have not seen it, or I would betray my office. But there are whispers in the court now that . . . hint at such a possibility." He tugged off his fur hat as they came into the great hall where an enormous fire blazed on the hearth. "The inn where I stayed last night, in Zaragoza, was as cold as a corpse. Not enough firewood in the place to cook an egg."

"This will be a pleasant change," Don Rolon said distantly as he looked around the room. Neither Padre Barnabas nor Don Enrique were to be found anywhere. With a resigned sigh, Don Rolon gave his attention to the messenger. "Good Herald, I don't know your name, or . . . ."

"I am Antonio Ursos, Alteza, youngest son of the—" the young man told him quickly, only to be interrupted.

"Of the Duque de Pamplona," Don Rolon finished for him. "I am honored to meet you, Herald. You come from a most distinguished family."

"With it being so large, it could scarcely escape some note," Antonio said a bit acidly. "My father has been blessed with eight sons and four daughters, and all but one of them have lived." He lifted his shoulders. "I do what I may, and Herald to the Royal

Presence is more than I ever hoped for."

"Then we are all twice fortunate," Don Rolon said, trying to think where Padre Barnabas might be. Most of the time he saw entirely too much of the Dominican priest, but now, when he had some use for the man, he could not find him. There was little he could speak of with the Herald; such conversations were strictly limited by the demands of their social stations and his office. "If you like, I will ask them to give you hot wine with honey. It is tasteless stuff, but warm."

"I would appreciate it, Alteza," Antonio said politely. "And if there is a little meat, I am famished."

"Of course," Don Rolon said, and having an excuse to leave the man to himself, he set out through the corridors, first to find the majordomo and request that the Herald be provided with refreshments, then to look for either of his companions.

He found Don Enrique sitting in an embrasure of the chim-ney of the minstrels' gallery. He had a cup of hot wine in his hand and was more than half drunk. A lute lay across his lap and he reached to strum it clumsily in accompaniment to his song:

Quando mi nombre llamaba
Su corazon de la vita
Y amor encontraba
Entonces . . .

"I forget what comes next," he said, looking up for the first time. "It isn't a very good song, anyway. Apprentices sing it."

"A messenger has come from my father," Don Rolon said without any of the customary preambles.

"Wants to know what happened to el Conde, does he?" Don Enrique asked, his words slurring as he took another drink.

"I don't think so. The messenger has another impression." He sighed. "Are you in any condition to witness my reading of the letter?"

"Probably not," Don Enrique admitted after giving it his consideration. "Better find the priest. He doesn't drink as much as I do." He plucked an inexpert chord on the lute. "This is a terrible instrument. Angels couldn't get melody out of it. That's probably heresy. Very well. Angels could get melody out of it, but they would have to perform a miracle. There. That's better." Abruptly he set the lute aside and lurched to his feet. "I'll go talk to the messenger. Who is it, by the way?"

"Antonio Ursos," Don Rolon told him, giving the name no particular emphasis.

"One of Pamplona's spawn? I used to know one of them, but it wasn't Antonio. I don't think it was." He began an unsteady progress toward the stairs that led down to the great hall on the main floor.

"Don Enrique . . . " Don Rolon warned.

"Don't be concerned. I will manage." He wiggled his fingers in a wave and staggered away, humming his song to himself as he went.

As much as he disliked the thought, Don Rolon suspected he would find Padre Barnabas in the chapel with the ancient and bewildered Padre Miguel. It had become a habit with the two priests to keep a vigil through the afternoon, reciting prayers and chanting. There was no heat in the chapel and the walls were clammy with damp, but Padre Barnabas was devoted to the task and had persuaded Padre Miguel to remain with him.

On his way to the chapel, Don Rolon encountered Capitan Iturbes, who was occupied with cleaning his tack. The Capitan gave a nod that might pass for a bow, then went back to his work.

"Your family wouldn't have a patent of arms, would it, Capitan?" Don Rolon inquired hopefully. There were enough minor nobles in the country that it was not impossible for Iturbes to be connected to one of them in some degree.

"No, no, Alteza. None of us ever rose above our station. One of my uncles married the niece of a Marquis from Languedoc, but that's as close as any of us has ever come to the nobility. Why?" He was rubbing tallow into the leather girths he had resting on his knees, working it until it took on a dull shine.

"I need a witness to my reading of this letter my father has sent me. Don Enrique is drinking and I don't want to interrupt Padre Barnabas at his prayers." It was not quite a lie, and for that reason he decided he need not confess it. "if you had some claim to a patent, I could ask you to act as witness, but since you have not . . . "

"I'll fetch the Padre, if you wish it, Alteza." He was already setting the girths aside and rising. "No reason you should have to summon the man. I'll tell him you're waiting in the . . . "

"Grand reception chamber," Don Rolon supplied. This elaborate name was used to indicate a small stone chamber just off the great hall on the back side of the huge fireplace. It was the most elegantly appointed room in the fortress—which was not saying a great deal—and used only for official acts and functions.

"That will bring him, certainly," Capitan Iturbes said with a wink. "You say there is word from el Rey?"

"Yes, and I must have a witness when I open and read the letter. It is required whenever the message is sealed with the Coat of Arms of España. He made a gesture to show how little control he had of the matter.

"If the army were as bogged down by protocol, Alteza, we would never take to the field, let alone win a war. If you will forgive me for saying it." This last was an afterthought, one that evoked a wan smile from Don Rolon.

"You are forgiven, mi Capitan. More than that." He looked at the letter he held and went on, more to himself than the other man, "This is simple, compared to some of the ceremony required."

"What about the jester. He has a title, hasn't he?" Iturbes suggested.

"Yes, he has a title, but in this case, it will not do. All such . . . entertainers are given titles, but they are not for . . . occasions like this." He needed little imagination to picture his father's wrath if he were told that Lugantes had witnessed the reading of his letter. There was little enough love between Alonzo and Rolon as it was; such a breach of courtesy would be more than enough to estrange them completely.

"What is the matter, Alteza?" Capitan Iturbes asked. He had studied the youth's long face, and although the question trespassed on Don Rolon's rank, he had come to like the Infante Real, and was concerned for his welfare.

"Nothing, good Capitan. C'est rien, as my father's wife would say." He tapped the letter against his leg. "At moments such as this one, I could wish el Conde alive again simply for my convenience. Perhaps we're fortunate that there have been no more losses at El Morro, or I would have to ride to Zaragoza to read this."

"You will have to ride there soon in any .case, if that message brings you orders to do so." Capitan Iturbes gave a brief salute. "I will fetch the priest for you."

"Gracias, mi Capitan," the Infante Real said formally, and went slowly back toward the grand reception chamber.

The room was warmer than much of the fortress because of its proximity to the huge fireplace, but it was chilly enough to cause gooseflesh to rise when Don Rolon took off his mantle. Properly he must not be dressed for riding when he read the letter. He rubbed at his face with cold hands, but neither hands nor face were warmed much, so he stopped and blew on his fingers instead. In his heart he was afraid that the Herald might be correct—that the letter would order him to accept a bride, to marry. All his life he had been schooled for this and he knew beyond question what was expected of him: he must marry the correct woman, from a sufficiently royal

House to be acceptable to the Spanish Hapsburgs as their German cousins; he must then produce legitimate heirs, male children in good health with intact minds who would repeat the pattern he had learned, and teach it to their sons; he must honor and strengthen the Church so that his country would be purged of all evil and continue to enjoy the bounty of God; he must be in all ways obedient to el Rey Alonzo II and teach his children the same obedience; he must love the Holy Coman Emperor, his Uncle Gustav, as much as he must not trust him; he must devote himself to the good of his people, but never permit them to come too close to him so that his high station could not be compromised; he must live austerely in the midst of opulence; he must . . .

"Capitan Iturbes told me I would find you here," said Padre Barnabas as he came into the room. His jaw was set in reaction to the insult of being summoned away from his prayers.

"Yes. I am sorry to have disturbed you, Padre," Don Rolon said, doing his best to placate the priest. "I have need of you. There must be a witness and Don Enrique is not . . . in the correct frame of mind to—"

"Drunk again?" the Padre interrupted, not requiring any confirmation. "Sots will find that they will have brimstone to drink in Hell when the Judgment comes."

"We must pray for God to show him his error and change his heart, then," Don Rolon said, hoping this would avert any sermon Padre Barnabas might be inspired to deliver. "I have here, as you will see, a letter from my father, el Rey Alonzo." He had lapsed into the more ritualistic speech of Court life, and, as always, felt that bleakness of spirit those formalities gave to him. The intention was to remind everyone of the majesty and permanence of the Court, but all Don Rolon gleaned was a profound distress and a sense of separation from those around him. "The Herald Antonio Ursos has delivered it not one hour past, and obedient to the dictates of the Crown, I ask you to witness my reading and understanding of the message it contains. Are you willing, Padre Barnabas, to be that witness?"

As much as the ceremony of court irritated Don Rolon it gratified Padre Barnabas. All earlier insults ware forgotten as his umbrage faded away; in its place was the first glow of satisfaction, which he could not believe was the great sin of pride. "I am the most humble and faithful servant of El Majestad after the devotion I owe by my vows to God."

"Very commendable," Don Rolon said as he held out the letter. "There is a seal upon this letter. Do you see it?"

"I do, Infante." He made a point of looking at the thing for a moment.

"Do you know the Arms of España? Would you recognize them if you saw them?" It was a foolish question, but one that was required, and he repeated it without much thought, wanting the whole incident to be over as quickly as possible.

"Yes, I know it and would recognize it." Padre Barnabas spoke confidently, his tones as ringing as when God visited him with eloquent expressions of faith.

"And do you verify that this is indeed the royal seal?" There were three torches in the room for light since the two high windows had been covered with moth-eaten tapestries to hold in what little heat they could. "Examine it closely, good prelate. El Rey demands it of you."

Padre Barnabas took the letter to the nearest torch and inspected the large blob of black wax that held two red silk ribbons crossed under it, sealing the letter within. He had never actually seen the royal seal before, but knew what it looked like from the countless times he had passed the Arms of España carved into the doors of his convent in Valladolid. He touched the hard wax, entranced by the deep impressions which were as ponderous as the titles incised around the Staff of San Diego and the Golden Fleece. *El Rey Alonzo, de esto nombre el Segundo, Fernando Luis Maria de los Hapsburgs, d'España y Corsica, Margrave de Saxony y Marashal in Camera al Gustav, el Emperador.* Padre Barnabas was awed by the might that seal represented and he showed his reverence by kissing the wax. "It is the royal seal," he declared.

"And it is properly affixed?" Don Rolon asked mechanically.

"Yes, Alteza." He rarely called Don Rolon by his title, enjoying his clerical privilege, which placed him above recognition of rank. Now, reminded of the enormous power of España, he gave the young man his due.

"Please give it back to me, good Padre," Don Rolon said, holding out his hand and noticing how reluctantly Padre Barnabas parted with the letter. "As you see, I am not tampering with the seal itself in any way." He had been taught how to use the ends of the ribbons to lift the seal so that it was not cracked or damaged, which was regarded as treasonously insulting as well as the worst omen to the Royal Family. Don Rolon pried carefully, and took the seal from the parchment, laying it on the table faceup as he spread the letter and read it—as he was required to do—aloud.

To Our most loved and esteemed son and heir, the Infante Real, Rolon Andres Esteban Angel Castelar de Asturias, Aragon, Leon y Castilla, our affectionate greetings:

Bearing in mind the destiny of our House and the duties a Prince owes to his House and country, we have entered into nego- tiations on your behalf to ensure your felicity and our continued favor granted by God. We are pleased to inform you that we have secured the troth of the third niece of the Doge of Venezia, La Donna Zaretta Melissina Colomba Patrecipazio, who brings with her a dowry of nine merchant ships, five estates, the incomes of her mother's fortune and ten percent of her uncle's, as well as the sum of sixty thousand Venezian ducats. Your joy cannot exceed our own at this marriage, which will mark the union of Venezia to all the Hapsburg empires, to our mutual benefit. To occasion the mar- riage properly, the Doge has signed a treaty that will bring about the end of hostilities between our ships and those of his country.

We ask, therefore, that you present yourself at Court once again upon the third week after Epiphany, at which time the direction for your celebrations will be made known to you, and you will be able to greet the representatives of Venezia and give them what assur- ances of your delight you may wish them to carry to your betrothed.

We pray God that you will show yourself worthy of the honor which is being conferred upon you, and will recall the duty you owe your House and your country. We humbly entreat the Virgin to show you how great is your favor in this world, that you may better conduct your affairs in a manner that will be satisfactory to us once again.

Until you kneel to kiss our hand once again, we are in all pa- ternal fondness, etc.

El Rey Alonzo II
by the hand of el Duque da Minho
at Valladolid

Don Rolon's hands were trembling as he put the parchment down and stared across the room at the flame of the torch placed there.

"We must offer a Mass of thanksgiving at once!" Padre Barnabas cried out. He went so far as to clap his hands together, but he covered this mistake by folding them in prayer. "Our heart- felt gratitude speeds to God for this great blessing that He has brought to our country."

Don Rolon crossed himself, and when he saw that Padre Barnabas was watching him critically, attempted to satisfy the priest. "It is . . . I am not deserving of this," he said finally, knowing certainly that Padre Barnabas would not understand him.

"It is good to see that you are obedient to your father's wishes and acknowledge your fortune so humbly. It will be remarked upon later." Also, Padre Barnabas thought, since I am the one who heard the letter, I will be called upon to testify that I saw the Infante Real open the document, and heard him read from it. That will surely show my superiors that I have sufficient merit to be granted a position with the Holy Office, where I might be more active in the questioning of heretics. Ambition was not an acceptable emotion for a priest, and Padre Barnabas knew it; however, zeal was, and he had no trouble mistaking one for the other.

"The niece of the Doge of Venezia," Don Rolon said slowly as he stood up. "He says nothing of her." He dreaded what that might mean, for often enough he had heard of unions between wholly un-suited persons for no reason other than to satisfy the requirements of blood and treaty. He was confident that this niece was young enough to have children, but that might mean she was thirteen or forty-five. There was no mention of her disposition. Was she intelligent or dull? Don Rolon's half sisters were unmarriageable—not even the Pope was willing to grant complete idiots dispensation to marry, no mat-ter how wellborn they were. Queen Margrit, the Emperor's wife, had a hunched back and two teeth left in her head.

"As we celebrate the Nativity," Padre Barnabas said, antici-pating the next few weeks, "we will add special Masses and devo-tions in thanks for this great honor. It will make the Holy Birth the more holy, for it will promise the joys of family life to you, and reveal to you the depths of your father's wisdom in arranging this match for you." Such service would also gain him attention that would benefit him later. Padre Barnabas was just beginning to re-alize what far-reaching use could be made of this lucky accident. At once he crossed himself and whispered a few words, for it was worse than heresy to assume such good fortune was not evidence of the Hand of God moving to reward him for his fidelity. "Come to the chapel now, Alteza. I am sure your heart is full and an hour of prayer will quiet your spirits."

Don Rolon did not have the demeanor of a man overcome with happiness, but he allowed himself to be persuaded. If he could find a way to resign himself to a marriage that he had always known must come, he would be able to greet his father without anger. Doubtless it was as galling to Alonzo as it was to him, for Alonzo longed to heap titles and riches and honors on his bastard son Gil; to have Rolon married well would infuriate him.

"You must send a message of your readiness to comply with el Rey's wishes," Padre Barnabas said, and turned back to pick up the letter, on the pretext of needing it for the reply, but actually for the pleasure of touching the document.

Unnoticed by both men, the edge of the parchment caught on the ribbons of the seal, and as Padre Barnabas turned away with his treasure in his hands, the black wax Seal of España dropped to the floor and shattered.

4

Lugantes was almost finished packing the two trunks that Don Rolon carried with him when he heard a tentative knock at the door. "You may enter," he called out as he folded up another set of sleeves.

"Is the Infante Real . . ." began the timid voice without opening the door.

"He is in the stable with Capitan Iturbes," Lugantes answered, then offered "to go inform him you wish to see him."

"No, no, Señor Lugantes," said Salvador Muñoz as he hurriedly slid into the room. As he closed the door, he looked nervously about, as if he feared to be seen here. "I have talked to the peasants today, Señor Lugantes."

It was rare that Lugantes was given any title but fool, and so it was not surprising that he was willing to listen to anything Muñoz had to say; his curiosity was piqued, as well.

"Is there some difficulty?"

"They do not wish the Infante Real to leave," Salvador Muñoz whispered, putting his hand to his mouth as if to shield his words.

"His father has ordered his return," Lugantes said firmly, but studied the majordomo for more information.

"Yes, yes, that is known, and we all thank Heaven for granting him so fine a bride and establishing a truce. It is most worthy and God will show His approval. That is not what is the matter." He moved away from the door in small, nervous strides. "You see, I said that I would not tell you, and so I am committing a sin to break that vow. But if I do not, then I will expose the Infante Real to great danger, here and on his journey, and that is a greater sin, I am convinced of it. Padre Hernan in the village cannot advise me, and he is an old man. He said the Masses for the unfortunate ones, and his prayers for their souls continue, but—" He fell silent abruptly, his face sagged with despair.

"What is the matter, Muñoz?" Lugantes asked, this time speaking more sharply than he had before. If there was risk here, he must know it, no matter how miserable Muñoz felt because of it. "Is it Plague?"

"Plague? No, would that it were." He planted his hands on his hips in helpless defiance. "El Conde, you saw him when he was found." Everyone at El Morro had, and Muñoz did not wait for Lugantes to confirm it. "A month after that, there was another, one of the children of the shepherds. I saw the body. It was the same. We brought Padre Hernan from the village and he said the holy words for her, and she was buried at the crossroads, with her face toward Hell and hawthorn in her mouth. And last week, the same thing happened. This time it was a traveler. We do not know who he was, but he was the same, with his throat gone and his guts pulled out. Padre Hernan did not want to pray for that one, but he has agreed, so long as the grave is not in sacred ground and there is no marker for it."

"A shepherd's daughter and a traveler," Lugantes said to himself.

"They were out alone, which is not wise at the best of times. With such a creature ravening, only a fool would—" Muñoz stopped. "But you see, the Infante Real will be traveling, and there may be a time for this creature, whatever it is, to attack him. If he must go, let el Rey send him more troops than Capitan Iturbes to escort him. I would count my soul lost if anything were to happen to the Infante." He wrung his hands suddenly. "There are those who say that the creature is hunting for the Infante, since without him, the Royal House would fall . . . . "

Lugantes made a motion to silence Muñoz even after he had stopped speaking. "You must not say this thing," he warned the majordomo. "It is true, and for that reason, it is most unwise to speak of it. All of the Succession depends on Don Rolon, and for that alone he is vulnerable." It was not fitting for him to add that there were those at Court who would be pleased to see others in Don Rolon's place, not the least of them his father.

"Then speak with him, Señor Lugantes. Warn him of the danger that exists in these mountains. Already they are saying that the Devil has sent this to try us, so that we will betray our trust and harm the Infante Real. There are also those who say that this is no beast at all, but men who are damned and depraved, who wish to make a sacrifice to the Devil of the Infante Real because of all the burnings and tortures that have been authorized by the Holy Office." He crossed himself quickly. "They are bad men who say this, but some who are weak listen to them, and then they do not tell all they know. Some of them fear that the same thing may happen to them."

Lugantes shook his misshapen head. "You did well in coming to me, Muñoz. And it is best that you do not speak to others." He frowned deeply. "Is it known that we depart at daybreak?"

"Yes. Stablehands talk, and cooks talk, and what can I do?" He shrugged then clapped his palms against his thighs. "I have told them that it is foolish, but that is all. They hear me and then they do as they wish. Each says 'My wife will keep the secret if I tell her to' or 'My friend will not speak' and before you know it, everyone from here to Zaragoza has been told." He sat on the edge of the bed, though it was most incorrect for him to do so. "I fear that this is not a beast who preys on the unwary. I have asked myself, what if I wished to kill someone of rank? I would not try them first, but I would practice one or two killings, so that I was certain I could do it, and so I was certain there was fear enough to keep others from coming to aid those I hunted. Then I would wait for the proper moment. There are those who say that the killings have been at the full moon to honor the Devil, but I think that a clever man might know this, and use it to his advantage. A man needs the light of the full moon if he is abroad without a lantern. A beast has no such trouble." Quite unexpectedly he started to weep. "I have prayed to God and the Saints to protect him, and I have burned candles for him, but it is not enough. I had to speak to you, Señor Lugantes. The Infante Real listens to you."

"To my jests, perhaps," Lugantes said quietly.

"He listens to more than that," Muñoz countered. "You have his ear far more than Hurreres does. With the priest, it is otherwise, but he is not a man to speak to, other than to confess."

"Very true," Lugantes agreed. "Well, Muñoz, what do you want me to do?"

"Warn him!" Muñoz burst out. "Oh, Dios!" he sobbed. "That he should suffer!"

Lugantes took pity on the man. "Muñoz, I will tell the Infante Real what you have told me, but I will not reveal your name if that is what you wish. I will tell Capitan Iturbes to be on guard while we travel, and once we reach Zaragoza, I will request that we have a full escort all the way back to Valladolid. It is not much, I know, but without being more specific, I cannot do more. I will tell Don Rolon in private about the unfortunates who have died, and if he wishes to take extra precautions, he will know what is best to do."

Inwardly, Lugantes. doubted that Don Rolon would ask for more protection than he already had, but that was not his decision to make, he knew, and he did not want to compromise the Infante Real to this man. He was aware that it was possible that Muñoz represented those he claimed most to abhor, one of the men sworn to bring down the House of Hapsburg in España and set up royalty more to their liking.

"Gracias, Señor Lugantes," Muñoz whispered as he wiped his face with the ragged cuff of his sleeve. "I am forever in your debt. You have taken a great burden from my soul, and I will remember you in my prayers for the rest of my life." He fell to one knee and kissed Lugantes' hand.

The only times this courtesy had been extended to Lugantes, it had been in derision, and now it made Lugantes want to pull his hand away and think of a stinging remark to avenge the insult. But he held his tongue and waited silently while Muñoz finished reciting the Ave Maria. "You are too good to me, Muñoz. I will do nothing that those who love the Infante Real would not do, were you to speak to them. It is my obligation as Rey Alonzo's subject to keep his heir alive." He stepped back from the majordomo and made a show of picking up a pair of fur-lined boots. "There are a few things left to do here, Muñoz, and I must attend to them."

"Of course, of course. I did not mean . . . " He backed toward the door as if Lugantes were a noble. "I thank you with all my heart, Señor Lugantes. For all my life, I will be in your debt."

"That is too much honor for so little a thing," Lugantes admonished him mildly because he was embarrassed.

"It is your great heart that says so," Muñoz told him as he opened the door and slipped out of the room.

Lugantes stood still for a little while after the majordomo had gone. It was important for him to decide what he would say now, for once he began, it might not be possible to weigh his words carefully. He knew far better than most—for he heard whispers and rumors more than half the courtiers combined—how hazardous the court of Alonzo H was to Don Rolon, and for that reason he hesitated. He did not fear for himself, but for his prince, who would be increasingly in danger as preparations for his wedding progressed. It was necessary to put him on his guard, but not to alert his enemies that he was aware of their efforts, for that would only serve to make them more desperate. He did not believe that the Devil was active in España, not as the good Churchmen believed, but he sensed the unrest of the people and he listened to the songs the soldiers were singing of late, and he feared that the Hapsburgs were in grave peril.

By the time he went down for the evening meal, he had decided what he would tell Don Rolon, and when. His mind was settled enough now that he was able to keep up a stream of witty patter while Don Rolon, Padre Barnabas and Don Enrique dined on veal and rice. Don Enrique was drunk again, but no one paid him any attention now.

❦

When Lugantes helped Don Rolon undress for bed, he broached the matter of the deaths to him, saying when he was finished with his recital, "I do not wish to add to your concerns, Alteza, but it would be best if you were not ignorant of what has happened."

Don Rolon paused in washing his face and turned to stare at Lugantes. "At the full of the moon? All of them?"

"That is what I was told. I did not see them for myself, except el Conde."

"But the full of the moon . . . " Don Rolon faltered, thinking with horror of the terrible dreams he had had the last time the moon was full. They haunted him still, and when they resurged in his sleep, it revolted him almost as much as it fascinated him.

"Robbers' moon," Lugantes pointed out, noticing the anguish in Don Rolon's eyes.

"And if they died for me . . . " It was more than he could bring himself to face. "Tell Iturbes that we must have a guard in our travels. And there must be some restitution for what has been endured here. I will leave funds with Muñoz to present to those families who have . . . that shepherd must not lose his daughter so terribly. Money will not buy him his child, but it may soften the blow he has suffered. The traveler is another matter. If Muñoz learns who the man was, leave instructions with him to send word to me, and I will see that his family receives my aid." It was not what his father would want, but Don Rolon was not as severe a man. "Must I confess what may be shared guilt? if these men did die for me, then I must share the blame with those who did the murder." He touched his hands together as if to pray, then dropped them.

"Alteza, you are too severe. A word with Padre Barnabas will put you at rest." Lugantes held up the outer robe for Don Rolon, reaching to lift the arms high enough for the young man.

"Perhaps it would be best," Don Rolon said thoughtfully as he reached for the cord belt to tie around his waist. He did not relish speaking to Padre Barnabas, for he was sure that everything he told the priest would be reported to the Inquisitor General when they returned to Valladolid. Yet his soul was heavy within him, and if he did not speak, he knew that he would tarnish his spirit.

"There will be time before Mass tomorrow morning if you still believe that you must do this," Lugantes reminded him, worried about the Infante Real.

"Yes. Gracias, Lugantes. I will talk to him." He drew back the fur comforter that covered his bed. "If there is another death here at the full moon, then we will know I am not the one who brought this disaster upon them, and I will pray that their trial will end soon."

Lugantes said only "May God keep you through the night, Alteza," but his heart was full of respect for the Infante Real.

❦

In the morning, all the servants of El Morro came out to see their prince depart. It was bitterly cold and the sky just after sunrise was the color of tarnished brass. All the servants received a blessing from Padre Barnabas and a golden coin from Don Rolon. From Capitan Iturbes, they had a salute and from Don Enrique little more than a sneer. Lugantes capered for them before scrambling onto his mule, and then the doors were opened for them and the noble party set out for Zaragoza.

The first night found them at a merchants' inn, where the overawed landlord offered to send all his other guests away for the honor of having the Infante Real and an officer of the Inquisition under his roof. Don Rolon put the man at ease and requested only that he be permitted to keep Capitan Iturbes at the head of the stairs to the floor where they were to sleep.

"I will keep watch as well, Alteza," said Lugantes as they began their supper. "I will be vigilant."

"And what would you do if you had to defend the Infante?" Capitan Iturbes asked with a chuckle. "Bite them in their knees, perhaps, or perform antics to distract them?"

"Very pretty, Capitan," Don Enrique said lazily. "Your wit is keener than I thought."

Lugantes was turning red, in part from anger and in part from shame. "I ask your pardon, Alteza. I intended nothing more . . . "

"I know what you intended, Lugantes," Don Rolon said quietly, "and I could think myself fortunate to have another devoted friend." This last was pointedly directed at Don Enrique, but he paid no heed to the barb.

"Do you think the Herald got back to Valladolid?" Padre Barnabas interrupted, not to prevent an argument, as he had not been paying attention to the conversation, but to give voice to a question that had been on his mind for the last half hour. "If he did return safely and in good time, there should be an escort awaiting us at Zaragoza."

"It is possible," Don Rolon said carefully, knowing that his father was capricious in such matters.

"On the occasion of your return at his behest, it would be appropriate," Padre Barnabas said stiffly. "It is fitting that he show his approval of your forthcoming marriage."

"As he is the man who arranged it, we may safely assume that he approves of it," Don Rolon said, more sharply than he usually allowed himself to speak.

"Naturally," said Padre Barnabas in an affronted manner.

Don Rolon sensed that he should placate the priest whose pride was so easily offended. "My father is not blessed in his . . . legitimate children, and so he does not always make too much of a show of them, for fear he should be disappointed again." The statement was an accurate one, and it hid the hours of humiliation and chagrin he had endured all through his youth. At the time he had told himself that he could expect nothing better than this neglect because of the curse that had marked his birth and killed his mother. The priests had told him that, his tutors had told him that and Reina Genevieve, his father's second wife, had railed at him for it when her two daughters were young, before she had resigned herself to their idiocy. He thought of the countless times he had seen his father with Gil del Rey at his side, his hand on the boy's shoulder. Gil, who was taller, blonder, sturdier, more accomplished than he, had won his father's heart from the day he was born. Don Rolon stared across the trestle table to the fire, letting his food grow cold. He had alternately adored and despised Gil; now he regarded him as his foe, and for that reason no longer hated or admired him.

"Alteza," Lugantes said, breaking into his thought. "Is something the matter? Do you want me to perform for you?"

Don Rolon turned to the little man. "No. A thousand thanks, but no, Lugantes." He thought of pouring more wine and changed his mind, not wanting to appear cut from the same cloth as Don Enrique.

"You would do well to spend the night in prayer, Alteza," Padre Barnabas suggested. "You are about to enter a new state of life, and at such times it is essential that you seek guidance of the Most High that you may come through your trials in a manner pleasing to your father and Him."

"True enough," Don Rolon said softly. "There are a few things weighing on my mind. Reflection, alone, might do much to . . . " He got up from the table, his meal unfinished, and nodded to the others. "No need for you to stop," he said quickly as he saw them start to rise with him. "This is not Valladolid and we are not at Court. You may continue to eat and drink as long as you wish. I need have no attendant."

"But Alteza," Lugantes protested. "A guard."

"A guard. Of course." He shook his head. "I suppose I must have one. Well, then, tell me what I must do to satisfy you. Shall I pray in the inglenook until one of you is ready to retire?" It did not suit him, but most of what was expected of him did not suit him. "Capitan?"

"If it would not inconvenience you too much, Alteza, it would simplify our position here. El Majestad would not forgive any of us if misfortune should befall you." He spoke through a mouth half full of roast pork, and when he finished speaking, he washed it down with a generous tot of wine.

"What if I retire to my room and lock the door with the bolt? One of you may come with me and be assured that I am quite safe." He wanted badly to be free of the company of these men, and this was the best way he could find to accomplish that.

When at last it was decided that Don Rolon might go to his room and bolt the door for himself, he was ready to howl with frustration. He felt hemmed in, as he had all his life. He trudged up the stairs, thinking briefly that he would like for once to live independently. He tried to imagine what it would be like to be a merchant who traveled the world unpampered by Courts and ceremony. How delightful such an existence would be! To go where he wished, when he wished, as he wished, to dine where he liked with only his purse to consider, at the time he liked, on the dishes he liked, in company of his own choosing. To be able to wed a woman of his own selection, a woman he knew and wanted, and was proud to wed him, and not simply the title of heir to the throne for the sake of a treaty. To be able to court her, showing her courtesy and in return being given favor. He had had one love affair, which had been as thrilling as it was disastrous, but it had given him a taste of real passion, not the desiccated promises of Court and Church, and he could not forget it. He gave a regretful sigh. He was intelligent enough to know that he was not prepared to live that life he longed for, but he could not wholly turn aside from the attractions it held for him. Perhaps he should travel incognito to Venezia and see his bride for himself, and woo her privately. He was still daydreaming when he opened the door to his room and saw a figure there start back. "What!" he burst out.

The figure cowered back, then dropped a deep and inexpert curtsy. "Su Alteza," she said quietly, her large eyes awed and admiring.

Don Rolon stared at her. In the lantern light she was pretty enough, with good features and clear olive skin. Her face was surrounded by a halo of soft dark hair and when she moved, her skirts rustled in a way no woman's Court gown ever did. And though she was only a chambermaid at a lowly inn, she was a woman, and a lovely one at that, one who faced him as a man, not Infante, though she used his title. He realized then that he was gaping, and recovered himself enough to say, "Who are you?" It was a poor beginning, but her smile reassured him.

"I am Inez Remos. My uncle is landlord here," she said, breathless at saying so much to their illustrious guest. She took one or two steps nearer.

Don Rolon was flattered by her attention; it was something he had never experienced from court ladies. He wished again that he were a traveling merchant, rich enough to be able to be generous to her, but not so rich that he traveled with a large train of retainers who would keep him from enjoying himself. A man, any man, needed the diversion pretty women provided, he told himself. "Your uncle is a good man?" he asked, thinking it was a stupid question but finding nothing else to say.

"Well, he took me in when my mother died and he has given me a place to live and work. It's better than begging or going into the Church. If that makes him a good man, I suppose he is." She took another step nearer. "Pardon, Alteza, but my legs are aching. I work hard, and the curtsy . . . " This confession made her blush and she started toward the door again. "I did not mean to disturb you. I was bringing the water for you, that's all, and . . . I wanted to see you."

Nothing like this had ever happened to Don Rolon, and it pleased him tremendously. Here he was, about to be married to a woman he had never met or seen, and he now found a beautiful—for she was growing more attractive in his eyesyoung woman who had made a point of meeting him, only to see him. He thought of his father's mistresses and the women who longed for the erratic attention of his half brother. "You don't need to go on my account," he said.

"There is work for me to do," she answered with a sad note in her voice.

Don Rolon stepped between Inez and the door. He felt wonderfully reckless, more like that merchant he wanted to be than the Infante Real that he was. With such an opportunity presented to him, the merchant would make the best of it, he was sure. Don Rolon was not naive, but he was keenly aware that his experience was limited. He had never known a woman who was not of the Court, certainly never any woman who served at an inn. "Don't go, Inez," he said, reaching out to touch her arm.

"Alteza, I am—"

"I am sure you are a virtuous girl," he told her at once. "And you do not wish to be . . . disappointed. But are you a faithful subject of España?" He had never used such an approach before and he was not certain it would be successful.

"Yes, as I am of the Church." She crossed herself and looked up at him.

"Then it is not wrong to show your devotion . . . personally." He saw her eyes widen and thought that for once, his life was going as he wished it to. He felt bolder and more handsome than he knew himself to be.

Inez hesitated. "I . . . do not know . . . how to . . . " She glanced toward the door. "My uncle may come."

Don Rolon turned and slid the bolt home. "Let him come." It was just what that merchant would say, he knew, and he liked the way it sounded. "It is a fortunate thing, isn't it, that I've come early to bed. Otherwise I might not have seen you and we would both be the poorer for that."

"Oh, yes," she murmured as he came closer to her.

Capitan Iturbes handed the purse of golden coins to the landlord. "You will say nothing, and the girl leaves with us in the morning. Is that understood? I will see that she is properly cared for and has no neglect."

"They say the Infante Real is to be married," the landlord grumbled as he took the purse and weighed it in his hand.

"That is not until the end of May, and he will have much need of a woman before that time. Your niece will not be cast aside, you have my word as a soldier on that." He looked around the kitchen. "From what I can see here, she'll fare better with the Infante than she has done here."

"I have done my best for her," the landlord insisted, pouting.

"No doubt. And so will the Infante Real. It is the way of the courtiers." He knew that this was far from true, but Don Rolon was not one to discard those who had served him well.

"She is only fifteen, Capitan," the landlord said petulantly.

"The Infante Real is only nineteen. A good age for both of them." He saluted briefly and started toward the kitchen door. "Not a word of this to the others, mind. They're to think that Don Rolon initiated the whole thing."

"Si. I understand you, Capitan." The landlord tossed the purse from one meaty hand to the other. "She does not work hard, in any case. This way is better."

"Yes, it is. Make sure that there is a mule saddled for her in the morning, along with the other horses and Lugantes' mule. She won't slow us down that way." He opened the kitchen door, ducking down to avoid the low beams by the pantry. "Think of your good fortune, landlord, and remember that your niece is fortunate as well."

The weight of the gold in the purse stifled any protest the landlord might have made, and by the time he thought of one, Capitan Iturbes was gone.

5

At Zaragoza there were banners and fanfares and church bells and Masses; Don Rolon accepted them in a daze. He was affable to hundreds of people, including a handful of Muslims who were among those to offer him their felicitations on his coming wedding. An escort of Imperial Cavalry, sent to España by the Holy Roman Emperor, joined Don Rolon's littly party, on the orders of Alonzo II, with instructions to bring them with all haste to Valladolid. Don Rolon professed himself to be delighted to accompany them, and attended a last, carnival night of feasting and celebration under the full moon.

In the morning, most of the company were too bleary-eyed to remember much of the riotous night before. Don Rolon, finding his hands bruised and dirtied, offered Inez an embarrassed apology for his behavior as they were preparing to leave the villa of the local Visconde.

"You did not return to me until dawn," was her sulking answer. "If there is someone you should ask pardon of, it is not me." She drew her shawl more closely around her shoulders and gave him an injured look.

"Oh, Inez," he said, with so much remorse that she smiled in spite of herself. "I don't . . . remember precisely what took place. There were so many cups of wine and the soldiers danced and danced."

"They didn't even make a gallery for the women. Not that I would have been permitted there, but still." She reached over and tweaked the lobe of his ear. "The soldiers danced, did they?"

"For hours, it seemed to me. And there was food and drink and singing and all the rest of it. If Don Enrique feels like this every morning, I wonder he does not enter a monastery to be free of it." His head was throbbing and he ached with exhaustion. The thought of spending a day in the saddle horrified him, but he knew it was what he must do. "You will be riding with Lugantes. He will amuse you."

"I would rather ride with you." She did not chide him, for she was a realistic young woman, sensible enough of her position in the world to know that she would never be more than a mistress to her royal lover. That was much better than serving at an inn, and she was determined to turn her opportunity to good use.

"I would rather it, too, querida, but it would not be wise, for me or for you." He touched her face. "You are a lovely creature, Inez, and I am very happy that you were willing to come away with me."

"You are Don Rolon. I could not refuse you." She did not tell him that her uncle had ordered her to go to his chambers and afterward announced to her that she was to leave with the hidalgos in the morning. That was a secret she knew well enough to keep to herself.

"Tell Lugantes that I want to see you smiling tonight." He kissed her quickly and easily, marveling that he could behave so with a woman. With marriage facing him, he was convinced he would need Inez more than ever. The only apprehension he had was for any children he might give her, for he was cursed himself and his two half sisters were little more than overgrown infants, though one of them, Leonora, was lovely as an angel and laughed readily. Impulsively, Don Rolon embraced Inez, kissing her again, with fervor.

"Su Alteza," she said breathlessly when they moved apart.

"Tonight, we will have more time together, I promise you." He was determined to spend as much time with her as he could before he reached Valladolid, for once back in the stultifying demands of Court life, he would not have much opportunity to keep company with her. "I will talk to Lugantes, and he will see that you have a proper place to live. You will have a house and servants and clothes

. . . But don't, pray, don't dress as the women do at Court. They are laced and boned and gowned until there is nothing human left to them. Let me see that you are still a woman, not a statue. Promise me you won't change that way."

Inwardly Inez was disappointed, for her ambitions included learning the ways of the aristocracy, but she did not argue. There would be time to ask for such favors later. "I will be just as you want me to be," she whispered, leaning against him briefly before moving back from him. "You had better go to the Marashal before he wonders what has become of you."

"You're right," Don Rolon sighed. "I would rather remain here, but we must depart within the hour. Most of my goods are packed, but they have yet to be put on the baggage wagons. You must have your case ready shortly, as well. Lugantes will come for you, never fear, and he will look after you."

"He's so . . . little and . . . ugly," Inez said, in spite of her intentions to keep her opinion of the jester to herself.

"Yes, but God teaches us that it is the soul that shines in Heaven, not the body, and I know that his is bright as the halo of a Saint. Don't speak ill of him, I pray you, Inez. You haven't a better friend in this world." He kissed her hand and hurried out the door before he could find another excuse to delay.

That evening was passed at a monastery and the night after in a sprawling castle built in the days of El Cid. Neither place afforded Don Rolon the chance to do more than exchange a few words with Inez, and then with Lugantes standing by. The following afternoon they reached Osma, and were once again treated to celebrations and a civic display that ended long after midnight in freezing rain. The next day they followed the Dour to Roa, which was their last stopping place before entering Valladolid.

There was a more extensive escort waiting at Roa, and a staff of servants that included Don Rolon's valet, Ciro Eje, and his confessor, Padre Lucien.

"Take proper care of her, Lugantes," Don Rolon ordered the jester before he went to meet the courtiers who el Rey Alonzo had sent out to Roa. "She will need a house and the rest of it. Do not be too expensive, for that would draw attention to her, and for her sake as well as mine, that should be avoided. The servants must be trustworthy and willing to follow instructions without harassment. You know the rest of it. Give her my greetings and tell her that I shall call upon her before a week goes by."

"She will not want to wait so long," Lugantes warned him.

"I know. Neither will I, but my father will not permit me time to see her. In fact, it would be best if he knows as little as possible about her. He has his mistresses, and Gil has three that I know of, but as I am betrothed, well, he wants me to behave." He laughed unhappily. "I will remember what I owe my family and my country, and he will have no reason to complain of me. But I will not give up everything that is beautiful in my life. He has not, and it is absurd to require it of me." He did not feel as brave as he sounded, but he knew that Lugantes would repeat to Inez what he told him, and this would reassure her as much as anything would.

Lugantes had hardly departed when Ciro arrived, bringing three large cases and promising Don Rolon more. "There is to be full ceremonial display, Alteza," he informed the Infante Real. "It's the most lavish I have ever seen el Majestad be, and I admit I am curious as to why. It is said that the Venezian emmisaries expect it."

"That would account for it," Don Rolon said nonchalantly. "You will forgive me for saying that you look tired, mi Infante. Have you been long on the road?"

"No longer than you might expect, given the responses we have faced every day. It was not at all the same when we left. Hardly anyone knew who we were, or cared. Returning, you would think that the Second Coming was expected from the display we were shown." He shook his head. "I hope you will not repeat that remark. Padre Barnabas would read me a sermon on my flippancy."

"I am hardly the one to do such a thing," Ciro reminded Don Rolon as he opened the largest of the cases and began pulling out the jewel-encrusted Court dress Don Rolon would wear the next day. "We conversos have learned to say little."

"Would that more Catholics might do the same." Don Rolon crossed himself. "It is not the province of men to read the hearts of men; God alone will know who is worthy to stand in His light." He considered what he had said and decided that it was not heretical. "What time tomorrow are we to depart?"

"Midmorning, or so I am told. The festivities in Valladolid are to begin at midafternoon, and will go on until the end of the night, most likely." Ciro avoided looking at the Infante Real as he spoke. "I have heard that there is a woman traveling with Lugantes."

"Yes, there is." Don Rolon fixed his eyes on the enormous quilt that lay on the canopied bed.

"Very pretty, so Capitan Iturbes tells me." Ciro went on unpacking the Court clothing, his tone as carefully neutral as if he were talking about the cut of a foreigner's cloak.

"She is pretty."

"Lugantes will not discuss her at all."

Don Rolon concealed a smile. "That is his privilege."

"Yes, it is."

Nothing more was said on the subject, and when Ciro aided Don Rolon in changing into Court clothes for dining, he made one minor remark only: "I will be happy to wait until you return, Alteza. The hour is not important."

"Do not trouble yourself. If I need assistance, I will waken you." He knew that it was not possible for him to get out of the elaborate clothing by himself, but if he were lucky, it would be Inez and not Ciro who would unfasten all the knots and brooches that held the elaborate clothing together.

Lugantes provided antics and jests while the fifty courtiers sat at their eighteen-course meal. The banquet went on for four hours, marked by formal, dull conversation and occasional exhortations from the various religious dignitaries who were among the company.

In all the gathering, there was only one man Don Rolon was glad to see, and it was not until the meal was half over that he was led to the dais to be presented.

"Su Alteza," the Pursuivant Herald announced while the partridges were being removed and replaced with veal-and-asparagus with onions, "it is my honor to present to you El Duque da Minho, permanent Envoy to the Court of Alonzo II de España. Don Raimundo Joao Carlos Dominguez y Mara."

Don Rolon rose from his chair, ignoring the murmur this courtesy evoked from those around them. "Duque, this is a great pleasure!"

The tall Portuguese went onto his knee and kissed Don Rolon's ring. "Infante Real," he said in his fine, carrying voice.

"Rise, rise," Don Rolon urged him. "It is not as if we are strangers." He had known Raimundo for most of his life, and although the Duque was seventeen years older than Don Rolon, the two had developed a fast friendship.

"You have been gone too long, mi Infante," Raimundo said as he got to his feet. "But it is happy news that brings you back to this city."

Don Rolon hated the traditions and tedium of Court life most at moment, such as these. What he wished most to do was to come down from the dais and spend an hour talking with Raimundo; it was not permitted: formal banquets ran by specific rules and it was unthinkable that they should be conducted in any other way.

The Herald made a signal indicating that Raimundo's time with the Infante Real was up, and proceeded to announce another of the guests.

Don Rolon resumed his seat and went through the motions of greeting the men presented to him. He knew most of them slightly and found the majority of them uninteresting, men without sense or curiosity beyond the current mode of court dress or the state of diplomatic relations with Flanders.

"It is my honor to present to you, Alteza, the Inquisitor General of España, Padre Juan Murador." The Pursuivant Herald stood aside and made a reverence to the man in the black habit who came forward. Most of the assembly copied the Herald.

"It is good to know that you have returned," Padre Juan said quietly, his downcast eyes bright. "I have spent the afternoon with Padre Barnabas who has told me much of your current spiritual understanding. There are issues we should discuss concerning your coming nuptials that will be to the benefit of your soul to heed."

"I will be grateful for your guidance," Don Rolon said, his throat feeling dry as he spoke the words. He could never encounter this middle-aged priest without feeling that he had been hit by a hard, cold hand.

"I will pray to God that your heart may be guided in the paths of virtue and your union fruitful and blessed." He made the sign of the Cross and stepped back. "It would be wise that we meet soon, Alteza. You are a young man, if you will forgive my saying it, and there are lessons you have yet to master."

"I will listen with humility," Don Rolon said, thinking that he sounded as idiotic as his sisters.

Padre Juan nodded with great dignity and stepped back, and as he walked back to his seat in the banqueting hall, there was no sound but the slap of his sandals.

Morning brought more frenzied activity, and Don Rolon, uncomfortable in the full Court regalia he was required to wear, paced his chambers while Ciro asked occasionally when they would depart for Valladolid.

"Be calm, Alteza. We will not linger here any longer than we must." He had learned over the years how to keep his noble masters from becoming distraught with the burdens of their offices, but today he sympathized with the Infante Real and was almost as eager to be moving as Don Rolon was.

"I spoke to Lugantes earlier," Don Rolon said suddenly. "He tells me that Inez is well and that she will want to see me as soon as possible. What am I to do? My father will insist that I remain at Court for two or three days before he tires of the sight of me again and sends me off on my own." He started to wring his hands, then recalled that he was wearing jewel-studded gloves, and stopped himself in time. "One day, I will change the rules about Court dress. These costumes are impossible."

"They are traditional, Alteza," Ciro said placatingly. "There is much to say in defense of them. If this were some upstart kingdom fending off the Turks or scrapping with its poor relations, then it might be appropriate for the Court to look as if they were all robbers, but this is España, the greatest power on the face of the earth, the conqueror of the Old and New Worlds, and the richest nation ever to rise since Rome!" He enjoyed the grandeur, and relished the pomp, but he knew that if he had to wear the clothes and wait in drafty halls for hours, then he too might wish for less elaborate rituals and garments.

"You're probably correct, Ciro, but my ruff is scratching my neck, and with these gauntlets on, I can do nothing about it. I can't sit down unaided and I can't walk upstairs without a page to assist me. It's too much to demand of a man that he live this way." Don Rolon did not often speak out so directly, and it bothered him that he permitted himself to tell his annoyances to his valet. "It's not necessary that you say anything about this."

"Naturally not, Alteza," Ciro assured him just as there was a knock on the door.

"We are here to escort the Infante Real to his carriage and bring him to his father El Rey Alonzo II, at Valladolid." The man wore the insignia of Major, and he carried the long sword that went with his rank. He stood aside politely as Don Rolon, moving as stiffly as a puppet, came out of the room and made his way to the court-yard of the villa.

"There will be many persons along the way desiring to see you, Alteza, and I must ask that you do not lean too far back on the seats, for these are the people who wish you joy and are awaiting your marriage with the same joy they would see fortune smile on their own children." The Major softened this order with a bow, but Don Rolon knew what his father expected of him, and he nodded as much as his ruff would permit.

"It will please me to see them and greet them," he said, because it was necessary to respond in some way. "It will be a great honor and tribute to my House that the people wish to stand in the rain and watch my carriage pass." He looked around, swinging his entire upper body so that he would not disrupt the fall of lace from his ruff. "Who will be riding with me?"

"That honor has been accorded to Padre Juan Murador," the Major answered with a deferential inclination of his head as the Inquisitor General stepped into the room and gave the blessing to them.

"Padre Juan. I see." Don Rolon's heart was heavy. For the next four hours he would be trapped in a carriage with the Grand Inquisitor of all España, who would read him sermons and homilies on his duties for his coming wedding. It was necessary that none of his trepidation be reflected in his words or manner, for then Padre Juan would do more than preach to him, he would question him, and that was much too dangerous a game for Don Rolon to undertake now. He lowered his eyes. "It is I who am honored by so worthy a priest."

Padre Juan gave a gracious little bow, as if in agreement with Don Rolon. "How pleased I am to see you submissive to the will of el Rey. Not all men are as fortunate in their sons. The burdens of royalty are great ones, Alteza, and piety is the only refuge for those who carry the responsibilities of the ruling House and the Crown. Do not forget, I beseech you, that we of the Church are your servants and promised to your cause after our service to God."

Why was it, Don Rolon asked himself as he descended the stairs, that Padre Juan could not open his mouth without giving a speech? He had never heard the man make a chance remark or a quip. It was impossible to think of a casual conversation with him: he discoursed rather than discussed. "The carriage, Alteza," the Major said, indicating a large, gold-ornamented vehicle drawn by six matched white horses.

"Your father does you great honor," Padre Juan pointed out needlessly. "It is not the State carriage, but it is used for visiting diplomats." This announcement was more for the benefit of the escort rather than Don Rolon, who was familiar with all the various royal equipages. "It will be most pleasant to beguile the hours of our journey in such a carriage," he said as one of the footmen let the steps down.

Don Rolon nodded to Padre Juan, then propped his elbow on the frame of the window so he would be able to wave to the people on the road. His sleeves were much too padded and stiff for him to lift his arm easily, and he had found that bracing his elbow from the first was the only tolerably comfortable way to get through such an ordeal.

"I had the opportunity to speak with Padre Barnabas, Infante," said Padre Juan as he got into the carriage and took the seat facing him. "He tells me that your spiritual instruction has been excellent and free of any questionable instruc-tion, but he has also found that you are often melancholy, and this is not what we hope to see in Christians, who are blessed with the Love of God and the knowl-edge of their Salvation. In these troubled times, with the Devil ev-erywhere in evidence and heresy strong in so much of the world, I perceive how you might come to feel that God has too many en-emies to triumph. But that is why the Church has acted as she has." The carriage began to move, rocking as if riding a swell. "It is for us to take the path of faith, confident that God will show us His Will and aid us in expunging the vile blots that have darkened our coun-try and our faith. If it is true that there are witches and heretics around us—and who can deny that there are, or that their insidious work contaminates much that would otherwise be laudable—at least we may say with true passion that we are working to pluck it out, root and stem, from our people. What other nation can say as much? They waver and cower and their courage fails them, and then they wonder why God no longer favors them. It is not so with España. We have undertaken a great work and God has shown us His blessings with conquest and riches that are the envy of the world. But we must not relent, for as high as we have risen, so much farther we can fall."

Don Rolon heard the shouts of many voices, and turned away from Padre Juan so that he could wave to the merchants who lined the streets, their hands filled with sodden streamers, which they waved enthusiastically. Some of the people threw flowers made of cloth, for it was still too early in the year to find them growing in the earth. As the cheers continued, Padre Juan went on.

"We must not shrink from our task, for God has summoned us to do His bidding in the world. We must show ourselves an example. Do not be disheartened, Alteza, that so many friends of the Devil flock to España; here is their greatest challenge, for it is here that the work of God is being done. We find witches because the Devil him-self works for our destruction. Be of good cheer, Alteza, that we have done so much to end heresy and deviltry, and do not doubt that as our cause is the cause of God Himself, we will be given the vic-tory." His black eyes were bright, and cold as a winter night.

Don Rolon did not answer; he watched the crowds along the

road, and from time to time he murmured a few senseless words while in his cool, passionless voice, Padre Juan ranted and exhorted him through the slow, rainy miles.

❦

Alonzo II, Rey d'España y Corsica, Margrave de Saxony y Marashal in Camera al Emperador Gustav, sat at his desk scribbling memos. He was forty-six, small, overly thin, with the pinched expression of one with chronically poor diges-tion. He has a man of ostentatiously austere habits, with nothing to show his rank but the crowned badge of the Order of the Golden Fleece on his stiffly padded sleeve. His quill moved nervously over the vellum, and the writing it left was crabbed and angular, like the man himself.

Beside him stood Gil del Rey. The young man was not quite six months' Don Rolon's junior, but presented a more promising figure than the slender, dark Infante Real. Gil had a bit more height, a greater breadth of shoulder and strength of physique that Don Rolon knew he would never possess. Gil's blond hair curled around his face attractively, and his short beard was beautifully trimmed and crisply curled. He was dressed with as much dash as the required black gar-ments of Court dress permitted, and he bore himself with that slight swagger that marked him as one of the hidalgos.

Both men looked up as the little page Esteban opened the door and announced that the Infante Real had arrived.

"Show him in," Alonzo snapped before leaning back in his tall chair and casting a quick, regret-filled glance at his adored bastard before giving his reluctant attention to his heir.

Don Rolon, weary from travel and half-soaked, entered the room in time to see his father's eyes move from Gil to him, and as always, the condemnation he read there stung him, although he told himself that he was inured to it. He bowed with well-schooled courtier's grace and kissed the hand that el Rey held out to him. "I ask your pardon, Majestad, for the state of my attire, but I was informed that you wished to see me as soon as I arrived."

"That is true," Alonzo said without inflection.

"I hope that I have the pleasure of seeing you well, Majestad." It was the proper greeting, but the inquiry was sincere.

"God is good," Alonzo responded impatiently, then launched into what he wished to say. "I was informed by my Herald that you received and read my letter, and I have received and read your reply. It is not inappropriate for you to be so much surprised at your coming union. The task of finding a suitable I wife for you has been one of my gravest concerns for more than a year now. I will now inform you of how the current betrothal was determined, that you may conduct yourself properly in the presence of the various Venezians who will be attending us in the coming months as preparations for the nuptials progress." He turned toward Gil. "You need not remain, my son, if it is not to your taste."

"I'll remain, if it's all the same to you." Gil grinned angrily at Don Rolon. "I must offer you my felicitations, after all."

"Thank you," the Infante Real answered stiffly.

Alonzo braced his elbows on the table and folded his hands beneath his chin, as if in prayer. "You must know, Rolon, that the welfare of the state is foremost in my mind. It was more than a year ago when the first offers from Venezia were made to us, and we considered them then and rejected them, for they were not to our satisfaction or the benefit of our House and country. The ambassadors forgot the matter awhile and then they approached us a second time. We were minded to refuse on your behalf again, but the proposals were more reasonable, modified in tone and offering a number of reasonable compromises. We then ordered you to El Morro while the discussions were in progress so that it would not be possible for the ambassadors to come to you for your answer until we were convinced that the interests of España were properly served." He never once met Don Rolon's eyes as he recited this information. Alonzo was a man unused to opposition, least of all from the Infante Real.

Don Rolon listened, the breath almost stilled in his throat. When it was apparent that Alonzo would say nothing more until Don Rolon had made some remark, the young man coughed once. "My father, I am grateful for all you have done for me, but I am troubled in my soul at this proposed marriage. You have told me many, many times that I am cursed, and that our blood is not clear. My half sisters are evidence of this, as you yourself have pointed out often. What do the Venezian ambassadors say of that, knowing that heirs will be desired of this union?"

"A year ago, we might have thought as you do, mi hijo," Alonzo said stiffly. "But you are my heir, my only heir, and if you do not wed, Otto will reign in España when you are gone. Otto!" He looked quickly at Gil, flushing as he did so. "You must marry, Infante, and there should be little delay."

"Two years ago, my father, I asked you if you wished me to seek a wife, and you said no." That was while Alonzo was still petitioning the Pope to legitimize Gil, before his request had been denied. "At that time you told me again of the curse and pointed to the example of my half sisters. You did not encourage me then, but now you are eager to see me marry. If that is truly your wish, I must obey it, but I beg you to recall the doubts you have had, and . . . " He saw the mockery in Gil's hazel eyes before he encountered the rage in Alonzo's.

"Your sisters are cursed. Your mother died bringing you into the world! The curse is not yours, it is mine!" He slammed his hands on the desk twice for emphasis, as great a show of emotion as Don Rolon had ever seen from him. "If you think of those two children, you will have all the more reason to produce heirs, for they never will." His ire faltered and at the end he turned toward Gil as if to reassure himself that his favored child had not deserted him. "It was the witch who did that to them, who declared that the innocents of the House should suffer as she did. Concepcion was innocent, and Genevieve's girls are innocent. You cannot make such a claim, Rolon, not if what your teachers tell me is true. You are a man of fleshly longings, and for that, marriage is the proper direction for such needs. All else is . . . " He could not finish his thought while Gil might hear it and be offended.

"I don't think it would be wise to marry," Don Rolon said again, wishing he could change out of his heavy, damp clothes.

"If you don't wish to marry, *brother*, turn monk," Gil said insolently.

"I *forbid* it!" Alonzo said. "Rolon, you will marry the Venezian noblewoman as we have already promised the Doge, her uncle, that you will. Our naval pact with the most Serene Republic will be sealed the day your hands are joined in church, and we must have that pact as much as our House must have heirs."

"If I had a vocation, what then?" Don Rolon asked, knowing it was useless.

"You do not have one. You are my heir," el Rey declared.

"And you cannot let me abdicate in Gil's favor?" the Infante asked with familiar pain. "The Pope may not grant him the legitimacy you desire, but if I were to resign in his favor?"

Alonzo looked again at Gil. "It is not possible."

"Why not, if I am willing? You would rather he ruled after you than I." Rolon stared hard at his half brother. "And you would rather as well, wouldn't you?"

While Gil shrugged, Alonzo grew rigid. "My brother Gustav has already indicated that he would not accept such . . . arrangements. Nor," he added in a resigned tone, "would the Doge of Venezia. It falls to you, Rolon, to perpetuate our line and bring credit to our House. You will do it. We have already informed you and you have indicated acquiescence. It is binding on you as it is upon us, and the honor of España rests with you." He looked grave at this prospect. "You do not know how little it would take to bring all we have arranged to ruin. We inform you now, Infante, that you will conduct yourself as befits a grandee of España, which you are from this time on. You are entitled to wear the Garter and Badge of the Golden Fleece. You are entitled to bear the Staff of San Diego on your arms. You are entitled to precedence over all in the land save ourselves. You have the right to—" He stopped as Esteban came into the roormonce more. "What is it? I was not aware that I had authorized you to enter."

Little Esteban quailed, but stood his ground. "It is the Duque da Minho," he told el Rey. "You asked to be informed the moment he arrived."

"Yes," Alonzo said, mollified by the announcement. "Very well. Dominguez y Mara may serve as witness to our investiture of our heir with full privileges of grandee of España."

Raimundo was already standing in the door, his acute eyes missing nothing of the conflict that simmered between the three men in the enormous room. He came up beside Don Rolon and addressed el Rey. "May God keep Su Majestad, and send you prosperous days and peaceful nights, for the glory of España." It was one of a number of standard greetings, but it was Raimundo's special genius to be able to make such statements ring with sincerity.

"Our thanks, Dominguez," Alonzo responded with a brusque gesture. "You come in a' good hour. We have just finished informing our Infante Real of the history of his coming nuptials. His bride, as you doubtless have heard, is Zaretta Patrecipazio, a noblewoman, you perceive from her name, of Venezia, niece to the Doge. We have been expressing ourselves on our expectations for their union and informing him of the obligations he owes our House."

Raimundo gave Don Rolon a quick, worried glance, then showed a smooth smile to el Rey Alonzo. "A triumph for all España, surely, Su Majestad. With Venezia as our ally, the world is open to us." Dominguez, being Portuguese, was not precisely in accord with Spanish expansion, but he had been at Court for more than twenty years and had developed an unfailing sense of survival.

"But my bro—the Infante Real is timorous," Gil said, catching himself before he had erred too much. In private Alonzo permitted his bastard every liberty, but did not extend the same leniency when others were present.

"As is every betrothed man," Raimundo agreed at once. "I recall now how terrified I was on the day when my father told me of Riopardo's approval of the match he had proposed. You will see, Alteza," he said to Don Rolon, "that all will be well."

"You are most kind," Don Rolon muttered as he stared down at his feet. He was chagrined by his father's manipulations, by the manner in which he had been treated. It was not the first time he had experienced Alonzo's implacable will, but this time he was shamed by it. That he should have been sent away while the negotiations for his future bride were in progress galled him. Worse, he suspected that Gil had been party to most every phase of the discussions, and that aggravated him more.

"The Infante Real has informed us that he is about to write his letter of joyous accommodation for the Venezian ambassador to present to the Doge on his behalf." This was said so pointedly that there was little Don Rolon could do but bow to his father and prepare to withdraw.

"Alteza," Raimundo said to him, "if you will be good enough to spare me a little of your time before you undertake your task, I have one or two matters that must be brought to your attention as well as el Rey's." Before either Alonzo or Rolon could respond to this astonishing breach of protocol, Raimundo had stepped up to the desk and held out a large, sealed letter. "I had this from Sir Charles Alister, Majestad, and its contents should interest you." He bowed once more and stepped back, giving a third obeisance from the door where Don Rolon waited.

"What is this, Dominguez?" Alonzo asked, about to hand the letter to Gil to peruse.

"It was purloined from the Queen's apartment, Majestad, addressed to Alexandre du Burgundy. It promises most interesting reading, I believe." Raimundo signaled Esteban to close the door, then motioned to Don Rolon.

"Is that what the letter really is?" the Infante asked quietly.

"Yes. El Majestad is worried that la Reina is still more French than Spanish. Since the treaty with Venezia is assured, French ships are likely to be in more danger than they were before, and it is not impossible for their merchants to suffer. She is an intelligent woman, and her concern is just. She is not one to sit by while her country is compromised by her husband, no matter what vows she made to obey him." As he said this, Raimundo was guiding Don Rolon along the tapestry-lined hallway toward a narrow staircase that led up into one of the galleries above the central throne room. "Do you want this marriage, Alteza?" he inquired intently when he was certain that no one could overhear them.

"No! I have thought about it, Dominguez, and I cannot want . . . I have not sought this match. It is my father's doing, after years of telling me that I am damned and therefore unfit for—" He turned away from the tall, polished courtier. "It is not what you may think. I do not prefer the flesh of men or children or goats, and I do not long for the religious life. It is . . . "

"Because of your half sisters?" Raimundo ventured, knowing it was not a very shrewd guess, but as familiar as anyone at Court of the tragedy of Reina Genevieve's daughters.

"In part. There are other . . . considerations."

"Is it your new mistress? Inez is your mistress, isn't she?" were the next questions.

"Yes," he admitted.

"Is all . . . satisfactory there?" It was asked so carefully that Don Rolon winced.

"God on the Cross! does everyone in España doubt my virility?" he demanded of the air. "Yes, yes, all things are satisfactory. And I would wear out my knees with penance if I thought she would never have a child of me from it." He had expected to be chastised for this impious wish, but he was taken aback when Raimundo nodded slowly.

"Are you confident that she is loyal to you?" He studied the Infante Real's shocked face, making haste to add, "I have no reason not to believe that she is, but I have been told that she is a country girl, and not entirely prepared for what might happen to her as your mistress."

"How do you mean, Dominguez, 'what might happen to her'?" Don Rolon stood more perfectly straight as he asked this.

"She is not used to the machinations of court life, and her goodwill could lead her to trust those who are not . . . worthy of it." They went a few paces farther before the Duque da Minho finished his thoughts. "Alteza, you are in great danger, and your coming wedding will only make it worse."

Don Rolon could not dispute this, but he wanted to discover what precisely Raimundo meant. "How is that possible, Duque?"

Raimundo sighed, and with a gentle shake of his head, explained his concern. "There are those, as you are aware, who do not wish our treaty with Venezia. These are not only our foreign enemies, but there are many within the kingdom as well. Your marriage will make the treaty binding, at least through the life of your bride. Many believe that when this occurs that they will have to forfeit the rich prizes they have so long claimed for themselves. If you were to die, however, perhaps through an unfortunate accident that could not be traced to their hands, if for example, you were set upon by bravos as you leave Inez one night, or were waylaid in your travels by bandits, then the treaty would no longer be a certain thing. And those who benefited by its collapse would run no risk of exposure while they continued to enjoy their predations. The Infante Real, dead by unlucky chance, would be held to be a victim, again, of the witch's curse." He looked over his shoulder and motioned Don Rolon to keep silent, and went on in a very different voice. "But, as you have heard, the women there are very gladsome and bold. You are expected to put your hands on their dugs when you greet them while you buss them soundly."

A servant walked by carrying a small coffer; his progress was slow.

"Bold women are not much to my liking," Don Rolon replied with a shrug, taking up Raimundo's tone. "Nevertheless, I am curious, I admit that."

"When the English suite arrives, you will see for yourself. They say la Reina does not allow such freedoms for herself, being the ruler of the nation, but for the rest of the Court, they are licentious and rowdy and much given to dalliance." Raimundo held up a finger of caution, and when he was satisfied that the servant was out of earshot, he said, "You are being spied upon, Alteza."

"I was spied upon when I was born. I've always been spied up," Don Rolon responded quietly.

"But it is greater now than before," Raimundo said, and saw the flicker of alarm in Don Rolon's black eyes. He pressed his advantage. "Yes. You must believe what I tell you, Alteza. You know that Gil has his groom follow you, and that el Rey has put more men about you—servants, for the most part. The familiar of Padre Juan Murador is often the companion of your confessor, and seeks to drink with him, since drink is the priests' vice. There are others as well, though I have not discovered all of them. Since your betrothal was—"

"Gil's groom I knew of, but not the rest. My father has long kept men around me, because, he has said, of the curse. I did not think, however, that the Inquisition would trouble itself with Padre Lucien." Don Rolon had an instant of terror as he thought someone might be following him once he arranged to visit Inez.

"You must have a care, Alteza," Raimundo warned him. "Those around you would not protect you, no matter what they say." His face, usually set in a pleasant courtier's mask, now clearly showed his concern for the heir to the throne.

"And why do you bother, Dominguez?" Don Rolon looked at the older man with more puzzlement than suspicion. "Surely you endanger yourself needlessly."

"You are the Infante Real," Raimundo reminded him with more feeling than Don Rolon had ever heard addressed to him by a member of his father's Court. "When you have a son, you will be Principe, and one day, el Rey. The right is with you, and there are no others, not in España. The Emperor Gustav in Vienna would not countenance Gil for the Succession, should Alonzo attempt to legitimize him again: his mother was a French dressmaker, after all, and not a noblewoman. Your sisters will not get husbands or children. It is you, or the Emperor's son Otto. España does not want Otto. Without you, there will be civil war." He rested his gloved hand on the elaborate hilt of his dress sword in an attitude at once resigned and militant.

There was a cold wind in the hall, and the wetness of Don Rolon's clothes turned clammy. "My cousin or me, what difference?" Don Rolon wondered aloud.

"Otto is Austrian; you are Spanish."

"We're both Hapsburgs. Is one so much more preferable to the other?" Before Raimundo could answer, Don Rolon cleared his throat. "I think that another day is more to my liking, as there are Court functions tomorrow. I will consider your invitation shortly, Raimundo."

"As you wish, Alteza," was Raimundo's practiced response as he caught the eye of the understeward coming up the stair. "My I present myself in your apartments tomorrow morning after prayers for your answer?"

"Why not come with me on my morning ride, instead? We will discuss it further then, when I have finished the letters my father has required of me. There must be a celebration, I suppose." He realized as he said it that it was true: he would be expected to show outward enthusiasm for his coming marriage.

"There must. It is a grand occasion," Raimundo agreed with a slight but significant smile.

"Tomorrow, then." He took a few steps backward, as was his privilege, then halted. "I am concerned about what you have said. Don't doubt that, Dominguez. It worries me only that you are my father's confidant as well as mine."

"I am your friend, Alteza. I am your father's counselor. Therein lies the difference." Courtesy required that Raimundo make a half-bow when honored by the heir to the throne, but he did not observe the custom—he only nodded and made a sign of approval before taking the usual three steps back and doffing his plumed black hat. "1 will speak of this more tomorrow; thank you for hearing me."

"It will be my honor, Duque." Don Rolon turned away and strode down the hall toward the wing of the palace where his rooms were, grateful that he could at last be out of his wet clothes.

7

Lugantes shook his stubby finger at Inez. "It is not right, woman, for you to behave so. You are mistress to the Infante Real, and should not tarry with any others." He paced around the open courtyard of the secluded house he had found for her. "He comes to you two nights a week, and that is enough for a good woman to want. It is not as if he is an ordinary subject, but heir to the throne. He is a man with more peril around him than you and I will ever see in a lifetime."

Inez thrust out her lower lip; the expression did not become her. "But there is little for me to do. I have servants and cooks and the rest of it, and I might as well have jailers. I have been here almost a month, and the only man who has come here other than Rolon is you, Lugantes, and . . . well, you do not count, do you?" She laughed, showing her teeth and pleased that she had wounded him.

"Inez, I am a man grown and I am twenty-nine years old. I may be no bigger than a child, but do not doubt that I am a man. If I did not honor my pledge to the Infante Real, you would discover for yourself that this is no idle boast. Do not play with me, Inez. And do not encourage Don Enrique or Capitan Iturbes to visit you. Unless you intend that they, not Don Rolon, should pay for your house and your servants. In that case, I should warn you that Capitan Iturbes very likely has a wife and family already and Don Enrique has less gold than a fishmonger." Lugantes sighed angrily. "You are a country girl, and you do not know the dangers here. It is folly to think you will learn overnight what the Court takes a lifetime to instruct." He climbed onto the stone bench and folded his arms over his thick chest. "You have entered a viper's nest. You think that you are caressed and sought after for love, but I warn you, that it is not so." He regarded her. "If you will not keep to yourself, Inez, I will speak to Don Rolon. I must."

She glared at him. "He would not believe you! I would tell him that you are lying."

"Inez, I am here at his request. I've remained silent because I know that you are not sensible of the world he lives in." He drew up his legs tailor-fashion so that they would not dangle childishly while he spoke to her. "He must have your fidelity, Inez, as much as if you were his wife."

"While he plans to wed a princess of Venezia," she countered angrily. "It is all very well for me to live as a nun, but he must have his foreign lady, as well." She put her hands on her hips and turned her back on Lugantes. "I have heard what the servants say, and I do not like it."

Lugantes did not answer her at once. When he did, he chose his words carefully. "The Infante Real is heir to the throne—the only heir Alonzo has. He must marry, and for reasons of state. We know nothing of this Venezian woman—who, incidentally, is not a princess, for they do not have such things there, being a republic—save that she is a niece of the Doge. Neither she nor Rolon have met each other, and little of her is known here, save that Ambassador has described her as lovely, which is only to be expected. Next month our emissaries will return with her portrait and letters of com-mendation from those who know her. Tell me, is that the way you would want to be courted?" He saw her shoulders droop a bit. "We know that she is a marriageable woman because the Church has vouchsafed the proposals and they would not if she could not produce an heir. We know that she is fair and that she prefers clothing of blue and green, which is unfortunate. That is all we know, Inez. That is all Rolon knows. And you wonder that he yearns for you."

"He has said nothing of this to me," Inez protested without heat.

"And what could he say?" Lugantes asked. "When he comes to you tonight, show him a pleasant face and do not be capricious." He got down from the bench. "I will attend him here, and I will remain when he leaves."

"But—" She put her hand to her mouth, recalling the fair-haired courtier who had stood under her window the night before, smiling up at her. He had left several sheets of paper, which she supposed were verses, and had promised to read them to her when next he came. She had found that sunny, arrogant face much more to her liking than Don Rolon's somber, dark mien.

"If you are planning mischief, Inez, abandon it at once." Lugantes had seen enough of the romantic intrigue of the Court to sense it in the air.

"I am not," she said, wishing she did not to have to lie. At home, the village priest would have made light of the sin, but here she was not so sure, for the eye of the Inquisition was apparent everywhere in Valladolid.

"See that you don't. I say that not only for the Infante's benefit, but for yours. You may not believe it, Inez, but it would pain me to see you . . . ill-used." He came over to her side. "You are beautiful, Inez. You are beautiful." Lightly he took her hand and kissed it. "You are so beautiful." With that, he bowed and hurried out of the courtyard before he betrayed himself further.

Inez stared after him, pleased with herself, but worried that she might have difficulties with the dwarf if he discovered what she planned to do when the Infante was not about. She clapped her hands, and was very pleased to see three servants coming toward her. One of them was new to her household, having joined the number just the day before, and it was this man she chose. "I want you to find me a covered chair so that I may leave the house when it suits me. I know I must not be seen abroad, but there can be no objection to a covered chair, since that is how the Court ladies move about the town."

"Very good," the man said with a subservient tug to his hair.

"And I am told there is a fair tonight outside the city walls. It would please me to go there, if my . . . friend is willing. The moon is full and we will have torches. With masks and capes, there should be no difficulty. You must get me masks and capes."

"As you wish, my lady," said the man, who glanced at the other two with a faint, cynical smile before he withdrew.

To the others, Inez said, "I want wine and bread here, now. And after that, I will rest for an hour." She was not really hungry, but it pleased her to be served food whenever she wished for it.

"At once, my lady," said the older of the two servants. "Perhaps a little chicken as well?"

"Why not?" She waved them away and sat down to think of the fair-haired courtier while waiting for her food.

Lugantes hastened back to the palace, but it took him more than an hour to make the journey through the crowds descending on Valladolid for the nighttime fair. He was accosted twice by beggars and once drew his dagger on a pickpocket, but encountered little more difficulty than that in getting through the jostling, noisy, restless people. Once within his own quarters, he called for his manservant to bring him his jester's costume, and changed into it as quickly as he could. Satisfied with his motley, he hurried to Don Rolon's chambers only to be told by Ciro Eje that the Infante Real was already in the grand reception hall awaiting the newest Venezian delegation.

"I will find him," Lugantes told the valet, and made his way through the anterooms and corridors to the grand reception hall.

"We extend to these good Venezians all the demonstrations of true hospitality," el Rey was saying to the group of brightly dressed foreigners who bowed before him, as Lugantes, breathless, came into the room.

"We are grateful for your magnificent reception," said the most splendidly dressed of the newcomers.

"It is our intention to present a grand festival on your behalf at the conclusion of the Lenten season. Being devout, it is not our intention to sully the Holy Days with any frivolity. From now until Easter, we will mark each of the Lord's days with an auto-da-fé, as a token of our zeal and our love. It is appropriate that you join us for these important occasions so that you will be able to bear true witness to the Doge that we are sincere in the profession of our religion." He stood up, his black clothing making him look like a high-ranking churchman rather than el Rey. "We will dine this evening two hours after sunset, of suitably simple fare. In honor of Venezia, we will serve fish." He stepped down from his throne and gestured to Don Rolon, who stood at the foot of the dais. "This is our heir, the Infante Real, who has been honored with the troth of your Doge's niece. It is our duty to make him known to you."

Don Rolon bowed as deeply as his clothing allowed. "I am pleased in all ways to meet those who come from the country of my promised bride." He sounded almost as wooden as his father, but the Venezians paid no attention. State occasions were stilted at the best of times, and most of them knew that receptions of this sort were awkward during Lent.

"You will be able to know him better in time," Alonzo declared, and held out his scepter to the doddering Duque de Zamora, his personal Herald. "For tonight, it is not fitting that he should participate, for such occasions are for grandees, not hidalgos. We will arrange shortly for you to converse with him." He did not look at Don Rolon in all the time he spoke, and now he made his way slowly down the enormous chamber, his long mantle of black velvet trimmed with ermine spreading out behind him while his Court bowed deeply to him.

Lugantes took advantage of the moment to approach Don Rolon. "I know where you are expected tonight," he said softly, then hopped around in a circle to distract the others around them. "I have seen a lady," he sang tunelessly, "and she is all that I desire, but poor me, poor me."

A few of the courtiers laughed, and one of the Venezians looked shocked, but Don Rolon clapped his hands twice. "Most excellent, Lugantes."

"I will tell you more later, when you cannot see my blushes, when she cannot laugh at me," Lugantes sang on, capering before the throne. "It is my fate to see her and to dream, but poor me, poor me."

"Climb up her leg and she will take pity on you," Gil del Rey suggested from his place at the rear of the line of courtiers. It infuriated him to have so low a place in the Court, although by rights he should not have been there at all. Angrily he tossed some coins to Lugantes, calling out, "If you have any success with this woman, let us know how you managed it."

The laughter was louder and less pleasant. Lugantes bent down to pick up the money, and looked Gil steadily in the eye. "Perhaps you should ask her yourself, señor," he suggested pointedly, and heard the rest of the courtiers guffaw.

"Monster!" Gil hissed at him, and turned away, signaling for someone to follow him. Don Enrique answered the silent summons.

"You're not amused," said a quiet voice in Don Rolon's ear.

He turned sharply and found Raimundo beside him. "No, Duque, not entirely."

"You're troubled." He had been watching the Infante Real for several days and had seen the little, well-concealed signs of worry in the young man.

"Of course. With the wedding, and my father . . . " It was an acceptable excuse to almost anyone, but not to Raimundo. "There is more to it than that. What is it?"

"Not here," Don Rolon answered curtly. "I will speak to you later, by the Moorish fountain. At sunset." This concession was impulsive, but he knew there was no one he would rather confide in than Raimundo Dominguez y Mara. "There will not be much time, but . . . "

"I will be there. At sunset." He slipped away from Don Rolon's side, and a few minutes later was bowing to Renato Grimaldi, the second-ranking member of the Venezian delegation.

Don Rolon waited the prescribed length of time before leaving the grand reception hall, then took the servants' stairs to his private apartments, where he tore off the wired ruff he had been wearing and tossed it to Ciro. "Simple clothing, Ciro. I'm going fairing tonight, or so I have heard."

Ciro raised his brows at this announcement. "But the Venezians . . ."

"Tonight is for old grandees only. We hidalgos, being only sons, are not to attend. Later my father will invite us." He was unfastening his sleeves. "Nothing obvious or too sumptuous. I don't wish to be recognized."

"The brown riding clothes, Alteza?" It was the simplest clothing Don Rolon possessed, and the valet shuddered to think of how little distinction there was in those garments.

"Just the thing!" Don Rolon said, showing more animation than he had in the last week. "It may be chilly tonight and—" He paused. "The moon is full tonight, isn't it?" He tried to keep the apprehension from his words, and failed.

"Yes, Alteza. And the sky is clear." He was uneasy at Don Rolon's sudden change of manner. "Is there some reason . . . "

"I have heard . . . those with afflictions of the mind are ruled by the moon, and when it is full, they are. . .maddened by it. At a fair, with a full moon, madness would be easy to . . . " He looked down at his hands remembered the dirt and broken nails he had seen there before.

"The Church cares for lunatics, Alteza," Ciro reminded him gently.

"The Church." He looked about him nervously. "And my sisters' attendants. My sisters are said to be . . . difficult when the moon is full."

Ciro nodded, relieved to hear this. "Yes. It is often the way with them." He picked up the discarded sleeves and heavy gold chain Don Rolon flung on the bed. "They have the most excellent care, Alteza."

"They are not the only ones in my family to be . . . troubled. There was my grandmother, Ciro, who killed three of her lovers." He began to unfasten his pourpoint. "It was said that she ran wild when the moon was full. That is what I have always been told."

"A most unfortunate lady," Ciro said, sure that he understood now. "Alteza, these afflictions have not touched you. It is true that your House has not been free of them, but you are not—"

"I was cursed," he said quietly. "That is something I cannot forget." He stood still, his eyes directly toward the window and beyond it the turrets of the palace. "Now, with my marriage coming . . . "

"You must not permit such thoughts to enter your mind," Ciro said sternly. "Here, I have taken the clothes you wanted from the chest, and they're waiting for you. It will be pleasant to have a night of fairing, all unknown." There would be precious little time for such diversions in future, Ciro knew, and he wanted to think of a way to make these last few, unfettered days as joyous as he could for his master.

"You're right, I suppose," Don Rolon said, and finished undressing.

By the time he met Raimundo in the garden by the Moorish fountain, he might have passed for one of his own stablehands. Only the shine of his hair and the neat trim of his small beard revealed that his station in life was higher than his clothes would indicate.

"Going fairing?" Raimundo asked as he approached Don Rolon. He was in full Court regalia, black and gold, with a heavy golden collar, with his official order of office depended from it. He could not move quickly, but he had uncommon grace and did not appear to be as hampered as he was. "I wish I might join you."

"You'd be welcome," Don Rolon said at once, meaning it. He had few men he could approach without courtly impropriety, but this man, who was a Duque of Portugal and not a grandee of España, was slightly removed from the rigors of noble society, and for that reason, the Infante Real, as well as el Rey himself, was at liberty to treat him differently than the rest of their inferiors.

"Some other time, perhaps," he said. "It would be more amusing than the way I will have to spend this evening." He paused and looked about, noticing that for more than twenty paces in all directions there was nothing taller than flowers growing. "This place is well-chosen. I had forgot it, since it's so remote. No one can approach us unobserved."

"Yes, that was my thought," Don Rolon said slowly. "I must speak to you about this marriage."

"Where is the difficulty now?" Raimundo asked, feeling irritated that the Infante Real had brought him out here for more dithering. He knew better than to reveal this, but there was a sharpness in his voice that Don Rolon heard, for he looked up sharply.

"It is. . .I believe that sometimes, not often . . . I have . . . odd moments. In my family . . . you know how things are . . . they might regard this as a bad sign." He stared at his long, thin hands with the blunt fingertips and short-bitten nails.

"How do you mean, odd moments?" In spite of himself, Raimundo was curious.

"I mean that . . . I cannot recall what I have done. I remember that I have been active, for my muscles are sore and sometimes my hands— He recalled the scrapes on his hands and the last time he had had such a spell. "I believe these occur when the moon is full."

"As it is tonight?" Raimundo suggested, beginning for the first time to be truly concerned for the Infante Real.

"As it is tonight. I have more than one reason to be grateful that I am not to attend the festivities my father is going to . . . If I should embarrass him now, I do not know what he would . . . "

"I see," Raimundo responded. "How often do you have these . . . spells?"

"There have been three, possibly four episodes that I have noticed. There may have been more, but I was not aware of them." He looked over the garden and gestured toward a line of trees, as if discussing them. To anyone watching, the Infante Real was suggesting something new for this neglected garden. "My father is determined to have this alliance with Venezia, and if I do anything to endanger it, he will have those who will aid him. So far, I have not mentioned my fears, even to my confessor, for fear of what might come of it."

Raimundo did not have to guess what Don Rolon meant—no Spaniard was beyond reach of the Inquisition. "And tonight?"

"I don't know. If there is another . . . problem, then it may come to . . . confession. I trust that it won't, but—" He gave a fatalistic twist of his hands. "What am I to do, Dominguez? Should I continue as my father wishes?"

"For the moment, yes," Raimundo said at once. "Do not give him reason to be displeased with you now. He is angry enough that it is you and not . . . "

"Gil; I know." Don Rolon pointed to the ordered beds of flowers. "He would always rather it were Gil."

There was no way that Raimundo could deny it. "Your father has—"

"He told me often how I was cursed, and how my mother died when I was born. Gil's mother lived to be married off to a rich Dutch merchant, and that is more acceptable to Rey Alonzo." There was little anger in his words and his long, somber face showed more grief than bitterness, but within he ached. "It is known throughout the court. Who am I to say it is wrong that he prefers a son with nothing but God's blessing to touch him? I think I might do the same, were I a father of two such sons." He turned away brusquely. "That is not self-pity, Dominguez, or not entirely."

"No, Alteza, not entirely." Raimundo might have embraced Don Rolon had he been any man's son but Alonzo's. The youth had become a distant, shy young man, diffident and self-effacing. That was the doing of priests, Raimund knew. Don Rolon had been in their care from his first day of life.

"I had hoped that you would tell me that I am being, foolish, Dominguez, subject to fancies and nightmares." He chuckled unhappily. "But you have not done this."

"I do not want to take your worry lightly, Alteza," Raimundo said. "You have been tormented by these . . . odd moments, and it would be callous of me to dismiss it all as nothing. I doubt there is need for concern, but it is wise to be cautious. Don't you agree? Isn't that why we are talking in this place?"

Don Rolon nodded. "You are said to be the most astute man at court, Dominguez. In all your canny wisdom, I hope there is some trust." He looked eastward, toward the place where the moon would rise. "I must leave. If I am to have another episode, I would rather it be at the fair, where no one will know me, and it will be thought that I am drunk or mad, or both." He took a few steps away down the narrow path, then turned back. "If they should ask what we were doing here—and they will—say that I have thought that planting a new garden for the arrival of my bride would be a proper gesture for the Infante Real to make, showing how she makes beauty of my life, or some such phrase."

"Of course, Alteza." Raimundo was pleased that Don Rolon had wits enough to account for his actions. As his marriage drew near, he would need more such excuses and evasions if he were to save himself from constant intrusion. "But why were you telling me?"

"Because . . . you are impartial, being Portuguese." He made a gesture of dismissal and continued on his way.

Raimundo watched him, frowning slightly, his eyes narrowing as he thought over all that the Infante had told him. He determined to visit Don Rolon before noon the next day, to find out, as discreetly as possible, what the full moon had brought to him while he was fairing.

8

When the night was almost over, Don Rolon Andres Esteban Angel Castelar de Asturias, Aragon, Leon y Castilla returned to his quarters, his leather doublet in rags and trailing horsehair padding from the peascod, his short stiff hose tattered, his tight leggings and high boots of soft leather entirely missing. He staggered toward his canopied bed and sank onto his knees on the brocaded satin spread, his hands pressed in horror over his face. He dared not let himself make a sound as he fell forward onto the elaborately embroidered Arms of España which covered the six plump pillows. As he sank almost at once into heavy sleep, he thought with despair, It happened again!

The first long rays of dawn spread through the cloudless spring sky and the most faint of the stars glistened and faded like the dew spangles on the leaves in the garden of the courtyard under his window. The first summons of church bells rang out over Valladolid, and the sound of chanting from the Chapel Royal drifted through the palace.

Don Rolon groaned as he drew his legs up under him and huddled on the bed like a wounded animal, and thanked God for the rising sun. Guiltily he crossed himself, and tried, vainly and with repugnance, to remember what had happened last night. He had met Inez, and she had been playful and happy at the prospect of going fairing. That much was clear. They had left the city with hundreds of other happy, jostling people, by the Leon gate, and had found the tents not far from the walls. They had walked together through makeshift booths where wonders of every sort were displayed and where rough-visaged men shouted hoarse promises of pleasure and wealth for those who ventured further. At one such booth a woman with a walleye offered to reveal the future to Inez, who had begged Don Rolon to pay for such a treat, and at last he had consented. What had the woman said? That Inez must beware of those she trusts and seek aid where she expects least to find it? Then there had been jugglers on stilts and a man with a trained bear who danced and stood on its front paws. Inez had been drawn into a party of dancers and then they . . . He shook his head. He could not recall what they had done after that. He pressed his head into the largest of the pillows.

A short time later the valet's door opened and Ciro came quietly into the room. "Su Alteza," he said respectfully to the miserable young man who trembled at the sound of his voice.

"Not yet," came the muffled response. "Not *yet!*"

"Su Alteza," Ciro persisted, still with proper deference but with determination, "your confessor will be here shortly and it would not be wise to receive him in this . . ."

"State," Don Rolon finished for him with detestation.

"Condition," Ciro amended, coming nearer. He had not yet had a close look at the Infante Real.

"Mercy of God," Don Rolon whispered, and lifted his head.

Ciro had seen the various ravages of his prince's face before and had become inured to the sight, but even he hesitated when he saw Don Rolon's countenance this time.

"Is it so very bad?" the Infante Real asked, seeing the disgust his valet had not succeeded in concealing from him. He had not yet been able to bring himself to look in the mirror or to touch the ruin of his clothing, for fear of what he would discover.

With a stern inner warning, Ciro made himself present a bland expression to Don Rolon. "No. No, of course not, Alteza." He cleared his throat and tugged at the peplum of his doublet. "It is simply that it will be . . . difficult to have you ready on time. Prayers begin shortly, and . . . "

"You mean you must make me presentable," Don Rolon corrected him sadly. "You need not deceive me, Ciro. You may say what is in your mind." His attitude was resigned now and his face slightly averted, as if to conceal the hideousness that might still cling to him. His long, narrow hands lay unmoving on the satin spread, the nails filthy and broken. Catching sight of them, he drew them self-consciously to his chest.

"Well, then, Alteza," Ciro said with false briskness, "we might do well to begin at once. Take off your clothes and let me have them." He wanted to be active, so that he could be able to order his thoughts; he must not allow himself to be distracted by the Infante Real's appalling appearance.

"You'll have to burn or bury them," Don Rolon muttered as he began automatically to unfasten his ruined doublet.

"I will do neither. The servants may notice and talk. The cooks have a way of seeing everything. Gossip at this time would not go well for you, Alteza." He reached out for the doublet as Don Rolon peeled it off.

"Of course." He nodded again as he looked down at his torn chamise. It was stained and the coarse linen had been raked into strips. One sleeve was bloody.

"I will tend to them later, Alteza. When there is no one to pay me heed, I will take them away from the palace and dispose of them, so that no one will know of it." The valet did not want to hold the garments too long, but he sternly disciplined himself to mask his revulsion. He gave the doublet a shake before dropping it over his arm, as if he feared vermin or worse were hidden in it.

"The chamise," Don Rolon said, fatigued by this little effort, as he tossed the thing to Ciro. In the increasing light, he was more lanky-looking than usual, a wiry youth with pale olive skin that showed scratches and bruises uncompromisingly. His face was hollow with exhaustion and his large black eyes red-rimmed and haunted. His dark hair was a disheveled mess, and Ciro could not imagine how he was to set it in order before the Infante Real met his confessor.

"I will hide these," Ciro assured Don Rolon, shuddering secretly at the thought of them.

"Bring me a basin," Don Rolon said as he stood up. He stared down at his bare feet in puzzlement, as if he had not been aware of the loss of his boots until that moment. "Madre de Dios!"

Ciro had rarely heard such distress in any man's voice and it was a moment before he could respond. "Is there something wrong, Alteza?"

"My boots. My leggings. What . . . ?" He breathed in through clenched teeth. "You didn't . . . "

"I have not—" Ciro began, only to be interrupted by Don Rolon's outburst.

"They are out there! No! Saints forgive me, they are out there!" He cringed where he stood, his long features turning a more waxen shade. "If they are found . . . " He did not know why the thought terrified him, but he could not free himself of that fear.

Ciro was alarmed, but he was sensible enough to motion Don Rolon to prudent silence. "Alteza, wherever they may be, they may not be found, and if found, certainly not recognized."

"And if they are?" He shuddered as he asked, and looked once about the room, as if seeking escape.

"If they are found, and identified as yours, I will spread some tale. Perhaps I will mention that you have had boots stolen." As soon as he said that, he rejected it. "No. That would attract too much attention, which we do not desire. If they are found and there has been a . . . misfortune, it can always be excused in some way. You are a young man, and you seek adventure."

"Do you know what they may look like? How can that be excused?" Don Rolon asked wretchedly.

"No, I do not know. Do you, Alteza?"

Don Rolon covered his eyes and shook his head mutely. "If they are found and need explanation, a bout with ruffians would account for anything that might have been done to them. No one will think to question you further, for you are Infante Real . . . "

He cut Ciro short. "And then what? It will be believed that the Infante Real was beaten and robbed, or worse, and his boots and leggings taken. No, thank you." He could imagine what fuel such a tale would give Gil, and the stiff disapproval of his father.

"Would you rather find out the truth?" Ciro inquired acidly, and instantly regretted the question.

"The truth?" What was the truth? He did not know, and what he guessed he loathed.

"Alteza," Ciro said apologetically, "it was not my intent to—"

"Was it not?" Don Rolon asked. "Oh, God. What is it? What is it?" He looked apprehensively at the valet. "You know I am at your mercy, Eje, and I cannot stop you from taking advantage of it. If I must tolerate your jibes, then I will, but if there is insolence as well, I will not have it."

"It was not my intention, Alteza, to be insolent. I most sincerely pity you. I would not mock anyone afflicted as you are." He had lowered his voice, and for that reason, his words were not easily heard, but he knew that Don Rolon was listening closely. "When have I ever traded on your favor, Alteza?"

"Never," Don Rolon admitted. "But then, you are assured of my affection, aren't you? I would be a fool to offer you any ground for complaint." He brought his chin up in a manner reminiscent of his father. Then he sighed. "I am not yet myself, Ciro. Ignore me, if you can." He began to unfasten the remains of his hose, but stopped and gave his valet an inquiring glance. "You have not asked me yet how this happened."

"Do you remember?" Ciro asked skeptically.

"No. That is the worst of it, I think. Possibly one or two things. I may have heard a child scream, but it might have been anything— the wind, a sow in her sty, my soul." He let the hose drop to the floor and untied his codpiece. He stood naked now, a slender, well-made man not far from gangly adolescence. "I must bathe. I stink of . . . " There were no words for the befouling of his life, and he did not go on.

"They will speak of it in the kitchen if I ask for heated water," Ciro warned him, but agreed that he must wash thoroughly. "Too frequent baths will earn you a sermon. The glorification of the flesh is a sin."

"Isn't there some occasion in the next day or two that would justify it? Is an ambassador paying a state visit, or are the Venezians planning a . . . celebration? Is there a Saint's Feast Day to be kept?" As he asked, he flexed his fingers experimentally, grimacing at the stiffness he felt in them.

"There is an auto-da-fé," Ciro suggested quietly. He had all Don Rolon's clothes now, and was about to order the water brought for his bath.

"Not another one!" the Infante Real burst out. "Who are the unfortunates this time? Peasants or Flemings?"

"A little of both. The apostate bishop of Badajoz will be one of them."

"Obispo Teodoro Lazarez?" Don Rolon asked, shocked afresh. "But they said he was not to burn."

"They have changed their minds, it seems. Padre Juan wishes to set an example for his clergy. Ciro was at the door now, but he paused before he opened it. "Be prudent, mi Infante. The Inquisitors would leap at the opportunity to test their strength against that of the throne, and . . . "

"And my royal father is not apt to oppose them on my behalf," Don Rolon asknowledged with old sadness. "Not if I will not accept the Venezian woman." He sat back on the bed and leaned over to inspect the abrasions and lacerations on his legs. Was it worse this time? And had there been so many before? "What of my face?" He looked up, but the valet's door was closed and Ciro was gone.

Padre Lucien was a member of the Order of Premonstratensian Canons, and profoundly dedicated to his calling. From the time he had entered the Order in its parent house Premonte near Laon, he knew his life was secure. The Order was an old one, older than the powerful Dominicans, and the Premonstratensians were viewed more fondly than their blackclad colleagues. Padre Lucien's first mission had been in Germany, where his Order was held in particularly high esteem, and there he became convinced of the propriety of his vocation. Since being sent to España, however, he had been assailed by doubt as his confidence waned. This was no place of jolly piety, as he had known at Aegidienkirche in Hanover, but one of somber, moody introspection where every action and thought were scrutinized for the least taint of heresy or Diabolism. To his consternation, Padre Lucien discovered he could be at odds with other clerics. At first he had assumed that it was the result of his exalted position of confessor to the Infante Real, but of late, he had come to realize that his Order made him suspicious to the Dominicans, for the Premonstratensians were few in number here and were not among those aiding the Holy Office of the Faith.

This morning, as he scrambled into his white habit, hurrying through his vesting prayers, he had to force himself to quell his worries, and beseech the aid of the Virgin in order to restore the tranquility his position demanded of him. It was the morning after the full moon, and he had observed once or twice before in his seventeen months at the Spanish Court, that these were sometimes difficult days for the heir to the throne. He knew enough about the history of the House to keep his own counsel. Padre Lucien tugged his rosary around his ample waist and rushed through his devotions before setting out for the Infante's quarters.

He found the young man squatting in a large wooden tub, sponging himself with tepid water. Padre Lucien coughed discreetly as he approached, and waited with all the patience he could for Don Rolon to give him his attention.

"Oh! Good morning, Padre," the Infante Real said, reaching out for the soap he had dropped at the sound of the closing door.

"Good morning, my son. May God send His blessings to you this day," he said formally and made the Sign of the Cross.

Don Rolon automatically copied the gesture, sighing as he did so. "I thank you, Padre, but I fear I deserve no such favor."

Padre Lucien had grown accustomed to hearing such sentiments from Don Rolon, and for that reason reacted with little more than an admonitory wag of his finger. "No, Alteza, it is not for you to question the benevolence of Heaven, which is promised to all true Christians."

"I wish I could be as certain of that as you are," Don Rolon responded as he took the silver bell beside his tub and shook it.

In answer to the summons, Ciro returned to the Infante Real's dressing chamber, and after giving Padre Lucien proper acknowledgment, he held out a sheet for Don Rolon to dry himself with. "Your pardon for this unseemly delay, Padre, but Alteza rose later than usual this morning."

"It is no concern, no matter," Padre Lucien said at once, doing his best, as always, to put Infante and his valet at ease. In Germany he had developed an easy rapport with those who came to him, but in España, everything he did was bound tight with rank and ceremony, and he often longed for that less circumscribed society. The cold formality of the Court of Alonzo II resisted every attempt he made to establish camaraderie with Don Rolon.

"I will be with you directly," Don Rolon promised the priest as he allowed Ciro to rub him dry.

"I am at Su Alteza's disposal," Padre Lucien said as he reached for the rosary at his waist and began his *Paternoster*. He murmured the prayers until Don Rolon approached him once more, now wrapped in a long robe and in the act of knotting a wide sash. "You are more patient with me than I deserve, Padre Lucien."

"Tush, tush," said the Premonstratensian with a gesture so French that he seemed entirely out of place in the gloomy stone room. "But, Alteza, think of your own soul, not of my convenience. You bathe frequently and this is dangerous to your body's health as well as the soul's well-being." He could not resist a little nod of self-approval for the neat way he had directed their conversation. "I am not reprimanding you, for that would not be seemly, but I wish you to think of the peril in which you place yourself."

"How is that, Padre? Where is my peril?" Don Rolon was giving the priest only half his attention as he sat on a covered bench, but he had learned always to convey an impression of courteous attention.

"You are aware," Padre Lucien said with deliberation, "that vanity is a great sin: nowhere is it more apparent than in the exaggerated concern that comes with bathing overmuch. I see that you do not agree," he went on as he studied the young man's face. "What is the issue of your argument?"

"That some things must be cleansed from the body before they can be cleansed from the soul, good Padre," Don Rolon said morosely as he allowed Ciro to begin dressing him.

"That is false, my son, and could lead you into great error. In youth, it is understandable that thoughts of the flesh are strong, for it is the nature of youth to be under the spell of fleshly things. And so it is with washing." Padre Lucien thought his admonition was nicely phrased, forthright enough to be worthy of his calling, and not so stringent as to suggest he had forgotten to whom he spoke.

"Our Lord washed the feet of His disciples, so that they could walk in their new path purely," Don Rolon pointed out. "Are we not to emulate Him in our lives? Is that not what our faith asks of us?"

"Of course," said Padre Lucien, thinking that perhaps he had at last reached this forlorn young man. "We must seek to live good and pure lives, mi Infante, and be humble before God and our Rey, no matter how mighty our station in this world, for nothing here can approach the majesty of Heaven. Yet, though we live virtuous lives, we are not His disciples, annointed by that holy Hand to do His work in the world. As you say, it was Jesus Himself Who washed the feet of His disciples, signifying His purification of them. Unless you believe that you are worthy of so great an elevation, my son, you commit the heinous sin of pride when you compare yourself to them." He studied Don Rolon's face as he spoke, seeking some unguarded turn of expression that would reveal the young man's thoughts.

"I know I am not worthy, Padre," Don Rolon said at last, more unhappily than ever. "Who among us can aspire to that sanctification? The desire itself makes it unattainable. And I am the least of those seeking God's way."

This daunting turn of their discussion upset the French cleric and he strove for a lighter touch in the hope that he might gain the confidence of the Infante Real. "You must not despair, my son. It is for God to judge us, not ourselves. Be sure that those little beneficences that you perform as a matter of course are as closely observed in Heaven as your failings. It is a mark of your modest nature that you do not choose to bring attention to your charities and good works."

Don Rolon stiffened. "What do you mean, Padre Lucien?"

"Ah, you think to keep such intelligence from me, but I have heard from the priests at San Andreas del Rio that you have provided them with monies and goods to distribute to their communicants. The Antonines are as much out of place here as this Premonstratensian is. Thus, we occasionally seek to cheer ourselves with the observances of our faith, and we celebrate Mass together. Afterward, Padre Martin tells me of the trials he and his Freyes face working in so poor a quarter of the city. The last time we did this, he told me of your generosity, and your request that no one should know of your gifts, for fear it would be thought you were using charity to gain popularity. Coming just when it did, after those two women and three children had been so savagely killed, your donations were the more treasured. As I am your confessor, Padre Martin of course believed I already knew of your good work, and—"

"He should not have told you." The gift had been made before he was sent to El Morro. "It was a private matter, not for currying favor." He was pulling on his pourpoint now, a fine garment of chaste black satin. He tilted his chin up so that Ciro could place the elaborately pleated ruff of black lace around his neck and tie it securely. "I do not wish it known that I have made such gifts, Padre Lucien."

"It is true that it was a private matter," Padre Lucien said querulously, "but it was an act you might have mentioned to me, in the course of our talks. It is not just that you ask me to advise you on spiritual matters when I do not know the full scope of your actions." He did not recognize his disapproval for the hurt feelings that engendered it, and instead decided that Don Rolon was being too capricious.

"Why? If the deed was recorded in Heaven, there is no reason for it to be known on earth," Don Rolon insisted as he tied the peplums to his pourpoint to the tops of his short hose. He reached for the bedpost to steady himself as Ciro brought out the tall, soft leather boots that were required for court wear.

"Your spiritual well-being is my first, indeed, my only concern, Alteza, and when you aid those in need, it re-veals . . ." He did not know how to continue, and so he crossed himself and gave a straight look to the young man.

"The other foot, Alteza," Ciro murmured when he had tugged the first boot into place.

"You must not let yourself be seduced by the appearance of humility that is in reality the most obnoxious pride," Padre Lucien said with more sternness than he usually demonstrated.

"Do you tell me that the people of the parish of San Andreas del Rio are not in need?" Don Rolon inquired sharply. "I have seen those streets, Padre Lucien, and I would be shamed to kennel my dogs there. A handful of coins and a dozen lengths of cloth are nothing against the suffering those poor families endure every day they live. My charity, as you call it, in the face of that, is nothing." He shrank at the memory of the squalor he had seen there, when he had come to himself the morning after the full moon, and seen the pitiful bodies of those three children lying not far away on a heap of refuse. The hovels were close enough to make him wonder what had happened, what he had seen—or done—that the wretches living there might have witnessed, but apparently violence at night was common, for no one paid him any attention when at last he had made his way out of the narrow, stinking lanes to return to the chilly magnificence of his father's palace. He had been even more appalled when he had gone incognito to San Andreas del Rio a few days later, and seen how overwhelming the poverty of the district was. What had he done, that night in October, that took him there?

"There are few of your station who give so much thought to the plight of those unfortunate souls who live in misery," Padre Lucien said with priestly condescension.

"That does not mean that because others neglect them, I must as well," Don Rolon said as he finished affixing a small, dark plume to his tall, narrow-brimmed hat.

"It is wise for a prince to concern himself with all his subjects, and to be acquainted with them, but there are tasks best left to deputies, and acts that do much to give heart to the people when they are known." Padre Lucien knew that it was time for him to begin their morning prayers, and he paused rather conspicuously until the Infante Real had once again given him his full attention. "Your father knows nothing of these acts, I suppose."

"No, and I would dislike it if he learned of them." He had seen how suspicious Alonzo was of such charity, and he was convinced that if he learned that Don Rolon was making such donations, he would want to know why. "Listen to me, Padre, I beg you," Don Rolon said suddenly. "You are not yet used to this Court, and you do not know how we live in España. Believe me when I tell you that it would be no service to me to reveal to el Rey what I have done. He and his confessors would subject me to many questions, and the result would be that I would wish never to give a gift again, and they would not trust any kind act I undertook. The Inquisition may seek to save souls for the glory of God, but they do not advise that we work to protect the body, or change the estate to which we are born. I am grateful to you for your kindness, but if you would wish to continue it, keep silent on what you have learned."

Padre Lucien stared in astonishment at Don Rolon, and could not bring himself to protest this outburst. He shook his head but at last said, "Very well, Alteza, I will keep my peace, but it goes against the grain with me. I will pray that there will come a time when you do not let yourself be ruled by these foolish fears."

"As will I," Don Rolon said fervently, looking once at Ciro Eje.

When Padre Lucien was satisfied that both Don Rolon and Ciro would not be distracted from their religious observances, he blessed them both and began, choosing a psalm to mark the day: *"De profundis clamavit, Domine . . . ."*

9

"We will set the day of her arrival as soon as Su Majestad approves one," the Venezian Envoy said with a flourish of his hand. "We are all agog to see the joyous day."

"We will also welcome the. event," Alonzo said flatly. "Venezia and España are by rights rulers of the ocean, and this marriage affirms that right."

The Envoy blinked but recovered neatly. "Yes, it is the great fortune of our two countries that we may have so glorious a . . . union." He could see no answering enthusiasm in el Rey's pebble-flat eyes, and gave it up—all the world knew that the marriage of Zaretta and Rolon was a political ploy, one designed to cement treaties and guarantee continued favorable relations, but in Venezia, they took the time to give at least the appearance of gallantry and romance. Here in España, it was most obviously otherwise. The Envoy, Nobile Rigonzetti, whose family had been diplomats for more than six centuries, decided that it would be best to accommodate the dour monarch. "We are eager to have the documents to present to il Doge for his review, and any letters that Don Rolon would want to have carried to his betrothed."

"We have already requested that he prepare one," el Rey said. "It will be in our hands by evening."

Envoy Rigonzetti sighed, bowed, and withdrew. He had a letter of his own to write and for all his courtly skills, he could think of no way to describe the Spanish Court that would fill Zaretta Patrecipazio with anything other than disgust.

As soon as the Venezian was gone, Lugantes let himself into the smaller throne room where minor receptions, such as the last one, took place. He capered up the long narrow carpet, turning somersaults and singing bits of courtly songs as he approached Alonzo.

"I am not ready for you, Lugantes," Alonzo said in a tired voice. "I must receive officers from Flanders, to hear their latest list of grievances, and then I will spend an hour with my confessor. There is the auto-da-fé to attend to, as well. When I dine tonight, you will be welcome."

"No songs, Majestad?" Lugantes asked, as if heartbroken. "What is poor Lugantes to do?"

El Rey looked up, startled by the question. "You have those in this palace who would be glad of your company. Find my son. He is likely to enjoy your antics." He was about to wave the dwarf away when the next question startled him even more.

"Does Majestad mean Don Rolon?" He asked it rolling his eyes and waggling his fingers, a performance that usually evoked a bit of a smile from Alonzo.

"Of course not!" he snapped. "Gil is off somewhere in the armory with Don Enrique Hurreres. You would be better company than that hidalgo."

Lugantes bowed at once. "As you order me, Majestad, so will I do."

Rey Alonzo paid very little heed to this; he waved Lugantes away and rang for his secretary.

As Lugantes threaded his way through the maze of corridors toward the wing of the palace where the armory was, he pondered the note tucked into his doublet. Since he had found it in his cup two hours ago, he had been trying to discover who had sent it, and why. It was cryptic enough: *Little man, it is most urgent that we meet. There is more danger than we know. Speak of this to no one, now or ever. Where the mermaid and the sagittary embrace, at Vespers.* Who would send it, and why? He was not so naive that he dismissed the possibility of a trap, but why, and to whose benefit? His caution and his curiosity were at odds; he had not yet made up his mind if he would answer the summons.

"Lugantes!" The voice, even when imperious, was beautiful, like the woman who possessed it. Reina Genevieve had just emerged from her private chapel, and now, attended by three ladies and Padre Juan Murador, she was returning to her suite of rooms. At thirty-six she was no longer the luminous beauty she had been when she came to Alonzo as a bride of twenty, but where there had been freshness and radiance before, there was now a stifled, obsessive sensuality that flowed from her like furnace heat. She, of all her company, did not wear black. Her stiff, jewel-studded gown was a deep, greenish blue, and her ruff, instead of being tightly pleated and gathered, was open and standing, framing her face, her neck, and the exposed white skin of her bosom. Her hair, which had once been bright as new copper, had faded to the color of peaches. It was dressed in the French style, with masses of tight little curls around her face and the rest gathered in an elaborate knot at the crown of her head. "Lugantes. Where are you bound?"

"El Rey has sent me to entertain his bastard," Lugantes said, permitting himself a little anger, for Genevieve's love of Gil was no greater than his own.

"He will do well enough without you," Genevieve declared. "I am weary and bored unto death. Do not reprimand me again, mon Pere," she said to Padre Juan. "I have heard your strictures all morning, and I have completed most of the penance you have required of me. I cannot spend the entire day crawling around the chapel in my shift. I have done it one hundred times, and have recited the Rosary each time I did. There are fifty more to be done, and I will tend to it before I sleep tonight."

Padre Juan straightened up, his eyes burning with some-thing more than zeal. "I will wait upon you, to see that you do. You must not neglect the care of your soul." He licked his lips abruptly. "You say that you have humiliation enough in your daughters, but you show no signs of repentance. Think of God's Hand."

"I do," she said, partly in anger and partly in despair. "He has blighted my life, and for no reason."

"You cannot say that to me. I am your confessor, and your transgressions are known to me. If it pleases God to chastise you, and to send you penance through me, it is not for you to question it, but to strive to greater perfection." His expression was adamant, and he turned to Genevieve's ladies-in-waiting. "You are good, chaste women. Let you be an example to your Reina, who has yet to master her . . . flesh. Show her that it is repugnant to God that she is wanton."

"I am not!" Reina Genevieve cried out. "I'm banished from my husband's bed and yet not permitted to return to my country. What I do has been done by other Reinas and they have been welcomed in Heaven. The English Queen has her lovers, and no one cries out except men like you, Padre." She gave him his title in Spanish with heavy sarcasm.

"Your family lives in lasciviousness and debauchery," Padre Juan insisted. "For this, there must be more penance. I had thought you were becoming more accepting, but I see that it is not so." He bowed and turned away, his sandals slapping on the inlaid marble floor, receding like the sound of muffled clappers.

Reina Genevieve put a trembling hand over her mouth; her eyes were wet. One of her women touched her shoulder, but she shook her head violently and moved away. Finally she said in a choked voice, "Leave me, my ladies. Lugantes, come with me. Sing me songs. Anything." She began to hurry toward her rooms, not looking to see if she had been obeyed.

Lugantes had to skip to keep up with her, and wisely remained silent until her two pages—twin boys of nine—opened her doors for her, then closed them behind her. Then he reached for her hand and kissed it. "Genevieve mia."

With that, Genevieve began to weep. She took her place on a hard-backed chair, paying no mind to her crushed skirts and misaligned farthingale, or that her eyes turned red and her milky skin became blotched. "Ah, Bon Dieu, what am I to do?"

"Genevieve," Lugantes said again, and went to sit on the carpet by her side. "Do not cry, my beauty, Reina mia. It will pass."

"Yes; when I am dead." She tried to dry her tears with her lace handkerchief, and discovered that it was useless for such a task. Petulantly she wadded it and flung it across the room.

Lugantes got to his feet and tore the flounce off his sleeve, then began to dry her eyes, crooning softly to her as he did it. "Be calm, mujer dorada. Hush, hush, querida. Mi vida. Mi vida. Yo t'amo." It was agony to say it, but worse pain to be silent, and so he said the words, as he had said them many times before, in whispers to himself and then in bantering, comic songs. When he could endure that no more, he had spoken and Genevieve had kissed him, very lightly. He had sung her other songs, when they were alone, songs that had been sung long ago, at the Courts of Love, which said that there was no greater joy on earth than the presence of the beloved, and nothing a man might aspire to more wonderful than the touch of her hand. Whoever had written that, Lugantes thought sadly, had not been a dwarf and a jester. Yet he could no more desert her than he could grow tall and handsome.

"Oh, my little treasure, what would I do without you?" Genevieve sighed when her eyes were dry again. "You are so good to me."

Lugantes felt a familiar coldness deep within him. He knew what these compliments presaged. "It is my love for you that makes—"

"You take care of me," she murmured. "You take such good, good care of me." She reached out languidly and touched his hair. "I am alone here in España. I have only you to help me. You understand me, Lugantes. The rest of them don't." She bent and kissed his forehead and he thought he had been branded. "I have been so alone."

"You have me, Genevieve," he said desperately, quietly. "I am a man who loves you and you have me."

"But you . . . " She sighed. "I can't endure it, all these days with priests and spies and whispers. I must have more in my life. Lugantes, why weren't you born tall and beautiful?"

"Were I that, hermosa, I would be a miller's son and we would never have met." He wished at times that he did not know her, did not love her, and never more than when she pressed him, as she did now.

"I would find you. Anyone with so loving a soul, I would find." She closed her eyes. "I have tried to image what that would be like, but I cannot see you as other than you are. And it is not enough."

"But I am a man, Genevieve," he protested again. "You are lovely, a vision of Heaven that fills my life, and you do not see what you do to me because all you see is a little man in whimsical clothes. Genevieve, please. Do not insist." It was useless; he knew it even as he said the words. He might refuse her for a day or two or three, but in the end, he would capitulate and bring her what she desired. "Who is it you want?" he asked in a thickened tone.

"Someone young and beautiful. Someone boastful." She stroked his hair and stared dreamily toward the huge painting of the crucifixion on the far wall without seeing the picture at all. "I must have someone soon."

"Genevieve . . . "

"They will not let me see my girls, but the priests tell me that they are a punishment. When I had them, I had done all that was asked of me. I was demure and obedient and chaste, and for that my daughters are idiots. My husband has not touched me for seven years, but he keeps me here. What am I to do? Pray until I wear out my knees and fast until I am more like a rail fence than a woman? And for what?" The outburst was not the first of its kind, but the anguish of it never changed.

"Who, then," Lugantes said softly. "Who this time, Genevieve?" He had tried twice to make love to her, and each time had ended in utter misery for them both. He did not have the courage to suggest that they try again.

"Someone, someone." Then she laughed, a breathless chuckle back in her throat that dismayed him. "I should have thought of this long ago. Oh, yes, yes, I must do it. Alonzo will be furious." She began to laugh. "Oh, little man, I will be revenged."

Lugantes listened to her with dismay. "Querida, who? Do not be unwise, I beg you, Genevieve."

"I'm not unwise. No. Not any longer. I will touch Alonzo where he can be hurt at last." Suddenly she was serious again. "You must do this for me, Lugantes. You must not object—and I know that you will—because I know what I must do. You will help me, if you love me."

Lugantes took her hand and kissed it passionately. "Whatever you desire, Genevieve."

"Whatever I desire." She looked down at the jester. "It was a mistake to bed Rolon last year. All it got for either of us was extra penance and Alonzo's wrath. He was not hurt by it. But there is a way."

"No, Genevieve," Lugantes said in spite of himself, anticipating what she would tell him. "It is too dangerous."

"No, not too dangerous. It is ideal. You must bring Gil to me. I want him. I want Gil. And I want to be certain Alonzo learns of it." She rose from her chair and walked the length of the room. "Think of it. Alonzo adores Gil. It would drive him to distraction if I were to bed him. If Gil should love me, Alonzo would be—"

"Querida, querida," Lugantes whispered as if frightened of being overheard. "Do not do this thing, I pray you. If you must have another lover, I will find you one, one who will delight you and give you hours of pleasure. I promise you, Genevieve, I vow it on all the Saints. But do not anger Alonzo. Please, please, please, do not give him reason to harm you, for I know that you would suffer for it, oh, so very much, and I could not bear that to happen."

"Don't be foolish, Lugantes," Genevieve said lightly, then smiled fondly. "You do care what becomes of me. That's truly endearing, little man, and—" There were tears in her eyes again. "Don't care so much, my little one. I am so touched by you. No one else would—" She dropped to her knees and they embraced with passion and sorrow. Then Genevieve pushed him away. "Do bring me Gil."

Lugantes swallowed his objections this time, and nodded dumbly. Very correctly he kissed her hand, hardly touching her fingers with his lips.

"And it must be soon, Lugantes."

"If that is your wish, Genevieve," he told her, aghast at his own compliance.

"Oh, Lugantes, you're so good to me!" Genevieve tousled his hair and gave a playful toss to her head. "It will be sweet, bringing that young devil to heel."

Lugantes could not bring himself to speak as he left la Reina's apartments, for his heart was full of fear.

El Rey read over his son's letter and grudgingly pro-nounced himself pleased. "The Ambassador Plenipotentiary is as encouraged by your actions as we are. He has asked for the honor of feasting you in state to demonstrate the pleasure of Venezia at your corning wedding. He has set the time for the evening of the seventeenth of March, which is less than a month away. That will give you enough time to have a gala suit of clothes made for the occasion. We will allow you to wear colors, my son, for the Venezians are much given to bright dress." It was apparent that Alonzo did not approve of this. "The Venezians lack restraint, and for the time being, we must not be intolerant of their modes. Because you are to be honored, and as a promised bridegroom, we recommend cloth-of-gold."

Don Rolon was not able to make any response, so great was the turmoil in his mind. The seventeenth of March was the night of the full moon, and then he would be in the throes of the witch's malediction. From the hour after sunset until the hour before dawn, the madness would claim him again, he was sure of it. What would the Venezian Ambassador Plenipotentiary think of the coming wedding if he saw the heir to the throne of España a raving madman? He felt his father's cold eyes on him, and repeated blankly, "Cloth-of-gold?"

"Do you have some objection?" Alonzo inquired, overly patient in his manner.

"No . . . " Don Rolon faltered. "I—"

"You will be provided the necessary funds and we will supply our own tailors to make the garments, so that you will appear in a manner proper to your rank and station." Alonzo waved his hand wearily. "We will inform our secretary of this at once, if you wish it."

In desperation, Don Rolon burst out, "That was not what concerned me, Majestad. No. I thought that . . . it would mean delaying the feast for a week, but what if I were to request Venezian silks for my clothes?" He had pulled the first notion that came to his mind, but he could tell by the slight squinting of Alonzo's eyes that he had caught his father's attention. "Wouldn't that be a more fitting act? Cloth-of-gold is the most magnificent fabric in España, but you have promised me to a Venezian woman, and I must do all that I can to show myself pleased with the match, or so you have told me. Would the Ambassador mind putting the festivities off for a week if it would make it possible to offer Venezia such a sign of esteem and . . . "

Alonzo nodded slowly. "You may be correct," he said flatly. "It is a suitable idea, one that will please the mission from Venezia." Admitting that Don Rolon had done well was not pleasant to el Rey, and his narrow mouth became even more pursed.

"Suggest it, Majestad. Say that it was my idea, if you fear they will be offended. Tell them that it was my eagerness to compliment my betrothed, and then if there are objections, the weight of them will fall upon me, as it should." This was the flimsiest of straws to clutch at, but he could think of nothing else to say. He tightened his jaw and forced himself to assume an expression of indifference. "You know that I do not want to marry, my father, but if I must, it ill becomes me to neglect the courtesies that are fitting to show a bride."

"It is true that the Doge would be gratified by your gesture, and it would do more good than a few well-turned phrases on parchment." He looked down at the letter Don Rolon had written, a thoughtful frown on his face. Alonzo was not a man who acted in haste, and more rarely still on impulse, but he had learned to accept opportunities when they could be turned to advantage. Pressed now, he was sure the Venezian Ambassador would be delighted with Don Rolon's request. "I will speak with the Ambassador and the Envoy shortly and inform you of their answer."

"Thank you, Majestad," Don Rolon murmured, preparing to leave his father's presence. His head had begun to ache.

"You will hold yourself in readiness to accommodate him, whatever he decides. The Ambassador does you great honor, my son, and I do not wish to see the honor of España sullied by improper behavior."

"Of course, Majestad." He bowed formally and backed toward the door, praying with fervor that the offer would be a welcome one. If it was not, he would have to invent another reason to delay the feast. Illness could not easily be claimed. Perhaps if there were religious duties, a retreat or a pilgrim-age he might undertake so he would be gone from Valladolid on the crucial night.

"You may leave, Rolon. And tell Gil that I will expect him to dine with me in my apartments after Vespers."

That last barb struck Don Rolon deeply, and no matter how he tried to convince himself that it was nothing new, and he had no reason to be given other treatment, still he hoped that his compliance would have softened Alonzo's heart toward him. He tried to think of an appropriate response, but none occurred to him.

"We will ask you to attend us the day after tomorrow, Rolon, for informal discussions with Cardinal Ayerbe on the preparations for your Nuptial Mass. It will be essential that Padre Juan Murador attend as well, for it may be wise to defer to Venezia on certain points of the celebration, but we must in no way compromise our faith so that there is danger of heresy."

"Venezians are Catholic, Majestad," Don Rolon reminded him with some asperity.

"Yet they are not as committed to the preservation of their faith as we are. It is apparent in the laxness of their court and the conduct of their people. Women appearing abroad in masks! They are easy prey for the Devil."

Don Rolon bowed in acknowledgment and made no attempt to argue. If he placed himself in opposition to his father now, he was afraid that Alonzo might insist that he wear cloth-of-gold on the night of the full moon, after all, and that would be disastrous. "I know so little of Venezia, but that it is on the water and their ships are excellent."

"You must learn," Alonzo said sternly. "We will see that you are instructed." With that, he motioned for Don Rolon to leave and did not glance his way to be sure he was obeyed.

10

"But I don't want to stay here day after day, locked up like a prisoner, while no one but servants surround me!" Inez flung a pillow across the room and paid no heed to the feathers that burst from it.

"I did not mean for you to have to live this way," Don Rolon told her, wishing he could apologize for neglecting her, as he knew he had done. "I have tried to be with you more often, but with the wedding—"

"Oh, yes, the wedding, the fine, royal wedding. I have heard nothing but gossip about that wedding, and the Venezian woman who is coming to be your bride. She is the main interest of every woman in Valladolid. They know you, Infante, but they have never seen her. Tell me, is it true that she has lost half her teeth?"

"I don't know," Rolon said quietly. "I have never seen her. They have not even sent her portrait." He had been worried at first for this glaring lapse, but it no longer seemed important.

"How sad," Inez said nastily. "You don't know who to look for when she arrives." Quite suddenly, she laughed. It was a hard, angry sound, and it made the room ring as if its walls were cracking. "And when she arrives, you will have to be the dutiful prince, won't you, and spend your time giving her heirs so that your House will be assured of its Succession on the throne."

"It is expected of me. That is one of the reasons I am being married. The other is to guarantee a truce and a treaty." He had not taken off so much as his short cape, and he did not know if it would be wise to do so. "Inez, I am not at liberty to be your lover every day. I wish I were. It would please me very much. And I cannot bring you to the palace. My father used to have his mistresses there, in discreet little suites of rooms near the back of the building, but I have heard that my mother was much despondent, and that the servants laughed at her for her misfortune. She suffered much because of my father. No matter what my wife is like, I do not intend she should be as poorly treated."

"And so you leave me for days alone, with servants to spy on me in case I should do anything that would not please you." She was turning sulky now, instead of irate. "I feel I am a suspect."

"It's true that you have servants to look after you, and I know you have little opportunity to go abroad, but you are not being spied upon, Inez. I am hemmed in with spies at Court. I could not wish the same on you." He reached out as if to touch her cheek, but held back.

"Then what do you call it? I cannot go anywhere, not to Mass, not to the market but Jacinto walks with me, always a bit behind me, never with my other servants. They pretend they do not see him, and do not speak to him." She pulled her camisado open in the front. "He watches me all the time. When I am alone, I find him staring at me, in a way that is . . . demeaning." She glanced down at her exposed breasts in a significant way. "When I wake in the morning, sometimes I see him in my antechamber, watching me."

"Have you told Lugantes?" Don Rolon asked, deeply concerned by what she said.

"What would be the point? He hired the servants for this house, and he must know what they do." Inez pointed to the branch of candles beside the bed. "If you wish to talk, Alteza, I will send for more light. If you would rather do something else . . . "

Don Rolon's smile was bright, an unusual thing for him. "I thought you were too angry with me."

Inez shrugged, but inwardly knew that she had been most unwise. If she caused the Infante Real to leave her, there were few who would be willing to keep her as he had done, and she had no desire to search for another protector in Valladolid where she knew almost no one. True, Lugantes had claimed to be her friend, and there had been one or two men who had sought her out, but they had not offered her what Don Rolon already provided. She sank back on the bed. "Do not be disappointed with me, Alteza. I am overwrought. I know that you are bound to your House, but the thought of sharing you with another woman distresses me so much, and living as I must here is so confining that I . . . " Her sigh showed him her breasts again, and she could see how hungrily he looked at them.

Don Rolon was not sure how sincere Inez was in her heart, but it pleased him to think she meant what she said. He knew Court women who were more artful, and told himself that Inez lacked their cynicism and expert handling of men, which proved her devotion was genuine. "I cannot stay too long. There is a Mass at dawn to mark the departure of the Herald Persuivant for Venezia, and I must attend. But I have a few hours. I'd rather spend them here with you than anywhere else."

"I am your most obedient subject," Inez said with a delightful, wicked smile as she pulled the blankets aside. "1 have been waiting for you to come for days, mi Infante, and I have laden my soul with sin for the thoughts I have savored." She opened her arms to him, whispering encouragements as he took off his clothes and laid them carefully aside. "Don Rolon, you do not know how much it pains me when you are not here. I am terrified that you will forget me and will cease to love me. I beseech the Saints to bring you back to me, to ease the desire that engulfs me."

Just as Don Rolon started toward the bed, he asked her, "And what of that servant? What was the name? The one you say watches you?" He meant to tease her, but there was more sharpness in his voice than he had intended, and Inez shuddered.

"Do not think of him, Alteza. If he watches, well, he has done so before." It worried her to say that, because if Jacinto were warned, he might become more crafty, and Inez would not know when he observed her and when he did not.

"Has he?" Don Rolon faltered. It was as bad as the palace here, where he had thought he had escaped the constant observations and intrigues.

"Mi Infante, please, I have been without you for days and I am weak from wanting you." Inez reached to touch his arm, trying to keep him from being distracted yet again. "Each day I hope you will visit me, and so often I am forlorn at the end of night."

Don Rolon bent his head and kissed her. There was passion in his kiss, but not his entire attention. "We must make the most of what time we have," he said, as much to himself as to her.

"Then don't dawdle," Inez suggested, catching his nearest hand in hers and pulling gently on it. "I know I must surrender you to another woman soon, which I do not want to do. But there is nothing to be done. For now, you are mine, and I am yours, as it should be."

He slid into bed beside her and felt the thrill of her nearness as he always did. "Be naked for me, hermosa," he whispered, his hand on her camisado. "I will take off my chamise if you will take off your camisado." It was a reckless notion, one that would earn him a lecture when he confessed it, but he had never seen or touched a wholly nude woman before, and had never wished to be so himself, except in his bath where it was acceptable to all but the most devoutly religious.

Inez was not shocked by the suggestion, which surprised Don Rolon. "If you wish me naked, Alteza, remove my camisado yourself." It was a challenge, but a playful one. "I wish to please you, but you must help me." She wriggled nearer to him, making sure the voluminous nightwear rode up her body, exposing her legs.

With his fingers shaking, Don Rolon reached for the hem of her camisado and pulled at it. He was breathing quickly, wishing there was something he could say that would reveal to her what joy he was feeling. "Inez. Hermosa." It was so inadequate! He touched her hip and tried to get her garment out from under her.

"Here, Alteza," she said, a bit impatiently. It was annoying to her when the Infante Real fumbled so. A more experienced man would deal with her camisado in one or two deft tugs. She slipped her arms out of the sleeves and rolled closer to him. "You can take it off me now, Alteza."

"Oh. I see. He grabbed the loose fabric over her head and pulled heartily, and finally the whole thing came away; he tossed it across the room, paying no heed to where it landed. "Inez. Inez." He wrapped his arms around her in a frenzy of delicious guilt. Everything he had been taught informed him that what he was doing was wrong, a glorification of the flesh and a gratification of the senses that could lead only to perdition. But if one must be damned, he thought, what a sweet way to go! He was slightly dizzy with it all, and the intensity of his arousal astonished him.

"Come Alteza," Inez said as she contrived to get him out of his chamise.

"Oh, yes. There. My arm is free now." He wrestled his pleated cotton chamise off, wadded it and sent it flying away from the bed. He could hardly contain himself now, and the warmth of her skin, the scent of it, the amazing nearness of her was better than too much wine. When he had made love to her before, he had been very satisfied, but this was so much more wonderful than anything he had known. Her knee, soft next to his; her arm against his side; her hand, warm and supple on his back; her breasts, her abdomen next to his so that he could feel only his hair between them—God, he was ecstatic with it all.

He reached down her body, touching all that he found, and every new discovery was a triumph for him. He did not notice that Inez was not as enchanted as he was, nor would he have believed her if she had told him. Anything that gave him such unspeakable rapture must be as marvelous for her as it was for him. Nothing else made sense. He was still aware, in one dark part of his mind, that what he was doing was morally and theologically wrong and that he would pay a heavy price for these splendid moments with Inez. He could not entirely ignore that knowledge, but for the time, any trial or punishment he might face seemed to be worth it.

It was over too soon, much too soon, and the hours Don Rolon had spent with Inez were less than minutes to him. He was horrified at the unfairness of it, and did not want to leave her bed to attend to the duties that waited for him.

"You must go, Alteza. You said you must, and I would not serve you well should I keep you here." She heard a noise and turned her head sharply. "Was that Jacinto? Could you see him?"

"There was no one," Don Rolon said, not certain that he was right. "I did not see anyone." What did Jacinto look like? He did not know.

"I don't want to send you off, mi Infante, but you must leave, or you will anger el Rey, and then you will think harshly of me for keeping you here when—"

"I will never think harshly of you, Inez," Don Rolon said ardently. "Never, never, never. I promise you."

Secretly she smiled, but her outward manner was more severe. "You have duties to attend to, and if you go to Mass and sleep, you will have to do penance for it. Come back to me soon, mi Infante, and love me again."

"As we did tonight?" He paused in the act of putting on his rumpled chamise and regarded her apprehensively. "You would not refuse, would you? It is wrong, I know, but it is so pleasant."

Inez had to force herself to keep from mocking him. He was older than she, but in so many ways, he was younger, much younger. Everyone knew that men and women slept together naked, no matter what the Church preached. Who were priests, but celibate men, with no experience of those few joys that made the drudgery of life bearable. A good meal, a warm, cozy fire in a stout house, a friendly body in bed, these were the rewards that could be found on this earth, before seeking the promise of Heaven. Those in the Church might scoff at such considerations, but country folk knew what to look for in life. She touched his hand. "Alteza, I would be glad for it."

This was so much more than Don Rolon had hoped for that he felt tears form in his black eyes. "Ah, it is no wonder that I love you, Inez."

She smiled, and let it go at that.

Not until the tremendous spectacle of Mass was over did Don Rolon have an opportunity to speak to Lugantes. He found the jester on the steps of the Catedrál, his humor more subdued than usual. "I must have a word with you," Don Rolon said as he came up to the dwarf.

"Of course, Alteza." Lugantes doffed his wide-brimmed hat and bowed, since this was a formal occasion. "Is it urgent?"

"Somewhat. Walk with me, Lugantes, and as we go, I will mention what is on my mind." He looked around and saw his father smiling with wistful pride at Gil. He turned away at once. "More . . . trouble, Alteza?" He asked as tactfully as he could without drawing too much attention to their conversation.

"Not of the sort you mean." They found themselves a place in the loose procession that was starting back for the palace. "I have seen our friend from the inn."

"Ah, yes. Is that where the matter lies?" Lugantes hoped that Inez had been faithful to Don Rolon, though he was not confident that she was. If the Infante had a rival, it would mean real problems for the young woman.

"Not with her, precisely." He bowed to the Venezian Ambassador and exchanged a few routine pleasantries. Then he resumed. "In the household of this person, there is a servant, one I did not know about, or had not been told of. It appears that our friend from the inn is worried about him. Did you think it necessary to place a spy among her servants?"

Since all the servants were paid to tell Lugantes what transpired at Inez's house, this question startled him. "Spies, Alteza?"

"The man Jacinto. He follows our friend everywhere, even into her chambers. She is offended and upset by him." He was exaggerating the matter, but he decided, that strong language was needed if the situation were to be corrected.

"Jacinto?" Lugantes asked. "There is no servant in . . . our friend's household by that name." As he said this, he began to feel that inward dread that warned him of treachery. "I am curious about this servant. Could you have mistaken the name?"

"No. From what I was told, I assumed he was . . . an afterthought." He placed his hand on Lugantes' shoulder and squeezed, silently warning his companion to say nothing. "It is an honor to see you with us, Padre Juan," Don Rolon said to the Inquisitor General. "Such ceremonies are not your chosen arena, and it is a great privilege to have you attend this one, for so much of the future of this kingdom rests with the success of our current venture."

"It is good to hear you say so, Don Rolon," Padre Juan said significantly. "You have a grave responsibility to your House, and it is best that every aid is obtained, especially the aid and blessing of Heaven." He gave the nod that passed for a bow with him, then moved away to take his place at the side of Alonzo II.

"Now, Lugantes. Tell me about Jacinto." Don Rolon had lowered his voice but did not bend down to say the words, for fear that one of the others in the crowd would notice this and make it a point to listen. "If he is not an afterthought, what is he?"

"I don't know, Alteza, and that disturbs me. There is no one named Jacinto in that household that I know of. If there is one such, I have neither seen nor met him." He was also sharply aware that none of the others servants had mentioned the man, and that troubled him even more, for the only institution that could command greater loyalty and devotion than the crown was the Holy Office for the Faith. If that were the case, what was a familiar of the Inquisition doing in Inez's household?

"Will you find out as much as you can and let me know what has taken place?" Don Rolon lifted his hand to acknowledge a cheer from an overhead window.

"I will, Alteza. I must know for my own peace of mind, in any case." He walked in silence for a little way, then said to Don Rolon, "It would be best to say nothing more to our friend from the inn, not until we are sure we know who the servant is. Otherwise, our friend might say or do something that would cause a more dangerous predicament. If you take my meaning?"

"Yes. I agree. There are other hazards already, and this is one more that would create notoriety." The Infante Real saw Raimundo in the confusion and signaled to him. "I must have a word with this man. Come to my quarters later, Lugantes, and we will discuss how this is to be done."

"Todas gracias, Alteza," Lugantes said, and moved away from him, looking now for la Reina.

"Is something the matter?" Raimundo inquired as Don Rolon approached him. "If you have need of me—"

"Only your good wishes," Don Rolon said, glancing quickly to his half brother, who walked not far from them, apparently unaware of them, but listening intently. "There are a few matters I would want to discuss about the, garden with the Moorish fountain. With my bride coming so soon to España, there are many things to be done, and I must arrange for someone to attend to my plans."

"Yes. The garden." Raimundo paused. "I am at liberty to wait on you in two hours, if you will not object to that." He added in an undervoice, "An hour from now, at the rear of the old chapel."

"That time should be satisfactory," Don Rolon said. "I will expect you, and those developments I have mentioned to you will be—" He broke off and turned his head to watch the ancient Duque del San Felipe Cruzado come tottering along the street toward el Rey. The Duque was descended from one of the most venerable Spanish noble Houses, one that traced its beginnings back to Visigoth Burgos. For this reason if no other, he was accorded the greatest respect; it was common knowledge that he hated the House of Hapsburg and regarded them as interlopers.

"You!" he shouted in his cracking, aged voice. "You. Stop at once!"

The person he addressed so unceremoniously looked at him with somber disapproval. "You wish to address us?" el Rey inquired with terrible civility.

"I wish to speak to Alonzo Hapsburg!" countered the Duque. "I want you to know that I think it's a disgrace that you should be marrying off one of your demented brats to honest Venezian nobility. Your whole family is crazed, Alonzo, and all the world knows it. Why wasn't the girl warned, and the Doge too, for that matter?" He had been walking with the precarious aid of two canes, and now he brandished one of them at Alonzo. "You've done nothing but cause heartache and misery since your House settled here. Holy Roman Empire or not, you've got bad blood in your veins, and you're trying to foist your get off on the world as capable of rule. You Hapsburgs are madmen, all of you." The old man shook his cane more furiously, then made a sweeping gesture at the grandees who waited uneasily around Alonzo. "You're as bad as he is, all of you. You disgrace this country. You have given allegiance to a tyrant and coward, a man who hides behind cassocks and crucifixes to keep himself secure. What needs Alonzo II with guards when he has the Holy Office to protect him? His enemies are in the hands of the Inquisition, where no one can aid them, and Alonzo may claim that he is guiltless." He stumbled and had to brace himself with his canes again. "Dogs! Insects! Vermin!"

Two burly officers of the Secular Arm came pushing through the crowd, both in light armor and carrying their truncheons at the ready. People gave way to them, and those who a few seconds before had pressed in for a closer look now stood back carefully, making an effort to be inconspicuous.

Padre Juan Murador came and stood at Alonzo's side, one hand on el Rey's shoulder, the other on the large golden cross around his neck. "Take that man," he said calmly, pointing at the Duque del San Felipe Cruzado. "It is the Devil who speaks through him." He then addressed the crowd at large. "How often you have heard your priests warn you that the Devil is everywhere among us, looking to bring down this Godly kingdom of España. The Devil is all lies, and he fills the mouths of his servants with lies."

"I serve no Devil!" the old Duque railed, trying to elude the two officers.

"It is the skill of the Devil that he may blind his servants into believing that they serve God Himself and not the Great Enemy. While no one can doubt that this honorable ancient is sure that he is free of the Devil, the Secular Arm will soon show otherwise." This ominous statement quieted the crowd completely, for everyone knew that the Secular Arm was the branch of the Inquisition that included jailers and torturers. "No doubt, under Question, we will learn that the Devil has ensnared the soul of this grandee and seduced him into these erroneous beliefs. From the pain of his body, we will wrest the purity of his soul." He signaled the officers, and they took the old Duque by his elbows.

"This is damnable!" shrieked their prisoner, but now no one listened to him. "You have no right! Only el Rey can—"

Alonzo gave one last look at the Duque del San Felipe Cruzado. "I am ever obedient to the laws of the Church for they are the laws of God. May Heaven forgive you your outburst today, and bring you to Grace." With that, he gave his attention to Padre Juan and studiously avoided notice of the struggle that the officers met with as they dragged the old man away.

Don Rolon watched in horror as the grandees and hidalgos once again resumed their walk from the Catedrál to the palace. He had heard it said before and now had witnessed it for himself—those whom the Inquisition condemned became invisible.

11

"They say there is a wolf loose in the city," Raimundo told Don Rolon when they were far enough ahead of the grooms that they would not be overheard.

"A wolf?" the Infante Real repeated. "In Valladolid?" His mind had been full of the reception he was being given the following night at the behest of the Venezian Ambassador, and until this moment, had thought of little but how fortunate he had been to be able to delay the event for a week.

"You're incredulous," the Portuguese courtier said, "and well you might be. So am I." He leaned a little closer to Don Rolon so that their horses were very close together. "The tale of wolves is a good ploy, I'll say that much. It prevents too many questions being asked."

"Then you do not think there is a wolf?" Don Rolon asked, scowling.

"Undoubtedly there is something, but not, I think, a wolf." He pointed toward the horizon where clouds were clustering. "We may have rain tonight, after all."

"It's possible," Don Rolon agreed. "If not a wolf, then what?"

"I think that there are subtle men, enemies of your House, perhaps, who have trained dogs to attack. There are those large, gray breeds in the north that one might mistake for a wolf. Think of it— everyone afraid of a wolf, and searching for such a beast—no one will notice that the Guarda is distracted from its task, and that the people are more concerned about the savage animal than the more subtle foes around us. I have been considering the matter since I heard the rumors." Raimundo continued to point out various features of the landscape as he spoke, so that those riding behind them would not guess the real object of their conversation.

Ahead there was a stream that ran through this part of the Royal Hunting Preserves, and Don Rolon drew in his Andalusian from a canter to a trot. "Do we cross?"

"Perhaps it would be best to stay on this side, in the open," Raimundo suggested.

"As you wish," the Infante said, and turned his mount away from the stream.

When they had gone a little farther, Raimundo said, "I think you are in some danger, Alteza. I've warned you of it before now. You know that you are being watched and that there are those who do not wish your marriage to take place."

"Yes. And none more than my father, if there were anyone else who would be acceptable to the Doge." His pride was still smarting from the insolent way Gil had treated him that morning at the welcoming of the Austrian Ambassador. Alonzo had seated his bastard at his right hand while placing Rolon at the foot of his dais, where he was required to stand. When the Infante Real had bowed to his father, both Alonzo and Gil had acknowledged it as their due.

"It goes beyond that, mi Infante," Raimundo said grimly.

"Ah, yes. You fear a civil war, as you have told me before. You have explained that to me, and I see the signs you have warned me of. But there are worse things than civil war; there are battles that are waged within the soul." He thought of the homily at Mass that morning, and he shuddered. Padre Juan had been most explicit about the fate of those who turned from God's Word and prostituted themselves—Padre Juan had used the phrase more than once—to the flesh and the Devil.

"Alteza!" Raimundo exclaimed.

"You do not agree with me? There are specters that haunt all of us. I see my father's daughters, and I fear." Five nights ago, the moon had been full, and he had wakened in the garden, his clothes torn and muddied, his appearance worse than it had ever been before. What had he done, that he had wakened there?

"Is there something the matter?" Raimundo asked, making a quick check on the grooms behind them.

"Nothing that was not the matter before," Don Rolon answered, deliberately vague. Padre Lucien has told me that each of us carries his own cross through life, and if that is the case, I am as much touched by that as any man. In any case, the burden must be borne . . . " He slapped the reins down so that his horse bounded ahead, snorting at the sting of the knotted leather.

When Raimundo caught up with Don Rolon, he did not conceal his anger as any other courtier would have done. "You're a rash young fool, Infante, and you must not permit such actions of yourself!" He took advantage of the rising ground to slow both of them to a walk. "The grooms will be up with us soon, and I will not be able to speak to you again for a time. Know this: Gil del Rey has hired men to ambush you as you return from Mass tomorrow morning. They are supposed to wound you, badly if possible, but they are not to kill you. Gil has promised them his aid in securing releases for conversos in the Inquisition's care. For the love of all that's holy, you must be careful now."

"Careful, yes, but I will not be intimidated." As Don Rolon spoke, he wondered if there were any way the men might be provoked to kill him when they attacked. It would be an honorable death, one that would not compromise the treaty España had negotiated with Venezia, and one that the Church could condone.

"Think for a moment!" Raimundo burst out after a desperate glance over his shoulder. "If it is learned that those who ambushed you are conversos or aiding conversos, then there will not be a Jew in all of España, converted or not, who would be safe from the people and the Holy Office. What is being done now to the Protestant Flemings is bad enough, but to house those poor Jews again as well, it could not be tolerated. Venezia has a large and powerful community of Jews on the Isola Ghetto, and they would require that the Doge repudiate the treaty if there were renewed persecutions of Jews by the Inquisition."

"Yes," Don Rolon said unhappily. "And I cannot turn cenobite or anchorite monk, not now. Very well. I will take precautions, as much as I am permitted to do, but I think my father will not want to provide too much for me. My father . . . " He saw the comprehension in Raimundo's eyes and did not continue. "A religious retreat for two or three days—I do not think he could object to that. Would that satisfy you, Raimundo? I must be in Valladolid for the reception next week, but there are three days I might persuade el Rey I need for contemplation." He heard the sound of the groom's horses as they drew near.

"It would not be unwise for you to spend a few solitary days at this . . . portentous time," Raimundo said quickly, then swung his horse around so that there would be room for the men behind them to pass on the trail. "A few days of contemplation and reflection, away from the world, might do you much good."

"Where would you suggest I go?" Don Rolon asked, heedless of the startled expression on the elder groom's face.

"San Juste is the obvious place," Raimundo answered so off-handedly that it was difficult to imagine how intently he had spoken only a moment before. Now he was the consummate courtier, elegant, vaguely unconcerned. "The monks there give excellent spiritual guidance and doubtless would be honored to have you stay with them for a day or so. The Superior there was your grandfather's confessor."

Don Rolon took the tone of his answer from Raimundo's manner. "I will give it my consideration and speak to el Majestad in a day or so. I trust that if he questions me, you will second my request?" He thought briefly of Raimundo's considerable influence with Alonzo and hoped that now it would stand him in good stead. There were many things that el Rey would deny his son out of hand but would grant to the Portuguese Duque. He was occasionally uncertain how he should deal with Raimundo for that very familiarity he had with el Rey, for it was possible that if matters became more difficult than they were, Raimundo might wish to side with Alonzo instead of Rolon, and if that were to happen, the Infante knew he was lost.

"You will not be disappointed in me, Alteza," Raimundo promised him, as if aware of Don Rolon's thoughts. He then pointed away toward the trees where the crushed branches gave testimony to the recent passage of game. "A boar, I think, Alteza. A most dangerous animal. Difficult to hunt, too."

One of the grooms allowed that he liked the boar hunts least of all. "Never know where you are with them. Smart, tricksy beasts with more cunning than temper. I'd rather face a lancer on horseback than a boar at a charge."

"But there are so many dangerous animals, aren't there?" Raimundo added with a quiet emphasis that was intended for Don Rolon and no one else.

"Wolves?" the Infante Real asked with a sad twitch of a smile.

"Among others," Raimundo nodded.

This time Don Rolon remained silent while those words echoed in his troubled mind.

Lugantes was waiting for Don Rolon when he returned from his ride, and he made no attempt to conceal his impatience. He paced the stableyard while Don Rolon unsaddled his gold-and-silver Andalusian, occasionally directing curt remarks to the Infante Real.

"At last!" he cried when Don Rolon gave the halter-lead to the senior stablehand. "I have been looking for you. Eje did not know when you would be back, so I came and waited here."

"I am grateful," Don Rolon said thoughtfully. "What is it, Lugantes?"

"Not here. Come into the orchard. We may speak there, freely." He reached up and tugged at Don Rolon's sleeve, a familiarity that would not be permitted most of the Court but was tolerated in the jester.

"Softly, softly, pequeño. We are observed," Don Rolon said quietly, though he followed Lugantes.

"No one notices dwarves, except to laugh at them. I could hand you the crown, and they would think nothing of it." He was fairly scampering across the flagging toward the nearest gate. "It is urgent, Alteza, or I would not trouble you so."

"Very well." Don Rolon walked faster, and shortly they were in the plantation of almond and apricot trees that grew on the south side of the palace. There were no benches to sit on, but Lugantes found a perch on a fallen branch and Don Rolon leaned back against the trunk of one of the almond trees, one foot braced against it.

The orchard was just coming into flower and there was a light breeze playing through it, bringing the soft scent of the spring hillsides. At the far end of the orchard beehives were set up and even at this distance it was possible to see activity there, a constant movement like a tawny coat stroked by an invisible hand.

"Jacinto was in the pay of Gil del Rey, not the Inquisition. It is Pascual who spies for Padre Juan. I have dismissed him, of course, and he has no choice but to leave. I paid him well for his information, and gave him a cart and a mule so that he could leave the city and make his way somewhere else." As he made this report, Lugantes struck his thigh with his fist.

"Gil? What did he hope to learn? I have known other women—not so obviously, perhaps, but . . . " He frowned. "What did Gil hope to accomplish, do you know?"

"Jacinto said that he wanted to have proof that you are not. . .fit to marry." Lugantes looked away and his olive cheeks turned ruddy.

"Not fit to marry?" Don Rolon repeated. "How, not fit?"

This was more difficult than Lugantes had anticipated, and his words came out in a rush. "He thought that the curse might have made you impotent, so that you could not be a husband to your betrothed. In that case, the marriage would be annulled and then you would not be permitted to have any wife . . . " He stared down at the grass. "You have not yet got Inez with child, and for that he still has hope."

"Veng' a me, Dios," Don Rolon muttered as he rubbed his eyes with one hand. "Won't he ever stop?"

"I don't know, Alteza. But I believe that if he cannot have the Right of Succession, he is determined that you will not have it, either." The flush subsided from his face. "He has very little time, Alteza. He is desperate, and will take more risks as the time of your wedding draws nearer."

"You may well be right, Lugantes," Don Rolon allowed. "He is not a man I would wish to fight, if it were my choice, but it appears that he has already challenged me. I must make preparations."

Lugantes cleared his throat. "Alteza, you must make some provision to protect Inez. Gil may seek to harm her in order to discredit you."

"But how?" Don Rolon asked, not following this new turn of Lugantes' mind.

"He has said that he might hire bravos to waylay her and . . . injure her, so that if she were with child, it would not be certain the child was yours." His small, thick hands twisted in his lap. "Jacinto told one of Gil's servants how to get into her house through the kitchen. As it is, he is trying to frighten her away." He shook his large head mournfully. "You have not had much time to see her, this past week, and she is growing restive."

"How do you mean, frighten her away." Don Rolon asked, not letting himself be distracted by the implied reprimand in Lugantes' last words.

The jester looked up. "There was a large dog circling her house for part of one night, howling. Half the neighborhood was terrified, and Inez said that all her servants wanted to flee, but they were too frightened to leave the house." He looked at Don Rolon strangely. "It was just that one night, when the moon was full, but none of the servants have ventured out at night since then, except Jacinto, who is more afraid of Gil than he is of mad dogs."

"I see." A memory flickered at the corner of his mind, just out of reach, and with it came dread. "A mad dog."

"Inez hid in her bedchamber with the door bolted." Lugantes cleared his throat. "She was afraid that you would try to come to her and be attacked by the beast."

"Was she?" Don Rolon said distantly. "I'm . . . touched by her concern." He made a distracted wave of his hand. "Lugantes, my friend, you have done much for me and I am in your debt—so much in your debt. I pray you, say nothing of this for the time being until I can decide what is best to do. You are worth an army to me if you keep silent on this." He put his hand on the little man's shoulder without condescension.

"You are my prince, Infante." It was all the explanation he could offer, and all that he needed.

"From my soul I thank you," Don Rolon said, and turned to walk out of the orchard.

❦

Ciro Eje jumped visibly as Don Rolon stormed into his quarters, his face darkened, his riding clothes still dusty from the saddle and the orchard. "Alteza," he stammered when he had recovered himself.

Don Rolon reached out, grabbing the front of Ciro's stuffed doublet and all but dragging the valet near. "You tell me," he said with quiet ferocity. "You must tell me!"

"Tell you what, Alteza?" Ciro exclaimed, casting a quick, worried glance toward the door. "You may be observed, Alteza."

"I am always observed," Don Rolon said bitterly, but it brought him back to his senses, and he released Ciro. With an effort, he was able to speak almost calmly. "There is a matter, an urgent matter of utmost importance. Do you understand me?" He kept his voice low but could not conceal the intensity of his emotions; he began to walk up and down the small room. "I have been told that there is a wolf running loose in the city. Duque Raimundo Dominguez suspects that someone is training large hunting dogs, teaching them to attack men and thereby spread dissension. But he is not correct, is he? Well?"

Ciro lowered his head, knowing what was coming. He crossed himself as he listened. "Alteza."

"It is not a hunting dog, but a wolf that runs through Valladolid when the moon is full. Isn't it? Isn't it?" He stopped in front of Ciro and stared at the valet. "Is it true? A wolf runs in Valladolid?"

"You may be overheard, Alteza," Ciro whispered. "It is difficult enough to conceal what . must be concealed without having such questions shouted to the winds and made . . . " He pointed to the door. "If they do not tell each other, they will tell that pious bastard Padre Juan. Contain yourself, Alteza, if you value your life and soul. Please."

Don Rolon stepped back, aghast. Ciro had not denied it, and what little hope he had nurtured within him failed. He had asked and indirectly been answered. "A wolf. Is that what happens?"

"We will discuss it later, Alteza, when we may be more private." Ciro took a shambling step toward the door, moving like an old man for all his youth. "Those of us who are conversos and the children of conversos learn to hold our tongues and our thoughts, Alteza. Best take a lesson from me now, if you can. It is folly to do otherwise, with the Holy Office so zealous in its duties." He said it simply, as if addressing a wounded man battling pain. "After the evening meal, while court is being held, meet me privately and I promise I will then answer your questions."

"And in the meantime you will invent lies to tell me?" the Infante Real challenged.

"No, Alteza. I will invent lies to tell, yes, but to tell them"——he cocked his head toward the door with a fatalistic look—"not you. Your behavior must be explained or . . . you will not want to answer the questions they ask, and you will not like the manner in which they ask them."

Don Rolon wiped his face with a trembling hand. "It is true." He looked toward the narrow window, but did not see the little courtyard and garden beyond. "I had thought it was beastliness, a madness like the lunatics endure, or an affliction like my sisters suffer. But it is worse."

"Alteza," Ciro insisted, exasperated. "You must keep silent. Stroll in the park or have wine and cakes or talk with Padre Lucien, or play at dice with Don Enrique, but do not say anything more now. For the sake of your good Saint, if not yourself." He put his hand on Don Rolon's shoulders in much the same way the Infante had put his on Lugantes' shoulder. "You must be cautious. Your safety depends on it."

"Yes. Of course. You are right." He moved away from the window and went toward the door, where he paused and said with the lightness of complete despair, "I will take a turn around the old garden, I suppose. I don't think I could eat. What can I gain from dice? What could I say to Padre Lucien?"

"Then let me give your excuses. I will tell them that you are having bridegroom's nerves, Alteza, and it will be accepted, perhaps joked over. They will enjoy thinking that your wedding means so much. The Venezians will be delighted." He offered this as the scant comfort he knew it was.

"Bridegroom." Don Rolon said the word stupidly. "How can I marry now, with this on my soul? I knew my blood was tainted, but this—" He lifted his hands in helpless resignation, then reached to open the door. "Bridegroom. You do not know how that word sounds to me." He turned abruptly and almost ran into the assistant chamberlain who was hovering a few steps down the hall. The man gave an embarrassed cough and bowed before hurrying off. Don Rolon watched him go with sickened eyes. "To whom does he report?"

"I don't know. I suspect he is one of el Rey's men," Ciro answered quietly.

"Do you think he overheard?"

"A portion. If he had . . . learned the worst, he would not have been here. Let me attend to him, Alteza."

"But—"

"Have your walk. I will find you in the old garden after the evening meal. That will be two or three hours after sunset." Ciro tried to find some words of reassurance, and could not.

Don Rolon swallowed hard. "I will be there."

The old garden was to the north of the long, cypress-lined avenue that ran from the palace to the monastery church of San Domingo. The waning moon hung in the east and Don Rolon stood in the garden staring up at it, fascinated by its hugeness. He leaned against a statue of San Diego, as if taking strength from the Saint and the stone.

"Alteza."

"Even tonight it draws me. I have been trying for the last hour to recall those nights when . . . I can feel the beast stretch and scratch within me, and I long to run. My thighs tremble to run." He said it softly, dreamily, the cold, pale light dappling down on his young features through the branches of the cypress, hiding his face one moment and subtly transforming it with shadows the next. "I thought it was the other, the madness that is the birthright of all Spanish Hapsburgs. So many of us are . . . crazed in one way or another. I was cursed in the womb, and I have feared that it was with mania. But it is the other."

Ciro came a few steps closer, moving as if he approached a

frightened animal. "You truly did not know?"

"Not until today. Perhaps I have suspected. You see, I . . . don't remember much. You have said once or twice that my face was hard to look on, and I thought it was because of the blood and bruises that I thought came with the madness. But that was not it, was it?" For the first time, he looked directly at his valet.

"No, Alteza, it was not that," was Ciro's subdued answer. "And you have known what it was, haven't you?"

There was little anger left in him, but what there was of it was apparent now. His black eyes brightened and his long, sallow features set in rigid lines.

"At first it was only a suspicion, but when the rumors began among the servants and in the marketplace, then I began to fear that it truly was . . . what it is, Alteza." There had been times before when he had considered broaching the matter, but as long as he was not certain, he could not bring himself to torment Don Rolon in that way.

"Buen Dios y Jesus," the Infante said in a whisper. "What am I to do?"

"Whatever is necessary," Ciro answered, although he knew the question was not directed at him.

"Necessary?" Don Rolon burst out. "It is necessary that I die and fall to burn in Hell forever. That is necessary. I should find a mountain gorge and throw myself down it, so that my bones would never be found and my name forgotten forever. Damned as I am, what matter now, if I take my own life?"

Ciro's face filled with alarm. "Alteza, you cannot—"

"Why? Because of the treaty? Because of my father? Because of my House? Because of the Church? Because of God?" Don Rolon flung the questions at him like stones. "Because of Venezia? What is my soul, my anguish, compared to peace with Venezia?" His voice subsided to a rough quiet. "What do I tell my bride, when she comes? That I am transformed when the moon is full? That I may fill her with cubs instead of children?"

Ciro held up his hand to stop the accusations. "Alteza, you need say nothing."

"Even to my confessor? How can I confess again, ever, with this on my soul? What do I say to Padre Lucien when he asks what my sins are that have offended God?"

"Nothing." Ciro let his answer hang between them. "You will confess as you have always done, of how you lie with Inez, of how you swear in the Name of God when it is wrong to do so, of your doubts and questions. If it is true you are damned—and it may not be so, Alteza—then it will not matter that your confessions are not perfect. You may make ammends now." His black eyes brightened and his long, sallow features set in rigid lines.

"At first it was only a suspicion, but when the rumors began among the servants and in the marketplace, then I began to fear that it truly was . . . what it is, Alteza." There had been times before when he had considered broaching the matter, but as long as he was not certain, he could not bring himself to torment Don Rolon in that way.

"Buen Dios y Jesus," the Infante said in a whisper. "What am I to do?"

"Whatever is necessary," Ciro answered, although he knew the question was not directed at him.

"Necessary?" Don Rolon burst out. "It is necessary that I die and fall to burn in Hell forever. That is necessary. I should find a mountain gorge and throw myself down it, so that my bones would never be found and my name forgotten forever. Damned as I am, what matter now, if I take my own life?"

Ciro's face filled with alarm. "Alteza, you cannot—"

"Why? Because of the treaty? Because of my father? Because of my House? Because of the Church? Because of God?" Don Rolon flung the questions at him like stones. "Because of Venezia? What is my soul, my anguish, compared to peace with Venezia?" His voice subsided to a rough quiet. "What do I tell my bride, when she comes? That I am transformed when the moon is full? That I may fill her with cubs instead of children?"

Ciro held up his hand to stop the accusations. "Alteza, you need say nothing."

"Even to my confessor? How can I confess again, ever, with this on my soul? What do I say to Padre Lucien when he asks what my sins are that have offended God?"

"Nothing." Ciro let his answer hang between them. "You will confess as you have always done, of how you lie with Inez, of how you swear in the Name of God when it is wrong to do so, of your doubts and questions. if it is true you are damned—and it may not be so, Alteza—then it will not matter that your confessions are not perfect. You may take Communion without perjuring yourself because God has read your heart and knows your tribulations, and will show you mercy. But there are those who will not be as forgiving, and they are nearer at hand. You must not give Padre Juan Murador the least excuse to invite you to his domain. His cure for anything from imbecility to witchcraft is the strappado and rack, which may release the soul from your body, but not the wolf. Alteza, think! You must live, and you must keep your Right as Infante Real and heir."

"Or there will be civil war? Yes, I have heard this. And it may be so." He turned away from the moon at last. He was haggard now, and walked heavily, motioning to his valet to follow him. "Perhaps there should be a war. If I fell in battle, there would be no complaint. My cousin Otto would be made Infante Real and the Emperor would ask no concessions from my father."

"And if you rode to battle and were not killed, and the moon turned full, what then?" Ciro inquired sternly.

Don Rolon paused, closed his eyes and shuddered with revulsion. "Gil would be willing, I think, to take advantage of any confusion to make an end of me, whatever . . . my form." Never before had he been grateful for his half brother's enmity.

"That would not settle the matter," Ciro said as he moved ahead of Don Rolon so that he could open the side gate for him.

"No, perhaps not. If my father ever learned of it . . . " He shrugged. "A monastery, if it were remote enough, might afford me protection if, not peace. Or a voyage to the New World. It would not be difficult to be lost there." He stopped before the half-open gate. "But it would not be permitted, would it?—now that I am to be married." His face was shiny in the moonlight. "0 God, what sin, what crime?" The curse, he had been told all his life, was to be visited on the innocent, so perhaps the fault did not lie with him. There was no consolation in this, for he could not bring himself to accept it. If there was guilt, it was his and his alone; he could not be a beast without guilt.

"Alteza, we must not linger. We will attract attention." Ciro bit his lower lip as the Infante Real passed through the gate and out of the old garden.

"Of course," Don Rolon said in a constricted tone. "I am always watched."

"We will guard you."

"We?" Don Rolon asked. "I fear I am lost." He lifted his hand to cross himself, hesitated, then with a miserable sigh completed the blessing.

Ciro closed and barred the gate, then followed the Infante Real into the palace.

Part II

April 1565 through August 1565

12

"It was a most sumptuous occasion," Nobile Rigonzetti said to his secretary, and waited while the man scrawled his words on a parchment sheet. "While it is true that these Spaniards are a most . . . dignified and sober court"—that was better than saying that they were pious, proud and dull, he decided—"nonetheless, their anticipation of this union is most sincere, and they undoubtedly welcome our treaties and pacts of trade as well as the joining of the great Houses of Patrecipazio and Hapsburg." He pursed his lips. "What have I left out?"

His secretary looked up. "The Infante? Do you wish to mention him?"

"Ah, Gennaro, you are my salvation. It must be said most precisely, I think, so that we give the proper impression of the lad.' He fingered his neat, crimped beard. "Let me see . . . " He walked the length of the room and came back. "The Infante Real, who showed us honor by wearing garments of Venezian silk, is a thoughtful and considerate prince. He paid proper respect to our musicians and complimented our cooks for the superior meal they served for his reception. It has been rumored that he has become a trifle nervous as his wedding day approaches, though he also expresses himself with elegance on the matter of his bride, whom he has assured me he will hold in suitable reverence. His manner is grave, but that is the manner of the Spanish Court, and for all his reserve, he has the reputation of being well-liked." He waited while Gennaro caught up with him. "Do you think that's enough?"

"Possibly," Gennaro said, who had learned long since to take his tone from his employer. "It might be wise to mention the retreat."

"Yes." Nobile sighed. "These Spaniards, with their constant religious practices. Zaretta will not like it if her bride-groom visits monasteries more often than he visits her. Wait!" He held up his index finger. "I have it. Ecco. I have learned from the Portuguese diplomat, Raimundo Dominguez y Mara, Duque da Minho, that the Infante plans to make a religious retreat shortly before his bride arrives. It is not unusual for the nobles of España to prepare themselves for marriage with a short time of prayer and reflection. Dominguez y Mara, who is in the confidence of the Infante Real, says that the youth is deeply impressed with the importance of this wedding and wishes to be of a committed and tranquil mind when he meets his bride at the altar." He thought about it. "Read it back to me when you are finished."

Gennaro nodded as he wrote. When he had the words down, he read through the letter, pausing now and again when Nobile held up his hand to consider again what he had said.

"Yes," was his conclusion. "I believe that it will do."

"Shall I seal it?" Gennaro asked, reaching for the wax and the candle.

"No. Not yet. There may be others in the mission—Renato, for instance—who may wish to add their observations to it before we prepare to give it to the Herald." Nobile looked down at his heavy signet ring with the arms of Rigonzetti cut deeply into the stone. "We must make the best of this awkward alliance, Gennaro. The Spaniards need our ships and we need their trade routes and their arms. We also need more strength to deal with Gustav, may God damn his pernicious soul. He has already attempted to take over Milano, and Venezia may well be next unless this treaty is firm. Still, I would not wish Zaretta's fate on any friend's daughter."

"It may be that after there are one or two heirs, Alonzo will permit her to spend part of her time in Venezia." Gennaro threw this out as the crumb it was.

"He has never allowed his wife to return to France, though he has not been husband to her for several years. If the rumors are correct." Nobile steepled his hands together. "The truce is necessary to us."

"But surely the Doge's niece will not have to live like a nun.

From what I have been told, Genevieve does not." Gennaro sniggered unpleasantly.

"Even if that is true," Nobile said quietly, "it is no credit of those of us here on sufferance, to repeat such gossip." "But I have seen—" Gennaro protested.

"And so have I," Nobile said less harshly. "It is best to remain silent." He looked up as he heard a sharp rap on the door. "Is anyone expected?"

"Not for more than an hour," Gennaro said as he rose to answer.

"Very curious," Nobile murmured. "Open it."

Gennaro was already at the door, and he obeyed with alacrity. He blinked at the man there, and gave a confused gesture to Nobile. "Ambassador Rigonzetti, it is the jester."

Nobile stared at the little man. "You have come . . . to see me?"

Lugantes nodded and bowed properly. "Yes, Señor Rigonzetti, I have." He came into the room and looked at the two Venezians with a critical eye. "I trust that I am doing a praiseworthy thing in coming here, but I am not yet certain of it."

This intrigued Nobile, who indicated one of the low padded benches by the window. "How can I tell you that until I know the reason for your visit?"

"You can't," Lugantes answered curtly. "I must try." He went and hoisted himself onto the bench and folded his legs, tailor-fashion, under him. "You are the one who keeps the Doge informed of all that happens here, aren't you?"

"That is one of my duties, yes," was Nobile's urbane answer. Covertly he motioned to Gennaro to have him withdraw from the room.

"Good." Lugantes folded his arms. "I have not discussed this with my confessor or anyone else. You are the only one to hear it."

Gennaro bowed slightly. "In that case, I will leave you." "Very good," said Nobile. "I will call you when you are wanted."

"As you wish." He went quickly to the side door, let himself through it and took up his post immediately behind it.

"Now then . . . uh, Lugantes? Is that the name?" Nobile ventured. "Yes."

"What is it you want of me?" He sat in an attitude of great attention, his blue eyes fixed on Lugantes' dark ones.

"I believe there are a few matters of which you are not aware," Lugantes began, his formality masking the difficulty he was having now that he actually addressed the Venezian Ambassador. "You are aware that el Rey has a bastard son—"

"It would be difficult not to be," Nobile interrupted. "He is called Gil del Rey, I believe."

"That is the man. He has great ambitions, that one, and he is determined that the Infante Real should not wed. I warn you of this because I have heard rumors, many of them dreadful, that impugn Don Rolon's honor and legitimacy and manhood. You will hear them soon enough if they have not reached you already." He scrutinized Nobile's handsome face and saw only bland attentiveness. "Well. I wanted you to be aware of the source of these rumors so that you would not suddenly worry that your Doge had made a poor bargain with el Rey. I know that the Infante Real is not of a . . . a lighthearted disposition, but he is a good man, and one who will do his duty to his House and his wife."

"You must be concerned to tell me this." Nobile was more interested in this answer than in the previous information. His own spies had already informed him of Gil's attempts to discredit Don Rolon; what caught his curiosity was that Lugantes should bother to speak to him of it.

Lugantes made bulky little fists of his hands. "There are few at Court who are the Infante's friends, though many of them are professing friendship now that it appears he will rule one day. They do not know him. They do not wish to understand him. All they look for is largesse when his time comes." Lugantes was distressed to say this, but he kept on. "And there is the Church. You know that the Spanish are a devout people. Don Rolon is a faithful son of the Church and deeply dedicated to the Church, but he does not always . . . see the necessity of punishing those who . . . "

"Are you trying to tell me that he opposes the burning of Flemish Protestants?" Nobile had been aware of this since the day after he arrived, but knew it was a dangerous opinion for anyone to hold in Valladolid.

"Yes," Lugantes said quietly. "He has said so, and has been willing to risk his own position for the benefit of those he believes are wrongly condemned." It was dangerous to say so much to this man, who might turn the information against Don Rolon, but he wanted Rigonzetti to hear it without the twists that might be given to it by others.

"You have taken a risk yourself, Lugantes." Nobile studied the dwarf.

"Not as much as you think," he answered with a bitter laugh. "I am a jester. I say outrageous things every day. No one will notice one or two more."

"Still, it took courage for you to come here. Is it so important to you that your Infante be reported accurately?" His inclination was to trust the little man and add whatever he learned from him to the letter he had been writing.

"It is. Don Rolon has always been . . . kind to me. I do not wish to serve him a bad turn for that kindness. If you believe half of what you may hear whispered here, you will decide that the Infante is not capable of keeping the terms of the treaty or his marriage, and he is not such a man." He looked around uneasily. "I cannot remain much longer, or it will be remarked upon. Gil is annoyed with me already—"

"Why is that?" Nobile interrupted again.

"Oh, I . . . argued with one of his servants." He had no intention of discussing the spy Jacinto with the Venezian Ambassador, for it would lead to questions about Inez that he did not want to answer.

"I see. Gil del Rey is not one to forgive such insolence?" He wanted to goad Lugantes into an impulsive answer, but the jester had been given far worse insults regularly and hardly noticed this one.

"He calls it that. It is his right to do so." Lugantes paused. "I hope I have done well by mi Infante, to speak to you. He will say nothing, I know that, and you may not have an opportunity to inquire closely."

"But that is what the Doge expects me to do," Nobile said quietly. "And what you have told me will aid me in giving a correct report. Do not be worried, Lugantes; you have done well by Don Rolon."

"Then may Heaven bless you," Lugantes said as he scrambled down from the bench. "1 will not speak to you again except in jest. I hope you understand why. And if I am asked why I came here, I will say that I wished to know more of what Venezians find amusing, so that I might better serve the Infante's bride."

Nobile grinned. "I fear I have underestimated you, Lugantes."

The jester smiled in return. "Others have done the same, Ambassador Rigonzetti. Most of them never realize it." He bowed deeply and strode to the door.

When the jester was gone, Nobile rose from the bench and stood in the center of his room, a measuring look in his eyes. He was beginning to wonder now why Padre Juan Murador wished to speak to him later.

Raimundo gave an impatient shake of his head. "No, Alteza, I cannot and I will not support your attempt to abdicate, not for any reason." He was superbly elegant this evening, preparing for a full procession that would mark the annual reception of Envoys and Ambassadors to the Spanish Crown.

"I do not believe that I will serve España as I would wish to." Don Rolon had a brief urge to tell Raimundo the truth and be freed of the burden of knowing what he had become, but he could not bring himself to speak.

"And who do you think will do it better?" Raimundo demanded with a scowl. "Do you think Otto would do as well? He knows nothing of this country and the people and has never shown the, least interest in it. He is pledged to Austria, mi Infante, and would not be accepted by anyone in España except the self-seeking courtiers, who would embrace a Barbary ape if it would bring them favor." He came close to Don Rolon and lowered his voice. "You cannot continue to behave this way, Alteza. Word will get back to those who do not love you, and they will shape your apprehensions to their advantage. You cannot do this, for your own protection."

"I am pleased to know that you are concerned for my welfare," Don Rolon said stiffly. "But what do you care for my peace of mind?"

"Peace of mind is not a benefit of royalty, Alteza. For that, we must trust to God and try to serve Him well." Raimundo crossed himself. "Speak to your confessor, Don Rolon, and pray for guidance."

"And God will hear me." He dared not reveal in his stance or inflection how hopeless he had become. "Padre Lucien has already reminded me of my obligations and responsibilities, and I do not wish to shirk them. However, I do not wish to undertake a task I cannot accomplish."

Raimundo lost some of the severity of his manner. "Who among us knows that he will achieve his ends? We strive, and do what we may toward our goals, but the rest is in the lap of Heaven." He permitted himself the familiarity of touching the Infante Real's shoulder. "You show me, through these searching questions, that you are truly worthy of your rank and position. One who treated his duties lightly would show himself to be unable to fulfill them."

There seemed to be a vise closing deep inside Don Rolon. His chest ached and his eyes felt hot. "Raimundo," he said quietly, using the man's given name which he had done few times in his life. "Listen to me. I know that you seek what is best for España and I am humbled to think that you have such great faith in me, but I tell you that to govern would be the most dreadful burden I have ever carried."

"That is the way with authority. To those truly capable of using it well, it is not an easy task. You do not have the makings of a despot in you." Raimundo faced Don Rolon squarely. "You are Infante Real, which gives you the Right, and for that I am sworn to defend the Succession. There is more, however. You are one who would bring greater justice to this country, and that alone makes you unlike the others who have a claim to the throne. Don Rolon, if you have any feeling for your people, don't abandon them to the predations of foxes and jackals."

"Predations. A curious way to put it." Don Rolon looked past Raimundo toward the painting on the far wall. It showed the soldiers coming to Gethsemane to arrest Jesus. The soldiers were massed and formidably armed, weapons and clothing more fitting to the previous century than the ancient world; Jesus, in a shapeless garment, knelt amid flowering trees, oblivious to the danger that approached.

"It would be no less than that. Your uncle wants to add power to the Holy Roman Empire, and what better way than through our explorations and expeditions?" Neither man noticed that Raimundo had said our: in matters of this sort, Raimundo was as much a Spaniard as he was a Portuguese.

"I know that, Raimundo." Don Rolon lowered his head. "I have asked to be permitted a retreat, and my father has granted me a few days to myself. In two weeks, I will leave for Santa Clara. The monks there have agreed to give me a cell to myself for five days." One of those days would be the night of the full moon. He hoped to be able to keep himself locked in, so that he would do no one, including himself, harm. "You said that you could not turn monk now," Raimundo reminded him.

"No, but I will find a little solitude before it becomes impossible for me to breathe alone." He had yet to determine how he would manage the public demands of his rank. He had tried to think of an explanation for his absences that would cause no questions to be asked, but none had yet occurred to him.

"I must leave you, Alteza," Raimundo said, cutting into Don Rolon's thoughts. "I thank God for you. If ever you need my aid, you may be sure that my sword, my honor and my life are at your service."

"So great an offer," Don Rolon said quietly. "Let us hope, Dominguez, that I never have need of any of them."

"Amen to that, Alteza." He bowed himself out of the room and hurried away to the ceremony. His concern for the Infante Real had to be set aside for the time being while he attended to the rituals of Court life.

❦

Padre Barnabas faced Padre Lucien across the simple plank table of the San Guittiere rectory. "It is good of you to join me, Padre. Frey Estaneslao will bring you whatever you wish to taste. The wine is very good—we make our own."

"A blessed thing to do; Our Lord made His own, too." It was a feeble joke and one that would ordinarily have given Padre Barnabas some offense, but this was not an ordinary meeting, and so he chuckled to show his appreciation.

"An apt observation. It might serve for a homily, one day. You French are more witty than we Spaniards, I fear." He motioned to the monk who hovered near the table. "We will have wine and wheaten cakes, Frey Estaneslao. If it is possible, see that we are not disturbed."

The young monk bowed and moved away from the two older men. The wine and cakes were already waiting, and once he had put them out, he had been instructed to stay near at hand and listen closely to what the two priests said.

"I have heard that you are encouraging the Infante Real to take this retreat he seems determined to have, in spite of the opposition of certain members of the court."

"Why, yes. He is a most serious young man, as you must have learned at El Morro, for that reason, I believe that it is beneficial to his soul to have a little time to himself before he embarks on the rigors of marriage and the greater demands that will befall him." He folded his hands. "We Premonstratensians leave more to the individual conscience than you Dominicans."

"Well, perhaps San Norbert lived in less harrowing times than San Domingo. You are not chartered for the elimination of heresy, as we are." Padre Barnabas could not keep from sounding critical as he said this. He had a contempt for Orders that were not as militant as his own.

"Pablo and Mateo found faith in different ways," Padre Lucien said quietly. "It is for God to inspire and for us to guide." He looked up as Frey Estaneslao put down a tray with a jug of wine, two cups and a plate of cakes before them. "Thank you for this service, Frey."

"It is for the love of Christ," the monk answered, and moved away.

Padre Barnabas gritted his teeth. "Perhaps, since you are a guest here, you would want to pronounce the blessing?"

"That is most gracious of you, Padre Barnabas," said Padre Lucien, and proceeded to make the sign of the cross over their refreshments. "In the Name of the Father, Son and Holy Spirit, we praise and give thanks for nourishment in body and soul."

Such a mild statement annoyed Padre Barnabas, but he took up one of the cakes and broke it in four parts before taking a bite. "You have not been in España long, have you, Padre?"

"Not very long, no." He could not help but wonder where this was leading, but he was not foolish enough to challenge Padre Barnabas for an explanation.

"It may seem strange to you, after France and Hanover." This was not quite a question. Padre Barnabas reached for the jug and poured wine into their two cups, giving himself somewhat less than he gave his guest.

"The country is more . . . austere than any I have encountered before, but there can be no doubt," he went on with a forced enthusiasm, "that the people of España are most devout."

"That is the Will of God, and the source of our prosperity." He lifted his cup and drank, encouraging Padre Lucien to do the same. "In Hanover, you were close to the Emperor Gustav, were you?"

Padre Lucien gave a self-deprecatory laugh. "I saw him a few times and he once attended Mass in our church, but it was hardly a frequent thing. I doubt I have heard more than a dozen words from his lips." He tasted the wine. "Very good," he said, but thought that the wines of his homeland were better, more tasty and satisfying than this vintage.

"A great honor, in any case." Padre Barnabas wanted to shake his fellow prelate but knew that would not get him the information he desired. "A rare opportunity, then, for you of all men to be sent here to be confessor to the Infante Real."

"As to that," Padre Lucien said when he had had more of the wine, "it was an accident of sorts. The Emperor spoke to my bishop, asking him to recommend a priest for Don Rolon, and wanted to know which of those under his authority were noted for the instruction of young men. In the end, names were presented to the Emperor. There were four of us. I don't know why I was chosen over the others, but so it was."

"Your good angel, it seems, has you in his special care." Padre Barnabas tried not to sound too skeptical.

"If it is so, then I am deeply grateful for such protection. I have recommended my soul into the keeping of the Saints and the Church, as all priests must do if they are to fulfill their calling." He took a piece of the cake and bit into it; it was crunchier than he liked, but he had found that this was often the way of breads in España.

There was nothing in what Padre Lucien said that Padre Barnabas could cavil with, and so he tried another approach. "You are closer to the Infante Real than any of the rest of us . . . ."

"Well, you were with him at El Morro," Padre Lucien said mildly.

"That is not the same as years of confession. It is true that the seal is upon those moments, as is only proper for such devotion, but you may say if you believe the Infante has shown himself to be in a proper spiritual state of mind for the changes that are coming into his life." He was skirting the edge with such a question, but he hoped that his high position with the Holy Office would have its own persuasion with the French priest.

"I believe I may say that he is aware of the needs of the soul as well as the body and that he is faithful to the Church." He was less comradely, for he thought that Padre Barnabas had overstepped the mark with such a question.

"I would not have asked, but while we were at El Morro, I had occasion to hear him and I noticed that he was of a somber turn of mind, but I have feared that he might be in the grips of despair, which is against the wishes of God. Those who are living virtuous lives need have no concern for their well-being." He poured them both more wine, again being more generous with Padre Lucien.

"If Don Rolon were a young merchant, then your doubts might be well-founded, but he is heir to the throne of the most powerful and rich empire on earth. It is just as well that he be of a careful nature, for to have a capricious or frivolous man Infante Real must be a misfortune for España." He drank more of the wine and decided that he truly did not like the taste of it.

"Your point is well-taken," Padre Barnabas agreed reluctantly. He was not achieving the ends he wished for. "His companion there, Don Enrique, is a sot. To see Don Rolon in such company must make every sensible man doubt—"

"But surely you know that Don Rolon's companions were not his choice? They were appointed by el Rey to accompany him because they were not closely connected." Padre Lucien set his wine cup aside. "It was the intention of Alonzo to separate Don Rolon from his usual associates"—Padre Lucien had been troubled by that, since he knew as well as anyone that Don Rolon was in the society of very few courtiers—"so that he could learn the ways of the world from them."

Padre Barnabas had been given a slightly different explana-tion of the journey, but kept what he had heard to himself. He was annoyed to see that Padre Lucien was taking no more wine or finished what was in his cup. It would not be pleasant to tell Padre Juan that he had learned so little. "Then this retreat—does he go in company?"

"His valet accompanies him. Since he will be at a monastery, there is no reason for me to go with him, and he has asked that he be permitted to travel without escort. El Rey has not allowed that, of course, but he has ordered that the soldiers who go with him are to stay at the nearest castle."

"A great concession for Majestad," said Padre Barnabas, pleased that he had one snippet of information for his superiors. "And rather foolish of the Infante Real, don't you think?"

Padre Lucien rose. "Don Rolon is not a fool, Padre Barnabas. He is a most considerate youth. You were most kind to offer me your hospitality and the hospitality of the monks here. I will remember you most particularly in my prayers."

Short of physical restraint, there was nothing Padre Barnabas could do to detain the French priest any longer. He said the proper phrases and escorted his guest to the door, all the while hoping that his lack of success—he could not quite call it a failure—with Padre Lucien would not be regarded with too much disfavor; he did not want to find himself ministering to a village of peasants in some remote part of the Sierra Morena, which had been the fate of more than one familiar of the Holy Office who did not give the Inquisitors what they wanted. Unbidden, a second, more troublesome notion arose—a village in the Sierra Morena was far, far preferable to a cell in Valladolid. He now regretted his decision to ask Frey Estaneslao to listen to his conversation with Padre Lucien, for he would report his observations and there would be no way that Padre Barnabas might put his information in a better light than it was. With these reflections for company, Padre Barnabas sat down at the table and finished the wine.

13

Santa Clara was located at the end of a narrow, steep valley in the ridge of mountains between Penaranda and Avila. The monks who lived there were of the Ambrosian Order, and much given to chanting and study. They gathered twice a day for meals and prayer; the rest of the time they spent in private worship, in copying music and religious texts, or in reading the inspirational writings in their extensive library. Their food was supplied by three little villages, for they did not work the land.

Don Rolon was given a retreat away from the main buildings of the monastery. It was set back against the hillside, near a swift-running brook that kept the Infante Real awake for the first night and lulled him after that. There were three small rooms in the retreat and Ciro established himself in the littlest of them, setting out those few items that he insisted he must have to give Don Rolon and his simple garments proper care.

For the first two days, Don Rolon rambled the hills or sat alone by himself, his gaze turned more inward than out. He spoke only to the priest who heard his confession.

"Alteza," said Ciro on the morning of the third day. "Are you well?"

"The moon will be full tonight, Ciro," Don Rolon answered grimly. "Are you prepared?"

"I pray that I am." He sighed. "Are you certain that this is what you wish to do? I will keep my word, but you know that I have reservations."

"Yes, I know that." Don Rolon put his hand to his forehead. "If this is not . . . successful, then I must find other ways. Barred windows and a stout, bolted door should be adequate. Remember, when the moon has been up for an hour, pay no heed to anything I say, or the sounds you may hear. If I beg or promise or beseech you, do not swerve from your purpose. I don't want the monks here to have their hospitality repaid by turning a ravening beast loose among them." He cleared his throat. "Ciro, if this does not work, as I think it must, then it would be best if there be an accident. Dominguez keeps warning me of those who are eager to do me harm. If I run wild tonight, I want you to do nothing to stop them. Do you understand?"

"I understand." Ciro looked away.

"But you do not agree." Don Rolon knew that evasive manner and though he respected it, he often found it impertinent, as he did now.

"I have said so before. I will do as you order me, Alteza, but I do not like what you require and I will not do one jot more than I must to follow your instructions." He picked up the large crucifix from the top of the chest by his cot. "I will see that this is put on the door, and I will put holy water in vials around the window before sunset. I don't know what good it will do, but it is better than nothing."

Don Rolon made a gesture of resignation and assent. "You are a good and faithful servant, Ciro, and what I have asked of you no master has the right to ask. But there is no one else I may turn to." That admission chilled him, though it was wholly the truth. If he had not had Ciro to assist him, he was convinced that he would now be in the hands of the Holy Office, answering Padre Juan's questions while the men of the Secular Arm broke his limbs. He had seen enough of their work in the ruined men and women led to the stake. He could not comfort himself with lies about their treatment of distinguished persons, for he had seen Obispo Teodoro Lazrez bumed with fifty other condemned heretics less than two months before. If the Holy Office would subject one of their own high-ranking prelates to such a fate, they would not hesitate to bum the heir to the throne.

"I think you do not appreciate your true friends, Alteza," Ciro said quietly.

"Oh, there are those who would shield me from my father, no doubt. But from Padre Juan?" He stared out of his retreat into the morning. It was misty still, and the valley was green. In these sheltered places, wild flowers grew, showing their shy beauty to deer and foxes. Near the brook, mossy rocks clustered in a hollow, making a perfect setting for a nymph or water sprite, though the only creature to visit it recently was a badger that had come to drink. Don Rolon walked quietly through the beauty of it, his mind seizing on the serenity and loveliness of the place, making it an anodyne for the torment in his soul.

Ciro watched Don Rolon for a little while, then went back to his preparations. He still wished that the Infante had agreed to let Ciro bring him a lamb or piglet, anything he might leave in the Infante's cell that night so that the . . . wolf would not be driven mad with hunger. Don Rolon had objected, saying that there might be too many questions asked if there were much of a mess in the retreat come moming. Ciro suspected that Don Rolon did not wish to see for himself what the wolf was capable of doing. Although he made a show of being religious, Ciro was not usually very devout, but that afternoon, as the sun dropped behind the mountains and the shadows announced the coming of night, he prayed humbly and sincerely, not only for his own protection but for the protection of his prince, who was in much greater need than the valet.

Frey Camilo was much shocked at the appearance of the Infante Real when he came to the chapel the next moming for Mass.

"Alteza!" he exclaimed, and then did his best to be more at ease. "What has happened to you?"

Don Rolon took a deep, uneven breath. "You may well ask, Frey Camilo." He and Ciro had improvised an acceptable story half an hour before, and Don Rolon decided that he would tell it now. "There is a large dog, a wild one, I think, who has been prowling about my retreat. Last night he attempted to break in. Doubtless he smelled the food left from our evening meal."

"A dog?" Frey Camilo asked, recalling the snarls and howls he had heard in the night. Then the monks had gathered in the chapel and prayed for protection from the Devil, for they knew as well as any clerics in España that at the full of the moon, the Devil and his worshipers went abroad in the land.

"It would seem so," was Don Rolon's response. "When the animal would not leave us alone, I determined to chase it off, or have a shot at it. I dropped my lantem in my pursuit, and, as you see, bruised myself and scraped my hands." He held them up for Frey Camilo to inspect his torn nails and scraped palms.

"God be thanked that there was no worse done than this," Frey Camilo said, crossing himself. "If the animal was a wild dog, you are fortunate that he did not tum on you." He paused, then plunged ahead, "But if the creature was of the Devil, then you were not merely brave but very foolish to venture after it, and it must be that Heaven has you in its care that you fared no worse than you did. Bruises and scrapes will heal, Alteza, but the mark of the Devil never leaves the soul."

Don Rolon looked away. "So we are taught, good Frey, and so it must be.- He genuflected before the altar and took his place in the chapel.

The monks who sang the service that moming could not keep their minds entirely on the ritual, for all of them were fascinated at the appearance of the Infante Real. Although he knew it was not proper to do so, Frey Camilo whispered some of Don Rolon's tale to Frey Valentin, who passed it on to Frey Blaz. By the *Agnus Dei*, all but two of the monks had heard of the Infante's exploits, which had improved in the telling. It was understood that a pack of maddened hounds, sent by the Devil to harass the monks of Santa Clara and kill Don Rolon, had fled before the outraged prince who had pursued them with the aid of San Jorge and San Ambrosio himself, who defended the Infante Real when he fell and was at the mercy of the Devil's monsters. The monks peeked and peered at the exhausted young man with awe and some little delight—it was the most exciting thing that had happened to their monastery since its founding. Clearly, it was the Will of God that this virtuous youth should triumph over the Devil and reign as a saintly man when at last he came to the throne.

But Don Rolon was not aware of this; and had he been, he would have been at pains to stop the story. Credulous monks in an isolated monastery might be convinced of his goodness by that recital, but the officers of the Inquisition were less gullible, and would want to look more closely into the event before they were satisfied.

"We are all most grateful to God for delivering you from your danger," Frey Blaz said to Don Rolon as they left the chapel at the end of Mass.

Puzzled by this emotional remark, Don Rolon gave a careful answer: "As am I, most truly."

"He has great humility," Frey Blaz reported to the other monks at the copying desks later that morning. "He does not claim that he is worthy of God's notice, only that he is grateful for it."

"A fine Infante for España," observed the oldest of the monks, Frey Jeremias. "He will be guided by Heaven."

The others agreed at once, and it was decided that a letter must be sent to the Superior General of the Ambrosians in España. "We must inform him," said Frey Blaz with enthusiasm, "of what has transpired. In these times, with heresy rife in the land and rumors of the apostates seducing the faithful, it will bring heart to our Brothers in Christ to know that the Infante Real is so godly a man and pleasing to Heaven."

There was some argument as to who would write this document, and resolved when Frey Jeremias recommended a group effort. "That way," he said in his measured manner, "each will be sure that all of the information is present. It would be a disservice to leave anything out."

By evening the letter was complete, and the next day, when the Infante Real and his servant prepared to depart, Frey Camilo approached him and asked if he would carry two or three letters for him to his Superior General in Valladolid.

"It is little enough to repay your kindness," Don Rolon answered, with a glance at Ciro. "My valet will see that they are delivered. Give them to him."

Ciro had finished loading the mule that carried their goods and was now tightening the girths on his saddle. "Yes, of course. I'll take the letters there as soon as we return."

"They are sealed," Frey Camilo said a bit more cautiously.

Since most of the documents Don Rolon saw were sealed, this did not seem unusual. "We will not open them; do not fear." The bruises on his face were very bad, but most of the swelling over his left eye had gone down, and he was able to give the monk a slight smile. "It is a privilege to be able to render you service."

Frey Camilo was not used to courtesy, and so made more of this statement than it called for. He turned ruddy and bowed before bustling back into his monastery, calling over his shoulder for the two men to wait but a moment; he would be back with the letters and would pronounce the benediction on them for traveling.

"What do you make of it?" Ciro asked once Frey Camilo was gone.

"They have few travelers here. He must not have much opportunity to communicate with his Superior General."

"Is that all, do you think?" Ciro had sensed the excitement that rustled through the monastery, like a wind scattering leaves. It bothered him to think that they might be the cause of it. "Alteza, what if he reports on the other night?"

Don Rolon sighed. "I am afraid that he will, but if I refuse to take the letters, he will be sure that there is something very much the matter."

Ciro patted his horse on the nose, gathered the reins and prepared to mount. "The letters could be lost, Alteza. It is not impossible."

"I've thought of that," Don Rolon said slowly. "It's tempting. But if I . . . lose them, eventually new ones will be sent, and with the loss to their credit to give weight to whatever the good monks have said. Men living as isolated as these do are known to make too much of events. But if you and I behave in a way that will give credence to their report, then it becomes much more difficult." He swung up into the saddle and tested his stirrups. "You're a cautious man, Ciro, and I am glad of it. You're also a brave one, and for that I thank God."

Ciro could think of nothing to say in reply. He put his mind to finding a way to delay delivery of the letters as long as possible, but could discover no acceptable way other than an outright lie, which was more unwise than anything. A lie was a sin, and if told to an ordained priest, could be interpreted as heresy, since the priest was the intermediary between men on earth and all of Heaven. Ciro did not like the notion that came to him as he watched Frey Camilo come hurrying back with three rolled and sealed scrolls under his arm: this was a very clever test, a trap set for the Infante Real, to discover the extent of his dedication to the Church.

"Here, Alteza," Frey Camilo said breathlessly as he held out the scrolls. "They are to be taken to our Superior General in Valladolid. We pray for your safe and swift journey, and for the blessings of God and the Virgin to attend on your marriage." Although he was not required to do so, he bowed to Don Rolon as the Infante Real took the scrolls, holding them gingerly, as if they contained venomous snakes.

"They will be delivered within a day of my arrival at Valladolid," he promised as he swung into the saddle. "Again, my thanks to you and your fellow Ambrosians for permitting me to come here."

"It is Santa Clara that is grateful to you for the honor of your presence, Alteza," Frey Camilo assured him, stepping back from Don Rolon's Andalusian so that the royal guest could depart.

Don Rolon signaled to Ciro, and they started off down the narrow, flower-flanked path toward the road to Valladolid.

Inez gave Don Enrique a long, measuring look. "You tell me that you will give me jewels and silks, but it is easy to promise such things."

"Oh, come," Don Enrique said with an unconvincing laugh as he strode about her courtyard. "As soon as Don Rolon is married, he will abandon you. His father will insist on it, you know, at least until there are heirs enough to ensure the Succession. By that time, his fancy will have changed. You must have noticed how temperamental our Infante is."

"He is good to me," Inez said stubbornly, her lower lip pouting enchantingly.

"While he is free. But that will not continue for long. You will discover that it will be otherwise. He has been gone for a week and is not expected for another day or so. As long as he is away, why not turn your time to advantage, chica, and vary your menu a bit; you have been fasting for some time." He chuckled at his own cleverness. "I am no Infante, but I can offer you a few pleasures I warrant Don Rolon knows nothing of." He caught the curl of his beard between his first and second fingers, tugging at the carefully trimmed hair suggestively. He was very elegant in dark-red velvet, piped with gold. His lace ruff stood out around his face like a lion's mane and he glistened in the sun. True, there were dissipated pouches under his cynical eyes, but he was not troubled by them, since few women were repulsed by his appearance.

Inez watched him closely, uncertain what to do. She was bored enough to enjoy the prospect of diversion with so elegant a courtier, but she recalled Lugantes' warning to her a few days before when the jester had come to see her. Then he had told her that Don Rolon had many powerful enemies, and that some of them might choose to woo her as a means to compromise the Infante Real. She knew that Don Enrique had been with Don Rolon when she had met him at her uncle's inn, but he had not called the man his friend then or since. She laced her fingers together. "I must have time to consider what you have said to me, Don Enrique. I am alone in the world but for the generosity of the Infante, and if that is taken away, I do not know where I will find another who will treat me as he has."

"I could do much for you," Don Enrique said with more bravado than truth.

"For how long?" Inez asked, far more pointedly than she knew. "You are interested, perhaps, Señor, because the Infanto Real protects me. But when he does not, why should I be of interest to you, when there are many beautiful women at Court, or so I have heard, who seek discreet men." Those various, whispered rumors had been the most tantalizing bits of gossip in all of España over the years. No one dared discuss those who were in the keeping of the Holy Office, lest it be assumed that they, too, should be taken and Questioned. But the life of those at Court, that was ripe fruit for everyone who had ever seen a grandee or hidalgo.

"Oh, you do yourself a disservice," Don Enrique said with less sweetness. "I am one who looks after his mistresses. There are those who abandon the women they have bedded, but I am not so dishonorable." It was a lie, but he consoled himself with the reflection that he always left his women a jewel or two to tide them over to their next lover. His family was too impoverished for him to do more, but had he been wealthy, he doubted he would extend himself for anyone more than he did now.

"And will you say that in half a year? Will you take any child I give you and see that it is raised well?" She had in her keeping already two pouches of gold angels and reals that Don Rolon had given her for the time she found herself with child.

"If I am not to your liking, you have only to tell me that, Inez, and I will not trouble you again." He was growing annoyed by her behavior, and it did not suit him to listen to her speak to him in such unflattering ways.

"Yes. It would be best, I think." She regarded him through the fringe of her lashes and saw him clench his hands. "If you decide that you are willing to provide for me so that I need not fear to be cast without resources on the world, then perhaps we will talk again. But the Infante Real will return soon, and there is still some little time before he marries, and I don't believe it would be wise of you to come here until the Venezian woman has landed in España."

"They say," Don Enrique told her with a touch of malice, "that she is quite lovely."

"Strange," Inez responded with a wide smile. "I had heard that it was otherwise. There are those in the market-place who swear that she is most ugly. But her portrait has not been sent, and so how are we to judge?"

"She has not seen Don Rolon's likeness," Don Enrique pointed out with satisfaction. "You would hardly call him a brute, would you?"

Inez shrugged. "What is expected of a man and what is expected of a woman are different matters. If this Patrecipazio woman is not pleasing to look upon, Don Rolon will have much to do to fill her with children. But that is the way of men, isn't it, Don Enrique?" she went on boldly. "They must please their eyes if they are to please their flesh."

Don Enrique would have slapped her had she been his to touch. "Those who are married by the laws of God and His Church do not have congress for pleasure. There is the wedding shift to be sure that they do not permit themselves to be distracted from the holy purpose of their union."

"Being that I am not a wife, I have no such shift," she said with a seraphic smile. "It provides holes for the act, doesn't it? And otherwise, the bodies do not touch." She had heard of this garment that the Church expected married couples to wear when they lay together, and if it were true, she did not blame highborn ladies for seeking lovers who would use them more enjoyably.

"It is sin for married couples to pervert the act of procreation," Don Enrique said with real distaste. There were times he was grateful that his family had as yet been unable to arrange a match for him.

"Well, then, it will not matter if the Venezian woman is fair or hideous. Don Rolon will not see her, in any case." Inez turned toward Don Enrique and favored him with a taunting smile. "He'll tire of that shift, Don Enrique. And he knows that I do not have one."

"There is nothing for me to say, then," Don Enrique said with a stiff bow. "I trust you will not regret your choice. Remember, however, that those who climb high have farther to fall." It was his parting shot, and as he went out the wrought-iron gate, he congratulated himself for thinking of it.

14

On the two long sideboards, a sumptuous meal was laid out, but Don Rolon had not been able to eat. He hardly heard the music played by the Italian musicians, and when spoken to, he gave disjointed answers.

"Well, Alteza, it is understandable that you should be caught up as you are," said Nobile Rigonzetti. "It will be less than an hour now, and you will see your promised bride. But think of her, as well, for you are as much a stranger to her as she is to you." Had Don Rolon been an Italian prince, Nobile would have patted his shoulder in comradely sympathy, but since the youth was Spanish, Nobile did not venture so great a familiarity. He contented himself with pouring a glass of wine and holding it out to his guest with a flourish.

"Tell me," Don Rolon said in as calm a manner as he could, "what sort of woman is the Doge's niece?" He was not certain what he should call her. Señorita Patrecipazio? Zaretta? My betrothed? All of them had a strange ring and he did not know what the Ambassador would think if he appeared to be too casual about his affianced bride.

"She is one of good understanding, with a discerning mind and educated discourses." That was dressing her up in flattering words, Nobile was well aware. "She is twenty years of age—closer to your own age than is many times the case in these political marriages. Her companions often look to her for entertainment, and she is unfailing in providing it." He took some wine himself and tried to think of other things to say about Zaretta. "She has good taste, but is fixed in her preferences. She has been taught from youth to be a worthy wife to a man of high station. She knows what is expected of her."

"Good," Don Rolon said quietly. "My father has instructed me to be at pains to welcome her. What would please her most?"

Nobile bit back the first response that came to mind and said, "She is a creature of light and warmth. Much of the Spanish Court is more . . . formal than she is used to. It would be wise, Alteza, if you permitted her a little time to become accustomed to your ways, and while she is learning, if you would not be harsh with her when she errs, I believe that would be best." He knew that this was good advice, for no matter how he approached Zaretta Patrecipazio, Don Rolon would have his hands full with his headstrong, indulged, pleasure-loving bride.

There were shouts in the street below, and a sober fanfare was sounded. Don Rolon turned slightly pale, and Raimundo Dominguez, who was standing near him, came closer. "The waiting is almost over, Alteza," he said respectfully.

"For her as well as me," Don Rolon sighed. "My father must be approaching her carriage now, to lead her in." He tried to imagine the scene as it was happening one floor below and half a block away. A woman—he would not recognize her if he passed her on the street—was being brought to him, to be his wife. He reminded himself that she knew as well as he what the purpose of their marriage was. If she would be content to live courteously but not too close to each other, he was half convinced that all would be well. If his taint stopped with him. If she did not expect him to dance attendance on her.

"Do not worry, Alteza," Nobile said as he refilled the Infante Real's glass with good Italian wine. "You will not be disappointed in your betrothed. She will deal well with you." He looked covertly at Raimundo for some sign of agreement, and the Portuguese nobleman did not disappoint him.

"You have had letters from the Doge, Alteza," Raimundo said, "that show clearly how well she has been instructed in her obligations to you. As you know yours to her, you will do well. I am certain of it." Secretly, he was worried about Don Rolon. For the last week, the Infante Real had been unusually quiet, taking long, solitary walks and seeking the peace of books more often than had been his wont. He suspected that more than this wedding was troubling him, but he had not found a way to broach the subject with the young man.

"Yes. Doubtless you're right and I am concerned over nothing." He looked around the room and noticed that most of the eyes were now turned toward the main entrance, through which Alonzo would bring Zaretta Patrecipazio. He noticed that Reina Genevieve was hovering near the portal, Lugantes not far from her side. As he watched, he saw Genevieve bend down and whisper something to the dwarf, who shook his head, frowning. "They're as nervous as I am," Don Rolon said in an undervoice.

Raimundo, who had also seen the exchange between Reina and jester, said, "Alteza, when there are weddings in the royal House, everyone must be concerned. It is not as if a man and a woman were being joined merely, but two Houses, two countries also participate in the union. That is enough to give anyone pause. A marriage between a common man and woman gives both of them joy and alarm. How much more, then, for you and the Doge's niece"—he used Don Rolon's designation of the woman—"who must anticipate the fate of nations as well as families."

It was tacitly understood that Raimundo's marriage to the daughter of the Duque del Riopardo was a failure, and had been from the first, and so Don Rolon listened to the courtier with more attention than he might have given similar advice coming from another. "If she understands the responsibilities that we must share, then . . ." he said dubiously. Now that the actual meeting was so close, he felt reservations that he had never known before.

"She knows, Infante Real, and she is prepared to do what is required of her," said Nobile with more force than he might have used.

"Good," Don Rolon said in order to say something acceptable. "Then all should be well."

On the other side of the room, Reina Genevieve stood straighter and adjusted the fall of her skirt. She was dressed in the French fashion, which Alonzo found insolent and infuriating, but which she claimed by right: her farthingale was smaller and higher than the Spanish equivalent; her ruff was open and wired to fan around her face; her outer sleeves trailed as tippets and the inner sleeves were a gorgeous light blue silk that matched the petticoat revealed at the front of the skirt; and the lavendar velvet of her overgown was lavishly embroidered with fleurs-de-lis and royal bees. She ran one ringed hand along the skirt and then made a sign to Lugantes to come nearer. "I believe," she said in a clear voice, "that el Rey and the bride are approaching."

As if to confirm this, there was a great bawling of trumpets and sacbuts followed by a noisy anthem on shawms and recorders. Somewhere on the lower level of the Italian palace, a chorus of boys burst into song.

"Most impressive," Raimundo said to Nobile. "You compliment both your countrywoman and the Spanish throne."

"I hope so; it was my intent." Nobile was studying the large doorway with some faint misgiving. So much ostenta-tion might not look well to the austere Spanish ruler. El Rey was noted for his restraint amid magnificence, and this was not in his manner at all.

"So Venezian a welcome," Raimundo went on with a trace of humor. "No one in España would dare to give such a demonstration. You, being Venezian, are not as limited in scope as we are."

"You are Portuguese," Nobile said tersely, hearing the singing boys draw nearer.

"Which is to say closer than cousins to España," Raimundo

commented, then addressed Don Rolon. "You should be at Señor Rigonzetti's side, Alteza, so that you may greet your bride at once."

"Yes. I must," Don Rolon agreed, though his mouth felt dry as flannel and his hands were suddenly wet. Obediently, with hardly a trace of thought, he took up his position beside his host, and licked his dry lips once and turned toward the main entrance to the room. He wanted to shout that he was not ready, that it was a mistake, that he wanted no part of the woman, but he kept the quiet, slightly morose expression that had long since become habitual with him.

Four ornately dressed pages entered the room, clearing a path, and behind them the chorus of boys followed, their strong, high voices extolling the woman they escorted. All who waited with the Venezian Ambassador fell silent, and then bowed in acknowledgment of Alonzo II as he came into the room, Padre Juan at his side.

Just behind them was a willowy woman in a gonella of blue-green silk, a color that was light and intense at once, and set off her lovely copper blond hair to perfection. The scooped neck of her garment had the suggestion of a ruff around it, and the puffs over the shoulders were slashed and jeweled with moonstones. Her face was meltingly beautiful, with features so perfect it was hard to believe they were not stolen from a too-flattering painting. She was like Venus wandering among the shades of Hades, for there was something pagan in her superb allure. On the train that spread from her shoulders were representations of the Patrecipazio arms and the Lion of Saint Mark.

Alonzo, his face wholly expressionless, came up to his son and motioned for him to rise. He took Don Rolon's hand and held it out to the gorgeous creature behind him. "Infante Real," he said harshly, "here is Zaretta Melissina Colomba Patrecipazio, your affianced wife, and niece of the Doge of Venezia." With that abrupt statement, he thrust Don Rolon's hand into the hand of the woman in blue-green.

Don Rolon's tongue could not move; he did not know if he would be able to breathe or if he would suffocate as he stared at her, and for the moment it did not matter. Was this the woman he was going to wed, the woman he was going to treat as a royal brood mare? This splendid, desirable sylph with the look of an angel? His hand trembled in hers.

"Donna . . . " he said in a strange, deep tone that startled him with its intensity, "it is my duty and honor to welcome you to Espana, and to greet you." He kissed her hand, as he had been told to do, though he feared his lips would burn when they touched her flesh.

Even her voice was beautiful. "I thank you, Infante Real," she said in what seemed to Don Rolon to be charmingly mispronounced Spanish. "I speak for all of Venezia to accept your gracious welcome." She did not curtsy, though Spanish custom required it. She turned and looked for la Reina. "You are Genevieve?" she asked in fluent French.

"Yes," la Reina answered, looking at Zaretta with awe and envy. "I am Reina."

"My uncle sends you his most particular greetings and asks that you permit him to address a letter to you, the better to eliminate any misunderstandings that might have arisen between my country and yours." She smiled sweetly and looked around the room. "How sober it all is. I would think I am in church but for my countrymen." She gave a trilling laugh and put out her hand to Nobile. "I have been asked to extend the special thanks of the Doge and the Council of Ten, Rigonzetti, for your service to the state, and to inform you that the grant of lands on Corfu has been given your family in recognition of your devotion."

Everyone in the room hung on her words, staring at this butterfly among crows. Raimundo cleared his throat and said quietly to Don Rolon, "You may count yourself a most fortunate man.

Don Rolon found it difficult to nod, for it meant that he could not watch Zaretta with perfect concentration. "Yes," he murmured as if in prayer, all the while wishing he had known how wonderful Zaretta was, for all his careful plans now were useless and unimportant to him.

"It is our decision," Alonzo announced in a barking tone, "that the wedding will take place, as we have previously arranged, on the tenth day of May, five weeks from today. Let all proper measures be taken to assure that this solemn state occasion be given the gravity it deserves, and the religious exercises that will ensure God's blessing on the union of Don Rolon and Zaretta Patrecipazio, niece of the Doge of Venezia." He swung around abruptly to face the Venezian bride. "You will make your home with the Duque da Minho and his wife until such time as you come to the palace as my heir's wife. The Duquessa will instruct you in the ways of Spanish customs and teach you a better command of our tongue."

"I am grateful," Zaretta said, but her light blue eyes flashed in brief defiance at these strictures. "It was my father's wish that I make my home here, with the Ambassador, until I am married."

"Your father is in Venezia and you are in España. It is fitting that you learn how to live as the wife of the Infante Real before the obligations of that station are thrust upon you. Doubtless, were the

Infante to come to you, the same stric-tures would be set upon him." He indicated the disapproving Inquisitor at his side. "Padre Juan will see to your spiritual instruction as well, so that your soul will not be neglected while your fine manners are perfected." He glared around the room once, and then went toward the door.

"Majestad!" Nobile protested, realizing that Zaretta, and with her all of Venezia, was being offered an insult by Alonzo d ' España.

❧

"What is it, Ambassador? I fear I have pressing matters of state that cannot be neglected for even so grand an occasion as this one. My Reina is here, and will act for us and stand in our stead." He signaled to Padre Juan before he made a general acknowledgment with his hand as he left the room.

Zaretta stood in silence for some little time after el Rey had departed, and the guests remained in their places, uncertain what they should do next. There was a suggestion of a frown on her smooth brow, one that she made no attempt to conceal.

It was Lugantes who saved the day. He cartwheeled across the floor toward Zaretta and sprawled at her feet, his bright eyes dancing. "You have won the first lists, child, and for that, we are all stunned. No army in the field has so completely vanquished el Rey as you have."

There was a burst of laughter, and it sounded a little too wild and reckless for the remark that had occasioned it. However, the terrible moment was over, and it was Raimundo who went to bow to Zaretta. "You will be the wife of the man I have the honor to call my friend, and Majestad has shown me great favor by granting that I be your host until the day of your wedding."

"You are da Minho?" Zaretta asked, putting out her hand to Raimundo.

"Raimundo Dominguez y Mara; da Minho is my title and lands. Here I am called Dominguez by the hidalgos and grandees, and it would please me if you would do the same." He motioned to Don Rolon to approach. "It is awkward, I fear, for you to meet so publicly, but that is the way of these important unions, and no matter how much you might prefer some little time with Don Rolon, for the rest of today, this reception must demand your presence."

Don Rolon forced himself to take the few steps required to reach Zaretta's side. He wished that he might find some imperfection in her that had escaped his notice at first, but the harder he stared at her, the more luminous she seemed to him. "I . . . I am profoundly grateful to Venezia for relinquishing such a treasure into my keeping." He was amazed at his own eloquence.

"It appears your father is not of the same mind," Zaretta snapped, then changed to smiles once more. "I was disappointed to be treated so."

Reina Genevieve came to her senses at last, and approached the young woman. "It was most kind of you to bring me word from the Doge. France is deeply concerned, as you might imagine, on what may—"

Zaretta interrupted her with a delightful giggle. "Oh, don't go on about it now. I have been hearing so much of statecraft that my head aches and I want to tear up every map I see." She looked once at Don Rolon and there was a petulance in her voice. "You're so dark. The clothes, the beard, the hair . . . They didn't tell me that."

"I beg your pardon for any offense that—" Don Rolon began, but Zaretta had already turned back to Reina Genevieve. "You are wearing velvet, and in this weather! How do you bear it?"

"One grows accustomed," Genevieve answered philosophically, then stared around the room. "You see how we are required to dress. At least I am not limited to black, as the rest of the court is."

"Black, black, and black. The whole world has turned priest," Zaretta complained prettily. "Will I have to do that, Dominguez? Wear black whenever el Rey requires it of me?"

"It would be wisest," Raimundo answered carefully, and was glad to hear Nobile speak up at his shoulder.

"Didn't the Doge tell you that you were to adopt the customs of España?"

"Oh, of course, but I didn't know that it would mean I would have to wear black all the time, and behave as if I were at a funeral." She sighed and looked around the room again. "At least this is Venezian. That's something." Her eyes continued to shift from one area to the next, until she saw the food laid out. "Oh! A meal! Thank God. I'm famished. I could not bear to eat a bite on the galley that brought me to España, and I have traveled so quickly from Valencia that there has been little chance . . . would you mind terribly, Rigonzetti, if I were to have a plate of chicken?"

"It would be my pleasure to see you have it," Nobile said promptly, and held out his arm for her to rest her own upon it.

"I wonder if there is any wine?" she asked as she let Nobile escort her through the crowd.

Raimundo stared after her, a thoughtful expression in his dark eyes. He glanced toward Don Rolon and what he read in the Infante

Real's rapt features caused him grave concern. He saw that Lugantes was watching Don Rolon as well, sympathy and deep anguish in his eyes.

"Dominguez," Reina Genevieve said in her most com-manding way, "the suggestion of our guest is well-taken. Pray escort me to the serving tables."

The awkward moment passed, and Raimundo complied at once, but as he guided the French Reina through the gathering, he looked back once at Don Rolon, now standing alone with Lugantes, and he worried all the more.

"I hear that she's the fairest thing to come into España since the northern fighters followed their battle-maids to Burgos," Gil del Rey said to his half brother the following morning when they met after Mass outside the chapel.

"She is most beautiful," Don Rolon agreed, hating the sight of his father's blond bastard.

"Count yourself fortunate. Not many princes have similar luck." He snickered. "Here I thought you'd get yourself a hag for a wife, and you end up with an angel. It should be a lesson to me." He fell into step beside Don Rolon, knowing that he made the Infante Real very uncomfortable, and relishing it. "You marry in May?"

"So el Rey has decreed," Don Rolon said stiffly.

"Well, for once you will be the man. But we all owe duty to the throne." He grinned slyly and planted the barb he had wanted to since he learned about Zaretta the day before. "If you cannot bring yourself to sully this Venezian beauty, be assured that I will do the work for you, to please our father."

Don Rolon turned on Gil. "It is enough that I will marry. I will not be made a cuckold, by you or anyone." His face had flushed and he tried to move away from Gil.

"Oh, this is raillery, Don Rolon, only raillery. It speaks poorly of you that you cannot discern it. Unless the lady plays you false of her own accord, you have nothing to fear from me," he finished with a smirk.

"By Heaven, if you address one more word to her than civility and courtesy require, I will tax you with your word, brothen" the Infante Real declared with more heat than he usually revealed to Gil.

"You're churlish," Gil insisted, knowing that this choler on Don Rolon's part proved his jibes had been successful. "I want only to be sure that no one trespasses on your preserves unless you neglect them yourself." He paused, then added one last dart. "I was simply thinking of what became of that Norman ruler of Sicily when he proved incapable of continuing the line. You do not want such a fate to be visited on you, my dear brother. They blinded and castrated him, if I remember it correctly." His lowered eyes concealed a glint of merriment. "That is what happened, isn't it?"

Don Rolon turned toward Gil with his face set in hard lines. "I warn you, Gil, that if you press me, you will regret it. My father may prefer you to me, but he prefers legitimate grandchildren to either of us. Do not forget that." He shouldered his way past Gil and hurried away, leaving Gil to consider what he had said.

❦

Lugantes found Don Rolon later that day in one of the smaller reception rooms near the western wing of the palace. "I have been searching for you, Alteza," he said after he made sure that they were not overheard.

"And you have discovered me," Don Rolon remarked as he put aside the large, metal-clasped book he had been reading. "I have not yet thanked you for the service you rendered my betrothed yesterday."

"It was nothing," Lugantes said, impatiently waving the Infante Real's gratitude away. "I must speak with you."

"You are at liberty to do so," Don Rolon told him.

"Not here. There is a person, a friend from the inn, who is . . . upset. It appears that word has reached this person's house of . . . recent events, and there . . . " How could he describe the shouts and tears Inez had displayed when he had gone to her house earlier.

"Friend from the inn?" Don Rolon asked, then turned two or three shades darker. "Oh. I see. I did not think that—" He stopped. Since he had first looked at Zaretta, all interest in Inez had left him.

"Someone visited our friend last night with very extensive tales of . . . " Lugantes came up to Don Rolon. "You had best make provision for her, and quickly, Alteza, or your enemies will, and you will suffer for it."

Don Rolon laughed. "What could she tell them?"

"Many things," Lugantes said, alarmed at Don Rolon's lack of concern. "Alteza, consider her safety, if not your own."

"But—" Don Rolon began, but the jester cut in once more.

"You have powerful enemies, Alteza, and . . . our friend is not clever. In her current frame of mind, she might be persuaded to do and say things she would later regret." He paced down the room. "You must attend to it."

The urgency in Lugantes' tone at last penetrated the haze of delight that surrounded Don Rolon. "Very well. I will attend to it."

"Soon!" Lugantes declared.

"Yes. Of course. Soon." He waved Lugantes away. "I must finish reading this before I speak to Padre Juan. Afterward, I will arrange something."

Lugantes bowed and withdrew, trying to mask the apprehension he felt by singing songs and doing inexpert dance steps as he went. But the songs he chose to sing were sad, and the dances were graceless, as if the weight in his soul had communicated itself to his feet.

15

Reina Genevieve sat in the smaller of the two music rooms in the palace. She held a viol in her lap and played at it in a desultory fashion. Her mind was not on the music, or on the setting; she kept thinking back to the night before, when Alonzo had presented Gil to Zaretta. She could recall with horrible clarity the avid look in Gil's eyes as he took Zaretta's hand. How blatantly he had put his lips to her palm—an intimacy Alonzo would have found unforgivable in anyone but Gil—and how obviously she had responded to his attentions. The bow shrieked on the strings, and she set it aside. Gil had followed Zaretta most of the evening, offering her courtesies, making her compliments. Even that deft and astute courtier Dominguez y Mara was not able to separate them for long. Genevieve cursed, remembering how attentive Gil had been to her for the greater part of two weeks. She had had hopes of making him hers and flaunting the attachment in Alonzo's face until Zaretta. Now she had no one.

There was a gentle knock on the door, and Reina Genevieve started up, aware that she ought not to be found alone anywhere. Her ladies-in-waiting were taking refreshments in her private garden, and had committed a great breach of trust by leaving Genevieve to herself. She was forming excuses for them in her mind when the door opened and Lugantes came into the room. "Oh! It's you, my little love."

Pain and adoration showed in his face. "I've been looking for you, querida. I hope that you are not angry with me?"

"Angry?" Genevieve frowned. "Why should I be angry?"

Lugantes was filled with hope. "I tried to bring Gil to you, but—"

Genevieve tittered. "That was not your doing, Lugantes. Alonzo introduced them, and it must have been for spite. Why else would he give his bastard distinction over his heir?" Her sympathy for Don Rolon was strong for the moment; in general she did not like the silent, reserved Infante Real.

"He has always done so," Lugantes reminded her, and went to her side, taking her hand and pressing it reverently to his lips. "I saw how you looked, and I wanted to transform the world for you, to change what had happened so that it would not have happened."

"Only God can do that," Genevieve said absently, and rested her viol on the floor on its side. "Lugantes, what am I to do? Padre Juan has spoken to me for two hours today, and I feel as if my head will burst with his words and his visions of punishment and Hell. He looks at me so! His face is all hunger." She gave a short, wild laugh. "You do not suppose that he, perfect priest that he is, has not subdued the flesh?"

Lugantes felt his heart turn to ice. "No, no, querida. No, do not think such a thing, do not imagine it for an instant. Those who tempt Padre Juan are punished for it. He does not forgive temptation." He put his arms around her waist and laid his head in her lap.

"I am Reina d'España," Genevieve said as if the title protected her.

"No," Lugantes said as his arms tightened. "No. It would not be enough. Majestad would not protect you from Padre Juan." There were tears in his eyes as he thought of how much danger Genevieve was in if she truly had caught the fancy of the Inquisitor General. "Listen to me, querida. There was a nun of the Benedictines who served as companion to Alonzo's mother toward the end of her life. Violante was modest and soft-spoken, patient and virtuous. She embraced her calling and her chastity as ardently as a lover. There was never a breath of impiety about her. Padre Juan saw her when he went to hear Druzella's confession, for the old lady wished to purge her soul of sin before she came to God. Thus Padre Juan and Sor Violante met from time to time. Over a period of a year or two—"

Genevieve interrupted him. "Alonzo said once that Padre Juan discovered heresy within his own House. Was this what he meant?"

"Yes, but it was not heresy. I had been here three years when it began, and I know what I saw: Padre Juan met a nun and conceived a lust for her. It was in his face, the way his mouth moved when he spoke to her, how he sat when he was in her presence. And because he was tempted by her, he punished her. She was accused of heresy and of apostasy. She was cast out of her Order and given to the Secular Arm. They racked her and crushed her feet in the boot, yet Padre Juan still desired her, and for that desire they tore her breasts from her body with pincers and knocked out all her teeth. And so that Padre Juan would be free of her, they burned her on All Saints' and threw her ashes onto the dung heap."

"Poor creature," Genevieve murmured as her fingers brushed through Lugantes' hair. It was difficult to tell if she spoke of the tragic Sor Violante or of Lugantes.

"Do not put yourself in peril with Padre Juan, querida, mi vida. He is as dangerous as a wounded panther." He twisted suddenly, and climbed into her lap. With utmost delicacy, he took her face in his hands and kissed her as if all the love in his heart could nourish her through his lips.

She returned his kisses, first in quick, light movements of her mouth, and then in a long, delirious pressure. At last she moaned and moved back. "No. No, no, no, Lugantes. You know what happened the last time."

The shame of it was still with him, but his desire for her was greater. "This time it will be different. I have thought of things, wonderful things, and they will please you, estrella mia. Your women will not disturb us, not if we are cautious. Who questions you with me? What am I but your jester?" Most of her hair was caught back under a formal headdress, but some of it fell around her face, and this he touched lightly with teasing affection. "An hour, Genevieve, that's all. If you are not pleased, we are no worse off than before. But if you are, then there may be a chance . . . "

"An hour, then," she capitulated, wishing he were tall and straight and beautiful, for then she would not hesitate to love him. "But you must talk with Gil. He can't have that Venezian, and he will want revenge. There is no reason he cannot take it with me."

Her words lanced his heart, but Lugantes nodded. "If it is what you wish, I will do it. You are taking more risks than I would like, Genevieve." He kissed her again, first her brow and eyelids, so slowly, so tenderly, then her cheeks and mouth. "I have listened to what the Venezian Ambassador says when he thinks he is alone, and it does not bode well for the Infante. Be wary, my dearest treasure, my goddess."

"Shush," she whispered, putting her hand on his lips. "Do not speak so, for the Holy Office would not approve."

"The Holy Office would condemn us for thinking about what we have already done,-" Lugantes said with soft bitterness. "This is treason and adultery, and other sins as well, no doubt." His kiss lasted longer. "Come. Before we lose our hour."

Genevieve rose as Lugantes bounced onto the floor. "My sewing room, then. It is small enough, and far away from where Alonzo is spending his time." She nodded toward one of the hallways. "As we go, tell me about a design or a flag or a tapestry, so that if we are overheard—"

"I am not a fool, mon ange, only a jester." He stood still for a moment, composing himself. "Very well. I am ready. But hurry." Then he laughed loudly, and clapped his hands. "Hurry," he repeated, then ran for the door and bowed her through it.

❦

There was an oblong fishpond in the garden, inlaid with small, bright tiles. Orange trees were planted on the far side of it, and costly Italian roses grew on the nearer. The evening air was heavy with the scent of blossoms.

Zaretta pointed down into the water. "Oh! There are fish."

It had been more than she had offered in conversation since they began their walk together half an hour ago, and Don Rolon was grateful for her effort. "Yes. Originally the Muslims had such ponds, and brought fish from the Arab countries to remind them of their homes. But they did not prosper here, and so others were found. The fish in the ponds now are a special kind that have been bred by the pool-keepers for more than two centuries."

"Do you eat them?" Zaretta asked.

"No doubt the gardeners do, but they are not supposed to. One of the Sanchos made it law, a long time ago, that nothing in royal gardens was game, and we have all chosen to abide by his rule." He hated the fading of the light, for it meant that he could not see her as clearly as he wished to.

She smiled mischievously and there were two adorable dimples in her cheeks. "I used to fish off the balcony of my father's palace. There was a room for the women of the household on the side of the palace, and I would get out on the balcony and hang a line over the edge. I never caught much, but I loved it." She stood on the edge of the pond now, her eyes trying to look beneath the winking, dark surface to what lay beneath.

"Were you happy there in Venezia?" Don Rolon asked, dreading her answer.

"It was wonderful," she said, unaware that her reply had wounded him. "It is very different in Venezia, though we haven't the liberty of the Florentine and Roman women. To be sure, there are priests, and we have an Inquisitor, but it is nothing like your society. No one here laughs, or sings. No one plays pranks." She pursed her lips. "I suppose I will grow used to it in time."

"I pray that you will; I would be . . . hurt to think that you did not feel at home here." He was speaking awkwardly again, not trusting himself to be open with her, fearing that she would mock him.

"My father said that I would. He thinks all a woman has to have is a child in her belly and she's as contented as an old cow." She folded her arms and stepped away from the pond. "I suppose that is what I must do, isn't it? Give you children so that the succession is guaranteed. I'll do my best to have sons. My uncle has already promised me hundreds of ducats for every male child I bring into the world." She made a quick, complicated gesture. "He said that your sisters—"

"My half-sisters," Don Rolon corrected her quickly. "They are Genevieve's children, not my mother's. She died the day after I was born."

Zaretta looked quickly at him. "What about the sisters?"

"They are . . . simpleminded. But they are not deformed or too badly afflicted in their bodies. Leonora—she's the younger one—is very pretty." He could not bring himself to meet her eyes and he felt his face grow dark.

"Are there any others?" Zaretta asked in a small voice. Don Rolon chose deliberately to misunderstand her. "No. La Reina has just two children."

"But in the family?" She knew the rumors about the Hapsburgs as well as any member of a European ruling House, and the reputation of the Spanish Hapsburgs was more distressing than the Austrian branch.

"There have been those who are . . . odd. But it is only the two girls who are truly inadequate.". It was a source of terrible embarrassment on the whole of Alonzo's House that the two girls had been designated unmarriageable by the Pope. Had it been Gustav who disapproved, they might still have found husbands in some of the lesser aristocratic or royal Houses, but with the Pope opposing any such unions, Alonzo was without recourse. "One of the convents of Annuciate nuns has offered to give them a home, when they should need one. Leonora has been there once or twice, but Genevieve has not yet agreed to permit them to go."

"But I thought she does not see her children," Zaretta said, perplexed. "She told me that it is not allowed."

"She visits them twice a week, but no oftener. My father and Padre Juan insist that she—" He could not finish, for the trouble in

Zaretta's face silenced him. "I did not mean to upset you, my dear. You will learn of this in time, and I hope that you are not too much overset by—"

"It is cruel for Alonzo and his Inquisitor General to keep Genevieve from her children. Mothers are to be with their own. That is what I have been taught since I was very young, and what my mother told me. I had my nurses, but that is not the same as removing the children from . . . " She looked at Don Rolon critically. "Can you do nothing?"

"Alas," Don Rolon answered. How could he explain his own weak position without lessening himself more than he had in her eyes? "When Padre Juan decides a thing, he speaks with all the power of the Church for his argument, and
my father has always his allegiance to the Church as well as to his House. And . . . there was the curse."

"A curse?" Zaretta asked, mouth forming a perfect 0.

"It happened long ago. My mother died for it, and my father has been much . . . tried by it." How long would it be? he wondered, until someone—and he thought Gil might be the someone—told her the whole story, and Zaretta began to regard him with the same cautious suspicion the rest of the Court had? He did not want to think about it, but the possibility stayed in his thoughts.

Zaretta clapped her hands and giggled. "A curse! It sounds like something out of one of the fables. Are you all condemned to wander the earth without rest, or to ride with the old gods, the way it happened in ancient times?" She moved away from him, turning a bit. "Are you cursed, too? Isn't it marvelous? Imagine, an heir to the throne with a curse hanging over him. I'll enjoy it!"

"But . . . " Don Rolon began, starting toward her. "It's not anything to—"

"And I was so worried that I would not be amused here! There are curses, and men with dark secrets. I'll enjoy this." She ran a few steps farther, then turned back to him, one arm extended. "You're so dour and glum, but it's different, I guess, if you're cursed. I'll try to remember that, when I'm bored." Then she went lightly away from him, half running, and her laughter came back to him with the call of night birds in the distant trees.

"Your suggestion is well-taken, Duque," Alonzo said to Raimundo at his very stiffest. "We will give it our consideration, of course."

"And do nothing more about it," Raimundo added, his manner as polished as ever, but with his eyes buming.

"We are gratified that the life of the Infante Real is important to you, but you must understand that we do not share your conviction that there are those seeking his life. He has not yet reached that station in life where those who intrigue at Court would think to attack him. He is too young, and his place is not yet assured. When he has given us legitimate heirs then we will guard him." Alonzo leaned back in his chair and regarded Raimundo narrowly. "We are most displeased, however, that you seek, however obliquely, to implicate our son Gil in your supposed plots. Gil is loyal to us and to our House, though his own place in it is not of importance here."

"The Emperor Gustav will not recognize him, Majestad, even if Don Rolon dies. You will have to bring in Otto, and that would bring disaster to your country, and to mine. The fate of España and Portugal are intertwined, and for the love I bear you as well as my love for my own country, I cannot stand by and watch all that you have achieved be ruined." He kept his voice even, his stance respectful, but his patience was growing short. "I do not say that Gil has done anything, or plans to do anything against his half brother. But there are those about him—impulsive, impetuous young men—who wish, misguidedly, to aid him, and believe that were Don Rolon to be harmed, Gil might become your successor. It is apparent that they do not understand how matters stand with you and the Emperor."

"It is not necessary that they understand. They are capricious young men, as you have said yourself, and we do not wish to dignify their argument with response." Alonzo tapped his toe once, twice, and studied his laced fingers, which was as much as he ever did when annoyed. "We would prefer, Duque, if you would cease to concern yourself with these issues and devote more time to arranging certain trade pacts with the Venezians, since the Ambassador has spoken to us recently of the desire of Venezia to have such documents prepared in time for the wedding of their Doge's niece and my son."

"Indeed, Majestad. It will be my pleasure." Raimundo bowed. "I am in all things submissive to your will, Majestad."

"Speak then, to Ambassador Rigonzetti, and do not waste your time with reflections that cannot lead to anything but disappointment for you and those you purport to aid." El Rey fixed his eyes on the large crucifix over the door. "We wish Rigonzetti to understand our displeasure. We were not told to expect a young woman of . . . the Doge's niece's sort. Women of high rank should comport themselves more modestly, with more reserve. It is not fitting that a woman of so . . . obvious charms should be sent to sit beside the Infante Real. It is not appropriate to our House that a woman of her stamp be part of it."

"I have thought that Don Rolon is fortunate in his bride," Raimundo said very carefully. "How many princes must content themselves with wives who will only serve to send them into the arms of harlots?" Since he knew that Alonzo heartily disapproved of Gustav's long list of conquests, he hoped that this argument might have some weight with el Rey.

"It is to be hoped that our son, cursed though he is, is nevertheless of greater moral strength than our brother, who has not had the benefit of the instruction of the Holy Office to guide him. It demonstrates what comes to those who adopt a tolerant posture to Protestant heretics, and reminds us all to be vigilant." Alonzo crossed himself before motioning Raimundo to leave him. "We would wish to see our son Gil, and pray you will inform him of this at once."

Raimundo bowed deeply and backed out of the lesser reception chamber. It was midafternoon, and that meant he would find Gil in one of the soldiers' quarters, drinking or gambling. He would have preferred to find Don Rolon first, but this was not the time to be lax in executing el Rey's orders.

"You'll lose your mare, if you keep that up," Gil chuckled to his companions as Raimundo came through the door. "I've got your saddle already."

Don Enrique shrugged and picked up the dice. "If I win, I get your mare, and that's enough for me." He shook his closed hand, then cast the dice down. "Turds of the Virgin!"

The three officers who watched this contest laughed at Don Enrique's misfortune, but Gil shook his head. "Don't' say things like that where Padre Juan and his friends can hear you. They don't—"

"A pox on them all!" Don Enrique declared, and reached for his wine cup. "You have the mare, don't bother me with the rest. I'd play you again, but I don't have anything left to bet with." He drank down the wine and called for more.

"Gil," Raimundo said when he was certain he would be heard.

"What is it?" Gil's face was surly as he looked up. "You lickspittle diplomat, there's nothing for you here."

"I agree," Raimundo said evenly. "Still, your father asked me to find you, and if this is where you choose to spend your time, I must seek you here." He gave a comprehensive and contemptuous stare around the room. "I've done as el Rey requires, and will excuse myself."

"What?" Gil jeered at him. "No bow?"

"In recognition of what?" Raimundo asked, and turned away with deliberate insolence.

"My father's goodwill?" Gil suggested as Raimundo got to the door. "You've been Rolon's advocate these last weeks, haven't you? My father does not share your liking for him—" Raimundo cut him off. "I have delivered your father's message."

"And one of your own as well." He stared at Raimundo as the older man left the room. "Don Enrique," he said when he had gathered up the coins he had won earlier.

"Yes?" His eyes were bleary as he regarded Gil over the rim of his cup.

"The woman you told me about? Can you arrange for me to visit her tonight?" There was a slyness in his face that disturbed those who watched him.

"If you wish," Don Enrique answered uneasily.

"Oh, I do wish it." He bounced the coins in his hand and they rang sharply. "Meet me in the alley behind the stables after the evening meal. It won't be much later than nine or ten of the clock since there are no receptions tonight."

"Very well," Don Enrique said, and lifted the cup to drink again.

Gil reached out and knocked it out of Don Enrique's hand. "No more of that. I don't want you falling down in the street tonight."

"Oh, very well," he conceded grudgingly. "But you know which is Inez's house. Why don't you just go there yourself?" This time Gil considered before he answered. "I need someone who will make her grateful I am there." Before Don Enrique could think of an adequate reply, Gil had tossed him a gold coin and walked, laughing, out of the door.

16

Ciro opened his hands and gave his most guileless stare to Padre Barnabas. "No doubt you are all correct to be concerned. I do not understand the subtle ramifications of such questions, Padre, and do not know what to tell you." He had been on guard from the moment the priest had come into his private chamber, and nothing that had passed between them had lessened his feeling of alarm.

"It is not unusual for a young man to speak of his doubts to those close to him," Padre Barnabas persisted. "It is essential that we know of these things before the wedding takes place, and it is not far off."

"Surely Padre Lucien is the man you must speak to, being the Infante Real's confessor. I am merely his valet." He tried to keep as candid a tone as he could, but his apprehension was increasing, and he could find no way to hide it. "Is there some reason you believe that Don Rolon has doubts of his true beliefs?"

"Not that we know of," Padre Barnabas answered smoothly. "And as his confession must remain under seal, then Padre Lucien is not the man we must address, but those not constrained by the Rules of Order and the Church for—" He paused. "In the past, Don Rolon has expressed himself on the question of Protestant Flemings, to his discredit."

"It is possible," Ciro answered. "I know he has mentioned to me that he has often been bothered that he must balance political expediency with religious convictions in order to maintain cordial relations with the Holy Roman Emperor, who is noted for his toler-ance of Protestants." This was one response that had been easy, and one which Ciro had planned with Don Rolon more than a year before. "The needs of statecraft are demanding ones."

"But not more than the service of God, surely," Padre Barnabas said curtly.

"Don Rolon is a young man with grave responsibilities. He does all that he must to accommodate them." It was precisely the right tone for a servant—just familiar enough to be credible, yet servile in attitude, and therefore acceptable to the priest.

"It would be a simple thing for him to fall into error," Padre Barnabas declared.

"Then it is for his confessor to admonish him, and el Rey. My place would not permit such interference." Ciro glanced uneasily toward the door. "You were with the Infante while he was at El Morro. Did he say anything there that made you suspect he was in sympathy with heretics?"

Padre Barnabas knew that it was not proper for this servant to ask him anything, but he preened under the humble attention Ciro accorded him. "It did not come to my notice, but Padre Juan has specifically requested that we be more . . . precise in our inquiries." He was taking advantage of the Inquisitor General's name, and knew it, but excused himself of vanity because of his high purpose.

"I do not know what I may do to aid you, good Padre, but if

there is something, I will naturally be at pains to do it." He sensed the satisfaction his timorous acceptance gave Padre Barnabas and shuddered inwardly. "I cannot compromise my position, good Padre, for then I would be of use to no one, but if it is possible, I will learn what I can."

Padre Barnabas did not want to push Ciro too far, since he wanted cooperation, not subjugation. "You must serve your master properly, and we would ask nothing else, because service is the heart of the Church. Yet if your master shows that he has been lured away from the truth and has been seduced by the promises of heretics and Diabolists, then your service requires that you dedicate yourself to the good of his soul, not his flesh. You conversos know best of all how God demands the most of His children that He loves best."

Ciro looked away. "Yes. We conversos know that."

"Well." Padre Barnabas rose from his place in the single chair. "I did not mean to shame you by referring to your grandparents' errors. Yours is one of the families that has distinguished itself in its devotion to the Church, and you may take, satisfaction in knowing that the zeal of your parents has done much to expunge the vile blot of faithlessness on the honor of España." He lifted his hand to bless Ciro, who knelt for him. "Be diligent in your faith and your prayers, Eje, and you will have nothing to fear from the Holy Office in this life or the Glory of God in the next."

"Thank you, Padre," Ciro said as he crossed himself. "I will remember all that you have told me, and benefit from your instruction." He rose and escorted the Dominican to the door. "If I might avail myself of your good counsel in a week?"

"Perhaps," Padre Barnabas said as he went down the hall.

Ciro sat in his room for the better part of an hour, his mind in turmoil. He had to find a way to warn Don Rolon, but knew that he must not appear to do so. For more than a month, he had suspected he had been watched and now he was certain of it. Whatever he said and did would be reported to Padre Barnabas, and if there were doubts of his actions or motives, he would be invited to explain them to officers of the Inquisition. What troubled him more than his own danger was the hazard Don Rolon faced. He could think of nothing that would make the Infante Real safe. With the full moon approaching once again, he did not know how he was to care for the young man.

There was a sound in the hallway, and Ciro looked up quickly, his heart thudding in his temples. "Who is there?"

"Lugantes." The jester came sauntering into the room. "I saw you had a visitor."

"Yes," Ciro said, his manner guarded.

"There are difficulties." He perched on the narrow bed where Ciro slept and pulled his legs up under him. "It is becoming more difficult, isn't it?"

"With the wedding and—" Ciro began.

"Don't treat me like an idiot, Ciro Eje," Lugantes said quietly, no trace of his bantering tone left. "You know that there is something the matter with the Infante Real. And it is worse than sympathy for Flemish Protestants."

Ciro said nothing; he moved to close the door.

"Not very wise, when there are those who make note of such things." He stared hard at Ciro. "No one followed me, and the guard who watches this part of the palace is putting his hand under the chambermaid's skirt. Padre Lucien is in the chapel and the other servants are preparing for the evening audiences. We have a little time to speak."

"You took care, if what you say is true." He studied the jester.

"You may check, but it will waste time," Lugantes said, reaching for one of the pillows so that he could lean against it. "Majestad thinks it's amusing that I cannot sit easily anywhere in the palace. He does not have a sore back."

Ciro nodded and went quickly into the hallway. When he was sure it was empty, he hurried back to his room. "What do you want with me?"

"Aid. Your master has always been kind to me and he is without friends at Court. Raimundo helps him, but that is for España; if he thought the country could be better served by his death, Raimundo would be the first with the dagger." He rubbed his dark hair out of his eyes. "When I was a boy, there was a man in our village. He had strange visions and fits, and from time to time, he would attack anyone foolish enough to be near him. Once the fit was passed, he had no recollection of it. Finally the priest sent him to penance at the Catedrál de San Ezequias, thinking that there he would be given care. The man was put to the Question. By the time they burned him in the plaza, he was mad as a rabid dog." He put his head on one side. "I don't think the Inquisitors have changed much since then."

"Why do you—" Ciro faltered, tasting bile at the back of his tongue.

"Is it the curse, that maddens Don Rolon when the moon is

full?" Lugantes asked very quietly.

"He is not maddened," Ciro replied. "Heaven forgive me for speaking."

Lugantes shook his head emphatically. "No. Do not think you have betrayed him. Upon my soul, you have not."

Ciro paced the room, trying to decide what he should do. "He is not maddened," he repeated at last. "There is a . . . change."

"Yes," Lugantes said, waiting for the rest of it.

"He is not himself then. Not himself. You would not know him, Lugantes." He put his hands to his face and strove to keep from screaming. "I have seen it for myself. I know . . ."

"And the marriage?" Lugantes interrupted.

"He can marry. For all nights but one, there is no danger." Ciro let his breath out in a long, trembling sigh. "He had planned . . . It makes no difference now, but he had decided not to visit his wife twice a month, as the priests recommend. He was going to be sure he could have time when he could absent himself without questions or disappointment." Ciro sat down abruptly.

"That was before he met the Venezian woman," Lugantes said with a stricken smile.

"If he had been told . . . if they had warned him, he would have prepared himself." Ciro struck his knee for emphasis.

"Do you think so?" Lugantes asked in such an anguished voice that Ciro was silenced. "What would have prepared him? It's done, and his plans are for nought."

"El Rey has said that he wishes proper conduct in the marriage. It helps a bit." Ciro pinched the bridge of his nose. "He was going hunting . . . hunting at the full moon. It was arranged. Now he does not wish to go. He has said that he will go to Inez's house and she will let him remain there without questions."

"Inez? After he has shunned her for three weeks? When all of España knows that he is enthralled by this Patrecipazio woman?" Lugantes laughed. "He will have to use care there at the best of times. Otherwise . . . " He got off the bed. "I cannot stay. It will be noticed that I was here. Do you play any instruments?"

This last inquiry was so unexpected that Ciro was taken back. "No. What has that to do with—"

"I play the viol and rebec quite well. You must let me teach you." He held up a finger. "No one will think it strange if I pass an hour with you from time to time while you are learning. And the sounds will let us talk without being easily overheard. If you play as badly as most beginners, they may even drive our intruders away." He chuckled, and the sound was almost convincing. "It may not be possible, but try to keep him away from Padre Juan."

"Yes." Ciro looked down at the jester, then said, "The Holy Office is watching him.

"El Rey still does not want Don Rolon to succeed him. Gustav insists. The Holy Office has long wanted to show its power, and Alonzo is blind enough to believe that they support his interests instead of their own. Padre Juan is willing to let him deceive himself. But you and I must not be deceived." He made a sign of encouragement to Ciro. "Get a viol. Tomorrow."

"I will." He glanced down the hall. "The way is clear."

Lugantes capered along the passage. "Oh, this time I want them to see me. I think 1 will enjoy teaching you, Eje. Dedicated students are so rare."

"Gracias," Ciro called after him, and then swallowed hard against the sickening fear that gnawed deep within him. He strove to compose himself, but all the notions he had led him to despair.

In Inez's bedchamber, the candles had burned low. There were scattered bits of a late meal on the circular table in the comer, but no one sat there now. Inez huddled on a padded stool; Don Rolon stood by the window, watching the moon through the screen.

"It will be full, day after tomorrow," he said to himself.

"And then it will wane," Inez said, growing more aggrieved as she watched him. "And I will not see you again for weeks. Will I?"

"It is the wedding. There are preparations," he said vaguely. Since he had arrived more than two hours before, he had not been able to speak to Inez about why he had come. "You are a good woman, Inez," he said lamely.

"Which is why you have neglected me," she responded, crossing her legs and pulling her robe more tightly around her. "You are preparing me for life in a convent, perhaps, so that I will be better?"

"No. Of course not." It was so much more difficult than he had thought it would be. "You have known that I am not free to follow my own—"

"So you tell me. That is not what the servants say, when they whisper among themselves and think that I do not hear them." Her annoyance grew stronger. "Then they say that the whole world knows that you have become enamored with that Venezian woman, and cannot wait to bed her. That is what my servants are saying." She made no attempt to control her tears. "Then you come here and lie to me, telling me there are too many ceremonies and receptions!"

"But there are ceremonies . . . " he protested. "I have not had any time to be alone." At first, it had been thrilling, but he was worried that he would not be able to break away for that night when the moon was full.

"You wish to be alone? Then why come here? Or were you going to spend the time by yourself?" She flung these accusations at him between sobs, wanting to hurt him because she was in such intense pain.

His hope for sanctuary here evaporated. "No. Inez, you must not believe that I do not care for you or would cast you off, or . . . " He started to reach out for her, but she pushed him away.

"No! I did not mind when you wanted me. That was well enough. I knew that I would have to share you with your wife. That was also acceptable. But you love her. I won't have it!" She got up, oversetting the stool, and blundered away from him. She was crying deeply now, shrieking at him. "I'm carrying your child, and I won't let you go to her!"

Don Rolon had been about to grab for her, but he froze at her words. "You're . . . you are . . . "

Now that she had said it, Inez tossed her head defiantly and smeared one hand through her tears. "Yes! Your child."

"But—" It was the one thing he had prayed would not happen. He stared at her, willing her to deny it. "You might be wrong."

"I know. I know. I know. Women don't mistake these things. And who has there been but you?" This last was a shout, and she watched him wince.

"It can't . . . Oh, God, Inez. What have I done?" He turned away from her, transfixed with horror.

"What a man does to a woman. And now you want to turn me out." She folded her arms again, her fingers digging deeply into the flesh above her elbows.

"No. No." He twisted his hands together and forced himself to look at her. "No, I will not turn you out. I would not ever turn you out, Inez."

"Not today or tomorrow," she said, making the words accusations. "But you will. Hidalgos promise readily, but they are not—"

"I will deal with you honorably," Don Rolon insisted, trying to overcome his terrible fear. "I will see that you are cared for, and that the child is raised well. You will not suffer more than you already have on my account." was an empty promise, he thought, knowing what he was what his heir might be.

"I don't believe that, Alteza. You will send me out of the city, and when it is convenient, you will send the baby to an orphanage, and I will be forgotten." Some of her sense of purpose had returned and she determined to get what she could from Don Rolon, who had been the author of all her woes.

"That's not necessary," Don Rolon said quickly. "If you wish to keep the child, then you shall. I will see that you have a husband, so that there will not be the stigma upon you." It might be enough to divert the intent of the curse, as well as offer Inez some protection he would not be able to give her. "Please, tell me if that is what you want and I will do all that I can." It would be little enough, he thought, castigating himself inwardly as he looked at her angry face.

"Then do what you will." She began to weep again, thinking that her life, which had seemed to have changed miraculously was now blighted beyond recall.

Don Rolon went to her and put his arm around her shoulder. "Inez, forgive me. I never intended that you should have to endure this. I do not want to see you in such travail. I won't let you bear the brunt of this alone." He tried to think of an officer who would be willing to marry her and live away from Valladolid, where no rumors would touch them. No one occurred to him. "I will speak to . . . a friend, and he will attend to it."

"A friend," she sulked. "And by the time he has taken care of it, all of Valladolid will know, and I will be disgraced forever."

Such things had happened before, Don Rolon knew, but he was also aware that often women who were the mistresses of well-placed men profited by their notoriety. "It will not be known. He will be sure of it."

"And then?" She pressed her head to his shoulder. "You will leave me, won't you? Nothing will change that."

"I must, Inez. I told you what is demanded of me. I may not refuse, or I will forfeit—" He stopped. He would have to confess this to Padre Lucien, and then insist that the priest aid him. That had been his first thought, but now he wondered if it was best to employ the Premonstratensian. Another, more worldly man, might do the work better.

"You will forfeit your Venezian woman," Inez said with a knowing look that made her young features appear much older than they were. "That is the sticking place, mi Infante, and well you know it."

There was enough truth in this accusation to shame Don Rolon into silence. "It is not in my power to refuse my father," he said stiffly when he had recovered himself to some extent. "I said that you will be cared for, and you will. But you and . . . and the child would be in danger if you remain here after I am married."

"Your father openly keeps mistresses, and has his Reina, and there are no objections," Inez pointed out, refusing to spare him humiliation.

"He has kept mistresses, he does not have one now, not one particular woman, nor has he for the last four years. He never kept them openly as a merchant might. And, Inez, he is el Rey, and must please only himself." That was far from accurate, Don Rolon knew, but it was what the people saw and believed. He had heard as much from the courtiers, as well.

"And when you are el Rey, will you call me back to you? Or will you keep to that Venezian woman and forget there ever was an Inez, who will raise your child?" She glared at him, relishing her anger now that she saw how potent a weapon it was against him.

"Don't be foolish. I could not forget you, ever, Inez." He wanted, oh, so badly, to walk out of her house and not see her again, but that was his father's way, and he could not bear to think he would conduct himself as heartlessly. "I will want to know, always, that you are well, and that the . . . child is well. I will make full provision now, so that you need never fear that there will be changes of fortune for you. I will see that there is money for you, and that it will be there always." He did not know how he would arrange this, but his determination increased as he spoke.

"I should be grateful, I suppose, and give meek thanks that you would do anything at all for me. I should, I suppose, be honored that you were generous enough to permit me to touch you. I should fawn at your feet for the baby I am carrying." Her scorn gave her courage and she faced him without a trace of fear. "If you go away, and there is no husband for me, I will look elsewhere for protection."

"No!" He knew by the curve of her mouth that she had misunderstood him and thought that it was jealousy in him that made him object. "There is too much risk."

"Others might be willing to take the risk. You did." She was beginning to feel powerful and her eyes brightened.

"Yes. And that is the risk. Those who know what has . . . passed between us, will seek to use you . . . " His hands closed tightly.

"But who knows of this? Don Enrique? I have told him I want none of him. He has a friend who said he would watch out for me. Which is more than you have done. A handsome hidalgo is better than a dwarf, mi Infante." She ran her tongue over her upper lip.

"Who is the hidalgo?" Don Rolon demanded.

"Why do you want to know?" she taunted him. "You have said that you will not be able to see me, and you want to send me away. Why should I not go to him instead?"

Don Rolon hesitated before he answered. "There are those who are enemies of the Crown, and who are enemies of mine. They are willing to . . . take advantage of you, or anyone who is close to me or el Rey. If I know who this hidalgo is, I will be able to protect you, should you need it."

"I do not know his name," Inez said, clearly lying and enjoying it. "I cannot help you, mi Infante. I know only that he is handsome and finds me beautiful. He has said that if he were free to marry, I would be his choice." Even when she had heard this she did not entirely believe it, and repeating it now, it sounded hollow. "I did not believe him, of course," she added quickly. "But I think he would care for me and keep me here."

"While you bear and suckle my child?" Don Rolon asked her. "What would that benefit him?"

Inez crossed her arms and shook her head. "You want to frighten me."

"No," he told her. "But were I you, Inez, I would be frightened. I did not want you to suffer, but it does not seem I have much choice in the matter. Someone has found you and knows that you are the one I visit—" He bowed his head. "Forgive me, hermosita, for causing you so much pain. It is not what I wanted to do."

"And that is all? You expect me to say you are blameless?" She wanted to scream at him again, and throw things, but she was not blind to the stupidity of such indulgence. "Do what you must. Find me the officer and I will tell you if it suits me to be his wife or if I will live with my hidalgo. You have no rights to me now, by your own admission. That may be, and it does not matter to me if you go to your Venezian woman and kiss her feet. I have the child, and as long as I do, you will care for him and for me, in the manner I wish. Do you agree?"

"I must," Don Rolon said softly. "Is there anything more?" He would have to discover who had found her and learn what he wanted. It was bad enough that Inez was with child; it was intolerable that she was no longer protected.

"I don't want that dwarf around here. The sight of such a creature is bad for my baby Inez insisted, taking full advantage of her pregnancy. Mantes was Don Rolon's spy, and she wanted no part of the jester.

"There must be someone to speak with you," Don Rolon said, and wondered how much he dared confide to Raimundo. Surely if anyone could find out who wooed Inez, it was Raimundo.

"If you will not come yourself, send a courtier. I do not want to speak to Lugantes again." There was an implacable note in her voice now, coming from her newly found strength. "I will tell you when I wish to have a visitor. One of my servants will come to the palace."

"Ita," said Don Rolon in Latin, accepting her terms with a formal bow. "I pray for your sake and the sake of the child beneath your heart that you are wise."

"Gracias," Inez spat, then turned on her heel and left him alone.

It was not the way Don Rolon had imagined them parting, though he had often tried to picture what would happen. He had thought she would weep, or show herself penitent, not be the willful, advantage-seeking woman she had revealed herself to be. Sighing, he went out of Inez's house.

17

With an elegant, insolent bow, Gil presented himself to Zaretta. "It has been difficult for me to offer you my felicitations, Señorita Patrecipazio, what with the demands of our court being what they are." His smile was all that was charming, his dress was superb and he kissed her hand with rare grace, never bothering to look at Don Rolon, who walked beside her through the throng in the largest of the formal gardens.

"Many of the same demands are found in Venezia," Zaretta responded, but with just enough of a smile that there could be no offense taken from this gentle reprimand. She liked fair men with dash, and Gil del Rey was the very image of a proper man.

"Accidents of birth, Señorita. All of us are victims of them, in one way or another." It was inexcusable of Gil to intrude in this way, and reprehensible of him to point out, obliquely or directly, his bastardy. His lips curved upward as much in satisfaction as amusement. "In another time or place, my half brother and I would be the most devoted of friends, but because fate has placed one stamp upon me and another one on him. Has it not, Infante?" This last, audacious challenge was delivered to Don Rolon's face, with the full impact of his sinister insouciance.

"Apparently," Don Rolon said haughtily.

"So I am illegitimate, which is unfortunate, but at least I am not cursed." With a parting bow, he turned away from Don Rolon and Zaretta and was quickly lost in the crowd.

"I have heard of this curse before," Zaretta said musingly, her thoughts still on the blond curls and handsome face of Gil del Rey.

Don Rolon was silent, not wishing to discuss the matter again. Their wedding would be at noon tomorrow, and he did not want to cast a pall on the celebration. It was only part of the reason, he admitted as much to himself, for it would be dreadful to have this glorious young woman become disgusted with him. As it was, he would have to leave her three days after their wedding, when the full moon would rise again. It was more than he could endure, anticipating the change that would overtake him.

"What is it troubles you, mi Infante?" Zaretta asked, misreading his frown for condemnation. "It is not unusual for a bastard to be angry at his plight, especially here in España where there are such rigid laws."

It galled Don Rolon to hear Zaretta defend Gil, but he held back the angry retort that hovered on his lips. "It is also not uncommon to be angry for a curse, Señorita." The answer was adequate, as far as it went.

"Oh, yes. That curse, that everyone whispers of. It was a poor godless woman, they tell me, who cursed your mother." She shook her head impatiently. "I have sat through two autos-da-fé, and that should be ample for the demands of the Church. I do not wish to see more of them, for they distress me. Don't they bother you?"

"Yes," Don Rolon whispered, "but it is best not to say so. Be prudent, mi paloma, and keep your questions to yourself, or suspicion might fall upon you. The officers of the Inquisition are most vigilant." He recalled all he had been told of the methods of the Secular Arm, and he hoped that Zaretta would never learn of them.

"We have the Inquisition in Venezia, but they are not so . . . so extensive as here," she said, then waved to one of her countrymen. "We Venezians stand out here, I am afraid," she said with pride. "You in your blacks and golds, and we in our bright colors; I am constantly surprised."

Don Rolon accepted the change of subject with gratitude.

"It is not our way to be gaudy." He knew from the way her chin rose that he had said it badly. "I myself admire the colors and pearls and slashings, but it is not our way in España." It was not enough, he could tell by the shine in her enormous eyes. He tried once more.

"When I was young, I wanted a pourpoint of scarlet, but my father said that only the Princes of the Church were entitled to deck themselves in red, and so I set my heart on a new saddle instead."

"Such a tractable boy," Zaretta murmured, still annoyed with him.

How could he tell her of the bleakness of those years, when he was cared for by nuns with only his tutors for company? Lugantes had not come until later, but he had been the only amusement he could remember in his life. "It is for us to set the example in duty and dedication," Don Rolon said, as he had repeated the lesson so many times before under the stem instruction of his first confessor.

"Gracious," Zaretta said, and laughed provokingly. "You must have been very dour, then. Now you are only a little dull." She removed her hand from his arm and slipped away from him. "I must find my ladies, Infante. Tomorrow I will see you again, at the altar."

There would be the three-hour Nuptial Mass, and afterward an evening of feasting and other entertainments. Don Rolon dreaded it. But the vision of that lovely, fair nymph in his bed compensated for all the other distress. His mouth was dry and his tongue felt too big behind his teeth. Everything he had learned with Inez, he would share with Zaretta. There would be tenderness and sweetness and such delight that the angels would sing for them. He stared into the press of guests, searching for the glimmer of her pale green gown.

"Infante," said a voice at his shoulder, and he jumped.

"Yes?" He met Raimundo's gaze with the expression of a startled deer. "Oh, Dominguez."

"I have been searching for you, Alteza," he said formally, with the proper degree of friendliness mixed with his courtly deference.

"Is there something urgent?" He hoped it was not the case, with his wedding so near and his thoughts in chaos.

"Not precisely," Raimundo said in his most polite and soothing manner. "You asked me to attend to a matter for you."

"Oh. Yes." A few days before, he had at last confided in Raimundo about his difficulty with Inez, and had been promised the aid of the Portuguese Duque.

"I believe the matter has been discharged. There is a Capitan Iturbes, who accompanied you to El Morro." He smiled and nodded, just familiar enough in his treatment of Don Rolon to discourage others from joining their conversa-tion. "No doubt you remember him. He told me that he thought Inez Remos a . . . personable young woman, and he is not adverse to raising your child, so long as there is adequate provision. He comes from Santander, and is willing to return there if there is money enough to make it worth his while. I have arranged for him to obtain a commission with del Circovar, and will see that there are funds paid twice each year. Iturbes has given his word that he will speak to Inez at once, and explain it all to her."

Don Rolon nodded, hardly able to take it all in. "I . . . thank you, Dominguez."

"I have also written to the Benedictines in Santander, indicating that, education should be provided for the child if male, and proper skills if female. That way, you need not fear that the child will be neglected." Raimundo bowed before Don Rolon. "I will continue to watch after your interests, Alteza. When I see Iturbes tomorrow morning, he will be able to tell me when he and Inez will leave for the north."

"It is good of you, Dominguez, and of Iturbes. I pray that Inez will allow herself to be persuaded, instead of hoping for her courtier to . . . " He sighed once. "I also pray that my betrothed will not learn of these sordid things."

"You would better spend your time in hoping that Padre Juan learns nothing of them. Women of noble Houses know that men are fleshly beings, but Padre Juan has no such tolerance, and his wrath is more dire than your bride's will ever be." Raimundo spoke with emphasis but his voice never changed from the polite tone he had been using throughout their talk. "If her courtier wants to implicate you to Padre Juan, you will be in more danger than if you had kept a hundred mistresses and spurned your wife."

"Do you think that?" Don Rolon asked. "With Gil paying court to her?"

"Gil is doing it to aggravate you." Raimundo wanted to make light of the most recent of Gil's trespasses, and this was the best notion he had.

"Most successfully," Don Rolon said. "I will try to be indulgent, but it might be impossible. I know that my father will not require Gil to be respectful, and so I must not complain of it, or . . . " He shrugged. "You know what Gil is, Dominguez. Would you want him paying court to your wife?" Too late, he thought back to the time, three years before, when Gil had been flagrant in his attention to Raimundo's Duquessa, and he flushed deeply.

"As I recall," Raimundo said, not quite able to conceal his discomfort, "I disliked it very much."

"I did not mean to . . . " Don Rolon began, but was cut short by the courtier.

"It is long past, and there is nothing that I can do now, or could have done then, to change it." He paused to swallow. "I will see that someone speaks to your bride, Alteza, and discreetly, so that there will be no difficulties over it, and we will determine that Gil will not bother her unduly." He bowed to indicate his withdrawal. "There are matters I must attend to for El Majestad before tomorrow. I will do myself the honor of waiting upon you after your Nuptial Mass, Alteza, for the purpose of extending my best wishes on the marriage you are undertaking."

"A thousand thanks, Dominguez," Don Rolon said perfunctorily, wishing he had an excuse to detain Raimundo. None occurred to him, and when he looked around again, he saw Nobile Rigonzetti making his way through the crowd, a determined smile on his face and a keen light in his eye.

They retired with great ceremony and ritual some time near midnight. The bells of the Catedrál were still booming out their approval, and merrymakers cavorted in the huge reception halls below. A procession of Dominican monks had accompanied them to their bedchamber, and there had been half an hour of prayers while the honored courtiers laid out the elaborate, many-layered bedclothes for Don Rolon and his bride. By the time they had been taken aside and their garments changed, another half hour had gone by and a few of the monks were beginning to yawn.

"It is the burden of those born to high station," Padre Juan intoned, "to have to ensure the Succession in the name of their House and their God. Therefore, we pray that this union be fruitful and sound, and that God will show his favor and blessings through the children He sends you." He made the sign of the cross over the newly married pair, then turned to the others in the room. "It is fitting at this time that we leave these two to their prayers and their vows." He motioned all toward the door. "We beseech God to give you His bounty."

"Is it over?" Zaretta asked when the door was closed and the chanting of the monks had faded in the echoing halls.

"I think so," Don Rolon said as he rose from his knees. "I am sorry that it has been so interminable."

"I thought we would be trapped at the banquet forever," Zaretta said as she went toward the bed and looked down at the embroidered linen under the satin coverlets. "They have gone to much trouble. I suppose in the morning they will hang out the sheets for everyone to see."

"No!" Don Rolon protested, then stopped.

"Well, they do in Venezia." She pulled at the lacing of her lace shift. "Must we wear these things all the time?"

"The Church requires it," Don Rolon answered, his voice muffled with embarrassment. "But . . ."

"The Church is filled with men who have no wives. If they really want God to give us heirs, there had better be more than this for us. One hole in the front of each! It's disgusting!" She sat on the side of the bed and tugged the starched cap off her head, tossing it carelessly toward one of the chairs by the fireplace.

"I know." He felt demeaned by their whole conversation. "About the sheets."

"Yes?" She turned her beautiful face toward him. "What about them?"

"Padre Juan will examine them in the morning." He hated to admit this; just saying the words made him feel slightly ill.

"The Inquisitor?" She was genuinely shocked at this, and made no effort to conceal it. "Why should he be the one?"

"So that if there is a question about the marriage, he will be able to present testimony that the marriage was consummated." He coughed, cleared his throat and tried to go on. "If he cannot say that it has happened, then—"

"Then what?" She flung up her hands. "This is hopeless! There are priests all around us, and you're looking glum as a miller in a drought." She began to unfasten the long series of ribbons that closed the front of her wedding shift. "This is going to take forever."

"They will look at the garments, too." He wanted to melt into the wall, or be transformed into a chair, anything that would remove him from the horrible shame that nearly overwhelmed him as he watched her.

"Then I will cut my finger or bite my lip and do whatever I must." She had got the first five of the knots undone and was working on the sixth. "I'm so tired, all I want to do is sleep, but if that Inquisitor is going to inspect the sheets and clothes, I suppose we'd better make sure he has something to find." She reached for the next bows and tugged them undone.

"Oh, Zaretta, if you would rather not, I will tell some tale about being sick with wine or . . ." He wanted desperately to be back in his old quarters, with Ciro tending to him and Padre Lucien listening to his confessions. There was so much he had not been able to tell the Premonstratensian, and now that he had taken Communion and entered into one of the Sacramental States, he was appalled at the sins he had brought upon himself and had compounded.

"That will mean going through the entire charade again," Zaretta said, crossing her arms over her head and tugging the shift off at last. "There. That is better. Do not be upset, my husband, for Mother Eve and Mother Mary looked no different than I do when they came to their spouses."

"They were not more beautiful than you," Don Rolon whispered, taking a few steps nearer the head of the bed.

"Very pretty," she approved. "Compliments are pleasant at these times." She pulled back the bedding and slid between the covers. "It is warm in here, but not too bad, you know." She drew the sheets up to her chin, then yawned. In another woman, it might have offended Don Rolon, but since it was Zaretta, the yawn was graceful and she was adorable for doing it.

"Shall I take off my shift, as well?" he asked, not knowing how to inquire indirectly. Everything he had been told about well-bred women warned him that she would be offended by what he suggested, no matter how she herself behaved. He braced himself for more rebukes.

"Oh, yes, please. I'd think there was a corpse laid out for burial if you were to leave if on." She pinched the bridge of her nose. "My head aches, too. And my feet are sore."

"I am sorry," he said, conscience-stricken that she should feel any discomfort on his account. "It is inexcusable of me to—"

"Why don't you rub my feet?" she interrupted him with a wide smile.

The suggestion was preposterous. Such work was done by servants, and lower servants at that. Certainly no one asked the heir to the throne to degrade himself in that way. He was about to object and explain to her how she had insulted him when he saw the beguiling smile and the softness of her mouth, and all his good resolutions of correct behavior disappeared. Who knows, he told himself, it may be that in Venezia, a suitor is expected to rub the feet of his beloved. He sat on the edge of the bed. "All right. Which do you want me to do first?"

"First I want you to get out of that absurd shift, and then I want you to be comfortable because I like having my feet rubbed a long time." Her smile was full of mischief but he decided that it was her youth and apprehension that caused her to appear so. He did as she bade him, putting the shift aside carefully while she stared at him. "You are very lean," she observed as he got into bed and moved one of the pillows.

"We are taught to deplore the needs of the body and think instead of the good of the soul." It was another one of the endless lessons from his youth, and he said it without thinking.

"Not all the needs, I hope," she said as she put her foot into his hands.

It was such a little foot, he thought, rosy and fragile, dainty, narrow, with rounded nails and long toes. He stroked it as if it were a little animal he held, or a bird. "You are very lovely."

"Press harder. I said that my feet are sore. They ache. Use your thumbs and press with them." She was both flattered and exasperated that he regarded her so reverently. "Don't your feet ever hurt?"

"Sometimes," he answered, using a little more force but afraid that he might hurt her. It was impossible to think of his feet and hers as being the same things. Then he thought of those nights of the full moon, and he knew with loathing that they could not be the same ever, for hers would always be the feet of a desirable woman, and his changed into clawed pads, as did his hands. It was sacrilege for him to touch her at all, considering what he was. He almost moved away from her.

"You're doing better," she encouraged him, noticing how he faltered. It was hard enough to persuade him that she was not made of glass, but if he did not use her as he was required to, there might never be children, and the Doge might end the marriage and use her to bargain with the Sultan in Constantinople, as he had threatened to do before. Given the choice of the Infante Real or a place in the harem of an Eastern potentate, she was determined to please the morose young man she had married.

"I don't want to . . . hurt you." He took her other foot and rubbed it gently, wanting to plead with her for patience. It was bad enough that he rub her feet, but the Infante Real could not plead with anyone but God.

"You are considerate, Don Rolon, and for that I am grateful. But it is expected that I will go through the travail of childbirth and bring your heirs into the world. Surely if that is to be my lot, you may be a little more . . . emphatic with my feet." She smiled at him again, trying to discover any hint of playfulness that might be hidden in his guarded soul.

"Don't think of it, Zaretta. I beg of you. When I remember that you are being asked to bear my children, I am horrified." He could not tell her how great his fear was, for he would have to tell her more than he dared.

"Women bear children. It is their"—she almost said lot in life, but caught herself—"destiny."

"Destiny," he repeated blankly. He stared into his lap and saw that he was aroused. He did not know when it had happened, and he could think of no way to tell her gently of his state. It was the duty of husbands to initiate their wives into the mysteries of union, but he could find no words to tell her.

"Don Rolon, come and lie beside me," Zaretta coaxed. `Here. Close to me. I am not a child, and my mother long since told me how to be a wife."

Once again, Don Rolon was shocked, but this time it was quickly followed by relief. At least he was spared one ordeal. He stretched out on the bed, reaching tentatively to brush her cheek with his fingers. "You are so beautiful, Zaretta." It was thrilling to say her name, that familiarity being as treasured as the access to her body. There were titles he would have to accord her in public, but while they were alone, he was permitted to call her Zaretta, and no one else could do so without his permission.

"Come under the covers, Don Rolon. I want to find out the sort of man you are." What she saw of him in the candlelight was promising though not what she had hoped for. Still, she would make the best of it, she thought, and it was better than many another man her uncle might have chosen for her.

Don Rolon moved slowly, afraid that he would yet do something that would turn her away from him. The linen was smooth under his nakedness, and when he touched Zaretta, he jumped as if a hot brand had been set to his flesh. He half expected to see her cowering away from him, but instead she made a gesture of encouragement, then leaned over to kiss him. He felt his mind dissolve, all his careful planning fizz away from the rush of desire that went through him like lightning through a tree. He could not touch or taste or explore enough of her.

As he swarmed over her, Zaretta was pleased at his passion. At least she had not married a monk, she thought, and remembered then to scrape open the small cut on her leg so that there would be blood on the sheets for Padre Juan to see the next morning.

18

"There are sins to confess?" Gil asked Zaretta as he saw her come out of la Reina's chapel four days after her wedding. "I would not have thought that my half brother would be able to . . . "

Zaretta stared directly at Gil. "My sins, whatever they are, are between my confessor, God, and myself, and they do not concern you."

Chastened, he nodded. "Of course. But you must not chide me for my surprise. Don Rolon has never been one of the mad young men at Court. Hidalgos are supposed to be a little wild, but he—"

"He is Infante Real, and it may be that he feels his responsibilities." She smiled pleasantly. "La Reina has been instructing me in the workings of the Court, and I find that I do not know enough yet. You are a most troubling man, Gil del Rey, and for that, Padre Barnabas has instructed me to keep you at a distance." They were walking down the corridor together, two ladies following them at the distance of five paces.

"You are speaking to me now," he pointed out with considerable charm while he inwardly cursed Padre Barnabas. He would have to deal with the priest later.

"Well, it would be rude not to," she responded a trifle self-consciously. "You are the son of el Rey, and in spite of your illegitimacy, you stand high in his esteem. I do not need a friend to tell me that Alonzo would prefer to see you in Don Rolon's place. I am a stranger here, and I would be foolish to be unkind to you." She stopped at the intersection of two hallways. "I will leave you here, Gil, and I will not see you until tomorrow."

"Y nada mas," Gil said in a low voice, making it a statement instead of a question.

"There is nothing more it can be," she answered, then favored him with a slight curtsy before hurrying away from him.

Gil watched her go with much inner conflict. That the Infante Real should have such a bride! He was determined to win her favor, and with Don Rolon once again gone from Court, he was convinced that he would be able to make the most of Zaretta's confusion. Now she had warned him,—however obliquely, that the Church was watching her, and that she must be circumspect. He felt strangely encouraged by this, for it told him she was concerned for him. He nodded to her two ladies who swept silently past him, then sauntered away in search of Padre Juan.

The Inquisitor was coming out of a meeting with the magistrates of Valladolid, and from the stony look on his face, he had been thwarted. He bestowed the most grudging of blessings and refused to linger for the usual polite conversation that concluded such gatherings. He was startled to see Gil standing respectfully a little way off, and used el Rey's bastard as an excuse to break away from the small party of staid men.

"Good Padre," Gil said with a slight bow. "I do not know how to speak to you."

"Without hypocrisy, I pray you," Padre Juan snapped. "Those liars there have spent most of the morning declaring that they cannot enforce the law, though to fail to do so is treason to the Throne and the Church. The law is clear and the penalties are concise. There is no room for argument, but they seek to object." He opened the door that led to an antechamber of the chapel royal.

"Lamentable indeed." Gil was unaware of what laws were involved, but he knew that Padre Juan would prefer the most rigorous enforcement of any of them, and so he said, "When laws are lax, the people are in greatest danger."

Padre Juan stopped and looked at him narrowly. "That is true, but you must forgive me if I am surprised to hear you subscribe to such opinions. You are the one who flouts the authority of your father and Our Lord."

"Because there are others in high office who do," Gil answered glibly. "You might not think I notice such things, but I do. If my father is willing to indulge me, then why should I not take advantage of his goodwill, since I will have little else from him, now or ever." It was a relief to show his malice; most of the time, he had to disguise it.

"Temper the wrath in your soul, my son, or you will fall into error, which would cause the greatest anguish to el Rey and your good angel," Padre Juan said. "In España, we must give the example to the world, and purge ourselves and our country of the evil that God has given to go to and fro in the earth." He was falling automatically into his pulpit tone, weighing each word for its power and worth and speaking as if to an enthralled congregation.

"Padre, you ask more of me than I can do," Gil said, showing his teeth.

"I do not ask it, no, Gil, not I. It is God Himself Who asks you to consider your sins and abhor them for the shame they give to God. You allow yourself to be seduced by envy. That is a great, cardinal sin, and for it you will suffer in Hell if you do not repent of it." He folded his arms. "I have warned you of this before. Why are you suddenly willing to listen to me?"

Gil chuckled. "Padre, my brother has recently got himself a wife. The match is pleasing to her country and España, but I do not know what either my brother or his bride thinks of the arrangement."

"They are both good and humble children of the Church, and they accept what God has given them to do for the benefit of their countries and their Houses, which is what all those of royal blood must do if they are to discharge their obligations with honor." He waited, studying Gil in the silence that was heavy between them.

"But will there be issue? And if there is issue, will they be like Genevieve's children, with minds more fanciful than a balladeer's, and never able to live without nurses?" He waved his hand. "No, I do not fear for the Hapsburgs, or not in the way that Don Rolon must do, but as one who has not yet lost hope that the mantle of greatness might still be laid upon my shoulders. For I know I will carry that burden better than my brother. Half the time he is afraid of his own shadow. It may be that he is also afraid of his wife, and if that is the case, el Rey must know of it, and proper steps taken at once. The longer it is delayed, then the more difficult it becomes to conclude all the—"

"The marriage was consummated," Padre Juan said stiffly. "I am satisfied that they are man and wife in the eyes of God and the Church. If Zaretta is barren, which we must pray is not the case, then it may be that we will have to seek other solutions, but the Pope requires at least five years of fruitless union before he will entertain any process on behalf of the throne. That is why it is essential that we persecute heretics with vigor, for well we Dominicans know how nefarious they are, and how they plot and scheme to blight this marriage. If you are too pointed in your opposition to the Succession, Gil, you stand in some danger from my Brothers in Christ. Frey Moises has been given the particular task of examining discontent in the court so that the influence of those fallen away from the True Church of Christ may be revealed. His testimony will be offered regularly to the Holy Office for their action; it would sadden me more than I can tell you to learn that Frey Moises included your name in such a report. The distress it would bring your father far exceeds any disappointments he has suffered thus far in his reign."

Gil tried to smile. "That sounds like a warning, Padre."

"It is, my son," Padre Juan said implacably. "Let me remind you that I cannot give you protection any more than I could protect Don Rolon or El Majestad."

"I understand, Padre."

"For the sake of your father, I hope you do." Padre Juan indicated the door.

"One thing more, mi Padre, and then I will leave you to your meditations." Gil paused for an instant, trying to think of the best way to word his last complaint. "My brother, though newly married, has gone off to hunt, taking only his valet with him. That is odd, but he has always been an odd boy. When the Infante Real hunts, he usually goes in a large party. Yet Don Rolon goes alone. I do not say that he has not told the truth. I do not accuse him of anything. But I wonder if hunting is all he does, since he has made no secret of his concern for the plight of Flemish Protestants."

"What do you mean?" Padre Juan demanded.

"Nothing. I only think it would be easy for my brother, while hunting, to find himself in odd company. I am not a godly man, and I have no pretense about it. But if I were as beleaguered as you are with heretics and Diabolists, I would set men to follow the Infante, the next time he takes to the hills by himself." Gil bowed his head and waited for the blessing that would dismiss him.

"Are you saying that you suspect him of harboring heretics?" Padre Juan asked, his voice turning harsh.

"I say only that he could do so, if he wished. And I recall that he has said before that it is wrong to burn Flemings. I am of an envious and suspicious nature, Padre, as you yourself have told me, many times. Yet even a man of an envious and suspicious nature may be correct in his suspicions."

Padre Juan started to speak, thought better of it, and simply gave Gil the blessing he waited for. "Now leave me."

"Of course, Padre." Gil was well-pleased with himself as he closed the door.

Raimundo entered Don Rolon's presence with more urgency than tact. He was still dressed for riding and he had not taken the time to remove the short cape that protected his clothes from the pull of branches and brambles. "You returned last night," he said when he had bowed.

"Fairly late," Don Rolon said, puzzled at this intrusion.

"You were gone for more than a week," Raimundo said accusingly. "Don't you know what that can make some of us believe? Your wedding was so recent, and you leave for so long a time hunting." He paced the length of the study that had recently been set aside for Don Rolon's use. "It is bad enough with Gil fostering questions about your potency but it is worse to find that you are trying to give weight to his innuendos by running off to the hills, leaving your new wife and—"

"Does anyone believe Gil?" Don Rolon asked wearily. "It's obvious that he is not disinterested, and only his friends think—"

"One of his friends is your father, Don Rolon," Raimundo snapped. "Don't you know how much Gil would do if it would mean he could occupy your place? Are you blind to what he is doing?" He very nearly seized Don Rolon by the shoulders to shake him, but as exasperated as he was, his years of courtesy kept him from venturing so far.

"My father believes poorly enough of me as it is. If my . . . wife does not complain and her confessor does not question me, then all we need do is produce the children el Rey desires and that will be the end of it." He sat down at the writing table and braced his elbows on its polished surface.

"Are you . . . displeased with marriage?" It was an awkward question, but one that Don Rolon would have to get used to answering if he left his wife alone too often.

"Not at all," the Infante Real said at once, and with such feeling that Raimundo was more reassured than he had been for some time. "I am more pleased than I ever hoped to be. But, Raimundo, you have a wife. You have two children. It is unfortunate that you and your wife do not agree, but others have learned to endure antipathy before now. Think of la Reina and my father." He laced his fingers under his chin and stared vacantly at the far wall. "My wife is . . . wonderful. That is what troubles me. I look at my half sisters, and the fear I have told you of returns a thousandfold. How can I wish such children on a woman like Zaretta?" His face clouded. "And there are others. If it were only the two of them, but there was my grandmother and my father's sister, the one who . . . well, you knew her."

"Alteza, there must be children," Raimundo said as compassionately as he knew how. "It is why you were married, and it is what you must do."

"But not yet!" Don Rolon turned to face him. "Is it so much to ask for a year of peace together before we do as our countries and our Houses demand? I know that spending time away from my wife's bed will lessen the chance of children now." He got up suddenly and reached for the door. The hall beyond was empty but there were echoes of hurrying feet.

"We may not have been overheard, Alteza," said when Don Rolon closed the door again.

"And we may have been. Well, so be it. Let the spy carry the tale wherever he wishes, it is all one to me." He leaned back against the door, as if his body would make them safer. "I have not yet told my confessor of my thoughts. He will not approve, nor will my father, but that is nothing new."

"Alteza." Raimundo started to bow, then looked closely at the Infante Real. "You are tired, Alteza?"

"I was born tired, Raimundo." He knew this was no answer, and sighed. "Yes, I am tired. The chase I was on was . . . rigorous. It exhausted me." He shuddered at the memory of coming to himself on a barren hillside, many leagues from the place where he had taken lodging with Ciro. He was ragged and filthy and there had been blood on his hands which he feared was not his own. What creature had he been, then? What had he done? He had sobbed in horror as he found his way back through the winding shepherds' paths to a village where the peasants refused to speak to him, and where the priest, an old man in monk's habit, held up a crucifix and commanded him to depart. That had been four days ago, and now as he thought about that moment, he felt his body grow cold, as if he were buried in snow, all cold and suffocating.

"Alteza," Raimundo said, seeing despair and revulsion in Don Rolon's eyes, "was there more than exhaustion?"

"Perhaps," he replied, not able to deny it, but growing upset again.

"Is it . . . a danger to you?" He had discounted the rumors that Don Rolon was meeting with Protestants, but now he wondered.

"What isn't dangerous to me, Raimundo. I have too much to do." He looked away; then, with his eyes still averted, he said, "I do not know what my father thinks of me, but I know it is not to my credit. How else should I live, but to the satisfaction of el Rey? That is what I am told I must do, and it is all that I am told my father wishes of me. Yet there is no way I can achieve these ends. I am not the man they said I am." He put his hands over his eyes. "I think I will run mad, my friend."

This soft, unutterably painful admission shook Raimundo to the roots. "Mad, Alteza?" There was madness enough in the royal family, and to have that afaffliction strike the Infante Real, and now, would be a blow that could bring down all that Alonzo and his father had striven to achieve.

"Not as the rest of the family, but still—" He stopped, thinking that he had said too much to Raimundo.

"Alteza, what . . . what makes you . . . " He did not want to ask anything more.

"Oh, it is an old fear, and now that I am expected to father children, I do not know what I am to do. He tried to make this dismissal believable, and saw that in part Raimundo was accepting it, so he pressed his point more forcefully. "I see my half sisters, and 1 know that my children could be the same. I listen to the words of my father, who has told me so often that I am cursed, and what curse could be more terrible than to see madness visited on my children?"

"And for el Rey, do you think he has the same fear?" Raimundo guessed.

"De seguro. I have dreaded this for years. When I confess, I ask my priest to examine what I tell him for—" He broke off, not trusting himself to say more.

"Poor Infante," Raimundo said quietly. "It has been more of a burden on you than ever I thought." He considered the silences of the Infante Real over all the years, his reluctance to demand more of his father, his disinclination to involve himself with the life of the Court and thought that at last he understood the youth. "What has your confessor told you?"

"Nothing to trouble me, not on that. But madmen are clever, and they often lie better than those whose minds are not . . . So it could be that . . . " He put his hands to his face. "Do not speak of this, Raimundo, I beg of you. I beg of you."

"I would not do so, mi Infante."

"Not even to your confessor. If word of this reached Padre Juan's ears, he would take me under his wing, and that—" The thought of an Inquisitorial Process being determined against him made him feel clammy all over. A month in the power of the Holy Office, and his true affliction would be apparent. Then it would be only a matter of whether the Question or the flames would have him.

"That must not happen," Raimundo said, knowing how much Padre Juan would rejoice to have the House of Hapsburg in his hands at last.

"No," Don Rolon said, for vastly different reasons than Raimundo had.

The Portuguese nobleman was not often indecisive, but now there were serious doubts rising within him. "Alteza," he said uncertainly, "do you think that you are mad?"

"No," Don Rolon said after consideration. "I fear it, but . . . there are worse things than madness."

"What?" Raimundo was worried at Don Rolon's last remark, and frowned as he thought it over. "How do you mean?"

Quickly Don Rolon changed his tactics. "There is the Holy Office, and what it might do, if—"

"Ah. Again the Inquisition. The whole of your House would suffer if they were to pursue a Process." Raimundo went once around the room. "If there is strength in my right arm and life in my body, I swear to you that I will defend you as heir to the throne."

Don Rolon turned amazed eyes on him. "Dominguez, you do not need—"

"You have my oath, Infante, and it is heard in Heaven. I cannot stand by and see all of España, and Portugal with it, come under the yoke of the Holy Office more than is already the case. We have jeopardized our position in the world badly enough as it is. If there is a clash of Church and the Emperor, most of this country will split in half, and perhaps Europe with it. I will not be party to that." He rested his hand on the hilt of his short sword. Because he was still dressed for hunting, this weapon was less elegant and more dangerously functional than the sword that was required as part of fashion; the gesture had the same efficient characteristic, and Don Rolon knew beyond question that Raimundo was completely sincere.

"I am grateful to you more than there are words to say or favors to show you, Duque, and as God will judge me, if ever I am permitted to show you honor from the throne, I will do so with a glad heart." He reached out and laid his hand briefly on Raimundo's shoulder, an act of such remarkable acknowledgment that Raimundo was wholly unable to speak.

He bowed deeply, as if to el Rey, and then turned away, leaving the study so quickly that he did not see the deeply worried scowl that creased Don Rolon's brow.

Lugantes shook his head. "You must not treat the instrument in that way, Ciro," he said patiently, and demonstrated his point beautifully on his own viol. "You see, thus."

"Lugantes—" Ciro began protesting, then was silenced by the quick, authoritative gesture from the dwarf. "I have been away and have not had much opportunity to practice. Do not be too severe with me." This last improvisation brought an approving smile from Lugantes, and so he went on. "I don't know what you will require."

"That you make dreadful notes until our observers grow tired of them," Lugantes said quietly, playing the passage again to cover his words. "Do not make an effort to improve too much."

Ciro very nearly laughed, but was able to confine his mirth to a crooked smile, for he had to admit that there was little to provide humor in his life. "I will do what I can," he said, and dragged the bow over the protesting strings:

"Excellent," Lugantes said under.the screech. "That should drive them out in no time." He smiled benignly as Ciro kept at the exercise.

"The journey," Ciro whispered as he continued to make terrible noises on the viol, "was . . . worse."

"Than before?" Lugantes asked, saying in a more normal tone, "Do try that last passage again, Ciro. You have not mastered the melody at all."

"Yes, than before," Ciro went on against the whine of the bass strings. "He did not come to himself where I was, and by the time he returned, there were many who had seen him,"

"That is most unfortunate," Lugantes said in a normal conversational tone, and anyone listening to the lesson would be forced to agree. "What happened?"

"He was not within doors when the . . . change occurred, and so I could not . . . we had made provision for him, but he was away, and so he . . . ran wild through the hills for the night. He said that one village chased him away." He stopped tormenting the viol, and said, "I don't know if I should hope for improvement."

"You must always hope, my friend," Lugantes said promptly. "Hope is all that we have from God; that and a place to die." He bowed three beautiful phrases. "You see, if my little hands can master this, think what you might learn to accomplish. Transformations are all around us."

"Sadly." He made a few more dreadful and halfhearted attempts with the viol. "It took him sooner this time. At first, it required at least an hour after the sun had set for the moon to have its way with him, but now there is much shorter time to be used before the alterations take place. That was why he was still out."

"Where was he?" Lugantes said, making a gesture for Ciro to continue with his playing.

"In the stables. I did not show him what became of the pack mule we brought. I told the peasants near the lodge that the animal became ill, and for that reason I could not spare the meat for them. They do not want to run the risk of bringing illness to their animals." He stopped his sounds again. "I was not prepared for it."

"A terrible thing. Next time, however, you will anticipate." He began to play an air, making his viol sing plaintively. "You hear this, my friend? You hear how the heart of the music cries out? Is it not the same way with the soul, that it too cries out?"

"Even the soul of the wolf?" Ciro asked, possessed again of abhorrence. He tried to shut out the memory of seeing that lean gray shape with blood-spattered fur go racing off through the night, but it was burned into his mind and he could not be free of it.

"Especially the wolf. Which of God's wild creatures sings more beautifully, or is more in need of salvation?" Lugantes stopped his performance. "You will try again, Ciro, and I will help you so that next time you will be better prepared."

"I pray it is so," Ciro said devoutly, and was about to set aside the viol when he felt Lugantes' bow tap his arm. "But—"

"We have only begun," Lugantes reprimanded him gently. "And besides," he added with a smirk, "most of our audience has fled. You did your task very well, Ciro. I applaud you. But I beg you will practice a little more for next time."

19

Alonzo subjected Raimundo to a long, stony scowl. "You displease us, Dominguez, and we regret that we must bring this to your attention."

"If you are unhappy, Majestad, I am desolate. It has never been my intention to offend you in any way, but to serve you and my Rey in ways that would meet with your gracious satisfaction." He lowered his head diplomatically. "No man, Majestad, wishes to find himself criticized by women, and when both are highly born and of much merit, the pain of their harsh words becomes more extreme."

"Yes." Alonzo crossed his arms and braced himself farther back on the throne. "From your remarks, we assume that you have already learned the nature of the complaint against you." He tapped his fingers twice on the gold leaf of the arm and waited for Raimundo to speak his defense.

"Majestad, I do not have the confidence of either woman, but I have spoken with them both over the last few days, and it is true that each has a reasonable grievance with the other. Sadly, I cannot resolve their difference. It is not my place to do so, and it would give me greater dismay to serve you poorly than to disappoint them." He would have liked to watch Alonzo's face as he spoke, but did not want to give el Rey any hint of impudence. "Tell me what you wish me to do, and it will be my greatest honor to do it."

"We are not certain that you can remedy the misunderstanding that exists between these two women," Alonzo said in measured tones, as if appeased by Raimundo's contrite attitude. "Our Reina has told us that she believes her station and rights have been infringed by the wife of the Infante Real. While it is true that our Reina is the daughter of the King of France, and therefore has the argument of birth to enforce her claims, nonetheless, France is not our ally and Venezia is, so that the greater moral weight is with my son's wife. From the whispers of my courtiers, I assume that both women wish to be permitted to receive the praise of the men of the Court."

Raimundo knew from long experience that when Alonzo lapsed from the royal plural, his pride was most vulnerable, and so he answered with all the skill at his disposal. "Majestad, you must consider. Here are two women, both of great rank and both noted beauties, and though"—he hastened on so that he would not be interrupted by Alonzo's strictures on worldly vanity—"only the treasures of Heaven have lasting worth, still these women are the objects of praise, which credits not only them but you as well, for your position as the most powerful ruler in the world is reflected in the adulation of these women."

"But," Alonzo said as he nodded thoughtfully, "they create dissension where none existed before."

"If you will forgive me, Majestad," Raimundo protested as diplomatically as he could, "there has been conflict, but not of a nature that would be worth your attention. The intrigues of courtiers are not for your concern. Were this an argument between Condessas, you would be entirely correct to ignore it as being beneath your consideration. But once more I must point out that these are the most esteemed women in España, and their lack of harmony must be reflected in the conduct of others, and for that reason, you must settle their complaints." He had not yet thought of a way to persuade Alonzo to insist that Genevieve and Zaretta stop jousting with words. "You must see, Majestad," he went on in the hope he would hit upon the right phrase, "that these women who have each enjoyed singular recognition are not used to having another who commands similar position and respect. So it is that they, now having Su Majestad's firm hand to guide them, flounder about and wound themselves and each other for lack of a decision you might make for them."

"They do not think clearly," Alonzo announced to the empty room. "It is the way of women to cavil at lifted eyebrows and ignore the fall of a kingdom." He glowered at his hands. "Don Rolon should have instructed his wife to show la Reina the deference she deserves."

"Majestad, I am sure he would do it if he knew himself what you wished to have done. It pains him to see his wife and your wife competing like harlots for notice and compliments." Raimundo had discussed the problem only in passing with Don Rolon, but he was sure that the Infante Real, infatuated as he was with his bride, was distressed to see her in this plight.

"If a man does not exercise his full authority at the first of his marriage, all will go badly," Alonzo declared with an underlying touch of satisfaction, as if he were pleased that his heir had once again disappointed him.

"And so he would want to do, but not in opposition to your desires, Majestad. He is a most obedient prince, O Rey, one who strives to do honor to his House and to uphold the kingdom in a manner pleasing to God and you." He faltered as Alonzo gave a slight, condemning shake to his head. "Majestad, you and your son have differences, but neither of you, I think, wishes for the war between your wives to continue."

"It is most aggravating that the women have so much forgotten themselves that they bring notice to their differences. But thus it is ever. We have seen it many times before, and know that the Church's dicta against women are for the protection not only of men and the family, but to protect the women themselves, who are as weak as their Mother Eve." He hooked the fingers of his right hand around the wide golden links of his Golden Fleece collar. "Very well. I will think on this and discuss it with my confessor."

Raimundo did not like to think that Padre Juan would be permitted to have a say in this, but he could not now object, having asked for Alonzo's judgment. He bowed formally, and added, as if it were an afterthought, "Another matter relating to this most regrettable situation, Majestad: your son Gil." This was the most awkward and hazardous aspect of this audience, and Raimundo called to mind all the skill he had learned at Court in the last twenty years; "It amuses him to see the two women behave . . . improperly. He does not comprehend how much such conflicts may disrupt a Court, and so he indulges them in turn, enjoying their distress." He wanted to tell Alonzo that his pampered bastard deliberately taunted and tantalized the two women, coolly and cynically playing one off against the other. Alonzo would not tolerate such flagrant behavior in anyone but Gil, and Gil exploited his advantage with ruthless delight.

"It is the waywardness of youth," Alonzo said with a faint smile. "He has often chafed at the restrictions of court life and has told me that his heart longs to prove his love for me and España on the field of battle. He has requested a commission on several occasions, but we have denied him this, and therefore believe that he seeks excitement closer to hand. In time he will learn better judgment."

It was difficult for Raimundo not to challenge this, to point out that Gil had no intention of exposing himself to the risks of battle, and made such statements only to curry favor with his father. It would be useless, he knew, and would lose him all that he had worked so long to gain. Yet there was a part of him that goaded him, reminding him of the satisfaction he would feel to see Gil's power broken at last. "As you wish, Majestad. It is my honor to serve you in all things."

"After God," Alonzo corrected him mildly.

"Of course, Majestad. After God." Raimundo bowed his way out of the smaller throne room, worrying as he went what Alonzo might do to stop the intense rivalry developing between Genevieve and Zaretta.

❦

"Who is Inez?" Zaretta asked Don Rolon late the following week as they sat in the withdrawing room of their apartments. Over the last month, the suite of rooms they occupied had grown from four to seven and there were hints that there would be more allocated to their use before the year was out. This room faced the south, and now that it was nearly summer, there was a hot smell of burgeoning orchards on the evening air.

"Inez?" Don Rolon asked, the breath all but stopping in his throat.

"Yes. Who is she?" Zaretta was looking dreamily out of the window at the treetops of the garden below them. The candles gilt her face and exposed bosom so that she looked to be made of precious metal miraculously made pliant.

"She is a woman I used to know." It was an honest answer, but he blurted it out so awkwardly that Zaretta gave him a long, questioning stare.

"Used to know?" she echoed, distrust in every line of her body.

"Yes. Once I married you, I saw her but twice, once to tell her that I would not continue to protect her, and once to . . ." He broke off.

"To have a farewell taste?" Zaretta suggested, ending the silence.

"No! No, she sent for me." He felt his face grow hot and his hands slicked with sweat. "She . . ."

"I was told—it is not important who told me—that she was pregnant. Is that true?" She asked it so sweetly, but it was plain that she demanded an answer from him and would not be satisfied until she had it.

"So she informed me." Don Rolon felt miserable. He had wanted to shield Zaretta from that part of his life, so that she would never know how far he had disgraced himself and thereby proved himself unworthy of her.

"Recently?" Zaretta asked.

"Not long ago. She is no longer in Valladolid. She is married now, and living in the north. I have provided money for her to raise the child, but that is all, I promise you that it is all." His eyes pleaded with her and he longed to embrace her to implore her forgiveness for his lapse. But he knew from the instruction of his youth that though men were prey to their animal natures, no woman who had been gently raised could tolerate knowing of the excesses of their men. Nothing he could say would exonerate him, and for that reason alone, he remained silent.

"My father has had six mistresses that I know of, and more, almost certainly, that I never knew about. That a man should want a woman for satisfaction or variety or pleasure, that is nothing to me. You Spaniards are so somber about such things, but we in Venezia know that there are appetites in nature, and that men and women are creatures of the flesh as well as children of God. I do not mind that this Inez was your mistress, but I do not enjoy learning of your future bastard through Court gossip. It is not proper for you to treat me so, that I must be made a laughingstock because all the world knows but your wife that you have fathered a child on another woman." She folded her arms, and although Don Rolon thought she looked beautiful that way, he also knew that she was determined.

"I am sorry, Zaretta," he said softly. "Here it is not fitting for a man to speak of such things to his wife."

"That is not what Genevieve thinks, Don Rolon, and she was the one who taxed me with the information. What was I to do? You had not warned me, and so I gaped like a girl in a nunnery. Everyone laughed." She cocked her head to the side, a stubborn light in her eyes. "I did not know what to tell them, and so they assumed you had tricked me, and that made it all the more amusing."

"Oh, Zaretta," he said, feeling more deeply saddened than before.

"Genevieve made much of it. You would be amazed to learn what she said, with her head up and her fine gown glittering with jewels. That petticoat she wears, with the pearl diapering and gamets, it must be worth a fortune alone. She said that it is better than anything the English Queen has. She is going to wear it when the English arrive for their State visit." There were tears in her eyes, but from anger, not pain. "I won't let her make me dowdy."

"She would not." Don Rolon tried to avert more misunderstandings. "Truly, she does know that the magnificence of the whole court will be required. You may have a new gown for it. You should have at least two, now that I think of it. You have the gowns of your dowry, but for such an occasion, you must dress in the Spanish mode. España is not Venezia."

"So I am discovering," she said impatiently. "I warn you, Rolon, I won't be made to look like a nun in black garments that gird me in like armor. I would think myself hideous, and Genevieve dresses in the French style, and so I must have the right to wear Venezian clothes."

"For most of the time, it is wonderful that you will wear your Venezian garments. No one would object to that. But there are occasions when all the Court, and that includes la Reina, must dress in the Spanish way, and you must not cavil at that. You may wear either silver or gold on your black, however, and there may be a great deal of it. Dominguez's Duquessa has a Court dress that is gold but for a borden of black scallops at the cuffs and hem. Even her ruff is gold. Dominguez told me that the whole thing weighs almost as much as their oldest child, but the splendor of it!" He put his hand out and touched her hair. "You would be a goddess in gold, mi amor. You would shine more than the sun and the fire together, and all the world would love you, so beautiful you are."

Zarettas shrugged, but was pleased. Don Rolon rarely became lyric in his praise of her, and when he did, she knew that she had won whatever contest was between them. "Rolon, I don't want to look like Dominguez's Duquessa. I want to look like a Venezian."

"And you do, but there are these few State occasions. You have had them in Venezia, I know. Your uncle has given huge banquets and balls and receptions. Word of them has reached España often, and their magnificance is the envy of half the world. But España does not want to be forever in Venezia's shadow, though with you here, part of España will always, be in Venezia's shadow." He smiled at her in quiet longing. He did not have words to tell her what the sight of her did to him, and how he wanted to touch her, be with her. It was not proper for the Infante Real to behave in such a way, for the role of heir to the throne was a strict one. There was always, in the back of his mind, the acidic fear of what she would do if ever she learned how afflicted he was. The idea that she might discover him at the full of the moon disgusted him beyond all consolation.

"You will speak to Genevieve?" Zaretta pressed. "You will tell her that she is not to interfere with me? You will tell her that I will conduct myself as I see fit, and not for her amusement? Will you?"

"If that is what you want." He did not want to argue with his father's wife. He had not entirely forgotten the brief affair he had

had with her, and to fight with her now, and over his own wife, would be awkward indeed. "But I might have to be careful, Zaretta. My father is displeased that there has been rivalry between the two of you, and I do not wish to give him further cause for complaint."

"Does that mean you will do nothing?" She folded her arms and stared hard at him. "Do you intend to indulge me now, and then set my cause aside in order to win the approval of your father and those priests who are forever hovering around him?" It was an unjust accusation, and she knew it, but she was irritated by his reluctance to come immediately to her aid, as any Venezian man would do. This was España, she knew, and the Court here did not indulge in such antics as were common in Venezia. That Don Rolon should want to be circumspect in his approach to his stepmother did not surprise Zaretta, either, and under other conditions, she might have approved his caution. But not this time, not now with the constant demands for demonstrations of respect and submis-sion that Genevieve hourly required of her. Zaretta was used to having men around her, handsome men who were eager to do her bidding. To have to sacrifice the few who dared to approach her with what was at best tepid gallantry to the vanity of la Reina, was more than Zaretta was prepared to do. Not for Don Rolon, not for her uncle the Doge, not for God Himself would she make a meek little urchin of herself.

"I will do what I can," Don Rolon promised her. "It is not always easy to accomplish such things at Valladolid. There are procedures." He put his hands to his forehead, feeling the first tug of a headache.

"Let me know at once what Genevieve says. I don't want to listen to more excuses. Even my confessor will not let me express my grievances." The last insult was also rankling her, for in Venezia her confessor had taken a familial pride in her, and had thought of her social welfare as well as the good of her soul. But Venezia, she reminded herself as if repeating a tedious lesson, was not España.

"I will, Zaretta. It might be a few days, but I will let you know as soon as I have had the opportunity to speak with my father's wife in private. If I choose any other time or place, it will only make matters worse. To tax la Reina where there are those to over-hear would be the greatest folly." He could remember the many times after Alonzo had left Genevieve's bed for good, that la Reina had upbraided el Rey at Court functions, since he stubbornly refused to see her at any other time. The court had moved more slowly and quietly than ever while those terrible confrontations went on, and Padre Juan had preached often on the devils of the flesh.

"I thank you, Rolon." She drew her finger down his cheek to the line of his beard.

"When it is done, you may thank me. Not until then, mi amor." He caught her hand in his and kissed her fingers, one after the other, glad to see her smile at last.

❦

Padre Barnabas knelt before the altar of the smallest chapel in the palace. He was lost in prayers this night, and could not help but be pleased that his devotion had made it possible for him to spend so much more time at his devotion than other Dominicans. He was preparing for his next conference with Padre Juan Murador and the other officials of the Inquisition. With piety and the approval of God, he might be promoted to become a member of that august body of interrogators, who were the most holy, most powerful men in España. He recited his *Aves* with fervor, and actually chanted the psalms.

"Oh," said a voice behind him, and Padre Barnabas turned to see Lugantes standing in the door.

"Jester." There was unending condemnation in his voice, as if Satan himself had intruded on this sacred place.

"Even jesters must pray, Padre," Lugantes said as he came into the chapel, leaving the carved door ajar. "At this time of night, there are few of the Court about, and for that reason, I had hoped to have some time alone with soul."

"I am not of the Court." Padre Barnabas might have been prouder of that statement if he had been given the chance to reject the glories of Court life, but as it was, there had been no such opportunity.

"Church and Court are not so far apart in España," Lugantes remarked, and started toward the door. "I will not disturb you then, good priest. If you will be kind enough, remember me in your prayers."

"For the Grace of God," Padre Barnabas said as a way of dismissing Lugantes. He did not like the little man, and found something unnerving about his size. There were other dwarf jesters at Court, but most of them were as stunted in mind as they were in body. Not so Lugantes, who had more than once unnerved Padre Barnabas with his mordant humor.

"Tell me, Padre," Lugantes remarked, not leaving as Padre Barnabas wished, "is it true that the Inquisition intends to preach of the evils of heresy to the English Queen when she comes with her court?"

"What the inspirations of God are in those matters is not for ears such as yours," Padre Barnabas said, pointedly lifting his beads.

"But I am part of the Court, and it must be that we will know some of this, if we are not to embarrass our Rey and Church with inopportune talk." He gave Padre Barnabas an inquiring look, then gazed toward the altar and the statue of Christ in the arms of His Mother. "When He was a child, His family fled the wrath of priests and ruler. How times have changed." He crossed himself and opened the door wide. "If you like, I will ask one of the pages to see that you are not disturbed."

"I thank you for your concern, but it is not necessary. I want only to be able to pray in peace." He knew that this was ill-mannered, and as such might earn him a few words of reprimand from his superiors, but the jester was infuriating him.

"As you wish. God give you His peace," Lugantes said and left the chapel. He did not at once leave the area, but walked a short way down the hall and then stepped into an alcove where he became nearly invisible.

A little while later there was a sharp sound on the servants' stair, and a cloaked figure stepped into the hall. It hesitated, then made for the chapel, moving cautiously in spite of the late hour and the deserted corridors around him.

"You may stop there," Lugantes said softly, coming out of the alcove.

The man turned with a stifled cry. "Who?"

"Lugantes. You wanted to speak to me, Dominguez. You have wanted to speak to me for some time, if your occasional cryptic notes are any indication." He looked at the Portuguese Duque. "What has perplexed me is that you have not approached me directly. Always those notes: *Meet me by the Moorish fountain an hour after sunset, See me at noon in the orchard, At dawn behind the stables.* I thought I had a lover, except that when I answered the summons, there was no one to meet me. In time, you must understand, I grew irritated. When this last one came, I decided that I would have to wait you out. And I will do you a service, but why, I cannot say. Padre Barnabas is at prayers in the chapel. It might be best to remain here."

"Padre Barnabas? But he is a familiar of the Holy Office." Raimundo spoke just above a whisper, and though he did not shiver, there was enough fear in his words to convince Lugantes that the man was sincere in his wish to see him.

"As are half the priests at Court. Surely I need not tell you that. Why have you been so determined to speak to me, and why have you failed so often?" He had been surprised to discover it was Dominguez himself who was looking for him. He was aware that the Duque was one of several nobles attempting to keep the differences between Alonzo and Rolon from becoming a rift in the Royal House. On the other side, Gil del Rey worked to destroy the tenuous agreements be-tween father and heir.

"I did not want to risk—" He looked about. "Is there nowhere less public we can go?"

"There is la Reina's confessional. No one is in her chapel at this hour, and if anyone should overhear voices, coming from the confessional, they must be considered sacred and not to be trespassed upon." What he was suggesting would merit an accusation of heresy if Dominguez decided to lay evidence with the Inquisition.

"An excellent idea," Raimundo said, and followed Lugantes through the corridors to la Reina's apartments. "You are more clever than some say."

"Don't correct them, I beg of you," Lugantes said, only partly as humor. "A man in my position is expected to be a fool. Anything else is dangerous." He opened the door to the chapel and let Raimundo precede him into the room. "Who's to be priest?"

"It does not matter to me," Raimundo said, after genuflecting and crossing himself. "Choose."

"Very well, I will be priest." He entered one side of the booth and hoisted himself onto the cushioned stool that waited there in the dark. "What is it that you want to discuss?" he asked as he heard Raimundo take his place on the other side of the darkness.

"Lugantes, you hear things in this Court, much more than most courtiers." He was not speaking to flatter, and there was not a hint of such intent in his tone. He was determined to be as candid as he could with Lugantes, for he knew that the jester saw through artifice and mendacity more quickly than anyone else he had met.

"Very likely. What is that to you?" He listened intently to Raimundo, to the way he spoke as much as to the words themselves. A hesitation, an emphasis, an unfinished word or sentence could tell him more than whatever else Raimundo had to impart to him.

"I need your aid. You know as well as anyone that Alonzo is not pleased with Don Rolon's wife, and he is looking for a reason to disavow the terms of the marriage. He had not realized that she was a beautiful woman—he did not want to provide his son with a beautiful bride—and for that reason, he wishes to have proof that the marriage is invalid." He sighed once, a short, aggravated sound that alerted Lugantes to the state of his mind. "He already knows that the marriage was consummated. He cannot demonstrate that Zaretta is a heretic, and would not dare to, for that would mean war with Venezia as well as a direct challenge to the Pope. Neither of these things are wise; and much as he dislikes Don Rolon, he cannot endanger what he has achieved thus far without open conflict here in España and with his brother. The Emperor is pleased with the marriage and has been anxious to arrange a marriage for Otto to one of the Doge's family, as well. Whatever it is that Alonzo does, it must come from some source outside the Court."

"In other words, the Church," Lugantes said quietly. "Preferably the Holy Office."

"For some time there has been resistance, because the older bishops do not approve of such interference, but since Obispo Teodoro Lazarez was burned, their authority has lessened, and the Holy Office does not hear their objections." He paused to organize his thoughts. "Before his wedding, Don Rolon went on retreat."

"Yes. For prayer and reflection," Lugantes said to let Raimundo know he was aware of the time of the journey.

"And during that retreat, something happened." He did not have the details, but he had learned a few days ago that a document of the Ambrosian Superior General had been sent, on request of Padre Juan Murador himself, to the archives of the Inquisition.

"Do you know what?" Lugantes asked.

"Whatever it was, the monks there decided that God had chosen to give aid and strength to Don Rolon in a supernatural battle," Raimundo said miserably. "They were convinced that the Infante overcame minions of the Devil with the aid of Heaven."

"Monks—" Lugantes began, but Raimundo cut him off.

"The Holy Office has decided that Don Rolon must be watched closely. They believe that it was the Devil and not God who rescued him that night. It may be that the good Ambrosian monks meant well by the Infante, but . . . He has not been warned, and I dare not approach him, not now, with the Holy Office determined to . . . " Raimundo faltered, once more finding it difficult to keep his mind clear. "This whole nonsense must be stopped, or—"

"Yes. And Padre Juan thirsts for might. To rise higher than the crown would be a triumph he would treasure." Lugantes tapped his stubby fingers on the wall between them. "I will see that he is warned. Do not be afraid, my friend. There are ways to protect him. He will know those who aid him, and he has a generous heart."

"That does not matter as long as España does not become the plaything of the Holy Office and the Emperor does not turn his might on the country. Both of those things are possible. Once he has an heir, it will be easier." He stood up hastily. "I must leave. It might be best if you wait a while before departing. It is not likely that either of us were seen, but if there are servants in the halls, or . . . " Raimundo stepped out of the confessional, made proper reverence to the small altar, and left the chapel.

Lugantes sat alone in the dark and remembered all that Ciro had told him of that retreat. If ever the Inquisition learned what had occurred, Don Rolon would be at the mercy of the Secular Arm of the Holy Office. The jester shuddered, and wished he could bring himself to go the few paces into Genevieve's quarters and seek comfort and oblivion in her arms. But it was late and she would be guarded. It was folly to think of it, and his mind was full of her.

20

The Progress of the Infante Real and his Venezian bride took almost eight weeks, and was thought by the court to be a triumph. The royal pair with full entourage went from Valladolid to Palencia and from there, taking two days, to Leon. Next they stopped at Oviedo, then turned east to Santander and Bilbao. They went to Vitoria in Alava and Pamplona in Navarra, and along the southern slope of the Pyrenees where the Infante was able to spend a few days hunting with a few chosen courtiers before continuing on to Barcelona and Taggagona. At Castellon della Plana there was a delegation of Moriscos who met with Don Rolon to plead with him on behalf of their relatives who had been detained by the Holy Office. As he listened to the continuing tales of despair and fear, Don Rolon's heart was wrung, and he wanted to cry out to them that he too knew the terror that haunted them day and night, for he shared it and knew that there was no salvation for any of them this side of Heaven. In Valencia there was a festival of boats and in Alicante there were gypsies who sang and danced in ways that would have cost them their lives in Valladolid. At Murcia one of the Governor's men so far forgot himself that he attempted to touch the breasts of the Venezian bride of the Infante Real, and for that he was rewarded with a long, public execution, which Zaretta watched in shock. In Granada the Moriscos were once again presenting petitions, but here there was more anger and less misery, and Don Rolon was glad that they were required to leave, for he did not trust the men around him, and with the full moon approaching, once more, he needed the safety of isolation. So it was that outside Cordoba he left his wife and entourage and sought out a distant spring in the mountains where it was said that miracles were worked in the name of a great Saint that no one remembered very clearly.

"It is probably left over from some pagan goddess," Ciro remarked when he and Don Rolon at last found the opportunity to speak by themselves.

"What do I care, if there is some relief?" Don Rolon asked. "The last time, east of Pamplona, I thought for certain that Padre Juan's men would find me before morning. I do not know that they believed the tale I told of crawling into a cave to escape a bear, but they did not have adequate reason to question me, and at least the only animals that were reported killed were sheep. If there had been another child or—" He could not go on. "How many men are following us this time?"

"Eleven, I think. But Lugantes is with them." He offered this last as consolation, and was pleased to see that the Infante did not want to argue with him. "He will be with us a few more days."

"After Badajoz, there is what? Small cities to Salamanca, and then Madrid. From that, we return to el Rey and the court at Valladolid. And it will once again be just ten days until the full moon." He held his head in his hands. "I am being driven mad, I think. Were it not already in my blood, six weeks such as these have been would be enough to make the least susceptible man into a lunatic. May God in Heaven rend me limb from limb if ever I sought to offend Him, or trespass against His Word. What have I done that His Church pursues me as if I were in the company of the very angels of Hell? What is it that damns me? Tormented as I am, I have never wanted to harm anyone. I have not wished anyone . . . or very few harm. But for that curse, I am more hateful than those who murder and lie and steal food from the poor. Was this what God wished when He sent His Son as sacrifice? Was it? Did not Our Lord teach us to love one another, and did He not promise that we were forgiven all our sins? Then why this?" The last cry was loud enough to carry all the way through the hunting lodge where they were to sleep.

"Alteza, you must calm yourself. You cannot have such statements repeated where they might be . . . misunderstood." Ciro had not noticed anyone following them to this lodge, but he was certain that someone had. Throughout the Progress, there had always been one or two men who stayed close to Don Rolon, but not so close that they would be apparent. They were faceless men, lesser courtiers with good manners and little else, nothing that made them remarkable in any way, but that they were so wholly unremarkable.

"Oh, God!" Don Rolon swung around on his heel and started toward the door. "I wish I were a drunkard, or a libertine, so that I would be able to walk out that door and into the night having nothing to worry about but their contempt. To have this hanging over me . . ." He glared at the floor. "What may I do that will serve any good purpose?"

"Alteza . . . " Ciro began, worried at the despondent tone of the Infante's voice.

"There are times, may God forgive me for it, when all I want in the world is to be free of this. I would throw myself off a bridge or walk into the enemy's guns or turn myself over to Padre Juan, only to have it over at last. I used to think of my grandmother, and the others in the family with their delusions, and I thought that if I had to, I would find a way to remove myself from the court and not endanger those around me. But that was not to be my fate, no." He took up one of their bags and flung it across the room onto the bed. "Nothing so simple as that."

"Infante, if you were to be discovered, there are those who would also suffer." He did not want to sound craven, but as a converso, he knew he would be the first to feel the oppressive hand of the Holy Office, should it be learned that the curse had wrought so powerful a change in Don Rolon. "Lugantes would be in difficulties. I would. So would the Duque da Minho. And your wife. She is foreign, and there are those who say that the lax behavior of the Venezian court would promote trouble in a man. There are also those who think that a man who is in love with a woman is one who has already given himself to the flesh and therefore is open to the Devil and all his works. If you wish to end your life, so be it, but you must not do so in any way that would bring suspicion, on others, unless you want to see them all . . . " He picked up the bag from the bed. "The Holy Office watches you now. They will be watching those you see often. No matter who they are or why, the Holy Office will want to know more of them. And let them discover that anyone who has become close to you, however briefly, has about them any touch of heresy or Diabolism, that person has his fate sealed. Do not doubt it."

"I don't," Don Rolon admitted, and suddenly calmed down. "I thought the Progress would help. Dominguez approved it, my wife approved it, Padre Juan approved it, even my father approved it, and it has been torture for me. There are always people, so many people. And those who do not want to gain favor through flattery are in such dire need that my heart aches for them, no matter what they have done. I hate my father for living in the palace as if behind barricades, but I cannot entirely blame him for it, not after these last weeks. Who can hope to alleviate all the misery he sees? And who can ignore that it exists?"

"There are many who can, Alteza, and do. Think of the officers of the Secular Arm who hear the cries and groans as they turn the rack another notch or tear living nails from hands and feet, and praise God that they are able to assist in bringing heresy to an end. They are no different than the hidalgo who finds the poverty of his own peasants disgusting, who increases rents and taxes so that he may have a second ermine-lined mantle for Court, or those who prey on the poor merchants, keeping them from earning enough to live and then purchasing their goods for as little as possible. You don't have to think of this, Alteza. But those of us who are conversos, we know of it all." He went to sit down, which was a breach of good manners in the presence of his prince. "There are very few who wish to aid us at all, and those who do, they are not always treasured."

Don Rolon stared at him. "You say this to me, knowing that I might accuse you of treason for it?"

"But you will not, Alteza. You have feared for so long that I would take advantage of what I know of you to use it to your discredit. Now you know the same things of me." He dropped into the chair and bent over to pull off his own boots. "You must forgive me, Alteza. My feet are so sore that I do not know how I am to use them at all. I have sore arms and I think both my buttocks are so bruised that they will never be the color of skin again." He rubbed at his feet, grunting with the awkward posture. "I don't know how you do it."

"I've ridden since I was four," Don Rolon said. "But, yes, I am sore, too. And after the next full moon . . . " He touched his forehead. "I did not want to leave Zaretta. She was not pleased that I did so, but she did her best to appear pleased. She told me last night that she was worn out, and that the Venezian entertainment that the Conde de Llerena was planning sounded to her to be horrible."

"It has been a very long journey," Ciro said.

"And it is not over yet." He sank onto the edge of the bed. "We ought to prepare for the full moon. I don't think I can repeat the story of the bear."

"Alteza, there is a chamber for underground storage, a stout room with thick walls and just the door for access. It is thick, to keep out the heat of summer, and if you were to permit me to bar it, then it could be that . . . there would be that . . . it would be possible to . . . confine you through the night." He kept his voice low and he did not look at the Infante, as if in doing so, he would reveal how little faith he had in his notion. He had to find a way, though, or it would be only a matter of time before the Holy Office learned of his changes, and took what they thought was necessary action.

"You propose to lock me in and stand guard?" Don Rolon asked, feeling weary to the depths of his soul. "Well, and why not? It may be that this is like any other madness and you need only find a prison strong enough to hold me until the . . . fit passes. And there were Saints, weren't there, who were immured so that they would not have to deal with the trials of the world. It might be said that in a small way, I tread the same path." He leaned back, his hands joined behind his head. "Tomorrow I will hunt, and that will give the spies who follow me the chance to see that I am only amusing myself. The Infante is known to like hunting, isn't he? And when the full moon comes, then . . . if I am confined, I might not make such a mess of myself as I have done. It would be less difficult to think of new explanations each time I return from those nights. It might be best to see that a sheep or other animal is left for me, so that the worst of the . . . hunger may be appeased."

"Is there hunger, Alteza?" Ciro asked softly.

"Yes, I think so. There is something pervasive and dreadful that ensnares me. I don't remember much of it, or not very clearly, but I do know that there is hunger. Along with everything else, there is hunger." He turned on his side, away from Ciro. "I do not know what else there may be."

"I will pray for you, Alteza." It was little enough to offer, for unlike many of the others, Ciro had scant faith in prayer. He had seen too many supplicants go unanswered at best; often it seemed to him that the Holy Office meted out punishment to those who had the temerity to address Heaven for aid.

"Thank you, Ciro." Don Rolon cleared his throat.

It was with trepidation that Ciro put the thick oaken bar across the door to the storage cellar. The night was balmy, though a bit too warm, or so it seemed to Ciro. He looked at the fading light with the air of a man who feared blindness. It was difficult for him to remember that he had an obligation to his prince now, with sunset upon him. He braced his shoulders against the door, as if the added weight of his body could keep the creature the Infante would soon become within the confines of the makeshift prison. Although it was unwise to do so, he murmured two prayers in Hebrew, and hoped that none of the spies were near enough to hear him.

The first hour was uneventful, and Ciro began to fret. He had expected difficulties, and now that they did not come, he was afraid that there was some greater evil coming. He wanted to lift the bar to look inside. It might be, he reasoned, that the curse had lost its power, or that it would not manifest itself tonight. He wondered if perhaps he should have risked the questions and procured a lamb or a piglet, so that he would not have to face a ravening beast, if beast there was. He recalled the way Don Rolon's countenance had altered the last time the curse had overtaken him, and he shuddered at the image in his mind. He sat down in front of the door, his legs crossed, and waited.

Not long after he had taken his place, he heard the restless padding of feet behind the door, and a voice that still had something human about it wailed at him, begging for release. Ciro steeled his heart against it, thinking of the familiars of the Inquisition in the entourage who would report anything amiss. Somewhat later, there were thumpings and howlings, no longer beseeching but enraged. Ciro was aghast at what he heard, and no longer had to force himself to keep the door tightly closed. Then came the scrabbling sound of frantic digging, and it was then that Ciro fled, running through the darkness to the little hunting lodge, where he cowered until the morning was far enough advanced to give him courage to step outside. He went first to the storage cellar and saw to his horror, if not surprise, that part of the door had been broken.

They hastily concocted a story between them, and when they returned to the rest of the courtiers, each told it reluctantly, so that the familiars would not be able to report that they were eager to be heard. Don Rolon said less than his valet, and when he did mention the men who waylaid him, he did not give much information, saying that he was shamed to have had such dishonor befall him.

At confession, Padre Barnabas tried to sound him out. "You were attacked by strange men, you say?"

"Yes." The Infante Real stared down at his feet, trying to imagine them as paws.

"How many were there, do you recall?" He tried to sound confiding and sympathetic and only succeeded in giving an oily eagerness to his voice.

"Less than ten, I suppose. It was dark and they struck me about the face—you may see the bruises they left—and then tied me, so I cannot tell if there were more. What has this to do with the state of my soul, good Padre?" It was just impertinent enough to lend credibility to his complaint.

"If you harbor resentment and anger, that may endanger your soul, Alteza," Padre Barnabas answered glibly; it was a favorite ruse of the Holy Office and one that he did not hesitate to use now.

"You mean that I must forgive them?" Don Rolon asked.

"Yes. Anger is a great sin, Alteza." He leaned a little nearer the screen that separated them. "It must be a genuine forgiveness, of course. To do otherwise would be to lie to yourself and to God, which is, a greater sin yet."

"Then what hope is there, good Padre? Surely these men did me an injury. That which gives us injury is—"

" . . . is the instrument of the Devil sent to tempt us from the paths of virtue and righteousness. We must cast it out for the godless thing it is." He spoke with zeal, and went on avidly. "Our Lord taught that we must forgive all injury against us and love those who do us wrong. If we do not, we embrace the Devil and all his works, and for that we will be damned. We must accept what is sent us, and bow our heads to God's Will, meekly showing our submission to His love. To do otherwise is to blaspheme. How often have we seen a good man corrupted utterly by his anger that the rest of the world is not as good as he. Thus our strengths become our weaknesses."

"Then I will forgive those men," Don Rolon said after a moment's pause. He thought of those pitiable men and women who languished in the prisons of the Holy Office, wishing he understood why his wrath was damnable and the Inquisition's was merciful.

"And you must do penance for the anger you have felt and the resentment you have harbored toward those men. It is true that they hurt your body, but unless you are tainted by anger, they have not corrupted your soul. It is the soul that must concern you, Don Rolon, and you more than most." He thought a moment. "How do you think they knew to find you?"

This was the question that Don Rolon had dreaded, but he forced himself to give the answer he had invented. "Highwaymen and other brigands know that hunters venture out on the night of the full moon. There are few places in that area where one may ride safely by moonlight, and they might have chosen such a spot for their ambuscado. It was foolish of me to hunt alone, I know, but the Progress was so long, and I was longing for a little privacy." It had sounded reasonable enough when Ciro and he concocted the tale, but now he had great doubts about it. There were flaws in the tale, and if they were questioned, Don Rolon did not know what he would say.

"You did not fight them?" If the Infante Real were a coward, Padre Juan would need to know of it.

"When a man knocks you to the ground and holds a knife to your throat, you are a fool to fight him, good Padre," Don Rolon answered steadily. "Or would you prefer that I oppose such odds? It would mean that I would have died and not had the chance to risk the lives of good men in battle."

"Yes," Padre Barnabas said steadily. "You are correct in that, I think." He was wholly unaware of the offensiveness of his tone, and Don Rolon did not choose to challenge him on it. He merely nodded and looked away toward the curtain that enclosed the confessional.

"So I am alive." He hesitated, then decided he would take the chance. "There are spies in my entourage, of course. I wish that one of them had had the foresight to follow me that night, for I could have used aid. Or did he simply hang back, so that he would not have to endanger his own life while those desperate men were—"

Padre Barnabas had asked the same question himself, and recalled that one of the two men whose duty it had been to watch the Infante Real that night had said that he thought that the heir to the throne was being stalked by the worshipers of the Devil, because he had heard the tormented cries of souls in anguish. "Tell me, are you sure that these men were highwaymen or brigands?"

"What else would they be, living as they did?" He hoped that he sounded indignant so that Padre Barnabas would not recognize the quaver in his voice for the fear it was.

"They might be followers of the Devil, who meet at the full of the moon to pay damnable homage to their lord." He spat, then crossed himself. "If you escaped from such as those, you preserved more than your life," Padre Barnabas assured him.

"And must I still forgive them?" He could not help but relish the silence that greeted his question.

Finally Padre Barnabas answered. "You must forgive the sinner and detest the sin and eschew all the works of the Devil without profaning the work of God." He had heard the same phrase so often that he had long since forgotten that he had no notion what it meant. He repeated it now with the satisfaction of familiarity, and shut out the other thoughts that troubled him.

"It is difficult to do so, Padre Barnabass," Don Rolon said, contriving to sound awed instead of confused. "Yet if you will give me a penance, I will perform it."

This was what Padre Barnabas liked best about his work—the assigning of penance. It thrilled him to see the mighty brought low, humbled before the altars of God at his order. "You must realize that you have erred, Alteza. For that reason, you will prostrate yourself before the altar here in a penitent's robe, arms spread in emulation of Our Lord on the Cross, and in that posture you will recite the Apostles Creed one hundred times, then you will listen while the novices here read you the Book of Job, to remind you that God does not permit men to trifle with His Will. At the end of that, you will make an Act of Contrition. In the Lord's Name, Infante, and for the good of your soul." He blessed the young man through the grille, then hurried away to find a penitent's robe so that Don Rolon could begin his penance at once.

"I *hated* it!" Zaretta repeated with more force when Don Rolon closed the door behind them. "What right had that man to make you lie there, with half the countryside coming to gape at you?"

"He is a priest and a familiar of the Holy Office," Don Rolon explained patiently, as he had been explaining for more than half an hour. "He is a man who must have obedience or the power of the Holy Office is nothing."

"Then it should be nothing," she said, turning on him with her enormous blue eyes burning at him. "It is not fitting that the Infante Real should be publicly humiliated. In my country, such abuses are not tolerated."

"Venezia is Venezia; this is España," Don Rolon said. His head throbbed and his throat was dry. There were new bruises from the stone floor that added their discolorations to the ones already marring his features. "I'm tired. I want to read alone awhile, my dearest, and then I want to hold you in my arms, to forget all that has happened until now and think only of you and your sweetness."

Ordinarily she would have accepted his blandishments, but not now. "I do not want to be with you just now, Don Rolon. I have seen my husband, the future Rey España shamed and disgraced at the whim of a Dominican who isn't even a bishop! It will take time for me to put this behind me and come to your arms as you would want me to." She picked up a shawl from the top of her traveling case and drew it about her shoulders, though the evening was warm. "I need to have time to myself. You are not the only one who needs to reflect."

If Don Rolon's pride were not already stung, he might have been able to set it aside long enough to persuade her to listen to him, but between the horror of the full moon and the ordeal of his penance, he could not bring himself to say the words that might win her over. "You will do as you must, mi amor. Should you change your mind, my valet will know where to find me." He swung away from her and went out of the room without looking back, so he did not see the shine of tears in her eyes as she watched him go.

Part III

21

Padre Juan's smile was as cordial as his surroundings; Padre Lucien quailed at both, for the antechamber to the Inquisitional Questioning rooms was regarded as being as ominous as the portals of Hell.

"Why have you sent for me, Padre Juan?" Padre Lucien asked as he looked nervously at the two burly officers of the Secular Arm who escorted him to the low stool in front of Padre Juan's enormous writing table.

"Do sit down, Padre Lucien," the Inquisitor General said without looking up from his documents.

The stool was like those assigned to children by their tutors, and sitting on it was not only awkward, but made Padre Lucien feel he was a disobedient child once again. He realized that this was precisely why he was being treated in this manner, and he resented his own lack of character, but he could not ease the feeling within him that he had transgressed his parents' rules, or the requirements of his instructors. "1 wish to know why—"

"In a moment, good Padre," came the answer as Padre Juan scrawled his name at the bottom of the document before him. When he had affixed his seal to the foot of it, he carefully rolled and sealed the heavy parchment, then handed it to the nearer of the two

Secular Officers. "If you will be good enough to dispatch this to Sevilla at once, I would be grateful. There are many heretics there who must be detained if we are to rid España of their despicable influences."

The man took the scroll and kissed it, then bowed himself out of the room.

"Now, then," Padre Juan said, turning toward Padre Lucien in a leisurely way. "I have wanted to talk with you for some little time, Padre, but the demands of my high office have made it difficult." He leaned back in his tall chair and regarded Padre Lucien through narrowed eyes. "You have been most busy, good Premonstratensian."

"I have tried to fulfill my duties and obligations," Padre Lucien said carefully, not at all certain what Padre Juan meant by his comment.

"To the best of your ability, of course. That is always the way with you French monks, isn't it? And priests too, of course. But then, you spent more of your time in Hanover, didn't you? And have served the brother of our Rey in some capacity or other." He put the tips of his fingers together in a prayerful attitude, which only increased Padre Lucien's apprehensions.

"I have seen Emperor Gustav, of course, but so have you, good Padre. He has come on State visits, and you must have served him Communion on more than one occasion."

If this scored a blow to Padre Juan, he gave no sign of it. "That was another matter, quite another matter. The Emperor was here on a visit, as you remarked, and because of that, it is not to be expected that there would be the least opportunity for discussion. He is not a man to listen to the Dominicans. He prefers Orders of lesser rigor, such as the Benedictines, and Franciscans. And Premonstratensians."

"There are many of my Brothers throughout the Holy Roman Empire and the German kingdoms," Padre Lucien agreed, still not certain he understood the thrust of Padre Juan's inquiry.

"You do not find it strange that you should have been asked to serve as personal confessor to the heir to the throne of España? You—a French priest in a German Order?"

"A French Order," Padre Lucien corrected him mildly. "Saint Norbert founded the Order in Laon in 1119, good Padre. That was not quite a century before Saint Dominic founded your Order, I believe." It was no real triumph, but reminding Padre Juan of this gave Padre Lucien a touch of satisfaction, though it was short-lived.

"But most powerful in Germany and Austria," Padre Juan said

sternly, "where there is much tolerance of Protestant heresies." He lowered one hand and tapped his fingers on the polished wood. "It is understood here in España that there are those of the Emperor's court who are anxious to see that it is Otto who Succeeds, not Don Rolon. There are those who believe that your coming here was intented to aid that advancement by the gradual corruption of the Infante Real."

"That's ridiculous," Padre Lucien said, though he turned pale as he said it, and his face grew shiny with sweat. If this was the accusation he faced, he was already a lost man, and there was nothing that could be done to save him. All efforts on his behalf would simply drag others down with him. Deep within his heart, he commended his soul into the keeping of Heaven and hoped that whatever the Holy Office did to him, it would not last too long.

"At first it would seem so," Padre Juan agreed with spurious compassion. "But then we must consider all that has transpired here in España. It is curious to see that it is the Infante Real who questions the actions of the Holy Office, but no one else in the court. Even Gil del Rey, who has no reason to love the Church, for it is our ruling that bars him from the throne forever, supports our actions and lends his soul to our endeavors. Yet Don Rolon, who will one day be el Rey, is moved to inquire into the mandate of Heaven. It is he who finds excuses when there are autos-da-fé, it is he who meets in secret with Flemings, to encourage them to persevere in their struggle against the Church and the throne. This is the man who will one day guide España, and already we see that his feet are on the path to eternal perdition. We know beyond doubt that our teachings have been of the most devout and strict, and so it cannot be from us that he has learned to despise all that is commendable in man. So it must be from another . . . " Here he looked squarely at Padre Lucien. "You are the man, sent from Hanover, to hear the confessions of the Infante Real and minister to his spiritual needs. You, the choice of the Emperor Gustav himself."

"I have said before that I do not know why I was chosen—" Padre Lucien cried out, but was cut off.

" . . . and trained by those priests who have made a mockery of our faith in all the German kingdoms. My predecessor objected to your coming, but his warnings were ignored because el Rey did not wish to offend his brother. Now we see what ruin this laxness has brought upon the royal House. You are the viper in the nest, Padre Lucien, and it is you who have turned Don Rolon from the light of God and brought him instead into the bosom of the Devil!" At this last, his voice rose thunderously, and, as if driven by the passion of his accusations, he rose to his feet. "You have filled him with doubts and polluted his mind with rationalizations that lead to the grossest of sins and offenses against the Holy Spirit. You, who come in the guise of religion, are the most foul and despicable being in any region of this world or the next, an apostate priest!"

Padre Lucien raised his arm as if to block an attack. "Padre Juan, I swear by the Blood of Christ, I did none of these things."

"Who would believe you, Judas?" Padre Juan scoffed. "You have been found out, and we, who have hoped that you would show our Infante the true path now know you for the spy and Diabolist that you are. It took those unworldly Ambrosians to show us the extent of your treachery, but we are now prepared to take vengeance for your perfidy. You will sing Hosannas again, before we are through with you, and they will be sung with a purified heart."

"Oh, God." Padre Lucien crossed himself, shrinking away from the towering fury of the Inquisitor General. "0 my Lord, if ever I offended Thee, I most heartily repent, and for this I supplicate through Thy Mother that I may see my sins so that I will never again cause Thee sorrow for my failings."

"Stop those hypocritical rantings!" Padre Juan shouted. There was a roaring in his head greater than the sound of his words, and he rejoiced in this surge. He was confident now that Heaven was firing him with holy zeal, showing him the way to cleanse the royal House of the last taint of godlessness. He had prayed to find the canker that he might burn it out with purifying fire and protect España from the depredations of the Devil. His exhilaration increased as he saw Padre Lucien tremble, for well he knew that no heretic could stand before the triumphant forces of God and the Holy Office.

"For Jesus sake . . . " Padre Lucien whispered, knowing beyond doubt that he was in the hands of a madman.

"Do not pervert that Holy Name with your lips, Padre! You have caused grief enough in Heaven, and it is for us to rectify your villainy. You are the servant of the Devil and have trampled on the Host to the delight of your master, who has already brought down the righteous in the German states. You have dallied with the Evil One, sharing his excremental couch for the satisfaction of your most unnatural lusts, and to reward your fornications and despoilings, the Devil gave you the favor of the Emperor Gustav, who will be damned until the end of time for his failure to root out the weed of Protestantism. I am only the servant of God, and I do not know the vastness of the abominations in your heart, for we mortals are not granted that knowledge for our own protec-tion. The Mercy of God shields us from such contamination. You have embraced such things as makes the mind shrink and fry with disgust," Padre Juan came around the end of his writing table and glared down at Padre Lucien. "I accuse myself of blindness to evil, that I did not see at once that you were the one who lured Don Rolon from all that is worthy in a prince. I blame myself for spiritual failings in that I permitted you to have daily contact with him, and thus leave him exposed to you and all the ghastly manifestations of your iniquitous ways." It was pleasing to watch Padre Lucien cringe, to see him sully his habit with urine and begin to weep in fright. He reached out to tug the bellpull that summoned another officer of the Secular Arm, and at the same motioned to the man who had remained, impassive, in the shadows while this diatribe went on. "See that this . . . vermin is closely guarded. Tomorrow we will begin Questions in the first degree. See that he is ready." He glanced toward the second guard who entered the room. "Do not be deceived by this man. He is the sworn servant of the Devil, and may call up imps and demons at any time, who will overwhelm you and steal your breath and your souls for the service of Hell."

Both of the men had heard this speech before and so paid little attention to it. The older of the two produced a length of chain and proceeded to secure Padre Lucien's arms behind him.

"Good Officers," the French priest said, making an effort to control the panic that engulfed him, "I tell you that I am not guilty. I have done nothing. The accusations are false." It was useless, and he knew it as he spoke, but he could not stop himself from making the effort. "Do not do this, good Officers. For the sakes of your souls and your peace in the world that is to come, release me. I am willing to end my days an anchorite, but as I am a Christian, do not—"

Padre Juan's voice cut through this plea. "If he speaks, gag him. His words are lies and snares for the unwary. Those who listen to him are led away from God's Word and enrolled in the ranks of those who worship the Devil."

The younger of the two men held up a gag, and the older fitted it in place, saying as he did, "We are familiars of the Holy Office, heretic, and we have learned to heed the admonitions of those good Dominicans who protect us."

With a wild shaking of his head, Padre Lucien made one last attempt to reach them. He resisted their pull on him and tried to be heard through his leather gag. Neither of the officers paid him any attention, dragging him implacably and inexorably toward the door that led into the prison.

"Chain him in the lowest cell," Padre Juan called out. "So that he may be nearer his master."

There was nothing in what Padre Juan said that was worse than the rest, but those last words, so lightly said, were the culmination of his nightmare. Without warning, his legs buckled as he fainted.

❧

Gil del Rey smiled as he knelt on the chapel stones. He hated the endless prayers and recitations, and found the ritual boring, but his new professions of devotion had already convinced Padre Juan that he was more suited to rule España than his half brother, and for that he was ready to endure much more discomfort and tedium. He raised his head as the Inquisitor General appeared and began to address the small congregation in the chapel royal.

"A great evil has been discovered, and thanks to the aid of God and His Good Angels, we are once again preserved from the peril of the Antichrist and his host of the fallen. Never before has the Devil come so near the throne, which we know from the confessions of his followers he has sworn to control. He had as his slave the false priest, Padre Lucien, who was confessor to the Infante Real himself. It is with a heavy heart that we realize we must warn the heir to the throne that he has placed his soul in the gravest danger and only our rigorous examination will preserve him from further harm. As it is, we must all be especially diligent in watching Don Rolon, measuring his words and his behavior to find any trace of Diabolic influence. He has for so long confessed to the damned Padre Lucien that we must not dare to hope that he is wholly without the stain of his confessor's apostasy."

Lugantes, who sat at the back of the chapel, listened with increasing dismay. He had been looking forward to Don Rolon's return from his Progress, but now he knew that mortal danger awaited him in Valladolid. He moved uncomfortably, trying to find a way to leave the chapel unobtrusively, and found none. There were Dominican monks at all the doors, and anyone found leaving would surely be followed by one of the familiars. He decided to speak to Dominguez immediately after the service was over. If there was anyone who would be willing to help him, it was the Portuguese Duque.

"It may be that the curse that has marked the Infante Real from his birth made him especially easy prey for the Devil's servants, who are ever searching for those they may suborn into their ranks. It is not for us to condemn the Infante Real, but to pray for the safe deliverance of his soul." Padre Juan crossed himself and bowed his head. "Let us all thank God with humble hearts and grateful minds that España has been spared the horror of his rule."

At this, Gil very nearly laughed aloud, but he forced himself to keep his head bent and his attitude submissive. At last the prize he sought was attainable. Bastardy and commonness be damned, within the year, he would be Infante Real. España would bow to him. And, he thought, he might just be willing to take up where his half brother left off with his Venezian wife. He joined his hands piously as he listened to Padre Juan drone on.

"Padre Lucien departed this world of the flesh without abjuring his faults and sins, and for that he will burn in Hell's eternal flames, never released from that agony that consumes and renews forever. Yet we have gleaned some few bits of worthwhile information, thanks to the zeal of Gil del Rey, who brought certain irregularities to our attention. Even now, as we pray for the soul of the Infante Real, officers of the Secular Arm are speeding north to detain the deceitful witch and sorceress who excited Don Rolon's lust and was mistress to him even while plans for his wedding were going forth. We believe that much will be learned from her that will shed light on the extent of the Infante's errors." Padre Juan felt himself grow flushed under his habit, and he knew beyond doubt that the malignant spells of the witch were working on him already. "It will be for the Secular Arm to wrest from her how she came to seduce the Infante Real, and to what extent she has persuaded him to participate in the adoration of the Evil One. If we should learn that Don Rolon has entered into a pact with the Devil, it will be essential that we cleanse him of this terrible blasphemy so that his soul may come to God free from the effluvium of his sins. It is our obligation to preserve España from the Devil and all those who labor in his name."

Raimundo listened to this with a mixture of disbelief and revulsion. He had not thought that Padre Juan would dare to attack the royal House so directly, but he had not reckoned on Gil's ambition. For a greedy priest and an envious bastard, España would be plunged into war! He ground his teeth at the thought, and all but shouted out his opposition to all that Padre Juan was saying. His silence infuriated him, though he knew it was absolutely necessary. His only hope lay in the possibility of keeping Don Rolon alive and free long enough to reveal to Alonzo the extent of corruption in the Church and Court that made such accusations as these tolerable. He was sensible enough to recognize how difficult a task that would be, but he refused to capitulate to the Holy Office and Gil del Rey after he had struggled so hard for the Infante Real and España. He discovered he had not heard the last of Padre Juan's homily, and had missed one response. To the curious Conde beside him, he murmured, "I am stunned by what I hear."

"Yes," the Conde replied as both men gave their full attention to the ritual being enacted at the altar.

"Duque," Lugantes said as he plucked at Raimundo's sleeve as they left the chapel royal, "if you have a few moments to spare for me, I believe we must talk."

"Of course," Raimundo said languidly, as if he had been bored by all he had heard. "I will take wine in an hour. If you will join me then, I will be at your service, little man." He did not remain with Lugantes, for fear their conversation would be noticed. Instead, he looked about for Alonzo and found el Rey with la Reina a little apart from the others. He approached the couple cautiously, for it was possible they were arguing and would not appreciate an interruption.

"Dominguez," said Alonzo with a signal for him to come nearer. "We would be grateful for a word with you."

Raimundo bowed deeply, first to Alonzo and then to Genevieve. He saw the distress in her pretty face and wished he were sure of her loyalties, for her aid would mean more to him than any other. "Majestad."

"We were saddened to hear Padre Juan address us as he did. For years we have prayed that our heir would be worthy of his station and rank, but it appears that Heaven has decreed otherwise, and it is for us to bow our head with humility to the dictates of God." He glanced toward Gil del Rey. "We have but one hope now, if the throne is not to go to Otto."

"You must pardon me, Majestad, but I truly believe that without Don Rolon you have no hope. None. The Pope has already said he would not recognize the legitimacy of Gil, and he is far closer to your brother than to you. Without Don Rolon, the throne must pass to Otto. There are those in this country who would oppose such a transition with the full might of arms." He saw Alonzo's hands clench, and he knew he had little time to pursue his point. "Majestad, you are el Rey, and that makes you the ultimate authority in España."

"Earthly authority," Alonzo said imposingly. He lowered his eyes. "The Power of God far exceeds that of any monarch, though he ruled the world."

"And because Padre Juan has questions, you are willing to throw away all that your father and his father gave their lives to achieve?" Raimundo knew he had gone too far, and almost welcomed the rebuke he knew would come. "I do not want to challenge you, Majestad. It is my sworn duty to uphold and defend the throne of España on behalf of Portugal. It is for that duty and love that I cannot keep silent, for to do so would mean I would have to watch the kingdoms I have dedicated my life to preserve pass into defeat and ruin on the whim of a proud Dominican Inquisitor."

"You have said enough, Duque," Alonzo informed him coldly. "We will not chastise you now, for you are full of choler and have not given yourself time for prayer and reflection. But until you are prepared to beg the pardon of Padre Juan and the throne, we do not wish to see you near us, or in the company of those we honor for their loyalty." He turned away from Raimundo and signaled to Genevieve to depart with him.

The French Reina put her hand on Raimundo's wrist. "I am sorry, Dominguez, truly I am. If there were anything I could do, I would do it. When word of this most recent folly reaches France . . ." She shook her head.

"I know," Raimundo said with resignation. "Your brother need only wait a year or two and España will be ripe for plucking." He bowed to her. "I must not detain you longer, or El Majestad will be more displeased than he is already."

"Have courage, Dominguez," Genevieve murmured, and hurried after her husband.

"Disappointed?" Gil asked, coming up behind Raimundo as Alonzo and Genevieve left the antechamber.

"Worse than that," Raimundo answered baldly.

Gil's smile was both sarcastic and smug. "Your man has not done well, has he? You should have given your support to me, Dominguez. Don Rolon never will rule. El Rey dislikes him and loves me. And when I rule, I will remember those who have loved me and those who worked against me." His beautiful features were hardened now, showing a coldness that was reminiscent of Alonzo, and for the first time, Raimundo knew what it was that el Rey so adored in his son.

"There will be time for that if you rule," Raimundo told him with no pretense of courtesy. "But any man who seeks to destroy a kingdom for pique is not the one I would choose to aid. And I am not alone."

"I do not want to destroy España," Gil protested indignantly, his chin coming up.

"No?" Without waiting for a response, Raimundo walked away from him.

Lugantes arrived in Raimundo's quarters at the appointed time, and did not bother with any of the polite civilities that were expected of him. "I must reach Don Rolon before- he can be detained. Lend me a horse and I will ride through the night to find him and warn him." Though he wore his motley and bells, there was nothing amusing about him and it did not strike Raimundo as ludicrous that the jester would make such an offer.

"And then?" He had been trying for the last half hour to think what to do with the Infante Real once he had been warned.

"I have spoken with Alteza's valet, who is a converso. We will see that he is safe." He knew that he must not reveal too much of what had passed between him and Ciro in case Raimundo were called to give testimony under oath, for lying then was punishable by the Question, and there were few who could resist the officers of the Secular Arm.

"Good. Send me word when you have him and I will prepare a dispatch for the Emperor, putting down all that has transpired." He had little hope that Gustav would do much, but the man was swom to protect the Succession, and could not completely ignore a direct attempt to change it.

"Send your missive under guard, Duque," Lugantes wamed him. "Gil has already convinced many that he should have the Right, not Don Rolon. He will not think kindly of those who interfere with him."

"He has made that plain," Raimundo said with a nod. "Get the Infante Real away as soon as you can. I will do whatever is possible here until the whole ridiculous thing is resolved."

"I will tell Don Rolon that," Lugantes promised him. "Which of your horses shall I take?"

"There is a rawboned chestnut in my string, with a common head and a scrawny tail. He is the strongest horse I possess. He has carried me in full armor for most of a day." Raimundo handed a scrawled note to him. "Give this to the groom."

"I will," Lugantes said, putting the note in his patchwork jerkin. "About Zaretta."

"Yes?" Raimundo had not satisfied himself on that front, and did not volunteer any suggestion.

"Perhaps it would be best if she retums to Court. This battle is not of her making, and her uncle might not take kindly to our dragging her into it. Would la Reina consent to protecting her?" Lugantes knew better than anyone that Genevieve disliked the young Venezian, but his natural caution kept him from saying this.

"The women do not get on," Raimundo said. "You know that."

"The whole Court knows that. But they are both foreign brides and for that they may be willing to set aside their personal disputes for safety." If anyone could persuade Genevieve to take Zaretta in, it was Raimundo and Lugantes hoped that he could convince the Duque to act, no matter how unpromising the prospects. "Together they might better withstand the actions of Padre Juan."

Raimundo looked sharply at Lugantes. "An excellent point, my friend."

"Make any use of it you may," Lugantes told him. "I should leave before the Guarda changes at the gates. I don't want the Holy Office to know where I'm going, as they must learn if I am seen by the afternoon Capitan."

"Yes. Go at once. And may God go with you, little man." Raimundo said this so sincerely that the jester was not offended at his reference to his size.

"I thank you. Speak to the la Reina, Dominguez. Don Rolon will not protest as much if he knows his wife will be protected." He hesitated at the door, then burst out laughing and clapping as he pulled on the latch. "Oh, excellent, excellent, most excellent! Under all that courtesy you have a sharp wit, Duque."

Raimundo knew what was expected of him. "I pray you won't repeat it, Lugantes. It is not wise to make jokes at the expense of such women."

"Of course, of course, but what a pity, don't you think?" He bowed deeply, then skipped away down the hall, whistling and chuckling by turn, as if he had nothing more on his mind than the antics of immoral women.

22

More than a dozen Orders marched in the procession to honor the Infante Real and his Venezian bride. They all sang, their chanted hymns blending with the shouts and cheering of the crowd gathered to see the heir to the throne pass. The banners of the Orders as well as the standard of España were borne aloft in triumph as the parade wound through the streets of Segovia.

Don Rolon, dressed in one of three state ensembles he had worn on the Progress, sat on his gold-and-silver Andalusian, riding beside the gilt carriage where Zaretta sat. He was tired, his head ached, he was hungry, and worst of all, he was bored. The Progress had been more successful than he had hoped, and he felt physically ill at the thought of ever having to go on one again. He bent in the saddle to speak to Zaretta, needing to shout to be heard over all the noise. "Two more days of this, mi amor, and we will return to Valladolid. Then you may spend hours alone, or wandering by yourself through the orchards or—"

"I want to bathe, and then I want to sleep," she yelled back. "And I want to burn these clothes. The look of them is loathsome." Her hand moved as if of its own volition, a constant motion of greeting that had no more to do with her than the flight of birds.

"Patience, dearest," he said loudly. "We are to dine in an hour or so."

"I'll faint before then," she predicted, and leaned back against the stiff cushion of the carriage, finding what little comfort she could there.

Ahead, the doors of the old castle were opening and it seemed as if the great pile of dust-colored stone was absorbing all the procession, making them part of the bulk that dominated that part of the city. Don Rolon quivered as he passed through the gates, and he put it off to heat and fatigue, though the melancholy only got worse when he climbed down out of the saddle and handed the reins over to one of the royal grooms who traveled on the Progress.

"Are you well, Alteza?" asked one of the courtiers in the entourage.

"The sun, I think. A glass of wine and I will be better." It was not quite a lie, for he was certain that the sun had troubled him, and he was thirsty, but whatever new distress gripped him, it went beyond these discomforts to a greater malaise. At least it was not the full moon, he thought, and there would be no chance for that to compound his current woes. He went to the carriage in order to hand Zaretta out of it. Such a minor gesture always earned the wholehearted approval of the people, and what had begun as a game had now turned into a ritual.

"Is there anyone here who can play the lute decently, do you think?" Zaretta asked when she had alighted from the carriage. "I will ask, if you like," Don Rolon offered.

She thought a moment, then said, "Perhaps not. It may be that they will send me one like I heard at Cordoba, who made the worst twangings, but wanted so desperately to please me. The hour I endured listening to him was agony. Never mind. I will try to have a moment to rest, and if my ladies will be certain I am not disturbed, I should be ready to face the entertainments this evening." She turned to the three women who had hurried to follow her.

"Eufemia, Mercedes, Justina. Find me a place where I can lie down for an hour and change my clothes. I'll die if I have to stay in this one minute longer than that."

Don Rolon held onto her hand as the three ladies bustled off to do as Zaretta had bid them. "Tonight, jewel of my life, there will be time for us to ourselves. I have already arranged it. Our host is anxious to say that the next heir was conceived here, and so he will leave us alone." He bowed to kiss her hand.

Zaretta gave a little sigh. "As you wish, my husband. But do not be too harsh on me if I fall asleep. I ache from traveling and I think that my . . . " She knew that Spanish wives did not mention such matters to their husbands, but she plunged ahead. "I think - that my courses are coming, and there might not be more than a day or so that we may still enjoy ourselves."

"Como tu quieres," Don Rolon whispered, stifling both embarrassment and disappointment within him. "But if it is possible . . . "

"Then of course." She looked away, frowning. She had avoided him since he had done public penance, the sting of his humiliation cutting her more deeply than it cut him. She had listened to his explanations that in España these things were to be expected, and though she had seen enough to know it was true, she could not accept it. No one in Venezia would tolerate such behavior, and it struck her as subtly improper that no one in this country should question such disgraceful abuses of power. Ahead Mercedes was beckoning to her, and she hurried toward her lady-in-waiting, hoping that the plump, proper young matron would not want to talk.

"There is a room, Altezita," she said, using the respectful nickname that had sprung up for Zaretta while on the Progress. "It overlooks the courtyard, where there is a fountain. No doubt you will be cooler there, and the host promises that you will have an hour of quiet before the banquet."

"That will do, I guess," Zaretta said, and permitted herself to be led through the narrow stone hallways, preceded by six of the castle servants and followed by her ladies. Would it be this dreadful every time she traveled she asked herself. Was there no way for a woman to find a few days when she might be alone, to garden or hunt as Don Rolon did, or fish off a balcony as she had done as a child?

"Here is the room," said the chamberlain, standing aside, his whole body quite rigid with pride. "It is one of the finest rooms in the entire castle."

"I thank you for it," Zaretta said with the automatic courtesy she had been taught all her life.

"A pleasure, a great pleasure," the chamberlain assured her, bowing so deeply that Zaretta thought for one absurd instant that he was trying to touch his nose to his knees.

"If you would be good enough to summon me a little while before the banquet is to begin, I would be grateful," she told the man as she made a sign to her ladies.

"Come, Altezita. There are things we have to attend to," said Eufemia, responding to the signal. "You must excuse us, chamberlain."

"Of course, of course," the chamberlain said, and went away to boast of his words with the wife of the Infante Real.

❦

"This is pleasant enough," Don Rolon told Ciro as they stepped into the apartments that had been set aside for his use. "There have been worse."

"Indeed, Alteza," said Ciro as he closed the door. "But I fear there will not be much time to enjoy them."

"Why? The banquet? True enough." He was already unfastening the densely pleated lace ruff, which had all but choked him for most of the afternoon. "I'm covered with grime. Is it always this way when the wind blows?"

"In summer, Alteza. In winter, there is mud." Ciro moved about the room, looking behind large objects, opening and closing doors and, chests.

"Why these precautions, Ciro?" Don Rolon asked, puzzled. "Have we got more spies?"

"No," Ciro said, then nodded toward a thickly woven curtain that hung over a narrow alcove beside the empty hearth. "It is nothing so simple."

The curtain moved and Lugantes stepped out, bowing briefly to Don Rolon. He was still dressed in his jester's garb, but now the patchwork cloth was travel-stained, and his eyes were dark with exhaustion. "I followed the procession into the castle and found Ciro. It is urgent that I speak to you at once." There was no formality in anything he said; the tone of his voice was husky but stern.

"What is it?" Don Rolon asked, his splendid, dirty clothes forgotten. "Why are you here?" As he asked, he tried to think what he might have done or said that would bring Lugantes to him. Had word already reached Alonzo of his public penance, and was there more to come? Had the familiars accompanying him on the Progress sent equivocal reports back to Padre Juan and the Holy Office? He could not bring himself to speak aloud, for fear the words themselves would make his fears real.

Lugantes stared up at Don Rolon, wishing now that he did not have to tell him. But there was no safety in silence. "Alteza, Padre Juan has preached against you."

"What?" Ciro demanded, more shocked than he thought was possible. He had expected treachery from Gil del Rey, but not from the Holy Office.

"Why?" Don Rolon asked at the same time, very softly.

"Padre Lucien was was taken by the Secular Arm for apostasy," Lugantes said, finding it hard to say the words. "He was Questioned. I heard Padre Juan say that in general he approved the rule that allows the application of torture but once; however, where corrupted priests are concerned, he believes that no such restriction should apply."

"Padre Lucien?" Don Rolon repeated, feeling suddenly very stupid.

"For apostasy?" Ciro asked.

"They say he was working on behalf of the Emperor, and had been in the ranks of the Devil's worshipers. For that, all his actions are to be reevaluated, along with his influence on you, Alteza." Lugantes looked away, toward the leg of the nearest chair, as if this were suddenly fascinating to him.

"But what of Padre Lucien?" Don Rolon said, thinking he had missed something in what Lugantes was telling him.

"They Questioned him in the second and third degree, or so Padre Juan said to Alonzo. I was in the room at the time. They paid no attention to me." Without warning his eyes filled with tears. "When the rack got nothing from him, they obtained permission to apply torture. They tore the nails from his hands and feet, and broke all his teeth. When he still persisted in saying that he was not a spy, that he was a true priest, they bumed his eyes out with hot irons. He died while they were doing it."

As he crossed himself, Don Rolon thought he must be underwater. He could not move quickly and surely he felt he was drowning. His throat and eyes were aching and tight. "When?" he managed to rasp.

"I left not quite two days ago. Dominguez loaned me his best war-horse and I rode hard to get here. There are officers of the Inquisition not more than half a day behind me, Alteza." He dragged the cuff of his sleeve over his face, which only made the dust turn into uneven smears. "Padre Juan is determined to Question you, to prove that you have been seduced by the servants of the Devil and are no longer fit to be Infante Real. Alonzo has drafted a letter to the Pope, provisional to your confession or . . . "

"Death," Don Rolon said for him.

Lugantes nodded. "It would put Gil del Rey in your place."

"Damn them both!" Ciro burst out.

But Don Rolon motioned him to silence. "It is what they have wanted all along, and Padre Juan has given it to them." He sighed once. "How long before they take me?"

"No!" Ciro cried out.

"Alteza!" Lugantes protested.

"What recourse is there?" Don Rolon asked them, thinking that he was not even twenty years ad. They are going to kill me, he said to himself. They are going to kill me and I have done nothing. I am innocent. He wondered if this were more of the curse.

"Alteza," Lugantes said, his voice so low and arresting that Don Rolon was jolted out of his brooding. "Before you went on this Progress, Ciro and I had many opportunities to talk."

"Yes," Ciro corroborated. "We had music lessons."

"I remember," Don Rolon said, baffled by this turn in the discussion. "What of it?"

"No one wanted to listen to so inept a pupil," Lugantes said with a grimace. "We had few interruptions and no listeners." As he saw some understanding come into the Infante Real's eyes, he gave a quick nod. "We made plans, Alteza, in case there should be trouble. We thought then that your . . . affliction might make it necessary for you to . . . leave quickly, and be kept safe. It is all arranged."

"What is arranged?" Don Rolon asked, trying to keep pace with these shifts. "What are you telling me?"

Ciro took up where Lugantes left off. "We knew that we had to prepare to get you away. We had not planned on getting you out of Segovia, but it should be less difficult than removing you from Valladolid."

"I am not a fugitive, to run from—" Don Rolon began to object, but both his valet and jester silenced him.

"You are a fugitive, Alteza," Lugantes corrected him. "With the Secular Arm coming for you, you must fly or be prepared to undergo the Question and possible torture. It is what Padre Juan wants, and your father will do nothing to stop him, though it is the greatest folly he has yet committed." He folded his arms. "There are those who will hide you until we can get word to your uncle—"

"But if my father does not want—" Don Rolon started, only to be interrupted once more.

"Dominguez will attend to it. He has no wish to see España plunged into war, as must surely happen if you are taken by the Inquisition."

Don Rolon stared bleakly across the whitewashed walls of the chamber. "Are you certain of that? Might not the people be glad to be rid of a cursed Infante?"

"Not after such a Progress as you have just had," Ciro said, forcing more confidence into his tone than he truly possessed. "The people do not want Gil because he does not have the Right."

"Then it will be Otto." Don Rolon rubbed his eyes. "At least it will be over."

"No!" Ciro said.

"No, Alteza!" Lugantes all but shouted. "No!"

"But you do not know, my friend, not all of it . . . " Don Rolon said, averting his face from them.

"You mean the wolf?" Lugantes asked bluntly, and saw that the Infante Real was badly shaken. "I have known for some time. What of it?"

"What of it?" Don Rolon echoed, amazed at the jester yet again.

"There are those of us who are misshapen every day of the year, not just one night a month," Lugantes said with a bitter laugh. "And priests burn witches in church plazas. What did you do at El Morro that could compare to it?"

"But—" Don Rolon broke off.

"I have an uncle," Ciro told his master. "He lives near Toledo. He has no reason to love the Holy Office, and he has agreed to take in whatever guest I bring to him. We will go there, Alteza. Until Dominguez can notify the Emperor of what is going on here. Then we will take the matter to Rome, if we must. We will not let Padre Juan decide this matter, or the throne will never be able to take action without the permission of the Holy Office again."

"Oh, God," Don Rolon muttered. He thought, suddenly and vividly, of Padre Lucien. To have suffered so much and so futilely! He was afraid he would vomit. "

"Listen to us, Alteza," Lugantes begged him. "I implore you with all my heart. You must do this, Alteza, or it will all have been for nothing."

Numbly he shook his head, not so much to protest, but to try to escape the images that danced in his mind. To be subjected to the strappado, with weights on his feet to make it worse, to be stretched on the rack until his joints were pulled from their sockets, and all the while to listen to the droning of the priests with their endless, sense-less questions until he was mad enough to agree with them . . . . He coughed and swallowed hard. "What do you want me to do?"

Ciro looked quickly at Lugantes, and the jester began to ex-plain.

❧

Zaretta had put on her second-best gown of Venezian silk. It was a beautiful dress of a light blue-green, heavily sewn with seed pearls in a pattern like waves on a beach. The neckline was too open and low for Spanish tastes, but Zaretta ignored the stares and whispered remarks as she followed Mercedes down to the cavemous banqueting hall, where tables were being laid for the feast. She noticed that the fastenings were a little tight and concluded that the enormous amounts of food she had been required to consume on the Progress were adding to her flesh.

Her host, though not technically master of the castle, which was one of those mandated solely to el Rey, nevertheless received her in the most fulsome terms when she made her appearance at the portals of the reception hall.

"It is the most memorable day of my life, dear Venezian, to be able to welcome you to Segovia and our hearts. We so rarely see members of the royal House, that when they bring us such trea-sures as you, our lives are made the richer for your presence." He waved his hands and a consort of musicians began to play a mourn-ful, stately pavanne.

"You are most gracious," she said, trying to recall the man's name and title. "When one is a stranger, it is especial-ly delightful to be treated with so much warmth and hospitality. In the Progress, I have seen much of España, and have learned to know the kindness of its people." She did not think her host heard the irony in her words.

"How could anyone not be kind to you?" the host asked her rhe-torically, and looked to the rest of the company to agree with him.

"You put me to the blush," Zaretta said with great deter-mination, hoping that Don Rolon would come shortly. She was awkward by herself, and she knew it. Having her ladies and the entourage about her was not enough. Only in the last few days had she discovered that some time during the Progress, she had come to depend upon her young husband, and when he was not at her side, she missed him.

"How wonderful," the host said, then proffered his arm for her to lay hers upon. "Do let me escort you into the banqueting hall, Doña Real."

Hiding a vexed sigh, Zaretta did as she was bid, though her thoughts wandered. "I am curious about the history of this place," she said, confident that her host would embark on a long, complicated and boring recitation that would require less than half her attention and would please her narrator.

"A most amazing city," he said at once, launching into the various anecdotes of the last six hundred years.

All the places at the long tables were taken save one, which was at the center of the high table. Guests were doing their best not to appear hungry or anxious, but the smells drifting to them from the nearby kitchens were tantalizing, and no one could entirely ignore them.

"Perhaps," Zaretta ventured, interrupting a long and pointless tale about a twelfth-century Saracen, "it might be best if you sent someone to the Infante Real's quarters. He was much troubled with dust and the sun today, and it may be that he has fallen asleep." She could not imagine why Ciro would hesitate to wake Don Rolon unless he were ill. Nevertheless, the gesture seemed a sensible and harmless one.

"Should we disturb him?" her host asked. He could not conceal the awe he felt at the prospect of intruding on the heir to the throne.

"Send Padre Barnabas to speak to his valet," Zaretta said, hoping that this menial task would offend the Dominican, since she had not yet forgiven him for shaming Don Rolon with a public penance.

Apparently her host was not comfortable with this notion, either, but he did as she suggested, signaling one of his pages and sending that apprehensive youth down the high table to Padre Barnabas to murmur a few words to the prelate before scurrying away from him.

Padre Barnabas rose from his place and came toward his host and Zaretta. "You are concerned for the Infante Real?" he asked of them both. He had taken on his sternest manner, so that the imposing weight of his office made him even more impressive than he was ordinarily.

"He may be resting. It is not like him to be mistaken in the hour," Zaretta said lightly. "However, he was much fatigued, and he said that the sun troubled him. It would be best to determine if he has other complaints, and find out how he wishes us to proceed here." She was deliberately copying the grand courtesy she had seen her uncle employ on state occasions, and was pleasantly astonished to discover that it worked almost as well for her as it had for him. "As you are his confessor, he will confide the true state of his health to you, where he might decide that for the sake of the occasion, he would dissemble to another."

This was solace to Padre Barnabas' pride, and he accepted it eagerly. "Yes. There is much in what you say. After the brigands used him so harshly, it may be that the difficulties of the journey lie heavily on him." He hooked his thumbs around the chain that held his crucifix. "I will learn what I can and return at once."

The host—Zaretta could still not think of his name—said a few grateful words, and turned back to Zaretta to resume his tale of the Saracen.

Padre Barnabas required one of the understewards to show him the way to Don Rolon's quarters, which irked him. It detracted from his dignity to require a guide, and that was made more intolerable because the understeward was a bent old man whose wits were not entirely his own.

At first, Padre Barnabas rapped gently on the door, waiting impatiently for a response. When none came, he knocked more forcefully, then called out, thinking that if Don Rolon were asleep, he might have lost himself in a dream. It was also worrisome that Ciro did not answer him, and he scowled at the understeward as if accusing the old man of some unknown duplicity in the silence. "I will have to enter the room," he announced, and did not tarry for approval. He opened the door and stepped into the withdrawing room. There were two chests, both with the Infante Real's arms upon them, dusty and scuffed from being dragged through the cities and roads of España. A third, much smaller case was missing, but he assumed that it was in the bedchamber. He took a turn about the room, not certain what he was looking for. Nothing was disturbed or untidy. He half expected the door to open and Don Rolon to appear, sleepy and apologetic, to say that he had only just wakened.

"Is there something wrong?" the ancient understeward asked.

"Not that I can see, except that the Infante Real is not here." He went into the second room where a writing table stood near the high, narrow window. Nothing in the room had been touched, though there was a trace of dusty tracks on the parquet floor. The bedchamber was equally puzzling. There was no sign of violence or disturbance, but without doubt Don Rolon and his valet were gone. Padre Barnabas stood beside the curtained bed and pondered. It troubled him that this could occur while he was present, for he might be held responsible for the disappearance—if disappearance it was—by his superiors in the Holy Office. One thing caught his eye as he stood scowling down at the floor. He bent down and picked up one small, tarnished bell. It made a high, forlorn clink as he lifted it. Padre Bamabas had a vague impression that there were bells on Don Rolon's parade tack, and he said, "Send someone to the stables. It may be that El Alteza is there."

"At once," the understeward said, gratefully leaving the MOM.

Padre Bamabas went slowly back to the banquet room, the bell tucked into the wallet that hung from his hempen belt. He was convinced that the bell was part of the puzzle, but he did not know how.

"But that's impossible," Zaretta said when Padre Bamabas had finished murmuring his news, to her.

"No, child, it is not." He gave her his most sober look. "Had you any notion that he was expecting to . . . "

She remembered the way he had spoken of his desire to be alone with her, and her cheeks grew rosy. "No. He said nothing to me." Her thoughts were suddenly jumbled. She knew she should say or do something, but there was nothing she could think to do. Rather distractedly, she turned toward her host. "Whatever is detaining the Infante Real is . . . more involved than I thought. It will be best to serve the meal and trust he will join us as soon as possible." She was not sure that this was proper in España, but in Venezia it would be expected of her.

"Is he not well?" her host asked with some alarm.

"Oh, no no. That is . . . not ill." She smiled a little confusedly and gave her attention to Padre Barnabas. "Is there anything I . . . should know?"

"They are checking the stables now, Doña. They will send word if . . . anything is found." Padre Bamabas inclined his head, thinking that he was demeaning himself to show her so much courtesy.

Zaretta gave a helpless little shrug and tried to put her concern out of her mind. Whatever had happened, there was nothing she could do now except wait, and the better she conducted herself, the more it would help Don Rolon. She was not entirely certain this was wise, but nothing else occurred to her.

The banquet had progressed to the third course of eleven when word came discreetly that the Infante's horse and tack were in the stable and undisturbed. No one had seen Don Rolon since he went to his rooms upon his arrival.

Zaretta's eyes glimmered with tears, but she choked them back. There would be time enough for weeping if the cause for his disappearance was learned. "It is most unfortunate," she said quietly, and rose to excuse herself. "Until you have word of him, I will keep to my apartments with my women. I do thank you," she said to her host, "for your hospitality, and I know that you will do everything possible to find . . . ."

🍂

Pages and equerries hurried through the city the rest of the night, rousing the people to search for the missing Infante Real and his valet. No one had seen either man, or could recall anything unusual that might indicate what had happened to them.

Had the officers bothered to ask, one or two of those questioned might have remembered seeing two Franciscan monks leading a lame child and a donkey out of the southern gate of the city, but such sights were so ordinary that they were often ignored, and when compared to the vanishing of the heir to the throne, wholly forgotten.

23

"We are glad to see you well again, Lugantes," Alonzo said to his jester as he came into the reception room. "Your wit has been sorely needed these last few days."

"I did not wish to carry any disease to you, Majestad," Lugantes said with a perfect bow. "It is enough that there should be Diabolism touching the Court. I do not think it would aid you or anyone to add illness as well."

"The strength of our faith is proof against such things," Alonzo said with the unctuousness of one who rarely suffered from anything but indigestion. "But there are those around us who are subject to the trials of the flesh." He crossed his legs and made a gesture to the dwarf. "Tell us, Lugantes, how you see this most recent difficulty. Where, do you think, is our son?"

News of Don Rolon's disappearance had reached Valladolid from Segovia the evening before, and the most fantastic rumors were circulating through the court, growing more outrageous with each repetition. "I do not believe that he has been spirited away by either angels or devils," Lugantes said making a great show of somber consideration that amused Alonzo for its presumption. "I do not think we will find him in Heaven, Hell or the New World. I do not think he was murdered and the body stuffed down a rathole. I do not think he was kidnapped. Yet he is gone. He did not take his things. His valet is gone, so we may be confident that wherever he is, he is properly dressed."

At this, Alonzo permitted himself to give a faint smile. "An important consideration."

"It is," Lugantes concurred. "How would it be to have the Infante Real, mussed and rumpled like any man, wandering the roads of España with no one to tend to him. Shocking."

"Our Inquisitor General," Alonzo said thoughtfully, "has suggested that the men who were said to have waylaid him while he was hunting were not simple bandits but those who worship the Devil. He believes that they have been sent to claim Don Rolon for their own, and are charged with delivering him to the Evil One." His face and voice were entirely expressionless, but there was a heat in his eyes that showed Lugantes how much el Rey wished to be rid of his son.

"It is the task of Inquisitors to look for evil everywhere, and for that reason, their hearts are often closed to the goodness that is around them. Padre Juan is most zealous, but he does not often extend himself beyond the duties of his office. While he is without doubt most devout and pious, remember that he is not a man living in the world, and he often forgets that those of us not swom to the Church must often find our way through mires and deserts he has never known." Lugantes cocked his head on one side. "What are we to make of our lives, who have not been called of God? We must listen to the priests and observe the rites and Sacraments and trust to God's Mercy to aid us now and in the life everlasting."

Alonzo nodded. "An excellent observation, Lugantes. But you forget that Don Rolon was cursed before he was born, and that has made his soul more vulnerable." He rose from his seat and paced down the reception room. "No matter what happens, I must soon send word to my brother. Doubtless his spies have already prepared their dispatches and have handed them to messengers, but . . . " He crossed his arms and stood still, as if posing for a portrait showing his determination. "You hear more than I do, Lugantes. Is it true that there are those who think that Gil arranged this, in order to have free access to the Succession?"

It required all of Lugantes' wisdom and tact to answer, and he chose his words most carefully. "It is not surprising that such things are said, Majestad. Gil has never made a secret of his ambitions, nor you of your favor. Gil has said openly that he is pleased that Don

Rolon cannot be found, and he suspects that he has been killed or imprisoned by the enemies of España, and there are those who cannot help but think that for Gil his friends might do . . . unwise things."

"He has done nothing," Alonzo insisted. "He told me last night that he in no way is responsible for whatever has befallen his half brother."

Had Lugantes not known precisely what became of Don Rolon, he himself might have suspected Gil of engineering the Infante Real's disappearance, but as it was, he could say with complete conviction, "I am pleased that it is so, Majestad. Yet you must not be condemning of those who think otherwise, since they have listened to Gil for the last two years announce to the world at large that he desires to succeed you."

"He would not resort to treachery," said el Rey in a tone that permitted no argument. "He is my son."

Privately Lugantes knew that Gil might be expected to do anything he thought was necessary to become Alonzo's heir, treacherous or not, but he held his peace. Instead, he changed the subject slightly. "What else has been done? The Guarda has been dispatched, but that is little."

"The Holy Office has sent men of the Secular Arm, as well. They are searching for known heretics and Diabolists." Alonzo gnawed once at his lower lip. "There are many places in España where such damned men might take refuge, perhaps among the Moriscos or conversos who are not so converted as they pretend."

This last alarmed Lugantes, but his expression remained unaltered. "Nothing else?"

"Not at the moment. If nothing is found, then we will apply to our brother the Emperor and the Pope for their assistance." Alonzo shook his head slowly. "We wished to be entertained, and instead we have embroiled you in our affairs. It would be better if you were to leave us. We will spend time with our confessor, and in prayer for the protection of the Infante Real and the forgiveness of our sins that may have contributed to his travail."

Ordinarily Lugantes might have found an excuse to linger, but this time he was grateful for the opportunity to tend to his own affairs. He bowed without flourish. "Majestad, may your mind be tranquil and your heart be comforted."

"Gracias," Alonzo said absently as he waved Lugantes away from him. "We will send for you tomorrow, or perhaps the next day."

Lugantes hurried out of the reception room and made straight for the apartments of the Duque da Minho, not caring if his movements were observed. "Where is your master?" he demanded of Raimundo's manservant when his impatient knock was reluctantly answered.

"He is—" the servant began only to be cut off by Raimundo's voice.

"Show him in, Leandro. I long for some amusement." He sounded irritated and a bit bored. "If I do not listen to him, I must read more or wait until the next bit of gossip is offered as a treat."

Leandro hesitated, then shrugged. "It is not forbidden," he said, stepping aside to admit the jester.

Raimundo was in his withdrawing room, wearing a long lounging robe of black velvet embroidered with gold thread. He nodded to Lugantes as he came into the room. "As you see, I have been restricted to my own apartments. Leandro, while a fine manservant, is more devoted to the Holy Office than to me. Gil has let it be known that I am one who opposes his claim and for that, he is determined to punish me." He indicated one of the three chairs. "You have been ill, I understand."

"Yes," Lugantes said. "It appears that while I was recovering, I missed more excitement than usually happens in a decade. I was hoping that you would tell me as much as you can, and without embellishments. The rumors are most . . . incredible." He got into the chair and drew up his legs.

"You have heard, of course, that Don Rolon is missing," Raimundo said. "He was at Segovia one moment and so far as anyone can determine, evaporated into the air." He hesitated, then added for effect, "I do not know who took him, or why, but their execution of it was masterful."

"So it would appear, if what I have heard is correct," Lugantes agreed, his eyes sliding toward the alcove where he saw the curtains move slightly. "No doubt it is of great concern to the entire Court, but—"

"But. Precisely." He fiddled with the long tassels of his belt. "The Holy Office is determined to find him. They wish to speak to him in any case, and now there is more reason to be diligent." He looked directly at the jester. "Those who did this will have to be more careful now than ever they were before, with both the Guarda and the Secular Arm taking part in the search."

"From the sound of it, I would have to agree," said Lugantes, trying to find a way to tell Raimundo that Don Rolon was safely hidden.

"There are also suspicions that it may be a plot on the part of the Emperor, as well as all the other plots you will hear mentioned.

They say that he wants Otto to rule here, and therefore has decided to be rid of Don Rolon. Of all the suppositions I have heard so far, that one makes the most sense. I doubt that Gil del Rey would be stupid enough to try to be rid of Don Rolon before his own position is guaranteed." He made a covert sign to Lugantes, and the dwarf nodded.

"It is possible." He would go along with Raimundo on that, and give more credence to the stories that implicated Gustav than to those centering in España. He wished he knew more about how much Raimundo had been restricted in his movements, and why. "You appear calm about all this," he said, making an invitation of the remark.

"What else can I be?" Raimundo answered with a dry laugh that was as humorless as it was quick. "I am bound to honor and defend the Succession on behalf of Portugal, and to carry out the orders of my Rei. We are bound to España, and therefore to the Holy Roman Empire, and there are obligations I have to those I serve." He gave an exasperated sigh. "For that, they think me disloyal, and what defense may I present except my service to my country, which apparently is not adequate for the men of the Holy Office."

"I see." Lugantes was horrified to think that Raimundo might be Questioned by the Secular Arm, but it was certain that he expected it. "It is a sad day for España when we cannot trust men of your honor, Duque. If there is anything you would wish me to do for you, you have only to say so."

Raimundo nodded quickly, minutely, so that the servant who watched them might not see his response. "No, I don't think so, little man," he said lazily. "I am not in the mood for jokes and until I know that Don Rolon is safe, I will not be. However, here is something for your pains." He held out his hand and there was something that clinked in them. Since Raimundo had never before paid him for his aid or skills, Lugantes made quite a show of taking it.

"That's what I like about you, Duque," he said heartily. "Always such a generous fellow. Well, send word if you should change your mind. I have learned a few new songs that I cannot sing for just everyone." He leered broadly. "There's no harm in them, but a man might find them a pleasant distraction."

"Perhaps later," Raimundo said. "And I thank you again for visiting me."

"Yes. Well, may we meet again soon under pleasanter circumstances." He all but scampered out of the room as he tucked the three keys into his wallet and withdrew two gold coins which he tossed in the air and caught for the benefit of Leandro, who held the door for him. "A fine man, your, master."

"Perhaps," the manservant answered as he closed the door on Lugantes.

❧

Inez screamed in outrage to hide her terror, her eyes shifting from one hooded face to another. "And I tell you again, I have done nothing! Nothing! NOTHING!"

"And the babe within you?" one of the urbane voices asked, paying no heed to her outburst. "Is it your husband's get?"

The crass word upset Inez. "Of course," she said, beginning to sulk again. She had been sitting in front of these three sinister men for the better part of the morning, and the dark room with the red-painted floors was wearing on her. Ever since the officers from the Inquisition had broken into her house in Santander, she had been fighting the sickening dread of what would become of her if it were ever learned that she had been the mistress of the Infante Real.

"Of course," the smooth voice agreed. "It is strange how we of the Holy Office may be misinformed. Yet our own familiar has said to us that he saw you at a house here in Valladolid where the Infante Real called often, in such rooms and hours as could mean little else but that he was your lover. Do you deny this?"

"Yes." She felt the infant twist inside her, and she smiled at his strength. For the child she carried, she would not be beaten by these men. Her own confessor had told her long ago that the Holy Office could not abuse a pregnant woman. She was growing annoyed with Don Rolon for permitting this to happen to her, and she wanted to speak to him, to protest the way she was being treated.

"We have been told," said the one whose voice was deeper than the others, "that you ensnared a virtuous prince on the very eve of his wedding, and bound him to you with vile spells. It is further suggested that you conducted yourself as a lewd woman, exposing your flesh to his lusts and passions which you yourself aroused, so that you might more truly dominate him to do the will of your master the Devil."

"Ridiculous!" she scoffed, but her voice shook.

"And our familiar has sworn that you lured other men to you, so that you might have more than one conquest to bring to the Devil, so that he would be the better pleased with you and all you had done on his behalf." The deep voice was almost soothing, in spite of the vile words. "We know that our familiar is the trusted servant of the Holy Office, and that your vows mean little if your conduct is any indication, for you are without virtue or honor."

"That's not so!" she objected, starting to rise. Two officers of the Secular Arm restrained her and forced her to sit on the lowered stool again.

"We will tell you when you may rise," the one who lisped informed her.

"I must . . . the babe presses on me." Her olive skin darkened now more than it had in anger. "Please."

"Make water if you must. We have seen worse here." The deep voice was almost amused, but there was something else in its tone, a curious satisfaction or justification that made Inez wince. "And then tell us whose babe it is that presses in you."

"I wish you would stop questioning me like this," she said, finding a little defiance in her discomfort.

"Oh, we are not questioning you, woman," the one with the deep voice told her in his calmest way. "We have not yet shown you the instruments that can be used to prod the truth from you, or explained how we will use them if you drive us to it. That is the Question in the first degree. Nor have we stripped you and bound you in chains with your hands far over your head and your feet shackled, and left you to stand thus for hours while you consider your transgressions. That is the Question in the second degree. You have heard of the rack and strappado and the knotted rag? That is the Question in the third degree. If those are of no avail, there is always torture. We may apply it but once, yet that is usually sufficient."

As Inez listened to this grisly recitation, she crossed herself, but found that she was stopped in the act by one of the officers.

"Do not blaspheme, woman!" snapped the lisping voice. "Until you have shown that your soul is untainted, do not bring futher misfortune upon you and your babe by greater sins."

She felt the wet warmth run down her thighs, and she screamed. "You Devils!"

"Take note, Padres," the urbane one said. "She accuses us."

"Yes!" She started to sob, hunching over to conceal both the wetness on her skirt and the swelling of her abdomen. "You call yourselves servants of God and you abuse His children. You pretend to hunt the Devil so that you may be masters of the world, which is Satan's domain." She wiped her face. "Why do you not simply kill me now? It is what you have already decided to do. Or are you like cats, who must torment the mice they catch before making an end of them?"

"If the babe is your husband's, it is innocent, and we may not touch you until it is born," the one with the deep voice informed her.

"And if it is not?" She thought that her world had once again been turned upside down. "I have said that the child is my husband's, and—"

"But it is a simple thing to say such things when there is no reason not to lie." The lisp grew more pronounced. "When you have been with us, and we have learned the truth, it will be time enough to determine if the child is cursed or not."

Inez felt the little courage she had harbored drain away. "But I have sworn . . . . You have heard me."

"But you stand accused of witchcraft and sorcery. You are not yet exonerated of these charges, nor will you be with one or two questions and a few facile answers." The deep-voiced Dominican turned to his two colleagues. "It is the opinion of the midwife that she will deliver in two more months. We may subject her to the Question in the second degree while the child is within her, but there is too much hazard if the third degree is attempted with her so advanced in pregnancy."

"Is it a true pregnancy, or a ruse of the Devil?" asked the lisping one.

"Apparently it is a true pregnancy. If it is not, we will know of it soon enough. The midwife said that she felt the babe move, and that speaks for its genuineness," said the third. "There are the servants to be examined. I have statements here from two of them who agree that the Infante Real was her lover, but there is not conclusive proof."

Inez listened to them discuss her as if she were nothing more than a wooden statue, and it increased her fear. Suddenly she felt she must not permit them to ignore her. She wanted to speak out, to tell them that they were without honor or justice, but she could not bring herself to do so; terrified that they would not notice her, that she would be invisible and inaudible to them. Her confusion was increasing as she listened, and little of what they said made sense to her. Yet she was left with the impression that they were determined to see her hanging naked in chains. She wanted to retch, but put both her hands over her mouth so that she would not. The one with the deep voice said that Capitan Iturbes had sent a protest to them, and the other two nodded their tall hoods significantly, ponderously. What did it mean? she wanted to know. Was her husband in danger because the Inquisition had taken her? Or was it something else? Vaguely she realized that one of their remarks had been addressed to her, and she tried to concentrate on what was being said.

"Answer me, woman," the lisping one demanded.

"Pardon, Padre. I did not perfectly hear . . ." She did not think it would be wise to tell them she was not listening.

"We must know who heard your confessions in Santander." The order was a stern one, and rapped out as if to a stranger.

"Uh . . . at Santa Paula, it was . . . uh, Padre Agustin. He's . . . he's old and he does not have his teeth. He . . . um . . . often reads from scriptures before saying what penance is to be done." She could not keep a clear image in her mind of the old man who had listened to her for the last few months.

"His teeth are not significant," one of the priests interrupted her. "What have you asked God's pardon for?"

Inez looked up sharply. "That is between God, my confessor and me." She was well within her rights as a Catholic to say this, but the three men all took exception to her refusal.

"You wish us to believe that you are an honest woman and a good Catholic, and yet you will not tell us, ordained priests, the extent of your sins?" said the smooth-spoken one. "You do not understand how great your peril is, woman. You come before us, accused of sorcery and witchcraft and the deliberate seduction of the Infante Real, which some would regard as treason as well as a religious crime, yet you do not conduct yourself meekly and with submission to the Holy Office, whose only desire is to see that España is kept free of the influence of the Devil and all his works. If you are the good Catholic you claim to be, you should be willing, even eager to aid us in our examinations so that the Church may more completely bring the reign of the Devil to an end. Yet instead you tell us that you are not willing to reveal what you know, and thus you increase our doubts as to your sincerity. You are shocked that we question you, and yet you behave as one who is guilty."

"I am not!" Inez said, wanting to sound confident and instead giving the impression of a poor liar caught in deception.

"We will determine that in due time," said the lisping one, and signaled to the officers of the Secular Arm. "You know what to do with her."

Nothing Inez had ever heard had such a sound of finality as those words, and she began to weep again, steadily, without passion, with utter despair, as she was roughly led away into the dark cells of the Inquisition.

24

Inside the walls of Toledo there was little activity, since it was far advanced into the night. The Cistercians went about their mandated task of burying the dead, and their chanting rang faintly and eerily through the narrow streets. At the shrine of San Simeon poor pilgrims slept huddled in their ragged clothes, waiting for the Mass at dawn that would bring them the intercession they sought. In the streets where the smiths worked, there was an occasional wink of red from the banked coals of the forges, and the sword smiths' apprentices lay on pallets immediately behind the barred doors to prevent theft.

At the far end of that district, where the gold and silver smiths had their businesses, there were a few rushlights still burning but in the courtyards of the little houses, not where they might be seen from the streets. It was Friday night, and the conversos were gathered to do honor to the God of Israel, though they risked their fortunes and their lives to do it.

Ciro tugged Don Rolon away from the upper window and nodded toward the bed. "It would be better if you do not watch. Then you will not have to lie to a priest if he asks you if you ever witnessed a Jewish service in the house of a converso."

Don Rolon nodded. "Then you are still a Jew?"

"I am a converso," Ciro answered. "I have been baptized into the Church and I go to Confession and take the Sacraments, as well you know. I also honor my father." He would not say anything more specific, and both of them were aware of it.

"Why did we come here?" They had arrived two days before, but Don Rolon was so exhausted that he had slept for almost an entire day and had only recently begun to ask questions.

"For help," Ciro answered at once. "If there is anyone in all of España who can aid you, it is my uncle." He pulled the shutters closed and the room fell into gloom. "There are candles. I'll fetch them, Alteza." As he left the chamber he called out for Elena to help him.

"What is it?" the old woman asked, responding to the summons.

"We must have candles. I do not want Don Rolon to see what Isador is doing, for fear of what he may be forced to reveal later." He put his hand on his great-aunt's arm. "I am sorry that this may bring misfortune to us all, but I could think of nothing else. If he were taken by the Holy Office—"

"Them!" she spat.

"Yes. They are the ones who want him. That is what I must speak with Isador about, mi caraota pequeña." With gruff affection he kissed her hand, then went into the dining room where four branches of candles were burning. None of them were needed for the ritual, and so Ciro took the nearest of them. "I will have to talk with Isador before tomorrow. He has not wanted to talk to me, but he must. Persuade him for me, will you, tia mia?"

"I will try. But your great-uncle and I have been man and wife for over forty years, and I tell you now that he does not persuade very easily." The old woman wagged her head roguishly. "It was easier when I was younger, oh, much easier. Now I must use logic, which is a great drawback."

Ciro chuckled. "Thank you. For me and for my prince."

Elena stared hard at Ciro. "You have risen very high for a converso, nephew. Are you never afraid?"

"Often. But just now, my fear is for Don Rolon. He is in far greater peril than I am." He held his hand to shield the candle flames. "He is afflicted and abandoned. Compared to that, being a converso is nothing."

"I have heard that he is cursed," Elena said, her mouth tightening to a thin line. "It is not wise to have those here who are cursed."

Ciro thought a moment, then said, "It was his father who was cursed, and the curse was given to those who are innocent. I have served Don Rolon for five years, and I know him well. His affliction is great and he suffers much, but still he is innocent, and the curse is his father's, not his, though he manifests it."

"I see," Elena said. "In that case, you are wise to come to Isador, who is adept in such matters, and I will do what I can on your behalf." She walked beside Ciro to the door. "But there is still the Holy Office."

"Yes. And the Infante has no more reason to love the Inquisition than you do, tia. It is dangerous for one in his position to do so, but he has spoken out against them, and the abuses they have done." He bent to kiss her forehead. "I must get back to him. He's restless and worried and has no friends he can turn to but me."

"No one else?" she asked, surprised for the first time.

"Perhaps one or two, but they are in Valladolid, and that place is not safe for him or his friends." He thought of Lugantes, who had returned willingly to the capital, and he hoped that the jester would be safe for a while longer. The little man was intelligent and courageous, but in the face of Padre Juan's Questions, that counted for nothing.

"Well, then, you tell him that he is welcome here. And tell him to remember that the Jews were kind to him when no one else was." She gave a quick, ducking nod to her head. "I will speak to you again at first light."

Ciro turned to her, surprised that she would plan to rise so early. "You need to rest, tia. Do not get up for us."

"I will not. But at my age, sleep comes less often and stays for shorter hours. Doubtless I am learning to welcome that other sleep, and will be glad when it comes. I am always up before the sun, Ciro. Whether or not you are here." She gave him an impatient shove. "Go back to your master. Quickly now."

"Yes, tia," Ciro said, and made his way back to the second floor and the corner room where he found Don Rolon pacing uncertainly in the dark.

"There you are," the Infante snapped when Ciro came into the room. "You were gone a long time. Is there some difficulty?"

"No. I had a word or two with my great-aunt and brought these." He held the branch of candles aloft so that their light would dispel the gloom. "Tomorrow we will talk with my great-uncle and tell him how it is with you."

The prospect plainly made Don Rolon uncomfortable, and he moved away. "It isn't wise. It is too much of a risk. What if either of them should be taken by the Secular Arm? What then? They have no reason to keep my secret, and—" He hated the craven sound of his protests, but he could not banish the dread that had been growing in him for months and had possessed him wholly since his flight from Segovia.

"Don Rolon," Ciro said in reasonable tones, "you need not worry. If the Holy Office comes for them, the simple fact that they still keep their Jewish books would condemn them, and would cause the Inquisitors to regard everything they said as lies. If they are taken, you are the least of their hazards." He put the branch of candles down on a small table with a round, inlaid top. "And your danger does not come from being with Jews, but from within the Holy Office itself."

The Infante Real nodded miserably. "You're right. God have mercy on us all, you're right."

Ciro drew up a chair and sat down in it. "My great-uncle is a very wise man, Alteza, and you are one of the few who might have use for his skills. But you may find what he does . . . odd. He practices a craft that—"

"Witchcraft? I will not have truck with witches!" Don Rolon crossed himself and made the sign to ward off the Evil Eye.

"My great-uncle is no witch. He is something else entirely. But you must not let what the priests have told you prejudice you against him or what he can do for you if you will permit it." Ciro was hard put to find a way to reassure Don Rolon, and to make it clear to him that Isador was the only hope he had. "He is a dedicated master of his craft, with abilities few ever achieve, even those most sincere. For that he is regarded with respect and love by the Jews of Toledo, and they come to him when they know that all other remedies will fail them."

"But Jews . . . " Don Rolon faltered and smiled apologetically. "I have heard Jews spoken against all my life, Ciro. My first tutors told me they were cursed. But they told me that I am cursed, too, so it may be just as well that I appeal to a Jew for aid." He could see that he had offended Ciro, and that troubled him, for he now felt a gratitude and affection for his valet that he had never experienced before. He had been told that servants owed a duty to him, and that as heir to the throne, he was entitled to the respect and obedience of any person in España, but he had never thought about simple friendship, and was baffled by it.

"That is a beginning. I should warn you that my great-uncle is a proud man and not very forgiving of those who scoff at his skills. Whatever you may think of what he does, respect it, I implore you, Alteza, or he may decide to leave you to your own devices." There was a distinct chance that Isador might do that in any event, but Ciro did not want to disappoint Don Rolon any more than necessary. "He has spent many years pursuing his studies at great risk to himself, and he is at an age when this should be honored."

Don Rolon stopped pacing at last. "Whatever your great-uncle is, and whatever he does, if it is not Diabolic, then I will be forever in his debt, even if he cannot alter the curse in any way. No one, in all my life, has bothered to try to change it, to lift the curse in some way. The priests have all said that it was the Will of God that the curse should touch me, and for that I must humbly accept what God has decreed. They also said that I was more prey to the Devil and his servants because of the curse. If any of them knew what I become at the full of the moon, they would burn me as a heretic and Diabolist without more ado. What more can I say to you?" He had been taught to keep a proper distance from others, and so was not able to do more than put his hand on Ciro's shoulder, but the gesture was as wholehearted as an embrace.

"Tomorrow morning, Alteza, we will learn what may be done." Ciro got up, trying to hide how overwhelmed he was at Don Rolon's appreciation. "You had better rest now. Vigils and fasting are often required for what my great-uncle does."

Don Rolon hitched his shoulders up. "I am in the hands of God. He has led me here, through your kindness, and He will deliver me through your great-uncle, if there is any deliverance in this world."

"I will tell him you said so, Alteza. He is a devout man, too." Ciro went to the door quickly, then added, "Do not be troubled if you hear chanting tonight. Monks are not the only ones who chant."

"All right," Don Rolon said, puzzled for the first time why he should be treated with kindness, when he had never encountered it in strangers before.

Lugantes turned cartwheels the length of the larger throne room, ending up at the foot of the dais where Alonzo sat in state. He bowed deeply to the smattering of applause that greeted him, and immediately produced three apples from a pocket in his parti-colored jerkin, and began to juggle them, all the while moving about and performing a capering little dance. Various of the Court officials watched him with traces of amusement, but more of them were striving to find a way to whisper without being overheard.

"Have you discovered why the Holy Office detained Dominguez y Mara?" one of the lesser ministers asked of another, but Lugantes did not hear the answer. He skipped away, trying to approach Zaretta, who stood with Nobile Rigonzetti and a small group of colorful Venezians toward the far end of the throne room.

"Eh! Jester!" called out Don Enrique. "Show me something new. You're always juggling apples!" He was decked out in his most impressive clothes and had been minding his manners very carefully, but now could not resist teasing the dwarf a bit. "Or are you afraid to juggle something dangerous?"

A few of the hidalgos around him added their encouragement to his challenge, and Lugantes caught all the apples, pausing to tuck them away. "What had you in mind, Señores?"

"Oh, I don't know," Don Enrique said slyly. "There must be something more dangerous than fruit in this place."

"Daggers," suggested one of the young men, for all of them wore dress weapons as part of their most formal Court garments. "And dirks."

"That's an idea!" Don Enrique said, as if it had never occurred to him. "Daggers and dirks. Out of the sheaths, of course."

"Of course," Lugantes agreed, a bit contemptuously, for he thought that there were a great many more dangerous things in the throne room, but did not wish to point them out. "How many? Two? Three?"

"Let us say five," Don Enrique decided with affected casualness. "That should make it more interesting, don't you think?"

"If daggers in the air interest you, I suppose so," said Lugantes. He was actually relieved that Don Enrique had chosen something so commonplace and easily handled as daggers, but he showed a slight hesitation, as if he were not quite confident of his ability, and saw that Don Enrique was smiling. "Who is going to give me his dagger?"

There was a chorus of immediate offers, and Don Enrique took charge of it. "You, Don Tomas, you have that strange dagger from the New World. Do you have it with you tonight?"

"Yes," said the young man smugly. "I always carry it."

"That will do, if you don't mind entrusting it to the jester." Don Enrique gave a malicious grin. "And if you don't mind, Lugantes."

"Any dagger will do." The answer was crisp enough, but Lugantes was now on guard against treachery. It struck him that there was more than the usual sport of the court rakes here, and he watched the men closely without seeming to.

"Of course, I may drop them or get blood on them, but that is the object."

Don Enrique laughed as if Lugantes had said something clever. "And you, Sancho. We'll have your dagger. It is not evenly balanced, is it?"

"No," was the curt answer as the impulsive young man slapped the weapon into Don Enrique's gloved hand.

"And let me see," Don Enrique went on, making a game of his selection. "What of you, Amadis? You have a boot dagger don't you? A long one?"

"The jester may try it," came the prompt response, and the weak-chinned young man bent to remove it from its jeweled sheath.

"That's three. Oliverio has one you may use, Lugantes. And mine makes five. Are you sure that will not be too many?" This time Don Enrique did his best to appear innocent and angelic, which made the impression he gave much worse than it had been.

"You have chosen five, and five it will be," said Lugantes. He held out his small, pudgy hands, thinking back to the many times he had handled throwing knives. The old carnival master who had taught him most of his tricks had told him long since that most men were impressed with fire and knives, and for that reason, if he were adept with them, he would never lack for money or patrons. He recalled all those lessons, as well as the training he had been given with less dangerous appearing instruments that were, in fact, far more hazardous. The first of the three knives were handed to him, hilt first, and he tested the weight of each. So far they were well-balanced and not too diverse in size. The fourth was the New World knife, which Lugantes could tell was a throwing not a stabbing weapon. So much the better. The fifth was Don Enrique's own dagger, and Lugantes was not entirely surprised that the balance was off on the hilt, nor that there was a trace of something on the blade. Doubtless Don Enrique thought he was being clever, Lugantes told himself, but such clumsy attempts would get him nowhere. Lugantes tossed the first two of the knives into the air and caught them expertly. He was aware of the mockery and anticipation in Don Enrique's face, and was suddenly angry that the courtier should try to do him an injury. He started the third and then the fourth knife into the pattern, throwing them so that they turned spectacularly in the air, making the whole appear more impressive. The last was Don Enrique's knife, and Lugantes threw it carefully because of the off-center balance. All around him, the court fell silent as the knife arched, flashed and turned in the air.

Several of the hidalgos were pressing closer, leaning as near as they dared to the dwarf and the knives. Lugantes sensed his danger, and began a more theatrical series of tosses and catches, causing the young men to move back out of range again. Whatever it was that Don Enrique had planned, he would have to do it soon, and Lugantes was glad of it. Quietly he began to sing, one of those taunting, monotonous melodies that had been left behind by the Moors. Lugantes spun it out, varying his throwing of the knives just enough to keep his audience at bay.

The disruption, when it came, came quickly. Don Enrique nudged Don Sancho, murmuring something, and was in turn nudged by his companion. He pretended to be knocked off balance, stumbling forward, not quite close enough to be too near the knives, but enough to force Lugantes to move suddenly to avoid him.

Lugantes stepped nimbly aside, and hardly shifting his stance, he sent all five of the weapons, one after the other, ripping into the hassock that stood, unused, beside the door in the north wall.

Around him, courtiers gasped, and someone leaped in front of Alonzo, although el Rey was nowhere near either the jester or the hassock where the knives were lodged. There were shouts and warnings, and one woman screamed.

Breathing quickly, with a line of sweat on his brow under the drooping locks, Lugantes tumed at once and made a deep and formal bow toward the throne. "Your pardon, Majestad. I had thought it was better that the knives went into the furniture than into flesh."

"Undoubtedly," Alonzo answered without intending to be humorous. But the tension in the throne room had been great enough that most of those gathered let themselves laugh, and several of those watching assured their companions that they were not deceived by the actions. One or two ventured the opinion that the whole episode had been got up in advance by Don Enrique and Lugantes, and within the day this was the accepted theory.

Genevieve waved Lugantes to her side and said loudly how impressed she had been with his skills. "You are ever a source of joy to us all, Lugantes."

"Then any other entertainment you desire will be my delight to perform." He did a few steps of a dance, then bowed to her. "Not frightened, I hope, mi Reina."

The wide smile and gentle laughter did not touch her troubled eyes. "Terrified," she said. She extended her hand to him. "Come to my apartments later, Señor Lugantes, that I may give you a token of esteem. Any man who handles weapons so valiantly should have a token from his lady."

Those around them laughed and Lugantes dutifully joined in, but there was only love in his face, not mirth, when he went on his knee to her. "I am ever your devoted servant, mi Reina; in life and death, in Heaven and Hell."

"The little man is a gallant," whispered one of the grandees standing near Genevieve.

It was becoming difficult for Genevieve to keep up the bantering tone she had been using, but she managed it with an effort. "At least he does not lack for courage. Or would you care to attempt juggling knives?"

"Oh, I cry craven on that," the grandee said at once. He bowed to la Reina and moved away for fear the capricious Frenchwoman might take it into her head to set him a task he would not like.

Genevieve bent down, saying softly to Lugantes. "Are you all right?"

"Considering Don Enrique was trying to kill me, I'm very well." He kissed her hand, hating to have to relinquish it. "Say nothing, mi vida. I will explain it all later." It was torment to move away from her, but he made himself cavort through the gathering, making light of the various remarks addressed to him, until he reached Raimundo, who stood somewhat apart from the rest.

"Keep your distance, little man," Raimundo said quietly. "I'm being watched."

"So are we all," Lugantes declared roundly, and came up to the tall Portuguese. He could see that the Duque was worried and exhausted. "What's the trouble?" he asked openly. "Didn't you like my little display?"

"Most . . . agile," Raimundo answered. "Forgive me. I passed a sleepless night. I kept thinking of a wolf being chased by hunters."

"Hardly the sort of dreams for a courtier," Lugantes said nonchalantly, though he was paying sharp attention.

"Yes. At the end of the evening, I had it in my heart to pity the wolf with such hunters after it." He made an equivocal gesture. "Who knows where such fancies come from. Padre Juan would say it is an uneasy conscience."

"He certainly would," Lugantes responded at once. "But one with his responsibilities would see it that way." He performed part of a jig. "Ladies have loved swine and men have bowed to horses, and for this they go down to Hell: others have adored angels, and for this they sing in Heaven. So praise God and avoid the farmyard." This got a laugh from everyone nearby but Raimundo, who was silent, watching Padre Juan in deep conversation with Gil on the far side of the throne room.

25

"But good Capitan, my hands are tied," Padre Barnabas said with every appearance of innocence. "I would help you if I could, but the matter is entirely out of my hands, and there is nothing I can do that would be acceptable to those officers whose task it is to root out the works of the Devil." He indicated the bench on the other side of the small, whitewashed withdrawing room. "Sit down, do."

Capitan Iturbes ignored the offer, continuing to pace the small chamber with concern. "Can you at least tell me where they have taken Inez, and why?"

"Not at present. I am a Dominican, true enough, and swom to uphold the Holy Office, but much goes on I know nothing of, and there are men who prefer that their work be kept away from public eyes." He gave up trying to accommodate the soldier and sat down himself. "Capitan, I pray you to be patient. All things are in the hands of God, and He will dispose of us according to His Will." Out of habit he crossed himself, though the motion meant little to him now.

"That's all I've been told since I arrived here. Be patient! I tried to speak to that courtier, Don Enrique, and he will not hear me. Don Rolon is missing, and no one will tell me where I may find him. I have few I may turn to, and you are one of them. You are in the Church, and—" He slammed his clenched fist into his open palm. "I have been searching for her."

"But why?" Padre Barnabas asked with a show of interest that was not quite genuine.

"She's my *wife!*"

"It was an arranged marriage, wasn't it?" Padre Barnabas inquired, puzzled at the attitude of the soldier.

"Yes. What marriage isn't? But a man grows fond . . . I liked her when first I saw her. She's a pretty wench, and pleasant to cuddle, if you get my meaning . . . . No, I suppose you don't." He came to a halt near the door, and he looked back at the seated priest. "If she were nothing to me but a whore, I would be concerned for her. A man has obligations, Padre. And not all of them are to God, not if you live in the world." He placed his hands on his hips and waited for Padre Barnabas to say something to him.

The priest folded and unfolded his hands. "You must try to understand, Capitan. Your wife is suspected of sorcery and witchcraft. It may be that she bewitched you as well as others, and if that is the case, then she must be—"

"You're not going to burn her!" Capitan Iturbes shouted.

"Those who worship the Devil—" Padre Barnabas began in his most pious manner, but was interrupted by the Capitan before he had the chance to make his point.

"She doesn't worship the Devil. She's a good woman who goes to Mass and says her prayers, like any Christian. Anyone who tells you otherwise is a liar!" He took two hasty strides toward Padre Barnabas as if he were about to do combat. He recalled himself almost at once, and drew back. "Pardon, Padre. I am so worried for her that I do not always remember—"

"The heat of the moment," Padre Barnabas said with a nod, but showing constraint now. "Do take a seat, Capitan."

This time Capitan Iturbes did as he was instructed, straddling the bench, head lowered. "I am sick with worry for her. I cannot find her, no one will tell me what I must do to free her. It's all been a mistake, and I want to correct it before there is greater . . . damage done. She is to deliver soon, and shocks are not good for women at such times."

"Concern for your fellowman is always commendable, Capitan, but this is not quite the same issue. We have yet to determine if there is any agency other than God and her own female wiles at work here. Until that is known, it would not be safe for her or for you, or for her babe, to release her. There are those who in their devotion to the Devil bring their new infants to the Black Mass and there cut the throats of the babes and drink their blood, which is twice blasphemous. If it is that your . . . wife is one such as these, the child she carries now is in the greatest of danger, and for its good as well as yours, and hers, we must determine where her alliances are." He stood up. "I am not authorized to tell you anything in advance of the decision of the Holy Office, but I will give you my word now that I will notify you as soon as a decision has been reached."

But Capitan Iturbes had not been listening. He sat, shaking his head and staring down at the floor in disbelief. "She would never harm that babe. Not that babe. And she would never offer it up, never. Not that babe. God save and protect her, she is not one of those you seek. She is kind and good, and if she has done anything at all deserving of punishment, it is to do those things all women do if they are not given to God. She is not—" He fell silent. "Save her, Padre Barnabas. You have seen her. You know her. You know she would not do those things."

Padre Barnabas said nothing, but blessed the Capitan and withdrew from the room, going then to the study of Padre Juan Murador who waited for him with as much impatience as he ever permitted himself to show.

"I have spoken to him," Padre Barnabas said when he was sure they were alone and unobserved. "He is adamant about finding the woman."

"That should not surprise you," Padre Juan said. "And the Infante? Did he say anything about him or the child?" It was of minor importance to the Inquisitor that Capitan Iturbes wanted to find his wife, but he was not convinced that the Capitan did not know where Don Rolon was. "Didn't that old woman say that the Infante had taken refuge with his loved ones? The only woman he has ever been loving with, other than his wife, is that Inez woman. She has said that she wanted to gain his favor, but there is more to it than that."

He leaned back in the chair and stared up at the ceiling. "How to discover it?"

"Padre Juan," said Padre Bamabas, "you must allow us more time with the man. He does not trust us, and he is not willing to admit that his wife had dealings with those who worship the Evil One. He still believes that she is a good woman. How he can do that, knowing that the Infante Real kept her as his mistress . . . "

"Unless she was also his mistress at the same time," Padre Juan pointed out.

"The servants said that the only men who called on her other than the jester were courtiers, and she did not accept any of them as lovers." Padre Barnabas hesitated. "We have not been able to learn anything that contradicts that. It may be that there were others, but if there were, she was far more clever and discreet than any of us have thought until now."

"The Devil teaches cunning to his servants," Padre Juan reminded the other Dominican. "We must forever be on our guard against smooth and lying tongues."

"We do learn the truth eventually," Padre Barnabas said with a trace of what he believed was justifiable pride. "When exhortation fails, the Secular Arm is most persuasive."

"They are," Padre Juan agreed at once. "The Devil ensnares so many, and with such skill that there are those who do not realize how far gone they are in perdition until they have been put to the Question. I have seen those who swore with the fervor of angels that they did not profane the Church, or desecrate the altars, or practice Black Arts, or corrupt the innocent. To hear them speak, you would think that those who suspected otherwise were monsters of malice. But once under Question in the second or third degree, then the truth comes out, and their confessions would make a harlot tremble for their degradation and perfidy. How many times have I seen our work justified by these confessions. To wring the truth from a liar and return a soul, purified, to God, that is indeed a task that makes a man humble. What can worldly honors offer to compare to this holy service?" He joined his hands and began to pray.

Padre Barnabas, who had followed some of what Padre Juan had been saying with difficulty, now joined him in prayer. It was good to know that he had done well and pleased the Inquisitor General. He hoped it would erase the blot against him that had been caused by the Infante's disappearance. When Padre Juan was silent, he ventured to speak again. "I will call upon Iturbes in a day or two, and see what I may learn of him. By then there should be something known from Inez, and this will tell us more of what Capitan Iturbes can do for us."

"Very good. I will pray for the success of your questions," said

Padre Juan. "Now I must have time to myself. We have just arrested a most subtle and powerful man, and I will need the help of God to perceive what is truth and what is not. He is a most intelligent and gently spoken man, and for that reason, it is difficult to catch him in deceptions, for his manner is always that of one interested and concerned with the welfare of others. Thus is the work of the Devil prolonged and made manifest. It will require all the guidance of the angels to examine this man."

"I will pray that you will accomplish it, Padre," said Padre Barnabas in soft but dedicated accents. "If I may in any way aid you in this good work, you have only to tell me of it."

Padre Juan motioned for Padre Barnabas to be silent. "No, no, my son. Your zeal is most commendable, but where the Duque da Minho is involved, it will require the most delicate touch. At first. He is of a stalwart soul, and though it is given to evil, still he has shown valor, and for that reason, it will not be an easy matter to learn of him. I anticipate a lengthy Process, unless God gives us a sign that will lift the veil from my eyes and show me how far gone he is in sin and heresy." He cleared his throat and sat a little straighter in his chair. "El Rey is not pleased that we have done this, for Dominguez y Mara ranks high in his esteem. Yet well he knows that evil may lurk near the throne, the more easily to bring down those excellent souls who dedicate their lives to the service of España."

"God has laid a great responsibility upon you, Padre Juan," said the other priest, hoping that one day he would be the man permitted to make these momentous decisions and be the spearhead of God's battle in España, and perhaps the world.

"It is one that I pray I will acquit properly, so that when my soul comes to God, I will be able to show I did not falter at my task." He motioned Padre Barnabas to leave, and almost forgot to bless him as he went, so intent was he on how he would delve into the secrets surrounding Raimundo's life.

"Alteza," Ciro said a week later, "the full moon is not far off, and you have yet to give my great-uncle your answer." They were sitting in the little courtyard of the house in Toledo, and Ciro had at last spoken, breaking into Don Rolon's reverie so abruptly that the Infante Real jumped at the sound of his voice.

"Oh!" He tried to dismiss his alarm. "I was preoccupied. I was thinking of Zaretta. It is strange to miss her, when I have not been with her very long, but . . . " His eyes fell. "It is not right that I should take so long to give your great-uncle my response, but you must see that this is so foreign to everything I have been taught to respect and revere that . . ." He put his hands out in front of him. "The nails . . . . Always I bite them, and I think that nothing more can happen to them, but at the full of the moon, when I come back, they are broken and torn. I think that I must grow claws like a wolf, and use them as a wild creature does." He dropped his hands into his lap again. "And this does not answer you, either."

"No, Alteza." Ciro could see how deeply troubled Don Rolon was, and understood a little of the conflict that was raging within him. "But my great-uncle has said that for the . . . work to be successful, it must be undertaken before the full moon, preferably the day before. There are things that must be prepared if you decide that you wish to go through with it."

"Yes." Don Rolon got up, stretching as if that simple act would alleviate some of the tension that was rising in him. "He told me a little about it, and I know that he is sincere. But there are so many things 1 have been taught that go counter to everything your great-uncle said, and I am . . . afraid."

Ciro could think of nothing to assuage his fear, so he gave what comfort he could. "It is a chance, Alteza. With it, you may be rid of the curse and can ascend the throne without apprehension, at least not from the curse. There are difficulties enough for those who rule without this added burden."

Don Rolon listened to him, and was moved by the devotion of his valet. "And there would not be Padre Juan to contend with, at least not over this. Perhaps later, we will clash over the Flemings, and his desires for more autos-da-fé. That is not the same as changing into a wolf. One can be debated, the other is clearly damnable." He walked the length of the courtyard. "Are there many Jews like this left in España?"

"You mean conversos who secretly keep to the old ways?" Ciro asked, not wishing to discuss his great-uncle unless he had to.

"No, I mean those who practice your great-uncle's skills. But I am curious about the other as well." He frowned, looking down at his hands again. "How did he learn to do this?"

"Well, he explained the Qabbalah to you, and—" Ciro faltered. "The discipline is very great and he is able to do much because of it." This was wholly inadequate and both of them knew it. "I do not have the inclination or the abilities to master the powers my great-uncle has. He has spent most of his life in the pursuit of that special knowledge, and because of that, he is more able to lift the curse from you than anyone living in España today. He would not undertake it if he believed he could not accomplish what he set out to do. Do not forget that. Also, he is anxious to improve the lot of the Jews in España, and you have given him your vow that you will end the persecutions of our faith when you are on the throne."

"I will do that in any case. He need do nothing for me. That you and he have harbored me is more than enough reason to act on your behalf." Don Rolon rubbed his face with quick motions that were as restless as they were useless. "I want to be rid of this. I have wanted it since I was old enough to know what the word curse meant. I want it so much that I am afraid to do anything that . . . ."

"Might rid you of it?" Ciro suggested, perplexed by the Infante's hesitation.

"No; that might hold out the promise and then fail. It would be more distressing than I can tell you, now or ever, to come close and then fail to put this behind me. I have kept myself in check thus far with the belief that no matter what else may happen, the curse was put on my father. If it turns out that your great-uncle cannot lift it, then it must truly be that I, not my father, am cursed, and I will be without hope, in this world or the next." He crossed himself. "It's foolish, isn't it? I have never before been offered such salvation, and yet I hesitate. But you see, if I must be . . . what I am, I had best let Padre Juan have his way, and end my life before I . . . harm anyone. I recall how el Conde looked when we found him at El Morro. He did not die easily, and when he was dead, he was treated so badly that 1 am ashamed to have looked at him. To know that it was I who—

Ciro cut into this. "No, Alteza: no. You did not do that. The curse that works through you made it happen, but it was not you."

"Why cannot I die in battle, or voyaging to the New World, where no one need think of the curse again, and I might be permitted to have some touch of honor in my life?" He sighed a little, forlorn sigh that barely moved his chest, but that carried more anguish than a moan would have. "But battles do not happen when you want them, and if a wolf should raven through troops, it would be bound to be noticed. And a wolf aboard a ship would attract attention. I have thought about all these questions, it seems endlessly. And what do I gain from it, but more despair."

"Let my great-uncle try. If there is no improvement, I will do whatever you ask of me to serve you so that you may be free of this at last." Ciro was confident that Isador Esdras would be able, through his Qabbalistic rituals and incantations, to banish the wolf from within Don Rolon. "España has need of such a ruler as you will be. Can you leave the kingdom to Gil, or Otto, and believe that it will go well for us?"

It was the one endless question that plagued Don Rolon, and he had turned it over in his thoughts many times. If all that he lost was his own life, then it would mean little to him that he was taken or accused of wizardry or heresy, but to see España pass into the hands of his half brother or his cousin, that galled him more than fear of his own affliction. And Zaretta . . . by rights, the man who succeeded him could wed her to ensure the continuing bond of España's treaty with Venezia. His Zaretta in Gil's arms! The thought of it sickened him. Or in Otto's—Otto with his sweaty hands and moist lower lip, touching his bride—it was too horrible. He looked up at Ciro. "Very well. Tell your great-uncle that I will do what he wants, where he wants, any time he wishes me to. If I must fast, I will fast. If I must pray, tell me what words to say, and when. If I must be confined, put me in the chamber you choose, even a dungeon if nothing else will do." He bent his head to rub his temples. "God, let this end soon. I don't know how much longer I can bear it, waiting for the moon to wax, trying to find an excuse to be away from the Court or anyone I might do an injury, then dreading who saw me, and what was seen. If I do not end this, I will be as mad as my grandmother was."

Ciro tried to comfort Don Rolon, but knew that the Infante Real was too much worried to be reassured only by words. "Alteza, you will be delivered, I know you will. In four days, when the ritual begins, you will learn how strong my great-uncle's power is, and from that you will take courage and faith. God hears virtuous men, no matter how they call him or in what guise. He will give you victory."

"I will pray for it," Don Rolon agreed at once, and wondered how he would explain to his father that the curse had departed. It would not be possible to tell him the truth, but there must be some tale, close enough to the truth to be acceptable and to keep him from being accused of heresy in having the curse lifted by a Jew. As he turned that idea over in his mind, he recalled the way Padre Juan demanded obedience of those who professed Christianity. It was still possible that there would be a Process against him, for Padre Juan had desire to test his might against the royal House; but if he were rid of the curse, Don Rolon might come through such an examination unscathed. He knew he was no heretic, and he hoped that little as his father loved him, he would not tolerate his condemnation.

"Alteza, Elena has said to me that she will aid you in any way she can. There is not a great deal she is permitted to do, but as far as ritual permits, she will assist you." Ciro hoped that this would give Don Rolon confidence, for his great-aunt had much impressed the Infante Real.

"I am grateful to her. I am grateful to you all." He tried to dismiss the somberness that had risen between them. "The gratitude of princes is often suspect, but you may believe me when I say that I will never forget my obligation to you and your family."

"I believe you, Alteza," Ciro said, and then, very simply, bowed to Don Rolon. "I have served you too long to be deceived by you."

Don Rolon looked away from him. "I hope that it will not be to your sorrow, my friend."

26

Though to speak was agony, Raimundo brought his head up and said, "As God is my witness, I am no heretic." Padre Juan 'shook his head sadly. "Thus you see, my Brothers in Christ, how the Devil instills the most stubborn lies in the hearts of his followers."

"I am no Diabolist, either." Raimundo knew that his protests were in vain, and that his fate had been sealed when he entered the castle where the Inquisition ruled absolutely.

"You persist in this insanity," Padre Juan said in his most solicitous way. "Duque, I had thought better of you. For so many years you have done your master's bidding, and thought that you were unassailable in your mighty position. Now you learn that God is not mocked, but you will not bow to the inevitable. This disappoints me, for I have assumed that though you are damned, you are a sensible man and one who would spare himself unnecessary suffering." He nodded to the officers of the Secular Arm. "Another two teeth removed, I think, and then the thumbscrews."

"You vermin! You unholy . . . " His shouts were muffled and then disintegrated into screams as the officers set about wrenching out his teeth.

"Now, then," Padre Juan said, smoothing the sleeve of his black habit as if to rid it from dirt, "be honest with me. You have five more teeth to lose, Dominguez, and if you do not respond, I will find ways to get the confession out of you." He motioned to the officers, and they held out the thumb-screws. "These will be next. It would be a pity to be forced to use them."

Raimundo's head was aflame with hurt, and he could not hear because of the rush and roaring of the pain. He tried to protest, but his vision grew cloudy and when he forced himself to speak, one feeble "No . . . " escaped him before he fainted.

"Bring him around with vinegar, and question him again," Padre Juan said to one of his colleagues who stood behind him. "I want a confession. I don't want to have to burn him on suppositions; he must condemn himself."

"As you say, Padre," the other priest agreed. "Where will you be?"

"We are burying the woman Inez this morning. I must make sure that we are not observed. We have still not learned all that we might from her husband." He started toward the door. "There is the matter of the infant, and that can be given to Capitan Iturbes for his care, if he wants it."

"But it was so early," the other priest said.

"Yes, and few babes live long, emerging into the world before their time. But we are not monsters here, and we must protect those who are innocent. God demands that the infant be baptized, and we have done so. We have found a wet nurse for it, but even she says that he does not suck as he should. If he lives, it is the Will of God. If he does not, then we will pray for his soul."

As soon as Padre Juan was gone, the second priest gave his attention to Raimundo again. "I have been told that he was a handsome man. Well, such things are vanity and detract from the betterment of the soul."

One of the officers held up a sponge. "Shall I bring him around?"

"Yes. We must finish this business by sunset, for we are not allowed to torture him more than once." He shook his head. "He is a great traitor, corrupting both the Church and the Crown."

The officer unceremoniously flung the vinegar-soaked sponge into Raimundo's face and picked it up as the Duque shrieked in anguish.

"We must resume, Duque," the Dominican said firmly. "There are certain matters which have not been explained yet, and—"

"No!" Raimundo made no attempt to soften his refusal. "No more."

"We will cease as soon as you have confessed," the priest said, eager to have so great an evildoer put his soul into so young a priest's hands.

"No!" The word came out of the depth of him. Raimundo leaned forward, retching, though there was nothing more his body could give up but blood. "No more."

"I will bring a clerk, and—" the priest began, and was aghast when Raimundo's eyes met his, alive with fury that transcended his suffering.

"No. Do what you will. I won't speak again." He wished now that he had had the courage to bite his own tongue off earlier, before they had pulled out his teeth. He saw the officer bring the thumb-screws and steeled himself against what was to come. Fleetingly he thought that he had always taken pride in his long, well-shaped hands, and chided himself for folly. He felt the metal fitted into place, and then agony ran up his arm like lava. He strained upward once against the bonds that held him, then dropped into un-consciousness for what little respite it would give him.

"We are most alarmed to learn of how great a sin Dominguez y Mara has committed," Alonzo told Padre Juan the next day when the Inquisitor General brought word that Raimundo had shown himself to be a heretic and Diabolist sworn to corrupt the royal House and bring down the Spanish Hapsburgs for the benefit of Portugal.

"It is ever so, Majestad," Padre Juan told him, then looked over at where Lugantes lounged against the wall. "It would be best if we were alone."

"We are alone," Alonzo declared, then saw where it was that the priest glanced. "Oh. We never dismiss Lugantes. Jesters are—"

"There is no one at Court who should know of this," Padre Juan told el Rey, and waited while Alonzo made a sign of dismissal. "When we require you again, we will summon you."

Lugantes bowed deeply and left the small reception room. In this instance he was glad to get away. What he had overheard distressed him profoundly, and he was afraid that a word or a change of expression would betray him if he had to listen to more of Padre Juan's venom.

"It's the little bravo," said a slurred voice from one of the withdrawing rooms. "Still crowing over your trick with the knives, are you?"

Lugantes did an excellent imitation of a cock at sunrise, and sauntered on past the room where Don Enrique sat drinking with Gil. Another time he would have been tempted to stay and banter with the dissolute young courtier, but his shock was too great to allow him to think as sharply as such a contest required. He heard a cry of disappointment as he went on, and decided that when he had the opportunity, he would exact his own sort of vengeance from Don Enrique. Inevitably his steps led him to la Reina's apartments, and he slipped into her private withdrawing room through the servants' corridor, taking care that no one should observe him. This was the one place in all of the palace where Genevieve was not required to have another lady in attendance, and the one place where Lugantes knew they would be undisturbed. He found a footstool and sat down upon it, dejection making his shoulders slump.

He had somewhat recovered by the time Genevieve returned to her apartments, and was able to greet her with more warmth that he had thought he would show at first. He took her hand and kissed it ardently, treasuring it the more for the precariousness of their joy. As she bent down toward him, he reached up, and holding her face in his small, chubby hands, he kissed her mouth, hardly moving while they remained close together so that nothing would distract him from the wonder of her.

"You are a marvel, Lugantes," she whispered as she broke away from him. "And you run great risk coming here as you do."

He blinked, hoping that she was not intending to dismiss him. "Have I offended you, querida?"

"No. Never that. It's just that everything is growing . . . worse. For the love of God, tell me something interesting." She sat down on one of the chairs and smoothed the side of her skirt in invitation.

He came and sank down beside her. "The Duque da Minho is to be burned," he said, unable to soften the blow.

"Raimundo? That absur—" Her first, light words failed her. "To bum?"

"Padre Juan has determined that he is a heretic and Diabolist." Lugantes' head lowered with his voice. "It will be soon, I fear. You will have to prepare. If I know El Majestad, you will have to be there."

"With Raimundo at the . . . stake?" She started to rise, then dropped back as if robbed of all her strength. "Raimundo?"

"I have just learned of it, mi vida." He took her hand again and held it against his cheek. "Padre Juan is out hunting."

"But of all men—" Genevieve began to weep. "He was the only one but you who cared for me. While he was my lover, I was safe. He isn't a heretic, Lugantes. It's so foolish . . . " She swallowed hard, then let the deep sobs come.

Lugantes stood beside her, stroking her rigidly confined hair and whispering to her, calling her "Mi vida," or "mi amor." He did not suggest that Raimundo might be saved, because they both knew it was no longer possible. "He is a good man, Dominguez. He did more than anyone for—"

"How can Alonzo let it happen?" she demanded of Lugantes, her face no longer pretty, but blotched red and white. "What is he thinking of? If Padre Juan can seize Dominguez, then he will next come after the royal House. It's what he's wanted to do for years, and now he will." She crossed herself. "And that—"

Gently Lugantes wiped her tears away with his linen cuff ruffles, and when she wept again, he kept at his task. "It isn't safe for you, querida. As you say, if Padre Juan is after the Portuguese Ambassador, then he will next look higher."

"He wants to be master of España, and the ruler of the royal House, so that España is his in everything but title." Her hands became fists and there was a touch of anger wakened in her. "He can't do it."

"He will try," Lugantes said with great certainty. "It is not safe here, and that is why we must talk."

She shook her head, not paying too much attention to him. "I want to see that proud man—he is no more priest than Gil is—brought down, and all his power with him. I want to see it, Lugantes, my little love, my sweet manlet. Tell me he will fall."

"I will tell you, if it pleases you," he responded carefully. "I will tell you that I will bring the moon down as a jewel for you and deck you with stars, for it is what I would want to do, if I had all the power of the angels to give you. There would be oceans of diamonds and kingdoms of gold that I would heap up before you, and it would not touch the smallest part of your worth to me. But that is the love I have for you speaking, not my good sense. You are Reina and I am a dwarf jester, and that is the truth of the matter. By the same token, I will say that it is impossible that Padre Juan should keep his power until the . . . next full moon, but that is not my mind you hear; but my heart. Listen to me, querida. You must listen to me." He brought her clenched hand to his lips and kissed it open. "You know that I would rather have the flesh torn from my bones than be separated from you, don't you, vida mia?"

Her smile was uncertain, but she let her fingers stray gently over his features. "Yes, little man. I know that is how you love me."

Lugantes wished he could permit himself to be distracted by her kindness, so that he could spend time in her arms, but the dangers were too close, and he knew he might regret a few moments of dalliance for the rest of his life if it meant that Genevieve came to harm. "Then think what it costs me to tell you that you must leave España."

The motion of her hand stopped abruptly and she frowned as she looked at him. "What? Are you proposing that we fly together?"

"I said nothing about myself," Lugantes murmured. "I cannot go, not yet, not while there are so many . . . things that are undecided."

Now she was worried. "Is it because of Raimundo that you say that?"

"And other things."

"Don Rolon." She shook her head. "He was killed, Lugantes. No one wants to admit it, but someone arranged to kill him and take the body away."

"No," he answered, with such conviction that she stared at him again.

"No? Do you know where he is?" She was amazed that Lugantes should speak this way, and more astounded when she thought how it was he was sure of himself.

"I know that he is not dead, and it is not wise for me to tell you more. Or even this much. You must say nothing to anyone. Not to anyone. If Zaretta should speak to you and—"

Genevieve shrugged. "That one keeps to herself and those few Venezian courtiers who wait upon her. She has no use for me."

Lugantes did not want to bring up the matter of their rivalry again, so he pressed one finger to her mouth. "Hear me out, querida. Please. She misses her husband, and she is alone in a kingdom where she is treated with courtesy, yes, but also suspicion and condemnation. She is frightened. I have seen her, and I know that this is true. Do not doubt me, mi amor, I beg of you."

"Very well." Genevieve tried to sit up more straightly in her chair. "What is it you want me to do for her?"

"Not for her, for both of you. You must leave, or Padre Juan may make a first sally on the royal House by coming after one or the other of you." He had feared this for some little time, but now that Raimundo was to be burned, he was convinced that one of the royal women would be next, in preparation for casting out Don Rolon entirely.

"He would not dare. Alonzo would never permit it." Color mounted in her cheeks and her chin came up.

"Would you have thought that Alonzo would permit them to take Raimundo Dominguez y Mara?" Lugantes asked, and waited while Genevieve lost her defiant attitude. "He is devoted to the Church and to Gil, and that makes a fool of him, for he will do anything that Padre Juan suggests so long as it gains the Succession for Gil. You know that as well as

"It is madness," she said softly. "To sacrifice everything for that young man." She pressed her fists together in her lap. "Oh, Lugantes, my little love, what will I do?"

"Let me guide you," he said at once, sensing for the first time that he had an opportunity to convince her that his plan was wise.

"Very well. Yes, I will listen to you. But please, don't say any more dreadful things to me. I don't think I can endure more than I have already." She leaned in her chair so that her head rested against his chest.

He could not begin at once; it was too much like parting from her, and he wanted to postpone that moment as long as possible. Finally he spoke. "Zaretta will want to return to Venezia until the question of what has happened to Don Rolon has been settled. It is in keeping with the terms of the treaty, and Alonzo cannot refuse her without causing very serious repercussions. It is not appropriate that she go unescorted, as well you know. And so you will be her escort, la Reina and the wife of the Infante Real, together shall . . . leave for Venezia. No, don't tell me anything, querida, not yet. Let me finish, or I might not be able to do so."

"As you wish," she murmured, wrapping her arms around his waist.

"Ah, it is the delight of my heart that you cling to me, mi vida. Hold me, I pray you, so that I will always remember how your arms feel."

"Don't, Lugantes."

He forced himself to continue. "Once you are in Venezia, it will not be difficult for you to go to France. It has been very long since you went to visit your brother, and doubtless he will want to speak to you, because of all that has transpired here. Stay with him as long as you can, querida. If it is possible, do not return here while you live, for I am afraid that it will be dire for you if you do. It may be that in time I will be able to come to you, if you will have me." He asked this last most hesitantly, since Genevieve was often more interested in variety in her lovers than in constancy.

"Yes! Do come to me, Lugantes. It would be my joy to have you with me, if in truth I must go." She looked up at him. "Are you certain that there is so much danger?"

"Yes." He met her eyes evenly. "I could not part from you if there were not so much danger."

At last she believed him, and the gravity of her situation became real to her. She nodded slowly. "All right. But Zaretta is no fonder of me than I am of her. How is she going to take to having me travel with her?"

Lugantes made a crooked attempt at a smile. "You must leave that to me, querida. I will let you know when it has been arranged."

"Will you be the one who arranges it?" She was a bit surprised that he would have so confident an attitude, and it struck her as strange that he of all people might know how to accomplish the negotiations, for surely she thought there would be negotiations. "Alonzo will want to be part of it."

"No, querida, because I will not mention it to him, not now and not when the Venezian Ambassador approaches him to present the problem. I will be as invisible as I always am, and for that you should thank God." He leaned over and kissed her forehead. "May I visit you tonight?"

"Oh, yes. Do come to me. With so much going on, I want time and—" Her mind was still in some confusion, so she made no attempt to say anything more. "I will be ready for you shortly before midnight."

"Gracias, mi amor," he said. "If I am a little late, do not fret. There are a few matters I must attend to." With one last kiss, he moved away from her. "You are the light of my life, Genevieve, and it will tear my heart to see you go. Do not forget that."

"I won't," she promised, and started to get up when there was a rap on the door. She gave a quick, frightened glance at Lugantes, then said in a shaky voice, "Who's there?"

"Gil del Rey," was the answer as the door opened. His smile was one that was sure of welcome and he looked only mildly surprised to see Lugantes. "The jester?"

"Naturalmente," Lugantes said at once. "La Reina told me she was bored, and I have been doing what I might to change that. At least I have been able to make her laugh."

"Which is nothing more than your job," Gil said without interest. He paid little attention to Lugantes, thinking that the dwarf was amusing for a fool, but hardly worth more than a passing glance. "And now that I am here, I will see to it that la Reina is entertained. Do not let me keep you."

Lugantes longed to give a sharp retort, but only bowed. He could tell from the way Genevieve looked at the handsome young man that she was determined to have him in her bed to punish Alonzo for all his years of neglect. It pained him deeply but he could not rebuke her, then or ever; she was the lady of his heart and nothing she could do or say would change his love.

"Lugantes," Genevieve called after him as he went to the servants' door, "I am very grateful."

"As Gil says, it is my job." He bowed and hurried away.

❦

Alonzo sat more stiffly in his throne and sighed. "I cannot agree with you about these rumors, Padre Juan, but I know that your concern comes out of your piety and zeal. Very well."

"Does that mean that you will send out the soldiers?" Padre Juan demanded, leaning forward across the huge writing table. "I am certain that there is nothing else that will discover where the Infante Real has been taken."

"And you are still convinced that he is alive?" Alonzo asked distastefully. "It may be that his curse has brought this end upon him."

"If that is the case, then the sooner it is discovered, the better. Already the Superior of the Ambrosians has written to me to declare that he is convinced that Don Rolon is under the special protection of Heaven for his battle with those ungodly forces that were said to have set upon him. It may be that those forces have found him again and are determined to do him injury, perhaps to his immortal soul as well as his body. It is the soul that concerns me, as I have told you many times before now, Majestad." He saw that Alonzo was wavering, and decided to press harder, "We have learned that his friend Dominguez y Mara has allied himself with the forces of the Devil, and you have seen the evidence we have presented. If so great a man as the Duque da Minho may be corrupted, a vulnerable youth like Don Rolon is even more subject to those depredations. For the protection of España you must release those soldiers to search for him. I will send the mounted familiars of the Holy Office to assist them."

Alonzo nodded twice, very slowly and ponderously. "I must have time to consider, good Padre. Tomorrow when we have our open Court, you may approach us again for our decision."

Long experience told Padre Juan that he would be given the things he asked for, since Alonzo had once again slipped into the royal "we." He stood up and gave el Rey his blessing. "May God guide your reflections, Majestad, and bring you to a wise answer."

"Amen to that, good Padre." Alonzo crossed himself, then added with much difficulty, "We have long hoped that in time the curse would pass from our son and heir, but it has not seemed to happen.

For that reason, we are once again petitioning the Pope and our Imperial brother for permission to alter the Succession to our beloved son Gil, and thereby grant him legitimacy. We pray that this will not offend you, for we know that the Holy Office and the throne must be of one mind on all matters for the good of the kingdom."

"Precisely so, Majestad," said Padre Juan, unaware that he was gloating. "It would not be contrary to the interest of the Holy Office to support the claim of Gil del Rey. If such assurance is needed, you may be secure; you have it."

"We are much relieved to hear of it, good Padre." Alonzo motioned toward the side door. "There are other petitioners waiting for an audience, and we suggest that you leave this way, in order to prevent intrusions that would only distress you."

Since Padre Juan already knew that Capitan Iturbes had obtained a brief right to an audience, he was sure that this was the man Alonzo was suggesting he avoid. For once he was in agreement with Alonzo's overcautious attitude, and inclined his head. "I am humbled that Su Majestad should concern yourself on my behalf." He went quickly to the door and let himself out, guardedly pleased with his success.

27

There were diagrams on the floor and a number of ritual containers set about the diagrams in a pattern that bewildered Don Rolon as he stood, naked and shivering, at the point Isador Esdras had indicated. He was light-headed from fasting and the doubts he had been able to banish for some time now returned afresh. He longed to go through the ceremony, but he could not conceal his Worry that for all the old man's efforts and skill, nothing would come of it. He started to cross himself, then, suddenly self-conscious, stopped the movement of his hand.

"Oh, you may bless yourself if you wish, Don Rolon," Isador growled at him from a dark corner of the room. "God is God and those who entreat Him will be heard." He took a brass container of salt and began to chant over it in long, singsong phrases that sounded unduly harsh to Don Rolon's ear. When he had finished, he looked at Don Rolon. "As we practiced it earlier, my son. Take your place within the Tree of Life, at the juncture I pointed out to you this afternoon."

It was only a matter of a few steps, and ordinarily Don Rolon would have thought nothing of such a request, but he knew that once he entered the pattern, he would have to remain there until Isador had completed his spells and prayers, and for that reason, he went hesitantly, as if covering great distances. He was struck by the odor of incense, and almost coughed.

"No, Don Rolon. Be calm in body and mind. Lie as I showed you earlier and extend your hands. I will place the candles in them just as I did this afternoon, and you will find that nothing has changed." Isador recited another series of prayers and adjusted the drape of his shawl around his shoulders. He then waited while Don Rolon followed his instructions, watching critically so that the Infante Real would not be incorrect in his part of the ritual. When he was satisfied, he began the prayers over the candles, taking great care as he placed first one and then the other in Don Rolon's outstretched hands. "There. Now you must be still. I will trace certain designs upon your chest, and you may find that you become dizzy. That is all as it should be, and you are not to be concerned when it occurs. Trust in the strength of God and you will persevere as you must."

"I will," Don Rolon said a bit uncertainly.

Isador shook his head once at this most unhappy prince, then began his long and arduous task, calling forth the various spirits and archangels for their help. He worked efficiently, wasting no movement, his concentration so fierce that whenever Don Rolon caught a glimpse of the old man's sunken, dark eyes, he thought he looked into banked fires.

There was at first the discomfort of lying on his back on a bare floor to distract Don Rolon, and then the drops of scented oil that Isador put on his chest and face. He could not tell for sure if the oil were hot or cold, but something in it felt like burning, and Don Rolon had to resist the urge to wipe it off, or move so that it would spread. The smell of it, too, was pungent and not quite pleasant, and where it mingled with the incense, it created almost a thickness in the air.

"Pray do not move your feet, Don Rolon," Isador said sharply. "You must remain still. And do not blink when I move this light over your face."

Don Rolon knew it was not wise to speak, so he showed he had heard and understood these orders by obeying them. It had alarmed him to think that he had been able to move without being aware of it, and now he put his mind to keeping all his body as still as he could and still breathe. He heard the sound of Isador's feet as he moved to the various cardinal points of the compass to invoke the protective beings that guarded them. His nose began to itch, and he wanted to scratch it, or sneeze. Resisting both those urges took all his attention until the worst of the sensations had passed, and by then, Isador was standing at the foot of the Tree of Life, intoning a long prayer.

"You will feel strange for a bit, Don Rolon," Isador informed him. "Do not try to stop it in any way. It is right and proper that you feel so, and any movement or change of position would be very detrimental to you and to me. Do you understand me? Do not answer, but move your eyes downward."

Very carefully Don Rolon did as Isador instructed him, thinking that there must be something happening, though he did not know what. His skin tingled, but it might have been from cold as much as anything else. His eyes, too, ached suddenly and he had to resist a desire to gnash his teeth and kick his legs. It was difficult to hold the candles now, as if his hands were no longer capable of grasping the tall wax columns. He did not want to examine too closely why this was so.

"Be still, Don Rolon, be still," Isador reminded him, and stepped inside the pattern of the Tree of Life. "I charge you to remain as you are, and to give up the wolf that possesses you. Let the curse fall upon those who are cursed, not those who are innocent. Take the shape of the man you are, and do not again succumb to the other. It is not you, Don Rolon, but the beast, and it will be cast out." The sound of his voice was huge in the dark little room, and Don Rolon was awed by it more than he had ever been by the sound of the choir singing in the vast and drafty Catedrál.

There was a sensation that was not quite an itch, and it started at the back of his neck where his hair bristled suddenly. Then there was a shiver that went through him and in spite of his best efforts, the candles wavered.

"Do not do that!" Isador commanded him.

Don Rolon almost protested aloud that he had not intended to cause the candles to move, but he recalled in time that he was not to speak. He did his best to tighten the hold of his uncooperative fingers and saw the flickering of the flame as the candles shook. He grew taut, his shoulder and buttocks becoming rigid against the floor, and to his deep chagrin he felt his manhood rise. He wanted to apologize for this great profanation, but Isador paid no attention, concentrating entirely on the words of his invocations and hardly looking at the Infante Real at all. Don Rolon tried to relax, but his muscles continued to tighten, almost thrumming with the pressures they created.

"It is coming; let it come," Isador said in a distracted way.

"Nothing will harm you while you are there. Nothing in Heaven or Hell or you will reach you where you are, Don Rolon."

At that instant, Don Rolon's jaw twitched and his teeth clattered and snapped together. His hands were even more difficult to control and when his face began ti he could not stop from moaning—but the sound he heard was a low, rumbling growl.

"Do not move!" Isador shouted, his eyes directedly on Don Rolon's. "I have said that nothing can harm you, and that includes this wolf. Do not move, or you will undo much of what we have accomplished. Think of what you may lose, if you do this."

Unbidden, the image of Zaretta formed in his mind, showing her in all her beauty and radiance. He longed to reach out to her, but fear of what he was held him fixed to his place, with his distorted features set in total dejection. His heart leaped in his chest as if it struggled to escape a prison, and when he breathed, the air tore through him, a tempest in its fury. His legs tried to move, but this time he was able to hold them steady, and he felt a twitching at the base of his spine such as an animal with a tail might have.

"You are mastering it, my son," Isador said stemly. "Do not relent now, or you will suffer for it." He retumed to his recitations as if the sight of Don Rolon, half-transformed, did not affect him in any way, and in fact, he knew that it was necessary that he not reveal how the sight of this half-lupine young man distressed him. Whoever had cursed him had been more than a discontented old woman. The nature of the curse was not one that was familiar to Isador, and for that reason, he was convinced that the woman had not been the student of any of the magical arts, but rather someone so driven by hatred that she had been able to thrust all of it upon Alonzo's son. These were the most difficult of all curses to lift, for they were not gound by conventions, or structured by rules and rituals. He gave a worried shake to his head and continued his work. As he reached that part of his ceremony where he charged the essence of the curse to come forth and let its grievance be known or forever be disbelieved and forgotten, banished out of the minds of men, Don Rolon gave a sudden leap upward, his arms and legs flailing uncontrollably while he howled and howled. Then, just as abruptly, he collapsed in a huddled faint in the darkness.

Frowning deeply, Isador bent to pick up the candles and set them in place again, and hastily recited the invocations to the guardians to give their protection. Next, he knelt beside Don Rolon and studied his features. His face was largely human, but there was a subtle change, hardly noticeable to one not looking for it. Isador could see that something of the wolf had left its mark now.

With a whimper Don Rolon returned to consciousness. He stared up into the darkness and could hardly keep from crying out in protest.

"No, my son. It is all right with you." Isador put his hand on the Infante Real's shoulder, giving him every sign of reassurance he could think of. "I wish you will lie quite still while I relight the candles. Then we will have to talk."

Don Rolon nodded, thinking that he had surely failed as much as it was possible to fail. "Am I . . ."

"A wolf? You could not speak if you were, and I should not be talking to you, but looking for a cudgel to keep you at bay." He had intended to make light of the trouble, but saw that Don Rolon could not share his attitude. "My son, what you have endured few men could bear without death or madness, and that speaks well for your honor and courage. Do not think that we have failed."

Don Rolon's haggard face came alive with hope. "Then it is over?"

Isador hated to dash his enthusiasm, but could not lie to the young man. "Let us say that it is well begun. You will probably change tomorrow night, but after that we may continue to pursue your trouble, and by the time a month has passed, you will not be in the grips of this dreadful trouble." He had taken flint and steel as he spoke and lit the candles again. Their light was welcome to both men, and seemed to dispel far more than the darkness that surrounded them.

"Indeed?" His voice was distant, polite without any real strength. "And if there is no improvement, what then?"

"We will find another way," Isador said. "You have forgotten that I have made a vow to bring your a ii iction to an end, and I will honor my vow, for that is the way of those of us who devote our lives to the Qabbalah and its disciplines. We, in our way, are not much different than those who devote themselves to the Church or the life of the court. Each has his own dedications, and all of us know that there are demands we accept."

Don Rolon had got to his knees, and he remained there for a bit, breathing hard and showing the glisten of sweat on his skin. "I feel I have run for miles up mountains of stone."

"That is not surprising," Isador said, trying to soothe the Infante Real. "You will have some of the same sense for a day or so, and it should not alarm you unless you find that you are becoming more fatigued instead of less." He held out his hand to help Don Rolon to his feet. "We will make greater preparations this time, so that you have more strength to withstand the force of the wolf."

"Is it possible?" He doubted now that Isador, no matter how gifted he was, would be able to do more than offer him a little solace and the benefits of his kindness. The curse was too deeply sunk into him, too much in control of his body and his life.

"It is," Isador said emphatically. "You doubt it now, but you will see. There is time enough for you to prepare and practice for the next attempt. It will not be as frightening next time, and that in itself will help you."

"I will pray for that, Isador. And I will thank God for your kindness and skill. It is the most I can do for the moment, but—"

"But it is more than enough," Isador told him as he handed him a loose cotton robe. "Now you must bathe, and then Elena will prepare a meal for you. After that we will discuss how best to proceed. Do not argue with me, young man. There will be ample time for that later." He pointed in the direction of the door. "There is fresh warm water waiting. Go on."

"All right," Don Rolon said, abandoning his protests. He went toward the two tiled chambers that housed Isador's baths, and did not look back to see if the old Jew frowned or smiled, for fear that he would once again lose heart if he did.

Nobile Rigonzetti was startled to hear a knock on his library door so late at night, and he hesitated before calling out, "Who is there?"

"Lugantes," said the jester. "Let me in at once before I am observed."

❦

Nobile complied immediately, curious and apprehensive. He had wanted to speak to the jester, but had not thought it wise to approach him. With so much turmoil in the Spanish Court, he doubted that Lugantes' visit would ease his mind.

"Good. No one saw me," Lugantes said as he slipped through the door and closed it quickly. "I have been trying to reach you for three days, but there are more familiars prowling through the court than there are fleas on, a stray dog."

"Then it is urgent?" Nobile asked, the apprehension becoming paramount in his mind.

"Fairly, yes." He looked around the room. "Very pleasant, Ambassador. You must enjoy your books."

Nobile was not of a mind to be distracted. "They are well enough. It is not books that bring you here."

"No, not your books," Lugantes agreed, moving one of the chairs so that its back was toward the door. He got into it and made a quick motion for Nobile to sit down again. "I think it is necessary for us to have a little candid talk, Ambassador. You may not entirely concur, but hear me out in any case. You know that I would not attempt to contact you trivially."

"Yes," Nobile said, sitting down again and making the precaution of lifting up the book he had been reading. "This may be useful."

"Good," Lugantes said at once. He had been trying to think of a way to explain to the Ambassador all those things he thought the man should know, and could find no simple and direct way. "You are aware, as we all are, that the Infante Real is missing."

"Of course," Nobile said with asperity. "It is a cause of much distress to his new wife."

"They say that he was kidnapped or killed, don't they?" Lugantes went on, his face intent.

"You have doubtless heard as many rumors as I have."

"Oh, many more, I am certain." He folded his hands. "I am going to tell you the truth on the condition that you give me your holiest vow never to repeat any of it to anyone. That includes your confessor."

"What?" Nobile said, alarmed at how stern the jester had become.

"You heard me. Give me your vow and I will continue. If you do not, I will ask your pardon for disturbing you and will find another way to do what I must do." He watched Nobile closely, knowing that the man was shaken.

"Very well: on the soul of my mother and the Virgin, I swear I will never repeat any of what you have told me." He did not quite know why he was willing to do as Lugantes asked, but he had long ago learned to trust his intuitions, and now he sensed that the jester was completely serious and reliable. "Is that enough, or do you want my word in writing?"

"No!" Lugantes said, distressed at the suggestion. "If the Holy Office should come upon it, neither of us would be safe for an instant. We are not much safer right now." He paused, wishing this were easier. "Padre Juan has decided to cooperate with el Rey and support Alonzo's petition that Gil be legitimized. That would make it possible for him to succeed his father, which currently is not possible. There is, unfortunately, the Infante Real to consider, but Padre Juan has agreed to begin a Process against him as soon as he is found. There are reservations, it would appear, in having the heir to the throne be under a curse. It is the intention of Padre Juan to show that the curse is heretical, and for that reason, Don Rolon would no longer be entitled to succeed Alonzo. You perceive how neatly it all comes together when it is laid out thus. Since the Infante Real is missing—said to be the victim of Diabolists or agents of the Holy Roman Emperor—it is not yet possible to Question him, but it is only a matter of time."

"And it may be that the Infante Real is already dead. I have heard that notion put forth," Nobile said. He had taken great care to mention none of these rumors to Zaretta.

"Don Rolon is alive," Lugantes said quietly, meeting Nobile's eyes with his own.

"But—"

"He is alive." He took a deep breath. "If it is possible, he will soon leave España for Rome where he will seek audience with the Pope. That is the only way he can escape detention by Padre Juan, and you know as well as I that when Padre Juan has determined that one is a heretic, sooner or later, the heretic will confess precisely what the Inquisitor General requires him to confess."

Nobile was badly shaken. "Surely he would not treat the heir to the throne. . It is unthinkable."

"But Don Rolon is under a curse, and Padre Juan had decided that Gil should be heir. He would have no reservations about Questioning Don Rolon."

"Dio mio," Nobile whispered, horrified. "That is monstrous."

"I won't dispute that." Lugantes watched the Venezian Ambassador closely. "You are aware that Padre Juan has already condemned the Duque da Minho to the stake. If he can so dispose of Dominguez y Mara, he would not hesitate to do the same to Don Rolon, particularly since he would then have a direct link to the throne. You do not think he intends to permit Gil any independence, do you?"

Nobile shook his head very slowly, not quite sure he was awake. Perhaps, he thought, I have fallen asleep and this is my dream. How else would I come to hear such dreadful things, if not in a nightmare? "He is a priest."

"He is also a man," Lugantes said. "He is a very ambitious man. He tells himself that it is his zeal and righteousness that make him so concerned for the throne, but I have watched him for years, and I know ambition when I see it."

"But to do what you are implying is—"

Lugantes shrugged. "Are there no priests in Venezia who deceive themselves? Are none of them vain or greedy or proud?"

Nobile bowed his head. "All right. I will hear you out." He could not imagine how Lugantes came to know so much, but he believed the jester.

"Good. For I need your aid." He stared down at his hands. "I do not know what Zaretta has told you about her husband, but I know that he is devoted to her far beyond what was expected of him."

"She has said something of this," Nobile said cautiously. He had seen her weep for Don Rolon, chiding herself for being unkind to him, and praying to all the Saints in the calendar to protect him and bring him safely back to her.

"As long as she abides here, she is in danger, both from Padre Juan, who will not hesitate to use her against Don Rolon, and from Gil, who has already secured Alonzo's permission to wed her once he is recognized Infante Real. While she is here, Don Rolon will not want to present his defense to the Pope for fear of reprisal being visited on his wife." There was a long silence between the two men, Lugantes studying Nobile while he weighed up in his mind what the jester was telling him.

"It seems impossible to me that Alonzo would consent to anything so unnatural," Nobile protested at last.

"But the treaty allows for it. It is regarded as expedient, Ambassador, not unnatural." He had overheard the discussion between Gil and Alonzo the day before and now was convinced that he had less than two weeks to get Zaretta out of the kingdom.

"What does Padre Juan say of this?" Nobile asked weakly.

"He has approved it, of course. He is willing to grant a number of treats to Gil so that he will later have many obligations of gratitude he may call upon at his convenience." If it were ever learned that he was the one who acted to thwart Gil in his plan, Lugantes knew he would suffer for it.

"Ah." Nobile cleared his throat.

"I would like to propose a strategy to you: while the fate of her husband is so uncertain, Zaretta will wish to return to Venezia, to be among her family for their comfort. She will request the escort of Reina Genevieve for her journey." He held up his hands. "Yes, I know that the women dislike each other, but it may be—"

"Genevieve has never left España; not since she married Alonzo," Nobile reminded Lugantes.

"She will leave." Lugantes felt the deep sorrow of separation already.

"Is it ... necessary?" Nobile asked. "Could not I simply take her on my own authority? Must it be Genevieve who accompanies her?"

Lugantes shook his head with vehemence. "Genevieve. Zaretta is not the only one in danger from Alonzo and Padre Juan. La Reina as well as Zaretta may be . . . put upon if she remains."

Nobile considered this. "You are quite certain that the Infante Real is alive?"

"Yes."

"And you swear that he is truly in danger?"

"As I pray for salvation and the forgiveness of sin."

There was a silence between them. Then Nobile made up his mind. "I will do what I can, jester, but it will take some little time, I fear. If that will content you, then you may rest assured that—"

"Do not take too long, Ambassador. For the sake of Zaretta as well as Don Rolon." He got out of the chair. "Remember, you must tell no one that I've been here. There are lives at stake."

Privately, Nobile thought that Lugantes was overestimating the hazards, but he could see that the dwarf was convinced of what he was saying. "I will speak to Zaretta after Mass. The final decision must be her own."

"Convince her," Lugantes said without apology. "I beg you."

Nobile nodded, and sat still while Lugantes slipped out of the library. When he tried to read again, he could not concentrate on the words before his eyes, so he returned the volume to the shelf, then sat for the better part of an hour, wondering what he could say that would convince Zaretta to return to Venezia.

28

The Plaza del Rey sweltered in the afternoon sunlight as the procession of condemned heretics began. As there were only thirty-two men and women to be burned, Alonzo felt moved to comment on this to Zaretta, who sat beside him as a sign of his affection and esteem for Venezia.

"We realize that this is a disappointing auto-da-fé, but there has not been time enough to conclude many of the Processes before the Holy Office. Doubtless in time those who are guilty and in sin will be brought to justice. We do not wish you or your countrymen to believe, Doña, that we are not strong in our devotion to the truth and the defense of our faith." He paused to bring his pomander to his nose. "On days as warm as this one, we are aware of the press of humanity."

"It's natural," Zaretta said remotely, horrified at the anticipation she saw all around her. She wanted to protest, to demand that even these heretics be allowed to die in a manner worthy of good Christians. Those whom the Inquisition executed in Venezia were permitted privacy at the end, not this humiliating display for the entire populace of the city.

"What is natural is not generally desirable," Alonzo said at his most stifling, and turned away from her to address la Reina. "You have told us that you are feeling the heat. When the fires are lit and the exhortations are over, we give you permission to withdraw with your women. Our confessor will spend an hour with you after the evening meal, so that you may purge your soul off doubts and guilt."

"Majestad," Genevieve said to show she accepted his decisions.

Zaretta looked as little as possible at the heretics, and so she almost failed to recognize Raimundo when he was brought past the royal stands.

He was carried on a hurdle because both his legs had been subjected to the boot and could not bear his weight. Shards of bone protruded through the bruised and mangled skin. His hands were nearly black, his fingers misshapen from the screws that had been applied to them. His jaw was broken and his face was covered with stubble. He was half-delirious and paid no attention to the two men who walked beside him, urging him to repent of his sins before the flames could take him.

"During the next weeks," Alonzo was saying, unaware that Zaretta was no longer listening to him, but was staring at Raimundo, her hand at her throat, her face turned the color of chalk, "our Guarda and the soldiers of the Church will be making a new effort to find the heretics that still sully España. It is our wish and the wish of our Inquisitor General that these vile beings, so long indulged and tolerated, but shown that it is no longer possible to mock God in this kingdom, and that we will not permit them to continue their abominations—" "Dominguez!" Genevieve whispered, horrified at the sight of him. "Christ and the angels!"

"It would be better if you were to invoke Our Lord to better purpose, Reina," Alonzo reprimanded her. "That man is a traitor and a heretic."

"Dear God," Zaretta said, turning away.

"See what our daughter-in-law does, Reina. It would be better that you were equally condemning. It is the lure of the flesh that taints your faith." He gave Zaretta a sign of approval. "We are pleased to see that you do not allow false pity to cause you to excuse crimes as heinous as the Duque da Minho committed."

"May God pity and forgive—" Zaretta began, then broke off, afraid that she would weep and make herself suspect.

"Yes, for such attributes are God's. We, frail men, must dedicate ourselves to the eradication of sorcery, heresy and witchcraft, which come from the Devil." Alonzo pointed to another one of the men about to be burned. "That man is a great sorcerer and has cursed many excellent Christians so that they ran mad, profaning churches and destroying the holdings."

"If he is so powerful, why is he going to be burned?" Genevieve demanded. "Why does he not deliver himself through his sorcery?" She knew she was being reckless, but the terrible sight of Raimundo filled her with anguish.

Alonzo chose to interpret this question as banter. "Well you know that the might of the Church far exceeds the power of the Devil. In the hands of the Holy Office, any sorcerer must lose his magical strengths."

"Why not banish them, then, and leave it to the Church to keep España pure?" asked Zaretta with a quick glance at Genevieve. For the first time the two women were in agreement.

"Oh, it would not be to my credit as a Christian ruler to permit such dangerous men and women to enter the kingdoms of others. Your uncle would hardly welcome the Diabolists who will die here today for their many evils." Alonzo crossed himself and looked toward the stakes where the first of the heretics were being chained. "In time, we will be rid of all of them."

It was both interminable and insanely brief, that time while all the heretics were brought to their pyres. Raimundo and two others could not be made to stand and so were placed with their legs crossed around the base of the stakes, their arms chained above their heads. When all was in readiness, Padre Juan Murador stepped forward to deliver his homily.

"Majestad," Genevieve whispered, "I fear I will be sick if I do not leave. The heat is overcoming me."

Alonzo shot her an irritated look, and motioned her to be quiet.

"I will be glad to bear you company, Reina," Zaretta said unexpectedly. "I, too, am not quite myself. As you say, it is . . . very hot. Once the fires are lit, I fear I may faint, and that would—"

"That would not be appropriate," Alonzo declared. "Very well. But we admonish you both to pray most heartily, for it may be that your sicknesses are the result of spells and curses leveled at us through you. Such a thing has happened before." He waved them away and gave his full attention to Padre Juan as the two women rose and found their way to the stairs at the rear of the royal stand. They had almost reached the bottom of the stairs when there was a rush of flames and a great shout.

"Oh my God!" Genevieve said, and doubled over, her arms across her abdomen. "Christ in Heaven."

On the steps behind her, Zaretta swayed and felt her thoughts go blank for an instant. The warnings that Nobile had given her, which had seemed ridiculous yesterday, now rang in her mind like tolling bells. She stumbled down the last two treads and refused the proffered assistance of the courtiers who waited for Alonzo to leave the auto-da-fé. "Reina," she cried out to Genevieve. "Please. I must speak with you."

Genevieve had recovered herself a little, and she nodded twice. "Not here. In my apartments." She signaled for her sedan chair, averting her face from the curious glances of the grandees and hidalgos gathered around her. "Follow me at once."

"I will." Her own chairmen were already pushing through the crowd toward her, and she hoped they would be quick, or she might collapse.

There were two more cheers; smoke and soot billowed into the sky, obscuring the brilliant afternoon sun. A heavy, charred odor hung on the air.

Even in the palace, the smell pursued them. Genevieve ordered her windows closed and orange peels to be scattered about the rooms, but the stench of the burnings penetrated the acidic sweetness. She fretted but dared not complain.

"You still wish to speak with me?" Zaretta asked when a page admitted her to Genevieve's apartments.

"Yes." She gestured to her ladies-in-waiting. "We are not to be left alone, it seems, and so I will not say a great deal." Her eyes challenged the women, but none of them reacted to it. "You see, they are used to my ways, and hardly bother to report it to Padre Juan when I am disobedient."

Zaretta tried not to appear startled. "I see."

"No one warned me about Dominguez y Mara," Genevieve went on. "I suppose they thought I knew, or would not care that my oldest comrade at Court was to be burned at the stake." She picked up a glass cup and hurled it across the room, smiling with satisfaction as it shattered.

"I knew nothing of it, either," Zaretta said in a small voice, the horror she had so long denied coming back to her in a rush. Her legs trembled and her hands began to shake badly. "I . . . I don't know . . . I can't keep . . ." She dropped abruptly into the nearest chair. "Forgive my . . . rudeness . . . ."

"Scream if you wish," Genevieve offered kindly. "I may. How I loathe this place!" She glared at the ladies on the far side of the room. "You tell el Rey that I said it. He has heard it before."

Zaretta forced herself to speak of her errand. "Reina, I must make a request of you. My Ambassador has already presented the request to the throne. My . . . situation here is very awkward while . . . Don Rolon's fate is . . . unknown. While he is being sought, I believe it to be my . . . duty to return to Venezia and my uncle." She caught her breath and made herself go on. "I beseech you to accompany me, for the honor of Venezia and España."

"Accompany you?" Genevieve said, astonished. Somehow Lugantes had done it. She had not imagined he would be able to, and yet he had. She stared at Zaretta. "You want me to escort you to Venezia?"

"Yes," Zaretta answered simply. "Yes."

Genevieve looked at the ladies-in-waiting. "You have heard the request of Don Rolon's wife. You know that I have listened to it. Now I want you to hear my answer: I will be honored to provide company and escort for the wife of Don Rolon to Venezia. Tell Alonzo that I have consented." She turned her back on the women and paid them no more attention than if they had been figures in paintings.

"Thank you," Zaretta murmured. Her relief was enormous, and the promise of ending her stay in Valladolid eased her mind.

"We have not yet gained the approval of El Majestad," Genevieve cautioned her. "He may object to it."

"But how? Why?" Zaretta asked, appalled once more.

"Alonzo has his caprices," Genevieve said, shrugging. "He does not always permit me to see my daughters when I request it. I know that they are simple and will always be so, but they are my children." She thrust her arms out, as if pressing away from the thought. "He may decide that I must remain here, or you must remain here."

"My Ambassador has told me that it would be very awkward for Alonzo if he were to refuse. And he wishes to continue his treaty with Venezia. If my petition is not honored, the treaty could be refuted." That was how it had been explained to her, and she was clever enough to know that there was a great deal of truth in what Nobile had said.

"I hope it will happen. There is little I can do, but I will inform el Rey that I support your request. The ladies will tell him how I've answered you." Genevieve put one hand over her eyes. "Poor Raimundo. Oh, God."

Zaretta's hands clenched. "Please don't speak of him. I can't bear it."

"How he looked!" Genevieve said, compelled to go on. "He was my friend, and they used him so."

"Reina!" Zaretta protested, her gorge rising.

"The worst of it is, he was also Alonzo's friend. And Don Rolon's. But, but, but he was not Gil's friend. That was his error." She stared up toward the ceiling. "He deserved better than this from Alonzo."

Zaretta could find nothing to say that would express how revolted she was, and how frightened. She stared hard at Genevieve. "Please. I can't endure this."

Genevieve blinked as if coming out of a dream. "All right. I did not intend to be so distracted by—"

"Reina," Zaretta said, "no more. Let me tell my Ambassador that you have said you will travel with me, and leave him to settle what must be settled with el Rey. It is not fitting that we should be so closely watched, but let it go. When Ambassador Rigonzetti has all in readiness, he will notify both you and me that ships will be waiting, and we have only to travel to Murcia or Barcelona to embark. Another three or four weeks at the most, and we will depart."

Genevieve looked away, suddenly very much moved that Zaretta would do this for her. She felt badly now that she had not been kinder to the Venezian woman, or shown her more courtesy than she had. It had been out of pique and jealousy that she had subjected Zaretta to her pranks, but now it embarrassed her to think of them. She turned to her guest. "I do not deserve to be used as well as you treat me now. It says much for your nobility of mind, and very little for mine. Gratitude under such conditions is always suspect, but I want you to know that I have the deepest respect for you, Zaretta, and I am aware of the honor you have done me."

"It is nothing," Zaretta said, knowing she was glad for anyone who made it possible for her to leave this God-forsaken kingdom. She would ask Don Rolon, if they were ever reunited again, if they might live part of the year away from the oppressive Court of Valladolid. He had told her that he wanted to initiate reforms, but she was certain that they would take long years to bring to fruition, and at the moment España was too dreadful for her to be able to live here much longer. No wonder Genevieve had become . . . Zaretta trembled. She had heard before that the people of España were quite mad, and at first she had thought it was only the prejudice of Venezians, who thought all others were beneath them. Now she knew that España was indeed a kingdom of lost souls in the terrible grip of the Holy Office, and that all of España was strangling from it. "Do you miss France, Reina?" She had not meant to ask, since it was an inexcusable intrusion, but the words were out before she knew she was thinking about them.

"Miss France? Oh, yes. My brother has come twice on State visits, but both times were brief, and I have not seen him in almost ten years. He has asked that I join him at Bordeaux for his annual hunting there, but it has not been . . . possible." She smiled at Zaretta. "There is a smell to the fields in summer that is like nothing else in the world. It has been years since I smelled it, but I cannot forget it. Occasionally I will pass a field here and there will be a trace of the smell, not so strong or as pervasive, but it will go through me like a sword, and I will be awake half the night with homesickness. It's foolish of me."

Zaretta could not agree. "If I had to stay away from the sea for years and years, I would not want to live. Just last night, I dreamed of the way the Ca'd'Oro is reflected in the waters of the canal, and I did not want to wake up."

Genevieve looked at her with more understanding than she had ever shown Don Rolon's wife. "It's like being exiled, living here."

"I think so," she agreed. "Well, I at least will have time to watch the gondolas and ships riding the water of Venezia. You will see how pleasant it is. There are shops on the Rialto where everything in the world may be bought, including trinkets from the New World, purchased from Spanish sailors."

"It will be a welcome change." Genevieve wanted to say more, but was afraid of what her ladies were hearing, and so reluctantly brought their audience to an end. "I do have the headache, Zaretta, and must lie down for a time. Tomorrow or the next day, let us talk further, and you will tell me what progress your Ambassador has made in the arrangements for our departure."

Zaretta was disappointed that they could not speak longer, but she knew better than to oppose la Reina when she was showing herself to be so cooperative. She curtsied deeply to show the extent of her respect, then withdrew, going not to her quarters, but to the herb garden where three of Rigonzetti's servants waited for her.

Alonzo had not made up his mind about Zaretta's request five days later when he set aside time to discuss with Padre Juan his petition to his brother, the Emperor Gustay. It was evening by the time the Inquisitor General was free to discuss the issue with el Rey, and he came to the palace in the manner of a man who had been asked to do something that was wholly against his interests.

Alonzo received him in his smallest reception room, two chairs already set out and waiting for their conversation. "You are most gracious to spare me time, good Padre," Alonzo said, making note of the frown the Dominican wore.

"It is my duty to listen to those whose confession I hear, the more so when their responsibilities are weighty and far-reaching." He did not wait to be shown to a chair, but took the nearer one, then waited for Alonzo to be seated as well. "Of late, there has been a greater resistance to our efforts, which is due in part, I think, to the power of the Devil being given so much tolerance in the kingdom."

"There were heretics burned just this week," Alonzo pointed out, shocked that Padre Juan should be so clearly displeased.

"So there were, and that is the same as saying that a blossom plucked from a flowering branch will stop the entire tree from bearing fruit. I tell you, Majestad, that there are worshipers of the Devil gathering in España in greater numbers than ever before, bringing new disobedience and heresies into the kingdom that will cause God to turn His back on us and remove the favors He has granted us for so long, and in their place send us punishments and suffering. And we will deserve it!" He watched as Alonzo sat down, aghast at what he had heard.

"Padre, I am not able to speak." It had seemed to Alonzo that at last there had been a little progress in his kingdom; to have Padre Juan castigate him now threw his thoughts into disorder.

In one of the halls, a door slammed closed, the echo of it tolling down the corridors.

"Then reflect on what has transpired. Just when there was hope that some of the nefarious heretics might have lost interest in their subversion of España, we discover that the evil has not retreated at all, but advanced. Where it was once unthinkable that men of high rank and station might reveal themselves as heretics, or that men of the Church should be publicly executed for their transgressions, now we find that there is not just one such, but several. Not only Obispo Teodoro was proved guilty of the most pernicious heresy, now it becomes apparent that the Infante Real's confessor was a heretic and a spy, and the Ambassador from Portugal was deep in treason against both Church and state. I have prayed to God to show me how I have erred that I did not sooner discover the danger that is present all around us." Padre Juan clasped his hands, his face a study in conflicting emotions. "I have been most diligent in my calling, or so I have told myself. I have pursued those Diabolists and heretics that I knew of with vigor and with the firm belief that at last the forces of the godless were being beaten back in España. But therein did I commit a great sin, for I opened my heart to pride, and the Devil made a nest there, and let me deceive myself, convinced that at last we were turning the tide in favor of true faith and God. How the Devil must have laughed at me. How the heretics must have rejoiced to see the Holy Office perverted to their ends."

Alonzo was horrified to see how distraught his Inquisitor General had become. "You are a man, and as men, we fail God. Thus have you taught me always, good Padre, and so must you remember yourself."

"But I am not simply a man, but a priest, with my life dedicated to the service of God. It is not as if I were not warned of the hazards around us, or that I was unaware. In all my years, I have been constantly looking to end the power of the Devil on earth so that we might the sooner show ourselves worthy of the Kingdom of Heaven. It has made me forget how much power and subtlety the Devil has at his disposal, and how relentless is his hatred of God and mankind. I am rebuked for my weakness, oh, most surely, and you, Majestad, would be praised for dismissing me, so great has been my failure to defend you against the forces of the Devil and the rise of heretics." He dropped to his knees before Alonzo. "My sins are great, my soul has gone astray, and there is nothing I may do that is acceptable to man and God to show how great is my contrition."

"You are not to blame yourself," Alonzo said severely. "You are without doubt the most sincerely dedicated Inquisitor General in my reign, and it humbles me to see that you are so willing to take the burden on yourself which undoubtedly is more properly my own. I am the one who has been reluctant to act, good Padre, not you." He straightened in his chair and smoothed the front of his black velvet pourpoint. "I have been hesitant to act in the matter of Don Rolon, thinking that if his marriage proved fruitful, it would show that the curse that brought him into the world had not visited any lasting harm on the House of Hapsburg. But there are rumors of his willing protection of Flemings who are in open defiance of the crown and the Church. Already we have learned that the divine aid that was supposed to have kept him from harm was more probably the forces of the Devil, preserving one of their own. It is my error that has brought this danger to España, and it is my duty to resolve it. I may no longer falter in my purpose. Your own devotion makes this clear to me."

Padre Juan had been watching Alonzo with narrowed eyes, but now he lowered his head in a show of acquiescence. "If there is anything I may do to compensate in part for my dreadful failings, you have only to speak of it, and I will extend myself to the utmost so that it will be done. Though the task is worldly and not of priestly concem, I will give myself to it so that Su Majestad may believe how profound my love is."

"I thank you, Padre," Alonzo said with a sigh. "We must address our brother once again, and pray that he will hear us without preju- dice, though it is not likely he will be so willing. The Succession must be altered, and Gil, not Otto made heir to the throne, or the suffering of the kingdom will be far greater than it is now, and not entirely from the machinations of heretics and Diabolists." As he said this, he felt the familiar, dull pain in his side, as if something small and lazy were gnawing at his vitals. It had grown worse in the last year, but he could not remember a time when it had not been with him.

"Let me add my supplication, so that I may in part expiate my sin," Padre Juan said, extending one hand toward el Rey. "It is often the way of brothers that they are suspicious of those of their House and blood, but will be less partial to a man of the cloth who is removed from the conflict."

"We are grateful to you, good Padre," Alonzo said absently as he rang for a servant so that he could have parchment, sand and ink brought to him. "Our Imperial brother and His Holiness must once again be approached, and the gravity of the situation here made plain. Otherwise there will be long and arduous conflict here that will lend aid and power to the heretics who plague us." He folded his hands and murmured a prayer, and heard, to his relief, Padre Juan echo his amen.

29

Soldiers stormed through the burning city on lathered horses, their lances at the ready and the delight of battle in their reddened eyes. Screams, moans and curses filled the air in counterpoint to the song of the fire. The air was acrid with smoke and greasy smuts that left a black scum on everything they touched. The Secular Arm had come to Toledo.

"At the next full moon," Isador was telling Don Rolon as his roof-beams began to smolder, "you are to complete the ceremony we began. Ciro has been taught all the ritual invocations and gestures. You have already achieved part of the freedom you desired, and you told me that you remembered some of your last transformation."

"Yes, yes," Don Rolon cut in, impatient for the old man's safety. "We know what must be done, and one of the things is that you must leave this place. For the sake of God and your own soul, as well as the gratitude I owe you and can never repay, go and join your wife. Please."

"In a moment, Infante. I have a few more matters to attend to." Isador would not be rushed, now or ever. He took a golden chain from around his neck and dropped it over Don Rolon's head; an amulet made of a curiously carved polished amethyst depended from the links. "This will protect you to some degree. It will not prevent the curse from acting completely, but it will modify what happens and from that you will be able to control your actions. If you are able to have time and protection so that you will not be discovered, it will aid you until Ciro can complete the exorcism. Now I ask God to—"

There was a crash at the front of the narrow house, and the ring of metal on stone.

"Go!" Don Rolon insisted. "The soldiers will not harm me, but you are in the greatest danger. Go!" He embraced the old man once, roughly. "I will keep my promise, Isador, with all the gratitude in my heart."

"May the God of our fathers look on you with favor and keep you," Isador said, more affected by Don Rolon's gesture than he could ever express. He looked toward his great-nephew. "Do not fail me, Ciro."

"I will not, father of my father's brother." Ciro made a movement, placing himself between the door of the house and the old man. "Out the backway. Quickly."

At last Isador moved, half running toward the corridors that led to the back entrance of the house. The air was already heavy with smoke, and there were shouts mixing with the clamor of bells. In the street beyond, men and women ran ahead of soldiers on half-maddened horses, Snarling dogs ran past the front of the house, one of them breaking off in whimpers and a howl of pain.

"Come," Don Rolon said to Ciro. "We must go stop this."

Ciro held back. "Those are soldiers of the Holy Office, not the Guarda. They will not respect—"

"They will not respect anything," Don Rolon said somberly. "But still we must stop them or more of these people will suffer, and it will be my fault." He touched the amulet that lay over his heart. "I had better put this under my camise or they certainly will impound it."

Again Ciro hesitated. "They may not believe you, Alteza. They may decide to arrest you out of hand."

Don Rolon turned and looked at his valet. "Yes, it's true that they may do such things. But if they do, they will be taking great risks, and most of them cannot bring themselves to accept hazards." He did not smile, but there was an unhappy irony in his eyes that came as close as ever he could to making light of the despotism of the Inquisition.

"As you wish, Alteza," Ciro said quietly, and followed him toward the front of the house where the soldiers had just succeeded in splintering the door.

"And I'm San Cristobal," said the Capitan when Don Rolon was brought before him almost an hour later. "The Infante Real!"

Don Rolon stood very straight in front of the thick-bodied man and regarded him with the contempt he had often seen his father show to inferiors. "I see that you do not believe me, which is very foolish of you. And if you should delay in bringing me to Valladolid, you will have to answer to it, not only to the Holy Office but to the throne. Now, fellow, tell me what you wish to do."

The officer faltered. He had seen hidalgos and grandees enough to recognize the manner. Whoever this puppy was, he was highborn, and for that reason, the Capitan hesitated. "The Infante Real would not be here, in Toledo, with no escort."

"My valet is with me. We were . . . " Until that moment, he had no idea of what he would say, but a story, clumsy and half-formed, came out of him. "We were taken from Segovia by unknown and foreign men, and held for some time in an isolated building, and only escaped with the aid of some peddlers, who happened to hear our signals, and came to find us. As both of us were ill with fever, Ciro thought to bring us here, where he knew physicians who could restore us to health, and so they have. It is only recently that I have had strength enough to leave my bed." He was thin enough, and pale, to make the story credible.

The Capitan knew as well as any soldier in España that the Infante Real was missing, but he never thought he would be the one so fortunate as to find the heir to the throne. Such an opportunity came but once in a lifetime, and he would be a fool to refuse it. He leaned back in the rough-hewn wooden stool and looked measuringly at Don Rolon. "How do I know that this is not some clever tale of yours, made to bring me to a sense of false success and thereby bring embarrassment on the Holy Office and ruin on me?"

"You don't, of course," Don Rolon answered. "But remember that if I am lying, I suffer far greater punishments than you do." He spoke with quiet conviction, and that alone swayed the Capitan.

"I suppose I better give you escort to Valladolid, in case your claims are genuine." He sighed, and shook his head.

"Think, Capitan. If I am who I claim to be, there will be rewards for you beyond the commendation of the Inquisition. Surely el Rey will want to bestow his thanks on you. And I will be pleased to inform your superiors of your skills and efficiency." He kept his tone even so that none of the irony he felt would be communicated to the man whose aid he needed.

"Rewards," the Capitan mused, blatantly greedy. "How much would they amount to, do you know?"

"My father is considered a just man," Don Rolon answered, and let the Capitan decide what that meant.

"Yes," he murmured. The young man had said 'my father' without faltering. That was strong indication that he had some claim on the throne, though perhaps not the one he claimed. Still, if this youth were masquerading as the Infante Real at a time the real heir to the throne was missing, it would be of interest to the Holy Office and el Rey. He decided to take a chance. "Very well," he said at last. "I do not know for sure if you are telling me the truth but I am willing . . . "—he was cut off by a burst of screams and shouts— "to escort you to Valladolid. That is all I am willing to do."

"I am most grateful. My valet will accompany me, of course." He had not been permitted to bring Ciro before the Capitan, but now he decided to assert his rights.

"Ah, ah, now then my pretty lad, none of that. You will ride with me, and that other man will be kept here. Until we're told for sure that you're the man you claim to be, I'm not taking any more spies than I must into the court." He got up and ambled toward the door to the tavern where he was keeping his headquarters. "I'll give you my word that he'll be looked after properly, unless it turns out that you're not the Infante, in which case, we'll see that he goes straight to the Holy Office."

"Then I must speak with him," Don Rolon insisted, knowing he had to pass on his story and find out when he would be able to undergo the next ritual. There would be a full moon in two weeks and without another ritual, he was doomed to undergo the transformation another time.

"For a few minutes. I don't want spies passing information under my nose, and if you're Diabolists or heretics, I don't want you to have the chance to put spells on me and my men. You see my point of view, don't you?" He was not quite insolent, but he was also a long way from respectful.

"If it is a point, Capitan, I see it." He wanted to upbraid the officer, but dared not.

"You may have a short interview with him. But nothing strange, mind." He held up a square finger in warning, then called for one of his underlings to show Don Rolon to the place where Ciro was being held.

❧

"Don't overestimate the danger we were in," Don Rolon said to Ciro when he had been able to go over most of the story he had told the Capitan. "I do not want those who are not responsible for our confinement to suffer."

"Yes," Ciro said, and added, "Though with the fever, it is hard to say precisely where we were, or how long." He lowered his head, knowing that Don Rolon had seized on this recommendation. "You were more ill than I, Alteza."

"Was I?" Don Rolon asked. "I don't precisely remember."

"Yes." He paused, wishing that they were not overheard. "Particularly around the full of the moon. I was afraid for you."

Don Rolon's hands clenched at the word. "Yes. There was that medicine your old friend provided. I wish I still had it, in case the disease is not yet passed."

Ciro nodded enthusiastically. "Yes. I see that you are being prudent, Alteza. We must secure more for the future."

"But your old friend has left. His house was burned." It made Don Rolon angry to say that, and worried that Isador might not have escaped the soldiers of the Holy Office.

"He has some skill. He will make his way, do not fear." Ciro was not as confident as he sounded, but knew that their conversation would be reported, and for that reason wanted to make certain that his great-uncle was not looked for among the captives. "He has those at Granada who will provide a home for him until he is able to return to Toledo."

"I will thank them for their service and advance them," Don Rolon promised, though he knew that Isador had not gone to Granada.

"Yes, Alteza." He could think of nothing more to say. It pained him deeply to watch the Infante Real go, but he had no reason to ask him to remain without creating more suspicion. "Alteza!" he called out to the retreating figure, "Go with God!"

"And you, my faithful friend," Don Rolon replied, not caring that such a breach in proper behavior would be dutifully repeated to the Inquisitors.

Zaretta's blue eyes grew enormous as she saw the door to her private chamber open. It was well past the middle of the night and no one had any right to be in her apartments but her ladies-in-waiting. She reached for the dagger she kept under the mattress near her head, withdrawing it carefully. If that odious Gil del Rey were thinking to compromise her, he would pay dearly for his rashness. She shifted on the bed, drawing her knees up so that she would be able to kick out at her assailant before she brought her blade into play.

"Querida," said a soft, plaintive voice in the shadows. "Zaretta. Altezita."

She could not move. Her pulse drummed in her ears and she told herself that this was the cruelest deception yet. Or she was still asleep, and this was the dream of Don Rolon; she had prayed so often for his return that she had brought him back in sleep.

"Zaretta," he repeated, coming nearer the bed. "Wake up, my delight, my dove."

"Don Rolon?" she whispered, surprised to hear her own voice.

"Yes." He moved closer, leaning over the bed. "I am supposed to be in my own quarters, but I could not wait until morning to see you, and then have to endure the whole long day and the evening meal before I could be with you. Forgive me."

"You frightened me," she accused him in a small voice. "You come in here, after being gone so long, and you make me worry and fret, and then you sneak into my room in the dead of night like—" She stopped and caught the sob in her throat before it could escape. She rose to her knees and held out her arms to him. "Oh, why were you away so long?"

Without thinking at all, Don Rolon went to her, embracing her with more fondness and longing than he knew he felt. He had thought that he would be happy to see her again, and enjoy reassuring her, but he had not understood how deep the love and tenderness he had for her was. Now it was the world in her smile, and all the sweetness of paradise in her touch. Where before he had lost himself in her, now he found himself, and her as well. The revelation was beyond the union of their bodies, though that was more overwhelming, more intense, more rapturous than he had ever known; for the first time in his life, his soul felt cleansed to him, and he gave himself without reservation or guilt to loving her.

She had never held him as she did when they were satisfied. Her head was pillowed on his chest and with her free hand, she let her fingers stray over his face, finding every texture of him. "Your hair wants trimming," she said at last.

"And my beard, as well. Did I scratch you?" He caught her hand and kissed it.

"Probably," she giggled. "Where have you been?" "Away," he answered, and hated himself for being evasive. "I was cared for, most of the time."

She had sense enough not to question him too closely. "How kind of those who did."

"It was," he agreed with conviction. "I hope that they will never regret their kindness, but that will depend on el Rey."

At the mention of Alonzo, Zaretta stiffened momentarily. "Don't let's talk about him. Just lie with me a little longer."

"But I must talk of this. I wish I did not have to, but there may be questions they will expect me to answer, and I don't want to cause any ... unpleasantness for you, joy of my life, You will need good advice, and I may not be able to give it to you. Speak to Raimundo—" He felt her pull away from him.

"Raimundo?" She spoke so softly that it was difficult to hear her.

"Yes, Dominguez y Mara. He knows more of statecraft than—" He stopped. "What is it?"

"They killed him." There was horror in her whisper.

"Who? What happened?" Don Rolon was shocked, and for the first time since he entered Zaretta's room, his fear came back.

"The Inquisition. They said he was a heretic. He would not confess, so they Questioned him, and tortured him. And burned him." She started to cry, then made herself stop.

"Raimundo?" Don Rolon said, thinking that surely there must be a mistake. There were men who might come under the scrutiny, but not Raimundo, who was not even Spanish. It was unimaginable. "El Rey would not—"

"He watched the burning," Zaretta said, her voice rising on the last word.

"An auto-da-fé?" His fear intensified. "There was an auto-da-fé and they dared to burn Raimundo publicly?"

"He was very badly . . . hurt." She had a sudden, intense memory of Raimundo being taken on a hurdle to the stake. "He could not have lived as he was."

Don Rolon stared up at the canopy of Zaretta's bed, very little in his mind but a blankness like panic. His thoughts were empty as a white page. "Raimundo. He was my ally. My friend." The sense he had had of being clean began to fade, and his inward despair returned, bringing with it blame and doubt. "Why did they—"

"It was very fast. His Duquessa had already said she will marry again. They were estranged, but still . . . "

Automatically Don Rolon shook his head. "No, you do not understand. If she does not marry again in a year, the Church may take all Raimundo's goods and estates. She has no choice, querida. She must find a husband or lose all." He thought for a moment of what might become of Zaretta if the Holy Office took him. "You must remember that, jewel of my soul. If it should happen that there is a Process against me—"

"Rolon!"

"Ssshshuu," he hushed her, putting his fingers lightly on her mouth. "If there is a Process against me, you must leave España so that—" He forced himself to go on, "so that my father cannot command you to marry his next heir."

Zaretta glared at him. "I would never do such a thing."

"But el Rey would, and it is his right to do so. The terms of our marriage treaty provide that you will be the wife of the heir to the throne of España, not simply to me, and my father could insist that he is protecting the throne from losing the revenues of the Infante Real. There is much land that goes with the title, mi amor, and there are those who would do much to control it."

"Don't speak of it now," she said in a small voice. It had been so wonderful having him with her again, and now he was dashing the last of her dreams with his talk of Processes and political marriages.

"But I must. I may not be able to do so again." He kissed her on her brow and cheek and nose. "I pray that there will be years of nights like this one, but it may not happen, and if it does not, I would not be worthy of loving you if I did not do all that I could to be certain that you were not left at the mercy of my father and the Church—"

She did not quite pout, but there was a sullen thrust to her lower lip. "Very well. I will listen."

"Good. Now, I have said that you must leave España—" "But that is all arranged," Zaretta interrupted.

"What?"

As Zaretta ran her fingers lightly over his chest, she explained, not paying too much attention to her actions or her words. She was trying to indulge her fancy a bit longer. "Well, it has been arranged that I will return to Venezia with Genevieve as my escort and companion. I was wrong about her. She is not the petty and vain woman I thought she was. She offered to travel with me, and somehow the Ambassador—you know Rigonzetti, don't you? Yes—arranged it to Alonzo's satisfaction."

"This is good. You must go." He hated the thought of being parted from her, but he wanted above all to know she was safe.

"No!" Her protest was immediate and she made no apology for its fierceness. "I only asked to go because you were not here. Now you are back, and I will remain with you." She was surprised at how strong her feelings were, since at first it had not seemed to her that she was much involved with the Infante. Her chagrin at his public penance had imparted a reserve to her attitude for a while, but while he was gone, she had come to realize how unlike the rest of the Court he was, and how worthy a prince he was. Just as she welcomed him to her bed, so she wanted to bring him into her life, so that she might know something other than the repressed austerity she saw around her, or the salacious despotism that was its dark counterpart.

"Yes. And I will thank God for it. You must go. If you were here, I would be so vulnerable; they would only have to whisper a threat toward you, and I would be their pawn to save you. But if you are safe and protected by your family and all the might of Venezia, then I will be able to do all that I must and know that you are not likely to be harmed on my account." He kissed her, tasting her lips with an emotion that approached adoration. "We do not have much time, querida. Let us not waste any more of it."

Zaretta could hardly bring herself to admit she understood the implications of his words, but she made the best of it she could, turning in his arms so that they could press the length of their bodies together and hear the soft, joyous, private sounds that confirmed their love in these few stolen hours they both treasured the more for their brevity than for their pleasure.

30

"You came as a thief in the night!" Padre Barnabas insisted, not giving Don Rolon a chance to speak. "First you are gone, no one knows where, and there is total disruption within the court, and then you appear, as if by magic . . . as if by sorcery, and tell me that you were detained by men you did not know, in a place you did not recognize, and were lost in fever!" The priest threw up his hands as if to banish all concern with Don Rolon.

"Nevertheless, good Padre, you may ask my valet when your soldiers are willing to relinquish him, and he will tell you the same. He will be able to make the matter clearer to you because he was not so overcome with illness as 1 was." Don Rolon had anticipated this interview with deep concern, but now felt that he might have permitted himself to become too worried. Padre Barnabas was clearly angry, but he had not yet made any accusations that would require a Process against him.

"All in good time, Infante. First there are a few matters that we must clarify so that we may tell your father how we view your spiritual state at this time." He tucked his hands into the sleeves of his habit and regarded Don Rolon carefully. "You know that your confessor was shown to be a heretic and Diabolist?"

"I heard that there had been a Process against him, yes, but I have not seen what his records showed. I am not a churchman, Padre, and do not have access to those records." He did not quite smile, but there was an air about him that annoyed Padre Barnabas most thoroughly.

"It may amuse you to make light of such enormous crimes, but as it is certain you did not escape entirely unscathed after so many years under his guidance, it would be more appropriate for you to assume a circumspect attitude until the degree of your culpability is determined and a suitable penance be decided upon." He was pleased to see Don Rolon become more serious at once. "I must report to my superiors that you have not received my first visit in a manner that shows profound devotion and submission to the laws of the Church and the demands of the crown."

"Then I pray you will let me speak to my father, so that he may tell me what he desires me to do," Don Rolon said, knowing that this was a reasonable request.

"It is my duty to inform you, Alteza, that El Majestad does not wish to see you until we of the Holy Office have made our determination in your case, and he is assured that your soul has not strayed far from your obligations." He took a seat on one of the narrow benches. "I have been given the space of four days to discuss with you any questions of faith and dogma that may disturb you. When that time is over, I will make recommendations to the officers of the Inquisition, and with the aid of El Majestad and God, your case will be determined."

"I see." Don Rolon could feel fear take hold of him again, wrapping him in gelid coils, constricting his soul in its icy, stifling embrace.

"Padre Juan is especially anxious to learn of you, Infante Real, for he has come to believe that he has not discharged the obligations of his office as he should, and is of the opinion that your case is crucial to his own faith and salvation."

Don Rolon's heart sank. Padre Juan had set his sights on him, and he would have what he wanted. Don Rolon was his offering and the token of the Holy Office's total control of España. If Alonzo would not receive him until Padre Juan did, he might as well enter his tomb now. "What questions must I answer, good Padre?"

"I am pleased to see you once again submissive to the Church, which strives only for your salvation and the saving of all mankind." He blessed Don Rolon, but indicated as he did that he was very much afraid that Don Rolon was not yet worthy of his blessing. "You must tell us all that you confessed to Padre Lucien, and it will then be determined if his penances and—"

"Confess again? After I have been absolved? Isn't that blasphemous? Doesn't it mean that I am not certain of God's Grace and forgiveness?" It was a desperate chance, and one he was not confident would work, but she saw the flicker in Padre Barnabas' eyes, and knew that for the moment, he had won. "Padre? Have I misunderstood?"

Padre Barnabas rose. "Your question is well-taken," he said in some agitation. He had not suspected Don Rolon of such spiritual sophistication. "It is not for me, a mere priest, to bring doubt to you, who are in my keeping. It is wrong for me to require this of you." He knew that if he pressed the matter and Don Rolon challenged what was required later, he might be in a great deal of danger with his superiors in the Church. "It is a great sin to doubt God's Grace. And absolution, coming from even tainted hands, if there has been ordination, must come from God Himself. The Holy Spirit has chosen many imperfect vessels to bring peace to the world. I . . . I must speak with my superiors, and they will decide how best to proceed."

"I thank you, Padre Barnabas," Don Rolon said, astonished that his bluff had worked so well, and hoping that he might yet come through this period unscathed. "As soon as I have seen my father, I would wish to make arrangements to withdraw from the court for a week or two, to an anchorite's cell, where I may pray for guidance. What you have said has disturbed me greatly, and it will require time for me to purge my heart of uncharitable thoughts." He did not add that his lack of charity was toward the Holy Office and not toward Padre Lucien.

"A wise notion," Padre Barnabas said, somewhat taken aback at Don Rolon's attitude. He had expected to have to argue, threaten and cajole in order to make the Infante Real cooperate with the Inquisition. "There are many Orders that would be honored to make their facilities available to you. You have only to inform me of which is the one you prefer."

This ready agreement distressed Don Rolon, who now believed that Padre Barnabas was hoping to trap him. As much as he wanted to return to the Ambrosians, he sensed that such a request would not bring the results he wanted. "There are three monasteries north of this city. One is Benedictine, one is Capuchin, and one is Cameldolesian. I will let you choose which is the most acceptable to the Holy Office." He had carefully refused to mention the Dominicans, so that he could not stay quite so closely under surveillance of the Holy Office. He had a shrewd idea that Padre Barnabas would select the Cameldolesians, since they were the most isolated and strict of the Orders, taking vows not only of chastity and poverty but silence as well.

"If you are willingly penitent . . . " Padre Barnabas began, then trailed off. This was not going the way he had envisioned it, and it both angered and distressed him. "I must request a decision from Padre Juan. This is a question for the Grand Inquisitor, not for me. He is far wiser than I am."

"I will pray for God's comfort," Don Rolon said, grateful that he had averted prison for the time being. Now if only Ciro could reach Valladolid before he went to the monastery and could complete the ritual for him, so that the curse would fade away. He still had the amulet, hidden away in a tooled leather bag on his belt where no one would notice it or comment on it. It might provide some protection, but he did not want to put all his dependence on the amulet, no matter how powerful it was.

"And I will pray, as well," Padre Barnabas said, getting up and taking a turn about the room. "I will call you again tomorrow. In the meantime, you are to keep to your apartments. It has been announced that you are not permitted to see any member of the Court."

"Not even my wife?" Don Rolon asked, longing to repeat the pleasures he had shared with Zaretta. "My father has been most adamant in the past on my responsibility to the House of Hapsburg."

"That . . . no, not yet. Padre Juan has not said that—" He wanted to get out of the room and away from Don Rolon. The questions the Infante Real had raised so innocently were disturbing him more than he was willing to admit. He had decided that he could not allow himself to be influenced by anything the young man said, but such an inquiry struck at the very heart of faith, and he could not find a response to it.

"Then may I send a note to my wife? She must have been told by now that I have returned, and doubtless is concerned that I have not yet called upon her." This he knew was a wholly reasonable request, one that both Padre Juan and his father would expect him to make.

"A note. You may do that, I suppose. I will read it and see that it is properly delivered." That much was acceptable and Padre Barnabas knew that agreeing would not cast him in an unfavorable light with the Inquisitor General.

So it was that late in the afternoon, Zaretta received this brief, formal missive from the Infante Real:

My most esteemed and cherished bride;

It is my duty and pleasure to inform you that I have at last returned to the Court after a prolonged absence. You may be sure that I am well and that I am looking forward to seeing you once more. You know that my feelings of devotion have not altered since we last parted. I ask that you pray for a swift and satisfactory conclusion to my hearing before the Holy Office.

I am in all things most truly your servant,

Don Rolon Esteban Angel Castelar de Asturias, Aragon, Leon y Castilla, Infante Real

Padre Juan had scrutinized the note carefully and found nothing to object to in its contents, and so added his seal and note of approval beneath Don Rolon's signature, and then admitted to Padre Barnabas that he was determined to begin a Process as soon as

Don Rolon returned from his retreat to the monastery.

"And I think," he said quietly, "that it had best be the Cameldolesian monastery, for there he will have more time to himself and will not be exposed to the sort of attention that made his stay with the Ambrosians so unfortunate for everyone."

Padre Barnbas nodded his approval. "And the servant? What of him?"

"You mean the valet?" Padre Juan tapped the end of his quill pen against the inkhorn. "It is best, I think, if he finds other occupation. I have never been easy in my mind having a converso serve one so close to the throne. While there is no record that Ciro Eje is one who has not honored the Church, still I believe he may unwittingly still carry some of the disastrous apostasy of the Jews, and for that reason must be removed from the company of El Alteza. There must be a ship's Capitan who would have use for such a man. So many converses have already sailed to the New World to add to the glory of God and España, that one more would not be unduly noticed."

"The New World?" Padre Barnabas said, shocked. "But the man is a valet. He knows nothing of ships and—"

"He is a barber and a tailor as well. There are plenty of tasks he can turn his hand to, from letting blood to mending sails." There was a note of finality in his voice that told Padre Barnabas the matter was already settled.

"Of course, Padre Juan," he said subserviently. "Doubtless God has shown you the way."

"I pray for it every hour of my life, Padre Barnabas, but I cannot hope that one so lowly as I will merit His blessing." He waved Padre Bamabas away and went back to the documents on his writing table, secure in the knowledge that he had solved yet another difficult problem.

The day after Don Rolon left Valladolid in the company of two officers of the Secular Arm, Padre Bamabas had another visitor in his cell, this time a tall young man with blond hair and a lazy, insolent smile. "You wanted to speak to me, Padre?" Gil asked as he lounged in the door.

"Yes," Padre Juan replied sharply. "You have not behaved as we agreed you would."

"Oh, no, Padre," Gil corrected him. "You have said how you wish me to behave, and I have not given you my word that I would.

I have promised that I would consider it, which I have done, and decided that I do not wish to do as you have asked." His face was smug but there was a guarded look at the back of his eyes.

"It will not serve, Gil," Padre Juan said more firmly. "If you are to accomplish your ends, you cannot abuse your position as you have done."

"How have I abused it?" Gil asked, attempting to appear naive.

"You know full well that I have warned about about being too forward with Don Rolon's Venezian wife. That is for later, when your Succession is assured. If you give her a distaste of you now, it will not be possible to compel her later to marry you and continue the truce. She still has the right to refuse you." He folded his arms and shook his head. "This is not an idle amusement, Gil. You are fighting for a birthright and a kingdom." He paused so that Gil could reply, and when he did not, Padre Juan continued. "You will do better to be respectful and solicitous, so that when Zaretta is in Venezia . . .What is it?"

"You're not allowing her to go, are you?" Gil sputtered, for the first time at a loss.

"Of course. If she claims she is being detained against her will, her uncle will not be inclined to permit her to marry you." He stood up. "You are not thinking clearly, my son. You are permitting the lusts of your flesh and the greed of your mind to lead you away from your wisest course. For that reason, you will not oppose her departure, either to me or to your father. Then you will, not speak against Don Rolon, for he will condemn himself before the Process is done, and you will not be called envious by those who will serve you when you rule. Do you understand me?"

"After a fashion," Gil replied. "You don't want my position called into question, is that it?"

"Something of the sort," was Padre Juan's answer. "You are not always careful of what you do and say, and when you are el Rey, you will have to think very carefully at all times."

"The way my father does? So that I sound like an articulate post?" He paid no attention to the consternation in Padre Juan's face. The people and Court like a ruler with a little juice left in him, Padre."

"A little juice, as you say, is another phrase for sin, and if España is to be an example to the world, there must be no more sin on the throne." He hit the table with his fist and his voice rose. "I have wanted to bring España a rule that was uncorrupted with heresy and Diabolism and the lures and lies of the flesh. You want to rule when your father is dead, and that is understandable. You are a young man of vision and invention, and it is not surprising that your ambition leads you to strive for the throne. In those matters, you have my understanding, if not my sympathy. But your brother is—"

"My half brother," Gil corrected him.

"Your half brother, then, is cursed, and that curse brings grave danger to all those in España who look to the throne for judgment and wisdom, for there is no justice in those whom God has forsaken. You would not be my choice, Gil del Rey, if there were another son of el Rey in España who could inherit the title. You are a man of lax morals and a scoffer, but you are blessed by the Church and your baptism is not in question, and for those reasons, and no other, I will give you whatever aid I may with the condition that you forsake your vices when you come to rule, and be devout in your practices. Is that clear to you?"

"Very clear." Gil said. "Now you will listen to me, Padre Juan. You, with your Holy Office and your torture chambers. You are the one who wants, even more than I do, to rule in España. You are willing to condemn Don Rolon so that you will have more control over my father, and then of me. You may do as you wish with Alonzo, who believes as you do, and praises the work you do in your dungeons. But I am not one of your sheep, to walk to the slaughter. If you press me when I am el Rey, you will find that you have an enemy to reckon with."

"I can bring you down now, Gil," Padre Juan warned, his face turning white and his eyes blazing out at Alonzo's bastard.

"You may try, but I don't think my father will stand for it. He does not mind losing Don Rolon, but you forget that he loves me, and that gives me strength." He laughed once. "One heir at a time, Padre, and one Rey." He wagged his finger at the Grand Inquisitor. "I have those at Court who are tired of your tyranny, and they will aid me when the time comes. Don't doubt that."

Padre Juan did not flinch. "The Holy Office has been in España very nearly three hundred fifty years, Gil. You and I are nothing compared to that. When each of us is dust, the Inquisition will go on doing the work it was founded to do, and our lives will mean little except as pages in its annals. God will judge us both, and our souls will answer for the lives we have led. While you turn on a spit in Hell, I will sing with the angels in Heaven and pray for the salvation of those lost in sin on earth." He pointed toward the door. "I have nothing more to say to you."

"Nor I to you," Gil said courteously. "We'll test our strengths again later."

When Gil was gone, Padre Juan sat fot some time staring at the far wall, his expression quite blank. Then he took parchment and began to write in the most flowery Latin to the Superior General of his Order in Rome.

❦

The full moon was two days past when Don Rolon returned from his retreat. He was pale and emaciated with fasting, and there were deep scratches on his arms and hands. He entered his quarters with a military escort to find that there was a new valet waiting for him, a squat, simpering middle-aged man from Bilbao.

"But where is Ciro?" Don Rolon asked, attempting to hide his alarm. He had endured one transformation on his own and doubted he could face another.

"Ciro?" asked the new valet.

"My manservant," Don Rolon said abruptly. "He was supposed to be here when I returned, or so I was told."

"I have been given the honor of serving you, Alteza," said the new man with a deep bow. "It is more than a humble man deserves, to come so near those great ones who dedicate their lives to the welfare of the kingdom and rule us with devotion and abiding care so that—"

"Yes," Don Rolon cut him off. "Who retained you?"

"It was on the order of the chief steward of the household," the stranger said, once again bowing. "I previously had the honor of serving the oldest son of the Marquis du Bonhomme in France, but that was more than a year ago, and—"

Don Rolon turned to the two soldiers who had accompanied him to his apartments. "Can either of you tell me what has become of Ciro Eje?" he demanded.

"No, Alteza," they answered in turn, both curious about the reason for the Infante Real's concern for a servant.

"He has been my valet for several years and I am obliged to him for that service. If he is in any difficulties, it behooves me to know of it so that I may honor the service he had rendered me." It was the appropriate reaction for a man of his position, and Don Rolon could see that the soldiers did not fully understand this. He put his hands on his hips. "There must be someone you may ask. If you do not, then I will."

"I will make inquiries, Alteza," the older of the two assured him.

"Good. Now." He turned to the new servant. "Who are you? I do not wish to know more than your name for the moment. The rest I will discover in time."

"Yes, Alteza," the man said with yet another bow. "I am Guittiere Perez. It is my honor and pleasure to be of service to you, and if there is anything that you require of me, you have only to let me know of it and—"

Don Rolon held up his hand to stop this outburst. "Yes. Guittiere Perez. Very good." He turned to the soldiers. "I anticipate hearing from you. Now doubtless your superiors are eager to hear your reports of me, so hasten to them, I pray you, and do not be any longer detained here. Until I have word from my father, I may not leave my apartments in any case."

The soldiers took his dismissal in good part, one of them going so far as to salute Don Rolon before stepping back into the hall.

"Alteza, Padre Barnabas left word earlier that he wished to speak with you, to hear your confession and to discover what you require of him and the Holy Office." He did not precisely bow, but he bent a little at the waist and looked about self-consciously as he did.

"I would prefer to bathe before I speak with Padre Bamabas. I fear I stink like a beast of the field." He was able to say it lightly, but there was a grimness at the corners of his mouth that made him appear older than he was and for the first time gave a cast to his face that was not unlike his father's.

"Too much bathing is an indulgence of the flesh and—" Guittiere looked away, knowing that he had revealed too much of his true purpose.

"I take it that aside from a manservant, you are also a familiar of the Holy Office," Don Rolon said, feeling very fatigued.

"I—"

"Don't add a sin of lying to your soul, Guittiere." The Infante Real began to unfasten the front of his simple black doublet. "I am not surprised. But I would still like to know what has become of Ciro." He could not say more, for fear he might give away that his interest was more than simple concern for a devoted servant. "If you should hear, let me know of it."

"Of course, Alteza," Guittiere said so smoothly that Don Rolon knew it was not the truth.

"And after my bath, and my confession, will you see if you can send the jester Lugantes to me? I have been alone with my thoughts for many days and I have need of a little humor in my life."

"The jester Lugantes. Yes, Alteza." Guittiere had heard that the dwarf was often called upon to amuse the Infante Real, and had no reason to deny Don Rolon that simple entertainment.

"Yes," Don Rolon said thoughtfully as he continued to remove his clothes, "no doubt I shall be glad of his wit." He cast his mind over his few allies, and came to the chilling realization that Lugantes was his last true friend at Court, and the only one he could turn to the next time his transformation came upon him. He caught the leather bag that contained his amulet and held it. The charm had worked to a degree. He had not run mad through the hills under the full moon. He had sufficient presence of mind to master himself to that degree. But there had been a dreadful price to pay—for the first time, he had real memories of the change, and what it did to him. More than anything else, that understanding steeled him to be rid of the curse forever, for now that he knew what he became under its influence, he could not bear it.

31

It was more than a week later that Don Rolon was summoned to the castle of the Holy Office to begin the investigation called a Process. By that time, he was almost glad of it, for the waiting and doubts had been wearing on him for some days, and the isolation in which he was kept palled on him before the first day of it was ended.

Padre Juan was waiting for him, along with two other Dominicans Don Rolon did not know. The Inquisitor General inclined his head to the Infante Real, but with little respect. "These are my Brothers in Christ, Padre Enaes and Padre Bernal."

The two priests acknowledged Don Rolon politely, and the Infante noticed that Padre Bernal had a slight lisp. "We trust that we will not be compelled to detain you any longer than absolutely necessary."

"Amen to that," Don Rolon said at once. "What is it you wish to ask me? Let us get on with it." He saw the priests exchange glances, and wished he had the courage to question them himself.

"We will go to a room nearby where we will not be disturbed," Padre Juan said with a motion of his hand indicating that they should proceed down the corridor. "There were some regrettable decisions that have been forced upon us recently, and, naturally, we are anxious that we should not have to make the same errors again."

"Errors?" Don Rolon asked because he knew it was expected ˄ of him.

"Yes. There are those who are so far gone in their heresy that they will lie to bring others down with them, and the ones they have implicated have little recourse but to comply with the demands of the Holy Office. There are times when those who are accused are at pains to blame themselves, for the sins of their lives are heavy on their souls, and in this they commit a greater sin, for they bring those of us of the Holy Office to sin ourselves by causing injury to the truly devout. You may see how such mischances might occur and you will understand . . . "—he indicated an open door on the right—" that we are concerned that such mistakes should be kept to a minimum."

"I see," said Don Rolon, aware that he could not give them a simple answer to their questions, or use the accusations of others as the base for his admissions to them. They were determined to use all their techniques with him, and would not be put off by his compliance.

"You have been informed, have you not, that your wife will be returning to Venezia until the matter of the Process is settled?" Padre Bemal asked as the three priests took their places at a long writing table.

"I have been so informed," Don Rolon answered.

"Let us trust that our investigations may speed that happy day," Padre Juan said, and crossed himself to murmur a few prayers before beginning his examination. "You may sit there," he told Don Rolon, indicating a low stool.

"As you wish," Don Rolon agreed, squatting down on the uncomfortable bit of furniture.

There was silence in the room for almost a quarter of an hour. The priests busied themselves arranging stacks of parchment on the table before them, but it was only to justify their silence. They said nothing to one another and did not address Don Rolon at all. For all the notice they paid him, he might not have been in the room at all.

This was supposed to bring out guilt and nervousness in one being brought before the Inquisition, and Don Rolon knew enough of their methods to be certain that any show of discomfort on his part would be interpreted as a sign of guilt. It was a great effort for him to remain calm, however, on that low, inadequate stool with his knees drawn up halfway to his chest. His legs would ache in another hour, but that was also what the Inquisitors hoped for, since the severity of their questions was gauged to increase with the physical discomfort of the person being examined. With as little movement as possible, he did what he could to ease his body, afraid to move too much since that would be suspicious as cramps in his calves later. At last he folded his arms, rested them on his knees and put his chin atop his arms. In this position he was tolerably comfortable and he knew he could maintain it a while without suffering for it later.

"Don Rolon," said Padre Bernal when he had judged enough time had passed, "there are some serious questions concerning your . . . spiritual well-being that must be answered before this tribunal before the matter of the Succession may be decided to the satisfaction of the Church as well as the crown."

"So I understand," Don Rolon answered with composure.

"And it is appropriate that we pursue the matter diligently." This was Padre Enaes, whose voice, Don Rolon noticed, was uncommonly deep.

"That is your obligation," Don Rolon concurred.

"And you will forgive us for saying things that in another instance might be regarded as treason. It is our duty to see that the Will of God is done in this kingdom, and it may require that we set aside high birth and rank so that a greater master than el Rey will be—"

Don Rolon interrupted Padre Bernal's flow of words. "You are forgiven any question that may be counted as treasonable for the duration of this Process. Beyond that, I cannot extend my word."

"Precisely," Padre Juan said dryly. "You perceive, Don Rolon, that we do not wish to confuse you."

"I accept that confusion is not your intention," Don Rolon answered carefully, looking up at the men in black. "I trust you will accept the same of me."

"That is for us to determine, Don Rolon," Padre Enaes said in the most forceful manner he had yet used. "You cannot want us to set aside our—"

"Then I pray you will get on with it. Let us end the doubts, for God's sake if not for the sake of el Rey and the Succession." He saw that his asperity was not expected, and it distressed Padre Bernal, who shook his head. "I am submissive to the Will of God, but I am often impatient with men."

"We have much the same experience," Padre Juan said in a tone so pointed that Don Rolon lapsed into silence. "Now then, Señor, we must first ask you several things in regard to the curse that was put upon you . . . "

"Your pardon, good Padre, but it was el Rey who was cursed,

and it has been assumed because my mother died bringing me into the world that the curse fell on me." Don Rolon looked at the irritated expressions on the priests' faces and added, "You have told me that precision is important. I only want to be certain that your language is precise."

Padre Enaes laid his hands flat on the table before him. "It is good that you are fastidious in your devotion to accuracy. Such is our aim as well. We have all noted that the curse was not specifically directed at you, and may have been expressed in the death of your mother." He nodded to his two companions. "The point is well-taken, and we are wise to keep it in mind."

"Yes," Padre Juan agreed. "Later we may delve more deeply into the curse, but presently we are most properly rebuked." He stared hard at Don Rolon. "Have you ever experienced the effects of a curse?"

Don Rolon swallowed hard. "I have been told all my life that there was a curse upon me," he answered truthfully. "For that reason, the curse has always been with me."

"But has there been any other sign?" demanded Padre Enaes.

"It is possible," Don Rolon answered carefully, not wanting to lie outright to these three men, for there was no safety in lies.

"How do you mean that, Don Rolon?" Padre Bernal asked at once.

"There have been occurrences in my life . . . illnesses and possible fits that could have come upon me because of the curse. My confessor said not, and my physician agreed. Still, it may be . . . " He could see the three Dominicans grow tense and he knew they were on the scent now. No wonder they were called God's Hounds!

"Yes. Your confessor. We must find out more about Padre Lucien." There was a note of satisfaction in Padre Juan's voice, and he looked to the other two priests for their opinions.

"Padre Lucien was found to be heretical by the Holy Office, and for that reason there are many doubts as to the state of your soul." Padre Bernal squared his shoulders. "We have heard your remarks to Padre Barnabas, and we have deliberated on your reservations. While it is true that to doubt the Sacraments and the Mercy of God are blasphemous errors and ones that must be punished with severity, still it is for us to judge if the source of the inspiration of Padre Lucien as it pertained to you, was celestial and therefore a mark of forgiveness or infernal and a token of damnation."

Don Rolon remained silent as the priests spoke together, then he dared to interrupt them again. "Why would my father's brother, who is a devout Catholic, want to send me an apostate priest as a confessor?"

"There is always the matter of the Succession," Padre Juan said smoothly. "It is wrong to assume that because he is Emperor that he is free of ambitions for his son, who would rule in your place if the Succession were to go unchallenged and you were to be found unfit to rule."

This was not surprising to Don Rolon, but he had not thought to hear it so baldly expressed. "Why not simply arrange, for a steward to give me poison? Isn't that the surer method? If I wanted to bring down a prince, I could find a more certain way than sending him a priest who might or might not corrupt him." He knew that it was foolish to argue with these men, but he wanted to plant these doubts in their minds while he still had all his wits about him. "I do not say that you are wrong in your suspicions, good Padres, but I do wonder that you credit my uncle Gustav with such determination and ambition and yet so little sense. I have met my uncle, and I know that he is not a foolish man."

"That is not in question," Padre Enaes said coldly. "We are not diverted from our purpose by these absurdities of yours, Don Rolon. It would be the better for you if you kept that in your thoughts."

"As you wish," Don Rolon said quietly, sensing the harsh temper of the man. It would take more time than he had to convince these men that they were being skillfully used, but not by the Emperor in Austria.

"To return to your former confessor," Padre Juan said at his most urbane. "I fear this will take some time, Don Rolon."

"I am at your disposal," Don Rolon replied, matching his manner in order to conceal his anger. "You are the ones who desire this clarification."

"And you do not?" Padre Enaes asked with a hint of snide condescension in his voice.

"Of course I do," Don Rolon replied. He shifted his position on the small wooden stool. "It would please me to settle this quickly."

There was no mistaking the slow, malific smile that Padre Juan showed him. "That, Don Rolon, is for us to determine. And in a case such as yours, we prefer to be thorough."

Lugantes held up the key that Raimundo had given him, and tried again to puzzle out where it came from. He had been trying to find its lock for more than a month and so far had not been able to. Ever since Don Rolon entered the portals of the castle of the Inquisition more than two weeks ago, he had been fretting, anticipating the night of the full moon, which would come again soon.

"What have you got there?" Genevieve asked as she looked up from her embroidery. "Is it that key, still?"

"Yes, mi vida." He held it out to her. "It is old and it is made of brass. That makes me suspect that the door is an interior one, but where?" More than a week before he had shown the key to her, and she had studied it briefly but without much interest.

"Don't let it distract you. Besides, if you're found with it, you may be in trouble for it." She reached out and flipped one of the long dags of his sleeves, and laughed at the sound of the bell hanging at the end of it. "Is it wonderful to jingle whenever you move? You're like a bush full of singing birds."

"There are times it drives me to distraction. And when I am in motley, it is no easy thing to go silently about the palace. I have learned how, but it means that I cannot move quickly or do anything suddenly." He got onto the hassock. "Does Gil visit you tonight?"

"No, tomorrow. Tonight he has been told by Padre Juan that he must make a full confession of his sins to the officers of the Inquisition, so that they may believe his intentions are pure." She pulled two lengths of floss from the basket at her side. "He won't confess anything they don't need to hear. He promised me that. Alonzo would not like the world to know that his precious bastard is enamored of his Reina."

Lugantes looked at her intently. "But you want him to know," he said.

"Yes, of course, but I want Gil to tell him, or for whispers to reach him, so that he cannot denounce me or claim that I have dishonored the throne." She looked away from the jester. "It is not I who have dishonored the throne. I do not want to see Don Rolon in prison, starved and racked and made to sleep on wet, slimy stones where rats come at night. I don't want to cast out that young man in favor of Gil. Oh, Gil is the more beautiful, but he does not have the Right, and there is nothing that Alonzo may do that will change it. Even if the Inquisition . . . burns . . . Don Rolon. May God keep him from that! Making one youth a heretic does not confer the Right on another." She shifted in her chair. "I should not have taken him as my lover. I know that it was not a good act. But I thought that if Don Rolon shared my bed, Alonzo would grow disgusted enough that he would send me away."

"But not back to your brother," Lugantes warned her, as he had warned her for three years. "Alonzo would choose one of those isolated fortresses of his. I told you about El Morro, querida. He would send you there, and if you press him too hard, he will still do it. And then what would become of us." He knew already that if Genevieve were banished to such a place, he would follow her there.

"It doesn't matter now, anyway. I leave for Venezia in three weeks. After that, I will go to my brother. You will come to me in France, won't you, my dear little man?" She reached out negligently and caressed his face. "I will miss you while we are apart."

"And I will miss you, mi amor. Wherever you are, you take my heart with you." He seized her hand and kissed her. "It will not be long, Genevieve. Then you will be safe, and my soul will be at rest."

"What will you think of my new lovers?" She drew her hand away and threaded her needle with a shade of peach.

"What do I ever think of your lovers? If they bring you joy, I will like them; if they cause you pain, I will want to kill them." He said it matter-of-factly, almost without feeling of any kind.

She set a few stitches, then sighed. "If I were a sensible woman, I would be content to have you love me, and I would want nothing more than that. But I am not a sensible woman anymore. I may have been once; I don't know. That was before my daughters were born, and before Alonzo left my bed."

"Do not speak against yourself, mi amor," Lugantes said evenly, turning his face toward her once more. "We are all what we are, and that is all we are. I do not love you for what you might be or have been or could become, I love you because you are Genevieve. There is no other reason."

She drew a trembling breath. "Don't. Please, Lugantes, don't."

"But—" He was horrified at the distress he saw in her face. "What is it, querida?"

"I—" She angrily brushed at her cheeks. "Oh, you terrify me when you speak like that. How can I bear to go away from you if . . . "

"If you love me, you will leave," he said at once, getting up and going to her. "When you are safe, I will no longer dread the sound of Padre Juan's voice, or the laughter of Don Enrique, or any of the rest of it. Through you I am vulnerable. If you are safe, then I am invincible." He leaned across her lap and kissed her tenderly. "Go with my blessings, querida."

"All right," she capitulated. "Yes, very well. I will go when Zaretta goes, and I will look for you to come to me in France. There. And now I will go and pinch my cheeks to make them rosy, and rouge my nipples, so that Gil will be more eager for me. Go along, Lugantes. But come back tomorrow, when I return from Mass."

"As you wish, Genevieve," he said, bowing to her with a feeling that approached reverence.

"And take that key with you. I don't want anyone to ask me about it." She gave an impatient toss to her head, then waved in the general direction of the door. "There are so many locks in España. What is one key, with all those locks?"

Lugantes laughed as he knew she wanted him to, but the sound was only to please her, not to indicate any amusement. What she had said was too much the truth to afford him any entertainment. There were far too many locks in España. Even the graves were locked. He turned the key over in his hand again, holding it up to the branch of candles that flickered on the wall. He held the key close to his face, examining it with more care than before. When he saw the little embossing along the underside of the shank, he thought at first it was only scratchings, a sign of use. Then he peered more closely, his eyes becoming slits of concentration. There was a crude representation of arms he knew, the lantern and rosary of the Cistercians of San Lorenzo en Alameda. Lugantes looked up sharply, for those were the monks whose task it was to see to the burial of those the Inquisition had killed—not the condemned heretics of the autos-da-fé, but the unfor-tunates who languished in the prisons and fortresses . . . their prisons! He almost shouted at the thought. To bury the dead, the Cistercians had to get into the prisons of the Inquisition, and to do this, they had to have a key. He held up the brass once more and breathed a prayer for the courageous soul of Raimundo Dominguez y Mara, who had given this to him. One day, two days, a week at the most and he would be able to penetrate the castle of the Inquisition. It would not be difficult to find Don Rolon then, and when he did, he would be able to release the Infante Real. He tucked the key back under his giddy-colored doublet. He would have to be careful, very careful, and this time he would have to work alone. His mouth turned grim. He cared little for his own danger, but he did not want to increase the risk to Don Rolon.

There was the sound of approaching footsteps, and so he began to stroll along the corridor, humming aimlessly to himself. From the sound of the steps, Lugantes thought that the person approaching must be a monk or a priest, for the hall resounded with the slap of sandals, not the crisp tap of heels or the thud of servants' clogs.

Sure enough, around the corner came Padre Barnabas, his head sunk low on his chest, showing that he was deep in thought. He barely roused himself to notice the jester, but made a tentative motion that might have been a greeting.

"God be with you, Padre," Lugantes said as he passed the Dominican, his bells making a soft, tuneless melody as he went.

Something about the bells stirred Padre Bamabas' memory, and he stopped to look at the retreating jester. There was an impression he had, one he could not place at once, that lurked in his mind, just out of sight. There had been a bell. Where was it? What did it remind him of? He cast his thoughts back to that long Progress, thinking that it must have been one of the many entertainments, another jester who . . . He resumed his walk, knowing that it would come to him in time. His brooding eyes were fixed on the endlessly repetitive pattern of the parquet floor, but his attention was elsewhere, trying to find the bell.

32

It had been a day, or possibly two, since the Holy Office had begun Questioning him in the third degree. Don Rolon lay on the filthy, matted straw of his cell and tumed his fever-glazed eyes toward the far wall. His body swarmed with pain, alive with it as with some vermin. For the last several hours, he had been trying to recall how long he had been in the Holy Office's keeping. Hours stretched and slurred in his mind, measured in agony, not minutes. He had been racked, and he felt as if it has been months or years that his joints stretched while the meaningless Questions droned on. Was it just one afternoon, as Padre Juan insisted when they brought him back to his cell?

There was a wooden trencher, long since emptied by rats, and a bucket of stinking slops. It should have been removed in the morning and a fresh one provided him, but Don Rolon had learned that one of the means the Holy Office had to make their prison even more unbearable was to mete out its few comforts grudgingly and capriciously.

He knew that he had told them nothing so far, but any pride he might have taken in his silence had deserted him many days ago, when his hurt became constant. Now he refused them out of anger and the stubbornness of complete desperation. It was terrible to be in their power, to feel himself slowly and inexorably robbed of every trace of his humanity, but for that reason alone, he could not permit himself to give in to them and become their creature. His suffering was all he would let them have of him.

His cell, never brighter than twilight, was fading now toward darkness, and he tried to keep his eyes on the window, near the top of the wall. It was hard for him to focus his eyes, for the thundering ache in his head and neck made him feel that there were rats inside his skull trying to eat and scratch their way out with every pulsebeat. Still, the light was something to cling to, that made him feel less forsaken and abandoned. All else was lost to him, but for a little while, there was the light. He tried to turn on his side, but the damage done to his shoulders made it impossible for him to move more than a few inches without intolerable pain. He groaned, glad for the sound, since it made him feel less alone. When he had first been locked up, he had wondered why he heard voices shouting and speaking and singing behind the massive doors, but now he knew. Sound was real. As long as there was sound, he was not entirely deserted. He groaned again, a little louder, and listened to the close echoes, satisfied that he was still alive.

Outside, night was coming. Vesper bells rang over the courtyard and the first chanting of the monks and priests marked the ending of the day.

Don Rolon stirred uneasily. There was something about night, this night, that he had to remember. He had submerged it in his mind, hidden it from the persistent and relentless priests, but now it demanded his attention.

The light faded, faded, tuming to engulfing darkness, transforming the narrow, stinking cell to a vast cavern, limitless because there was no way to see its walls.

Rats chittered nearby, bringing Don Rolon's attention back from the distances it had fled into. He hated the rats and longed for the strength to strike out at them, to break them and crush them even as he was being broken. There was worse to come, he knew. In time they would get permission to try torture, and though there would only be one day, from sunrise to sundown when they might deliberately break his skin, using pincers and thumbscrews and the boot, that day would be unendurably long, and dreadful beyond anything he had known thus far. The day would be eternal, and at the end of it, he would be consigned to the flames, or . . .

He turned abruptly, a growl low in his throat, and snapped at the rats that were starting to creep into his cell.

Dread flooded through him. It was the night of the full moon! He moaned in a spasm of despair, and heard the sound he made; he recoiled. In the dark cell, he could not see his feet and hands, but he could sense the changes in them. The officers of the Secular Arm had long since seized the amulet Isador had given him, and now he was exposed to the whole weight of the curse, without any protection.

"Dear God," he tried to say, and the whimper that escaped him reminded him of the sounds his hound-bitch's puppies made when they first ventured into the world. He tried to clap his hands over his face, but flinched back when he felt rough pads on his forehead instead of hands. Under his penitent's robe, there was the rasp of bristles and fur. Then there was an ache at the base of his spine, something entirely different from what he had felt before. A twitch ran through his buttocks, and he felt movement under the cloth that came from no part of him he could recognize. There was a soft thump as his tail grew and wagged once more.

Revulsion coursed through him like corrosive poison. The Secular Arm inspected cells three times during the night, and it was less than an hour until their first check. What would they do if they found not the son of Alonzo but a wolf crouching in the darkness, maddened with hunger and hatred of confinement. He was still human enough to shudder as he thought of it. He would face the stake for sure, and there would be no excuse, no recourse for him but to die.

Something deep within him slipped away and there was a fury in place of his anguish. As his hands turned to paws and his skin grew a pelt, as his face lengthened and his beard broadened into a ruff, all that was wounded in him took on the fury of a hunted and trapped animal.

In the narrow hall outside the cell, Don Rolon's pricking ears caught a faint sound, a light step under the sound of the chanting and the quiet peal of the bells. He froze, belly low to the floor, thin lips drawn back to show lengthening fangs. A rumble of distress went through him; then there was the quiet sound of his panting, his black, wet nose quivering. He was hungry, very hungry, but it was for more than food that he hungered.

Another sound caught his attention, the snick and scrape of a key turning in the lock. The huge iron hinges protested as the door was opened a crack.

"Alteza?" Lugantes whispered, peering into the dark of the cell.

It took all of Don Rolon's remaining will not to lunge at the small figure in the door, and the effort it cost him was as painful as the damage done to him by the rack.

"I could not be here sooner, Alteza," the jester whispered. This time his growl was a warning, and he slunk toward the gray light where his escape lay.

Lugantes stepped aside just in time; a lean, swift shape hurtled past him and into the hallway, pausing to sniff the air before sprinting away toward the tunnel that led from San Lorenzo en Alameda to the prison of the Inquisition. Lugantes cringed back, ashamed of his own cowardice, but unable to face what his prince had become. He started to call out, but the thought of those baleful yellow eyes stopped him, and he hung back in the shadows, praying to a God he did not believe in to watch over the wolf that ran through the underground passages of this damnable place.

With his keen sense of smell to guide him, the wolf found his way to the Cistercian monastery without mishap. He was vaguely aware that the monks would not be about and for that reason he could move with impunity past their chapel and out into the huge enclosed field that was their burial ground. Pausing at the verge of the trimmed grass, he gave a whining cry as if troubled by the bodies of the unfortunate men and women who lay in the unmarked graves. Dimly he sensed that this would be his resting place, too, when his work was done. An urgent twinge went through him, pricking him as if to remind him that his time was short and his errand demanding.

There were sentries at the side gate of the royal palace, and they stood at guard in that attitude of boredom that revealed their long experience. Two of them flanked the entrance while a third lounged by the massive beam that served as a bolt in time of war and siege. None of them had ever had reason to be diligent in their duty, for Valladolid was the safest and most impregnable of all the royal holdings. So it was that by the time any one of the three had realized it was not a dog that had entered the palace but a wolf, the animal was already speeding along the main hall toward the grand corridor and the major reception rooms.

Even had Don Rolon been able to speak, he could not now have explained what it was he felt compelled to do. He ran swiftly and without hesitation, but the perceptions he had could not have been spoken, for they were the lust of hunter for prey, and nothing he had known as a man prepared him for his overwhelming need to run his quarry to earth.

Lugantes made his way out of the prison of the Inquisition :eat care. He was terrified now of what he had released to run free in the world, as much for those who might happen the wolf as he was for Don Rolon himself. Where he had had doubts before that Don Rolon altered so completely, he knew he had underestimated the ·extent of the transition the Infante Real experienced at the full of the moon. He also knew that if he were found in these hidden corridors, he would have to answer questions that would him in great danger. He had pulled on a cloak though evening was warm, so that the bells of his motley would muffled. He had wanted to put on less noticeable clothing, but: the time had been to critical for such a luxury, and now he ed he would not regret his decision. There were those he wanted to warn, but he did not believe he would have the chance, for he was convinced that Don Rolon—or the wolf he had changed into—was bound for the palace.

The jester stopped in the outer hall of the San Lorenzo en Alameda, feeling a little winded and disoriented. He thought strange that so little exertion should bring such a response him, but he could not dismiss the apprehension that weighted him down. He heard the sound of scuffing feet, and looked up to see a procession of monks come from the chapel.

"Who are you, and why do you disturb our devotions," said the oldest monk who marched at the head of the double line.

"I am the jester Lugantes, and I have seen a thing that makes me believe your services will be needed before the night is over," he answered, and began to weep.

"What thing is this?" the old monk asked for them all. "A beast," Lugantes cried out, and hid his face in his hands.

There were men chasing the wolf now, and their shouts were alternately loud or soft, frightened exclamations. Servants rushed wildly through the corridors, some of them calling out to their patron Saints, some of them grimly silent in the hope that they would not reveal themselves to the animal or animals that were said to be hunting men in royal palace.

"This is an outrage," Alonzo said in measured accents when a breathless chamberlain dared to interrupt him private prayers.

"It is," the servant nodded frantically. "And there one to stop it."

"But how could such a creature find its way to the pallet alone through the streets of Valladolid?" He recalled vaguely a warning he had been given some months ago Raimundo—he did not like to think of the dead Portuguese Duque—about trained hunting dogs that could be used bring down members of the Royal Family. "Who has seen this wolf, or dog, or whatever it is?"

"There are two soldiers who came to the servants' quarters, and they both swear that they saw a large gray wolf bolt through the gate . . . " the chamberlain broke off with shudder, crossing himself for protection.

"Soldiers are not always sober, and when they speak of wolf, it may be that a half-grown hound has wandered into the grounds of the palace." He spoke in his usual measured tones, and paid no attention to the expression of terror in the chamberlain's eyes.

"Majestad, 1 beg of you, come away," the chamberlain pleaded, twisting his hands in the folds of his long tunic. "If there is such an animal, then—"

The door was flung open and Gil rushed into the chapel. "What's all this nonsense about a wolf?" he demanded of his father. "Half the palace is in an uproar."

"So we have been told," Alonzo said with a long-suffering look at the chamberlain. "We are being asked to retreat."

"Not retreat, Majestad," the chamberlain protested miserably. "Pray, Majestad, do not expose yourself to more danger. I cannot answer for it if you do."

"Brave soul, isn't he?" Gil asked with a sneer. "Are the rest of the staff as valiant as he?" He put his hand on the hilt of his sword. "I don't think a dog, even a mad one, will be more than my sword can deal with."

"You must not—" the chamberlain insisted, but was cut off by el Rey.

"Send for the Marashal and his staff, if there is any real danger. It is their task to protect us." He signaled to his bastard son. "Come. We will withdraw into my library while it is decided how best to proceed."

Gil bowed, but said, "I believe I will patrol the halls. La Reina should be told of this, since she may be in some danger, too." He was relishing the chance to tell her and to enjoy her gratitude for his concern for her. "It may require a little time to rout out the beast."

"As you wish, my son. But do not endanger yourself. I don't believe that the risk is great, but I would prefer you were careful." Alonzo sketched a blessing in the direction of Gil, then followed the chamberlain out of the chapel at his usual careful pace. Nothing would cause him to hurry in an unseemly manner.

When Alonzo had gone, Gil went quickly in the direction of Genevieve's apartments, his thoughts already filled with the pleasure he anticipated at her hands. He was eager to tell her of the animals—he thought it best to exaggerate the number a trifle, so that she would be more excited—running loose in the palace, making it seem as if they were defying the gods and fate itself to bed each other at such a time. He knew Genevieve well enough to recognize she wanted to hurt Alonzo more than she wanted to give herself to her lover. Certain that Alonzo was in hiding while she rutted with his cherished son would add passion and pleasure to their union, and he was determined to make the most of the advantage he was offered now.

"Gracious," Genevieve said as she admitted Gil through the side door. "I had no idea that you were—" She had, in fact, been expecting Lugantes. Earlier that evening the jester had warned her that she might be in danger that night, and had offered to come to her so that she would not need to be alone.

"Hermosa," Gil said ardently, shutting the door behind him. "Let me take you now, while everyone is consumed with fear." It was abrupt, but he could see her eyes grow bright with appreciation of his audacity.

"What are you speaking of?" she asked. "I have been so occupied with packing for my journey that I would not know if we were under massed siege, I think." It was thrilling to be so much pursued.

"It is said that there is a pack of rabid dogs running in the corridors of the palace. No one knows how they got in, but we are all in the gravest danger from them. I want to be with you, Genevieve." He reached out and grabbed her roughly, pulling her up against him without finesse. He felt her resist, and that lent its own pleasure to his game. "Come," he said in a husky tone against her cheek. "Bed me, Genevieve. Never mind the dogs that foam at the mouth. Never mind any of it. Open your arms and your legs to me. Now."

At another time, Genevieve might have been stirred by this forceful demand, but her mind was distracted. "I am not interested in—" she began and was cut off by a light but direct blow to her cheek. She stared at Gil in total disbelief. "You cannot strike me."

"I've done so," he answered coolly, "and I will again, if you make it necessary. You and I are going to take pleasure of each other. Now. Here. And you're not going to fob me off with excuses. I want you now. Do you understand me?"

"Get away!" Genevieve said loudly. She could not believe that Gil would treat her so reprehensibly. No one had struck her before: no one had dared.

"Take off your gown, Genevieve. If you don't, I will tear it off you." His threats were exciting him as much as her presence. He had occasionally forced himself on serving wenches and country girls, but never on a highbom woman who could bring him harm if she complained. But he doubted that Genevieve would complain, not to her confessor, not to her husband. He laughed aloud. "Come. Undress at once, and I will not hurt you again."

"No!" She thrust him away, and began for the first time to be afraid of him.

There were running footsteps in the hall, and cries that a wolf had been sighted, though the words were too confused to know where.

"All right," Gil told her, and reached for the top of her low French bodice, pulling down on the heavy fabric with a jerk so that it tore. Lace and jewels dropped from it like morning dew from leaves. He liked the way she screamed her protest and tried to break away from him.

"There it goes!" bellowed a servant some distance away. The voice boomed in the corridor with the force of thunder.

Genevieve could not bring herself to reach for the dagger she kept in her sewing basket. It was too ridiculous that this should be happening to her, though her blood hammered in her ears and her face hurt when his blow had landed. Never before in all her life had she been treated in this way. She was Reina. This could not be happening to her.

Gil lunged forward and fixed his fingers in the muslin-and-boning of her corset. He tugged at the fabric, but it was not as delicate as the other had been, so instead of ripping the cloth, he pulled Genevieve off her feet, and she fell against her chair. "That will do," Gil said, gloating at the sight of her, now that her fright had reached her eyes. He listened to the shrieks from beyond the door, and he grinned. "It's like a town being pillaged."

"Get out!" she shouted at him, trying to reach her basket. "When I am done," he told her as he unfastened his beaded codpiece.

Lugantes ran through the halls, but his short bandy legs did not provide much speed, and the anxiety that possessed him robbed him of that extra burst he needed so much. Stairs slowed him more than anything, and there were three flights to climb to reach Genevieve's chambers. It was folly to go to her, but his heart prompted him to seek her out, and he could not deny it.

"There are mad dogs in the palace!" a cook shouted at him, his face white and staring as he tried to hold Lugantes on the second floor. "You can't go up there! Soldiers are searching the palace. The Infante's wife and el Rey have left for San Domingo."

"And la Reina?" Lugantes demanded, prying the man's grip off his arm.

"I don't know! With el Rey!" The cook fell silent as a long, low howl wound and echoed through the palace. In the next instant, he had bolted for the nearest door, crying aloud to God and the Saints to protect him from demons.

Lugantes spared no more attention for the cook, but resumed his climb toward Genevieve's apartments. He mocked himself as he went, thinking that it was most likely that she was indeed already out of the palace, but unable to make himself depart. He heard the shouts of soldiers occasionally, and then the cry of the officers of the Secular Arm, who had been called to join in the search.

"What the Devil?" Gil demanded as he heard the second howl. He had flung himself atop la Reina and was still trying to get his knees between hers as well as get her petticoats out of the way.

"Oh, God," she moaned, striking out again at him, and feeling his fist on the side of her head for her efforts. Her vision muddied and her mouth turned dry and coppery to the taste.

The ululating cry arrested Gil once more, and for the first time it troubled him. He braced himself with thighs and elbows placed to hold Genevieve down, then he turned enough to glance toward the door. At the sight of Lugantes running toward them, disheveled and outraged, he began to laugh, throwing his head back and jeering at both the jester and the woman who struggled weakly beneath him, so he did not see the large, gray shape that hurtled around the door, jaws agape, eyes blistering with fury.

"No!" Genevieve cried out, and then the breath was knocked out of her as Gil was flung back under the snarling, ravening force of the wolf.

Gil tried to scramble back out of range, striking out repeatedly with his fists and feet, not caring now for the hurt he gave himself or la Reina. He saw the jaws of the wolf open and close on his forearm, sinking through to the bone. He heard the crunch as the teeth bit home, but the damage was not real to him. There was a spray of blood as the wolf released him and fell back half a step, preparing to launch his attack again.

"No!" Lugantes was shouting, not quite daring enough to try to restrain the big animal, not while it attacked Gil and not Genevieve. "Mi amor!" he called out to her. "Come to me!"

Genevieve was too dazed to do more than shake her head

slowly, as if trying to clear her ears of water. She strove to breath deeply, but could not do more than gasp and cough. She heard the snarling above her, and once or twice the impact of bodies falling against her, but there was no reality to her.

When the pain hit Gil at last, it struck with the force of a maul wielded in battle. It traveled up his arm and seemed strong enough to explode under his head and lift it from his body. He had not thought he could endure such pain, but there was worse to come. As he reeled from shock, he felt the wolf strike again, and this time the fangs went deep into his shoulder, rending, breaking, beading the gray muzzle with drops of blood.

Man and wolf rolled together to the far side of the room, and in that moment, Lugantes rushed forward and tried to drag Genevieve out of the chamber. "Come, mi amor, mi vida. Come, come. Come away."

It took every last reserve of her strength, but la Reina was able to pull herself toward the door, hanging on to the dwarf jester with one arm and trying to steady herself with the other. She gasped for air, almost choking when at last she was able to fill her lungs with air.

"Querida, do not look. Come away with me," Lugantes crooned to her, trying to ignore the howls, screams, scuffling, blows, curses, and then a deep, gurgling cry that made his hair rise on the back of his neck. "Hush, querida. It is nothing, nothing."

There were running footsteps now, not the chaotic flight of servants, but the sound of disciplined troops. "There is a door open!" one voice shouted, strong and clear, the voice of a man used to command in battle. "Hurry!"

The footsteps came faster.

Now Genevieve sat, propped up against the side of the door, one hand to her bruised and puffy face. Lugantes smoothed her hair back and did what he could to cover her so that she would not appear as abused as she was. "0 my dearest," he said to her, making sure his body blocked the sight of the battle in her rooms.

Gil felt his blood running in hot gouts down his chest and back, and it did not bother him very much. He was light-headed and elated, and he knew that he was above his wounds and the murderous teeth that snapped at his neck. His breath was ragged in his throat and his legs wobbled under him, but none of this concerned him; his pain was almost gone and he could sense that victory was within his grasp.

"That's the wolf!" the officer of the Secular Arm declared as he brought his men up in the doorway. "Crossbows ready!"

There was a flurry of activity, and then the men stood to attention, unmoved by the grisly sight ahead of them.

"Don't," Lugantes began as he realized what the officer intended. "No. Don't shoot him." He reached up, but it was too late.

Eight heavy quarrels thudded and ripped through bone and sinew, throwing the wolf into the air even as they killed him. There was one dreadful howl from the animal, as if it were from a man in ultimate agony.

Gil gave a high, cackling cry of glee, then collapsed in a spreading pool of blood, which ran and spread with the blood of the wolf.

"No! Por Dios, no, no!" Lugantes shouted, pushing past the soldiers and racing to the side of the great gray beast.

That is where they found him half an hour later, seated with the gray muzzle cradled against his chest, blood sticking to his garments. Genevieve watched him, weeping in a steady, hopeless way, but Lugantes had no words of comfort for her.

And that was how Padre Barnabas saw him, and remembered at last how it was he recognized the little bell he had found on the floor in Segovia.

Epilogue

THE JESTER

Christmas 1565

Blustery rain had been falling on Valladolid for two days, and so the faggots piled around the stakes had been covered with tarred sails to keep them dry enough to burn. With the Solemn High Christmas Mass almost finished, the officers of the Secular Arm began removing these covers so that the fires could be lit for the auto-da-fé. A few of them complained of the weather, but not loudly, for they did not wish to be overheard by the familiars and monks who gathered in anticipation of the glorious moment.

One monk, a young man from Salamanca with a hare-lip, watched these final preparations with ill-concealed excitement.

"So the little piglet is rooting for pearls," one of the older men from the Secular Arm said to the young Dominican.

"That's an irreligious attitude," Frey Feliz responded self-consciously, hating the sound of his own speech.

"This rain is irreligious," the other man said, not rising to the tone in the young monk's voice. "Fifty-two heretics to burn, and God gives us rain."

"It is December," Frey Feliz reminded him. He had never seen a large auto-da-fé, only small burnings of ten or a dozen damned, nothing like the splendor of this great occasion in the Plaza del Rey. "The wood is dry enough. And if it is a little damp, so much the better, for it will be slow to do its work."

"Oh-ho, what a militant little monk we have here," the officer declared, winking at two of his fellow officers. "Listen to him, my friends."

Frey Feliz folded his arms. "I am only concerned that faith and the Church should triumph in España. What is there to mock in that goal?" He did not add that he loved the magnificence of the fire and the great thrill he believed was inspiration that he felt when he saw the condemned heretics chained to their stakes for the end.

A fanfare from the Catedrál announced the end of the Mass. At once the doors were thrown open and a double line of monks and priests emerged, followed by el Rey and the Court.

"So that's the new heir," the officer said in disgusted accents.

"Can't say I think much of him," one of the others agreed. "He's got shoulders like a donkey."

"Whatever he looks like, he's the Emperor's son and el Rey's nephew. And our new Infante Real." The older officer shrugged. "It's all one to me, who sits on the throne, but he's not much to look on."

As if young prince Otto had been able to hear these remarks, he cast his blue eyes in the direction of the stakes and the officers of the Secular Arm who lounged there waiting for the penitential procession to begin. He was of medium height, with broad shoulders that he carried a little stooped. He had a wide, soft mouth and a lower lip that was perpetually moist. When he laughed he had that hearty bray that encouraged others to laugh with him, but since coming to España, he no longer indulged in mirth as he used to. He waved in a vague manner, then turned to his uncle, the better to hear what Alonzo was saying.

"Are they going to marry him to Don Rolon's bride?" the younger officer asked his superior.

"She says she won't leave Venezia, and this lad claims to want a Dutch wife." The older man shook his head. "A Dutch wife. Fleming, I'll be bound, and you know that they're all heretics. There isn't one that Padre Juan wouldn't have chained to a stake in a minute if he were given the chance."

Frey Feliz could contain himself no longer. "If that is so, why doesn't the Holy Office put a stop to such blasphemy?"

"The Emperor likes the Dutch.. He likes the Flemings. He doesn't want war. And el Rey is dependent on him for expanding our holdings in the new World. When Don Otto is Rey, then it may be different."

"You mean," Frey Feliz said urgently, "that he might relax our posture, and extend the tolerance to España?"

Both the officers laughed. "No, no, little monk," the older one declared. "You'll see none of that gutless tolerance here in España.

Leave that for the disbelievers in the Germanies and Austria. In time they will suffer for their leniency and we will show them that God is just."

"I pray you are right." He turned to watch the Court take its place in the various covered stands around the Plaza del Rey, and then began to recite the prayers for the dead as the procession of those about to be burned made its way into the Plaza.

An old man was the first, and he walked between a Duque and Obispo Antonio, showing how evil he was believed to be. There were terrible bruises about his forehead where he had been Questioned while knotted, barbed cords were tightened around his skull. Because of his age, he had not been subjected to the strappado or rack and thus was able to bear himself with some dignity.

Frey Feliz watched the old man, knowing that he was one of the Jews who had so far blasphemed that he had claimed to be one of the conversos rather than the Jewish magician he proved to be. He had been taken in Barcelona but was known to be one of the Jews who had escaped from Toledo. Frey Feliz crossed himself for greater protection against the Devil and his workers, and decided not to look directly at the old man, in case he should still be able to send imps to torment him.

Padre Juan Murador entered the Royal viewing stand and took his place beside el Rey, murmuring now and again into Alonzo's ear while the procession continued.

The seventeenth heretic was pale and terribly thin, but there was no sign of mistreatment. He was one of the few who had confessed voluntarily and had not denied any of the charges leveled against him. He stopped before the royal viewing stand and looked up into el Rey's austere, unmoving face. He capered once, as he had done many times before, but there was no response from Alonzo. "You are dead, Majestad," Lugantes told him simply, with a shake of his head. "You have only unmarriageable daughters to come after you. The daughters, and your nephew. But it isn't the same, is it?'

"It is God's Will, dwarf, as your size is," Alonzo replied grudgingly, not wanting to speak at all.

"God's Will?" Lugantes asked sadly. "No, Majestad. My height may be, but this ruin of España, it has nothing to do with God. There are despots in España who cloak their tyranny in righteousness, but it is tyranny nonetheless. God is the source of all love and mercy, not a cruel—"

"You continue to be obstinate in your heresy!" Padre Juan shouted at the jester, bringing his hand up as if to strike a blow.

"Naturalmente," Lugantes answered. "As you are in yours. I thought we had settled this weeks ago, when you had Anathema pronounced on me." He stared at the Inquisitor General as if the man were a stranger, then bowed to el Rey. "You will not believe me, Majestad, but I grieve more for you than I do for myself. And far more for your son than for either of us. He was a good prince, Rolon was. Do you know, he never laughed at me—oh, he laughed at the things I did or said that were amusing, but never at me. That, if nothing else, should make a place for him in Heaven." He looked up at the two men who were his escort. "Conde, Padre, there is very little time left. Rather than tell me anything more about the climate of Hell—which I will soon discover for myself in any case—permit me to regale you with one or two anecdotes you may find entertaining." With a last, casual nod to Alonzo, Lugantes turned away from him and strolled toward the stake, chatting amiably and reducing the men on either side of him to ill-disguised laughter.

"That dwarf," the older of the two officers remarked to Frey Feliz, "he used to be the best of el Rey's jesters, but he aided Don Rolon, the one they say kept trained wolves to do his bidding. One of these familiars turned on him and killed him. It goes to show that you can't trust the devil."

Frey Feliz shook his head and crossed himself, saying piously, "They tell us that fiends and imps are little men, like that one."

"He's unscathed," the younger officer noticed.

"He wasn't Questioned," the older said. "Confessed without coercion."

"Confessed?" Frey Feliz repeated incredulously, "Without the Question?"

"I was there," the older man said with obvious pride. "He came right out and admitted it all. Except flying through the air. Padre Barnabas said he would have had to fly through the air to get to Segovia so quickly and then spirit Don Rolon away."

"What was his answer to that? Didn't they put him to the Question for such a grave accusation?" Frey Feliz was shocked at such a lapse on the part of the Holy Office.

"The jester said that he wished he had flown through the air because he hated being in the saddle day and night. He had been given one of Dominguez y Mara's horses—you know, the Portuguese Duque who was burned a few months back—and allowed that the beast might have been enchanted."

"Then he does not repent of anything?" the younger officer asked.

"He's being burned, isn't he? And in a pretty cocky frame of mind, too, from the look of him." He pointed to Lugantes, who was wiping the moisture from his face and adding one last touch to his jokes.

"Undoubtedly he is in the service of the Devil. See how he enthralls the godly men who walk with him. He will not listen to their exhortations, but instead makes them laugh—laugh!" The young Dominican's face grew flushed with his indignation.

"Well, he won't be laughing when the fires start," said the younger officer laconically.

"Pray God that he does not do anything worse than laugh," said the older, recalling that day long ago when el Rey had been cursed.

Lugantes had reached the stake where he was to burn, and the pile of faggots was taller than he was. "Well, Señores, one of you will have to boost me up."

The Conde bent and offered his joined hands as if he were going to toss the jester into a saddle. "Permit me, Lugantes. You are a heretic and for that I despise you, but there is enough of the hero about you that I would not want to see you lose your dignity now."

"Muchas gracias," Lugantes told him, and put his foot into the Conde's hands.

Frey Feliz watched with excitement as all the heretics were chained in place. A few of them fought or screamed and had to be beaten into silence, but most of those condemned to the flames accepted their fate without protest, and for this Frey Feliz was pleased, He began to make the sign of the cross over the torches that would light the pyres, calling on God to make the sign of the cross over the torches that would light the pyres, calling on God to show His might in the strength of the fires.

Lugantes felt the rain on his face and was able to smile once, though there was more longing in his heart than anything else now. He had learned a scant three days before that Genevieve was in France at her brother's Court. It pained him that he would not be able to keep his promise and join her there, but he took what consolation he could in knowing she was safe at last. Genevieve. He filled his thoughts with her, with her face which he treasured more than the light of the sun.

At the foot of Lugantes' pyre, Frey Feliz paused with his torches and brazier, saying prayers as he lit the wood, then moved on to the next.

The first flames hissed as the rain spattered down on them, and heavy black smoke rolled up toward clouds that were almost as dark. Lugantes coughed and his eyes watered; he told himself that it was the smoke alone that caused those tears. He heard the screams and prayers of others around him, and somewhere a steady, firm voice recited words in a language the jester did not know. He thought that it was the old Jew, completing the last of his rituals.

A sensation like tickling but more acidic went through his feet and up his legs, and then grew painful—the greeting kiss of the fire. Lugantes steeled himself against it, but knew it was only a momentary victory. He felt the chains that held him turn from cold to warm to hot, seering his arms and wrists, and then his clothes began to char. There was no resisting the pain now, and he gave himself to it, surrendering to it as if to an embrace. And because it no longer mattered, he answered his agony with his love, calling "Mi vida," calling "mi amor," calling "Genevieve" until there was no more breath to call with, and only the fire remained.